PRAISE FOR *BURNING ANGEL*

"BURKE IS OFF ON A CHASE THAT IS AT ONCE ENGROSSING AND . . . CONVINCING."
—Jonathan Yardley, *Washington Post*

"*BURNING ANGEL* IS CRIME FICTION AT ITS BEST."
—Betty Ann Kevles, *Los Angeles Times*

"BURKE IS A BRILLIANT DESCRIPTIVE WRITER, PERHAPS THE BEST IN MODERN AMERICAN FICTION."
—Jeff Baker, *Portland Oregonian*

"LIKE THE BLUES OF NEW ORLEANS, BURKE'S MYSTERIES ARE FRESHENED BY

RIFFS AND VARIATIONS FROM THE DEPTHS OF THE SOUL."
—Henry Kisor, *Chicago Sun Times*

"BURKE HAS CRAFTED AN INTRICATE WEB OF RELATIONSHIPS, POSSIBLE CONNECTIONS, AND METAPHYSICS THAT WILL KEEP READERS ENGROSSED FROM START TO FINISH."
—Susan L. Rife, *Witchita Eagle*

"BURKE IS A PURIST WHO WON'T BACK OFF FROM HIS ETHICAL STANDS. SUPPORTED BY HIS SUPERB WRITING, HIS BOOKS ARE A JOY TO READ."
—Bob Hoover, *Pittsburgh Post Gazette*

"*BURNING ANGEL* CONFIRMS BURKE'S REPUTATION AS A MYSTERY WRITER OF THE FIRST MAGNITUDE."
—Kim Cushman, *Albany Times-Union*

"*IN BURNING ANGEL*, BURKE SHOWS WHY HE IS ONE OF THE TOP FIVE WRITERS OF CRIME FICTION ALIVE."
—Oline Cogdill, *Ft. Lauderdale Sun-Sentinel*

"BURKE SKATES SKILLFULLY ALONG THE EDGES OF MAGIC REALISM . . . PROVING ONCE MORE THAT WITH EACH NEW CHAPTER IN DAVE ROBICHEAUX'S STORY, [HE] IS BUILDING ONE OF THE GREAT MODERN HEROIC SAGAS."
—Robert Skinner, *Mostly Murder*

"ABSORBING AND VIOLENT . . . BURKE'S LUSH, HUMID PROSE AND THE CONTROLLED, OTHER-WORLDLY ASPECTS OF THIS PLOT DEFTLY CAPTURE THE INHUMANITY OF THE BAD GUYS AND THE MORE COMMON FRAILTIES OF ORDINARY FOLK."
—*Publishers Weekly*

"BURKE WRITES LIKE AN ANGEL. . . . LIKE A 1940S RAYMOND CHANDLER MOVIE WITH BOGIE AND BACALL THAT HAS YOU HOPELESSLY ENTANGLED IN PLOT, BUT COMPLETELY MESMERIZED, *BURNING ANGEL* WORKS ITS MAGIC."
—Maureen Conlan, *Cincinnati Post*

"A TOP-RATED CRIME THRILLER."
—Rick Eymer, *San Mateo Times*

"BEAUTIFULLY WRITTEN . . . BURKE HAS A GIFT FOR TELLING A STORY."
—Susan Marx, *Orange County Register*

"A MUST FOR MYSTERY READERS."
—Tom Corcoran, *Bookpage*

"BURKE'S WRITING CRACKLES WITH STYLE AND AUTHORITY."
—Lewis Beale, *New York Daily News*

"IT IS A PASSIONATE, EXCITING ADDITION TO A SERIES THAT HAS SET NEW STANDARDS IN THE GENRE."
—Gary Dretzka, *Mobile Register*

"HE IS A GREAT PLEASURE TO READ."
—Bobbie Hess, *San Francisco Examiner*

"IT IS NOT TOO EXTRAVAGANT TO SUGGEST THAT JAMES LEE BURKE IS THE MYSTERY SCENE'S POET LAUREATE. HIS LYRICAL, OFTEN HAUNTING EVOCATION OF MODERN LOUISIANA, WITH HER CORRUPT AND SEDUCTIVE BEAUTY, AND HER PEOPLE, IN WHOM PAST AND PRESENT ARE FOREVER TRAGICALLY INTERTWINED, RANKS HIM AMONG THE MOST ORIGINAL AND POWERFUL WRITERS IN THE FIELD."
—Robert Wade, *San Diego Union Tribune*

"BURKE IS UNSPARING OF BOTH HIS CHARACTERS AND HIS READERS, AND THESE NOVELS, ABSOLUTELY REEKING

WITH THE SMELL OF OUR OWN TIME IN HISTORY, ARE AS GOOD AS SERIOUS POPULAR FICTION GETS."
—Alan Ryan, *Atlanta Journal Constitution*

"THERE IS A PASSION IN BURKE NOT USUALLY FOUND AMONG THE CYNICS AND MISANTHROPES WHO PLY HIS PARTICULAR TRADE. AND HE KEEPS GETTING BETTER."
—John D. Gates, *Winston-Salem Journal*

"THE ROBICHEAUX SERIES IS A MUST-VISIT FOR THOSE WHO BELIEVE THAT CRIME FICTION CAN BE INTELLIGENT, EVEN LITERARY."
—Dave Addis, *Virginian Pilot/Ledger Star*

"BURKE FLIES MILES ABOVE MOST CONTEMPORARY CRIME NOVELISTS, EXCELLING AT CREATING MEMORABLE SECONDARY CHARACTERS AND WRITING ATMOSPHERIC PROSE."
—Nancy Pate, *Orlando Sentinel*

BURNING ANGEL

ALSO BY JAMES LEE BURKE

Half of Paradise
To the Bright and Shining Sun
Lay Down My Sword and Shield
Two for Texas
The Convict
The Lost Get-Back Boogie
The Neon Rain
Heaven's Prisoners
Black Cherry Blues
A Morning for Flamingos
A Stained White Radiance
In the Electric Mist with Confederate Dead
Dixie City Jam
Cadillac Jukebox
Cimarron Rose
Sunset Limited

BURNING ANGEL

A Novel by

JAMES LEE BURKE

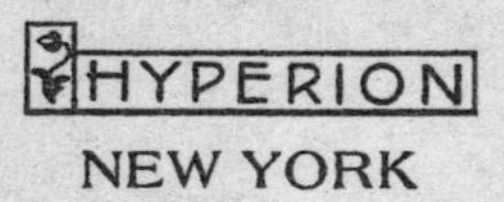

NEW YORK

The individuals and incidents portrayed in this novel are fictitious. Any resemblance to actual incidents, or individuals living or dead, is purely coincidental.

Printed in the United States of America. For information address: Hyperion, 114 Fifth Avenue, New York, New York 10011.

FIRST MASS MARKET EDITION

10 9 8 7

Original hardcover design by Holly McNeely

FOR *Rollie and Loretta McIntosh*

Commending myself to the God of the oppressed,
I bowed my head upon my fettered hands,
and wept bitterly.

—From *Twelve Years a Slave,*
an autobiographical account
by Solomon Northup

Chapter 1

The Giacano family had locked up the action in Orleans and Jefferson parishes back in Prohibition. Their sanction and charter came from the Chicago Commission, of course, and no other crime family ever tried to intrude upon their territory. Hence, all prostitution, fence operations, money laundering, gambling, shylocking, labor takeovers, drug trafficking, and even game poaching in south Louisiana became forever their special province. No street hustler, grifter, second-story creep, Murphy artist, dip, stall, or low-rent pimp doubted that fact, either, not unless he wanted to hear a cassette of what Tommy Figorelli (also known as Tommy Fig, Tommy Fingers, Tommy Five) had to say above the whine of an electric saw just before he was freeze-dried and hung in parts from the wood fan in his own butcher shop.

That's why Sonny Boy Marsallus, who grew up in the Iberville welfare project when it was all white, was a kind of miracle on Canal back in the seventies and early eighties. He didn't piece off his action, pimp, or deal in drugs or guns, and he told the old fat boy himself, Didoni Giacano, to join Weight Watchers or the Save the Whales movement. I still remember him out there on the sidewalk, down from the old Jung

Hotel, on an electric-blue spring evening, with the palm fronds rattling and streetcars clanging out on the neutral ground, his skin as unblemished as milk, his bronze-red hair lightly oiled and combed back on the sides, always running some kind of game—craps, high-stakes bouree, washing Jersey money out at the track, bailing out mainline recidivists licensed bondsmen wouldn't pick up by the ears with Q-Tips, lending money with no vig to girls who wanted to leave the life.

Actually Sonny practiced the ethics that the mob falsely claimed for themselves.

But too many girls took a Greyhound out of New Orleans on Sonny's money for the Giacanos to abide Sonny's presence much longer. That's when he went south of the border, where he saw firsthand the opening of the Reagan theme park in El Salvador and Guatemala. Clete Purcel, my old partner from Homicide in the First District, hooked up with him down there, when Clete himself was on the run from a murder beef, but would never talk about what they did together, or what caused Sonny to become a subject of strange rumors: that he'd gone crazy on *muta* and *pulche* and psychedelic mushrooms, that he'd joined up with leftist terrorists, had served time in a shithole Nicaraguan jail, was working with Guatemalan refugees in southern Mexico, or was in a monastery in Jalisco. Take your choice, it all sounded unlike a Canal Street fixer with scars in his eyebrows and a coin-jingling rebop in his walk.

That's why I was surprised to hear he was back in town, fading the action again and putting deals together at the Pearl, where the old green-painted iron streetcar made its turn off St. Charles onto the lovely hard-candy glitter and wind-blown palm-dotted sweep of Canal Street. When I saw him hanging in front of a game room two blocks up, his tropical suit and lavender shirt rippled with neon, he looked like he had never been under a hard sun or humped an M-60 or rucksack in a jungle where at night you burned leeches off your skin with cigarettes and tried not to think about the smell of trench foot that rose from your rotting socks.

Pool-room blacks leaned against parking meters and storefront walls, music blaring from boom boxes.

He snapped and popped his fingers and palms together and winked at me. "What's happenin', Streak?" he said.

"No haps, Sonny. You didn't get enough of free-fire zones?"

"The city? It's not that bad."

"Yeah, it is."

"Drink a beer, eat some oysters with me."

His accent was adenoidal, like most blue-collar New Orleans people whose English was influenced by the Irish and Italian immigrations of the late nineteenth century. He smiled at me, then puffed air out his mouth and cut his eyes up and down the street. He fastened his eyes on me again, still smiling, a man gliding on his own rhythms.

"Ouch," he said, and stuck a stiffened finger in the middle of his forehead. "I forgot, I heard you go to meetings now, hey, I love iced tea. Come on, Streak."

"Why not?" I said.

We stood at the bar in the Pearl and ate raw oysters that were briny and cold, with flecks of ice clinging to the shells. He paid from a cash roll of fifties in his pocket that was wrapped with a thick rubber band. His jaws and the back of his neck gleamed with a fresh haircut and shave.

"You didn't want to try Houston or Miami?" I said.

"When good people die, they move to New Orleans."

But his affected flamboyance and good humor weren't convincing. Sonny looked worn around the edges, a bit manic, maybe fried a little by his own velocity, the light in his eyes wary, his attention to the room and front door too pronounced.

"You expecting somebody?" I asked.

"You know how it is."

"No."

"Sweet Pea Chaisson," he said.

"I see."

He looked at my expression.

"What, that's a surprise?" he asked.

"He's a bucket of shit, Sonny."

"Yeah, I guess you could say that."

I was regretting my brief excursion into the illusionary pop and snap of Sonny Boy's world.

"Hey, don't go," he said.

"I have to get back to New Iberia."

"Sweet Pea just needs assurances. The guy's reputation is exaggerated."

"Tell his girls that."

"You're a cop, Dave. You learn about stuff after it's history."

"See you around, Sonny."

His eyes looked through the front window onto the street. He fitted his hand over my forearm and watched the barman drawing a pitcher of beer.

"Don't walk out now," he said.

I looked through the front glass. Two women walked by, talking simultaneously. A man in a hat and raincoat stood on the curb, as though waiting for a taxi. A short heavyset man in a sports coat joined him. They both looked out at the street.

Sonny bit a hangnail and spit it off the tip of his tongue.

"Sweet Pea's emissaries?" I said.

"A little more serious than that. Come into the can with me," he said.

"I'm a police officer, Sonny. No intrigue. You got a beef, we call the locals."

"Save the rhetoric for Dick Tracy. You got your piece?"

"What do you think?"

"The locals are no help on this one, Streak. You want to give me two minutes or not?"

He walked toward the rear of the restaurant. I waited a moment, placed my sunglasses on top of the bar to indicate to anyone watching that I would be back, then followed him. He bolted the rest room door behind us, hung his coat from the stall door, and peeled off his shirt. His skin looked like alabaster, hard and red along the bones. A blue Madonna image, with orange needles of light emanating from it, was tattooed high up on his right shoulder.

"You looking at my tattoo?" he said, and grinned.

"Not really."

"Oh, these scars?"

I shrugged.

"A couple of ex-Somoza technicians invited me to a sensitivity session," he said.

The scars were purple and as thick as soda straws, crisscrossed on his rib cage and chest.

He worked a taped black notebook loose from the small of his back. It popped free with a sucking sound. He held it in his hand, with the tape hanging from the cover, like an excised tumor.

"Keep this for me."

"Keep it yourself," I said.

"A lady's holding a Xerox copy for me. You like poetry, confessional literature, all that kind of jazz. Nothing happens to me, drop it in the mail."

"What are you doing, Sonny?"

"The world's a small place today. People watch CNN in grass huts. A guy might as well play it out where the food is right."

"You're an intelligent man. You don't have to be a punching bag for the Giacanos."

"Check the year on the calendar when you get home. The spaghetti heads were starting to crash and burn back in the seventies."

"Is your address inside?"

"Sure. You gonna read it?"

"Probably not. But I'll hold it for you a week."

"No curiosity?" he said, pulling his shirt back on.

His mouth was red, like a woman's, against his pale skin, and his eyes bright green when he smiled.

"Nope."

"You should," he said. He slipped on his coat. "You know what a barracoon is, or was?"

"A place where slaves were kept."

"Jean Lafitte had one right outside New Iberia. Near Spanish Lake. I bet you didn't know that." He stuck me in the stomach with his finger.

"I'm glad I found that out."

"I'm going out through the kitchen. The guys out front won't bother you."

"I think your frame of reference is screwed up, Sonny. You don't give a pass to a police officer."

"Those guys out there ask questions in four languages, Dave. The one with the fire hydrant neck, he used to do chores in the basement for Idi Amin. He'd really like to have a chat with me."

"Why?"

"I capped his brother. Enjoy the spring evening, Streak. It's great to be home."

He unlocked the door and disappeared through the back of the restaurant.

As I walked back to the bar, I saw both the hatted man and his short companion staring through the front glass. Their eyes reminded me of buckshot.

Fuck it, I thought, and headed for the door. But a crowd of Japanese tourists had just entered the restaurant, and by the time I got past them the sidewalk was empty except for an elderly black man selling cut flowers out of a cart.

The evening sky was light blue and ribbed with

strips of pink cloud, and the breeze off the lake balmy and bitten with salt, redolent with the smells of coffee and roses and the dry electric flash and scorch of the streetcar.

As I headed back toward my pickup truck, I could see heat lightning, out over Lake Pontchartrain, trembling like shook foil inside a storm bank that had just pushed in from the Gulf.

An hour later the rain was blowing in blinding sheets all the way across the Atchafalaya swamp. Sonny Boy's notebook vibrated on the dashboard with the roar of my engine.

Chapter 2

THE NEXT MORNING I dropped it in my file cabinet at the Iberia Parish Sheriff's Department unread and opened my mail while I drank a cup of coffee. There was a telephone message from Sonny Boy Marsallus, but the number was in St. Martinville, not New Orleans. I dialed it and got no answer.

I gazed out the window at the fine morning and the fronds on the palm trees lifting against the windswept sky. He was out of my jurisdiction, I told myself, don't get mixed up in his grief. Sonny had probably been out of sync with the earth since conception, and it was only a matter of time before someone tore up his ticket.

But finally I did pull the jacket on Sweet Pea Chaisson, which stayed updated, one way or another, because he was one of our own and seemed to make a point of coming back to the Breaux Bridge–St. Martinville–New Iberia area to get in trouble.

I've never quite understood why behaviorists spend so much time and federal funding on the study of sociopaths and recidivists, since none of the research ever teaches us anything about them or makes them any better. I've often thought it would be more helpful simply to pull a half dozen like Sweet Pea out of our files, give them supervisory jobs in mainstream society, see how everybody likes it, then perhaps consider a more draconian means of redress, such as prison colonies in the Aleutians.

He had been born and abandoned in a Southern Pacific boxcar, and raised by a mulatto woman who operated a zydeco bar and brothel on the Breaux Bridge highway called the House of Joy. His face was shaped like an inverted teardrop, with white eyebrows, eyes that resembled slits in bread dough, strands of hair like vermicelli, a button nose, a small mouth that was always wet.

His race was a mystery, his biscuit-colored body almost hairless, his stomach a water-filled balloon, his pudgy arms and hands those of a boy who never grew out of adolescence. But his comic proportions had always been a deception. When he was seventeen a neighbor's hog rooted up his mother's vegetable garden. Sweet Pea picked up the hog, carried it squealing to the highway, and threw it headlong into the grille of a semi truck.

Nineteen arrests for procuring; two convictions; total time served, eighteen months in parish prisons. Somebody had been looking out for Sweet Pea Chaisson, and I doubted that it was a higher power.

In my mail was a pink memo slip I had missed. Written in Wally the dispatcher's childish scrawl were the words *Guess who's back in the waiting room?* The time on the slip was 7:55 A.M.

Oh Lord.

Bertha Fontenot's skin was indeed black, so deep in hue that the scars on her hands from opening oyster shells in New Iberia and Lafayette restaurants looked like pink worms that had eaten and disfigured the tissue. Her arms jiggled with fat, her buttocks swelled like pillows over the sides of the metal chair she sat on. Her pillbox hat and purple suit were too small for her, and her skirt rode up above her white hose and exposed the knots of varicose veins in her thighs.

On her lap was a white paper towel from which she ate cracklings with her fingers.

"You decide to pry yourself out your chair for a few minutes?" she said, still chewing.

"I apologize. I didn't know you were out here."

"You gonna help me with Moleen Bertrand?"

"It's a civil matter, Bertie."

"That's what you say before."

"Then nothing's changed."

"I can get a white-trash lawyer to tell me that."

"Thank you."

Two uniformed deputies at the water fountain were grinning in my direction.

"Why don't you come in my office and have some coffee?" I said.

She wheezed as I helped her up, then wiped at the crumbs on her dress and followed me inside my office, her big lacquered straw bag, with plastic flowers on the side, clutched under her arm. I closed the door behind us and waited for her to sit down.

"This is what you have to understand, Bertie. I investigate criminal cases. If you have a title problem with your land, you need a lawyer to represent you in what's called a civil proceeding."

"Moleen Bertrand already a lawyer. Some other

lawyer gonna give him trouble back 'cause of a bunch of black peoples?"

"I have a friend who owns a title company. I'll ask him to search the courthouse records for you."

"It won't do no good. We're six black families on one strip that's in arpents. It don't show in the survey in the co'rthouse. Everything in the co'rthouse is in acres now."

"It doesn't make any difference. If that's your land, it's your land."

"What you mean *if*? Moleen Bertrand's grandfather give that land to us ninety-five years ago. Everybody knowed it."

"Somebody didn't."

"So what you gonna do about it?"

"I'll talk to Moleen."

"Why don't you talk to your wastebasket while you're at it?"

"Give me your phone number."

"You got to call up at the sto'. You know why Moleen Bertrand want that land, don't you?"

"No."

"They's a bunch of gold buried on it."

"That's nonsense, Bertie."

"Then why he want to bulldoze out our li'l houses?"

"I'll ask him that."

"When?"

"Today. Is that soon enough?"

"We'll see what we gonna see."

My phone rang and I used the call, which I put on hold, as an excuse to walk her to the door and say good-bye. But as I watched her walk with labored dignity toward her car in the parking lot, I wondered if I, too, had yielded to that old white pretense of impatient charity with people of color, as though somehow they were incapable of understanding our efforts on their behalf.

It was two days later, at five in the morning, when a cruiser pulled a man over for speeding on the St. Martinville highway.

On the backseat and floor were a television set, a portable stereo, a box of women's shoes, bottles of liquor, canned goods, a suitcase full of women's clothes and purses.

"There's a drag ball I haven't been invited to?" the deputy said.

"I'm helping my girlfriend move," the driver said.

"You haven't been drinking, have you?"

"No, sir."

"You seem a little nervous."

"You've got a gun in your hand."

"I don't think that's the problem. What's that fragrance in the air? Is it dark roast coffee? Would you step out of the car, please?"

The deputy had already run the plates. The car belonged to a woman named Della Landry, whose address was on the St. Martin– Iberia Parish line. The driver's name was Roland Broussard. At noon the same day he was brought into our interrogation room by Detective Helen Soileau, a dressing taped high up on his forehead.

He wore dark jeans, running shoes, a green pullover smock from the hospital. His black hair was thick and curly, his jaws unshaved, his nails bitten to the quick; a sour smell rose from his armpits. We stared at him without speaking.

The room was windowless and bare except for a wood table and three chairs. He opened and closed his hands on top of the table and kept scuffing his shoes under the chair. I took his left wrist and turned up his forearm.

"How often do you fix, Roland?" I asked.

"I've been selling at the blood bank."

"I see."

"You got an aspirin?" He glanced at Helen Soileau. She had a broad face whose expression you never wanted to misread. Her blonde hair looked like a lacquered wig, her figure a sack of potatoes. She wore a pair of blue slacks and a starched short-sleeve white shirt, her badge above her left breast; her handcuffs were stuck through the back of her gunbelt.

"Where's your shirt?" I said.

"It had blood all over it. Mine."

"The report says you tried to run," Helen said.

"Look, I asked for a lawyer. I don't have to say anything else, right?"

"That's right," I said. "But you already told us you boosted the car. So we can ask you about that, can't we?"

"Yeah, I boosted it. So what else you want? Big fucking deal."

"Would you watch your language, please?" I said.

"What is this, a crazy house? You got a clown making fun of me out on the road, then beating the shit out of me, and I'm supposed to worry about my fucking language."

"Did the owner of the car load all her possessions in it and give you the keys so you wouldn't have to wire it? That's a strange story, Roland," I said.

"It was parked like that in the driveway. I know what you're trying to do . . . Why's she keep staring at me?"

"I don't know."

"I took the car. I was smoking dope in it, too. I ain't saying anything else . . . Hey, look, she's got some kind of problem?" He held his finger close to his chest when he pointed at Helen, as though she couldn't see it.

"You want some slack, Roland? Now's the time," I said.

Before he could answer, Helen Soileau picked up the wastebasket by the rim and swung it with both hands across the side of his face. He crashed sideways to the floor, his mouth open, his eyes out of focus. Then she hit him again, hard, across the back of the head, before I could grab her arms. Her muscles were like rocks.

She shook my hands off and hurled the can and its contents of cigarette butts, ashes, and candy wrappers caroming off his shoulders.

"You little pissant," she said. "You think two homicide detectives are wasting their time with a fart like you over a car theft. Look at me when I talk to you!"

"Helen—" I said softly.

"Go outside and leave us alone," she said.

"Nope," I said, and helped Roland Broussard back

into his chair. "Tell Detective Soileau you're sorry, Roland."

"For what?"

"For being a wiseass. For treating us like we're stupid."

"I apologize."

"Helen—" I looked at her.

"I'm going to the john. I'll be back in five minutes," she said.

"You're the good guy now?" he said, after she closed the door behind her.

"It's no act, podna. I don't get along with Helen. Few people do. She smoked two perps in three years."

His eyes looked up into mine.

"Here's the lay of the land," I said. "I believe you creeped that woman's duplex and stole her car, but you didn't have anything to do with the rest of it. That's what *I* believe. That doesn't mean you won't take the fall for what happened in there. You get my drift?"

He pinched his temples with his fingers, as though a piece of rusty wire were twisting inside his head.

"So?" I opened my palms inquisitively.

"Nobody was home when I went through the window. I cleaned out the place and had it all loaded in her car. That's when some other broad dropped her off in front, so I hid in the hedge. I'm thinking, What am I gonna do? I start the car, she'll know I'm stealing it. I wait around, she turns on the light, she knows the place's been ripped off. Then two guys roar up out of nowhere, come up the sidewalk real fast, and push her inside.

"What they done, I don't like remembering it, I closed my eyes, that's the truth, she was whimpering, I'm not kidding you, man, I wanted to stop it. What was I gonna do?"

"Call for help."

"I was strung out, I got a serious meth problem, it's easy to say what you ought to do when you're not there. Look, what's-your-name, I've been down twice but I never hurt anybody. Those guys, they were tearing her apart, I was scared, I never saw anything like that before."

"What did they look like, Roland?"

"Gimmie a cigarette."

"I don't smoke."

"I didn't see their faces. I didn't want to. Why didn't her neighbors help?"

"They weren't home."

"I felt sorry for her. I wish I'd done something."

"Detective Soileau is going to take your statement, Roland. I'll probably be talking to you again."

"How'd you know I didn't do it?"

"The ME says her neck was broken in the bathroom. That's the only room you didn't track mud all over."

I passed Helen Soileau on my way out. Her eyes were hot and focused like BB's on the apprehensive face of Roland Broussard.

"He's been cooperative," I said.

The door clicked shut behind me. I might as well

have addressed myself to the drain in the water fountain.

Moleen Bertrand lived in an enormous white-columned home on Bayou Teche, just east of City Park, and from his glassed-in back porch you could look down the slope of his lawn, through the widely spaced live oak trees, and see the brown current of the bayou drifting by, the flooded cane brakes on the far side, the gazebos of his neighbors clustered with trumpet and passion vine, and finally the stiff, blocklike outline of the old drawbridge and tender house off Burke Street.

It was March and already warm, but Moleen Bertrand wore a long-sleeve candy-striped shirt with ruby cuff links and a rolled white collar. He was over six feet and could not be called a soft man, but at the same time there was no muscular tone or definition to his body, as though in growing up he had simply bypassed physical labor and conventional sports as a matter of calling.

He had been born to an exclusionary world of wealth and private schools, membership in the town's one country club, and Christmas vacations in places the rest of us knew of only from books, but no one could accuse him of not having improved upon what he had been given. He was Phi Beta Kappa at Springhill and a major in the air force toward the end of the Vietnam War. He made the *Law Review* at Tulane and became a senior partner at his firm in less than five years. He was also a champion skeet shooter. Any number of demagogic politicians who were famous for their largess sought his endorsement and that of his family name. They didn't receive it. But he never gave offense or was known to be unkind.

We walked under the trees in his backyard. His face was cool and pleasant as he sipped his iced tea and looked at a motorboat and a water-skier hammering down the bayou on pillows of yellow foam.

"Bertie can come to my office if she wants. I don't know what else to tell you, Dave," he said. His short salt-and-pepper hair was wet and freshly combed, the part a razor-straight pink line in his scalp.

"She says your grandfather gave her family the land."

"The truth is we haven't charged her any rent. She's interpreted that to mean she owns the land."

"Are you selling it?"

"It's a matter of time until it gets developed by someone."

"Those black people have lived there a long time, Moleen."

"Tell me about it." Then the brief moment of impatience went out of his face. "Look, here's the reality, and I don't mean it as a complaint. There're six or seven nigra families in there we've taken care of for fifty years. I'm talking about doctor and dentist bills, schooling, extra money for June 'Teenth, getting people out of jail. Bertie tends to forget some things."

"She mentioned something about gold being buried on the property."

"Good heavens. I don't want to offend you, but don't y'all have something better to do?"

"She took care of me when I was little. It's hard to chase her out of my office."

He smiled and put his hand on my shoulder. His nails were immaculate, his touch as soft as a woman's. "Send her back to me," he said.

"What's this stuff about gold?"

"Who knows? I always heard Jean Lafitte buried his treasure right across the bayou there, right over by those two big cypress trees." Then his smile became a question mark. "Why are you frowning?"

"You're the second person to mention Lafitte to me in the last couple of days."

"Hmmm," he said, blowing air out his nostrils.

"Thanks for your time, Moleen."

"My pleasure."

I walked toward my truck, which was parked on the gravel cul-de-sac by his boathouse. I rubbed the back of my neck, as though a half-forgotten thought were trying to burrow its way out of my skin.

"Excuse me, didn't you represent Bertie's nephew once?" I asked.

"That's right."

"His name's Luke, you got him out of the death house?"

"That's the man."

I nodded and waved good-bye again.

He had mentioned getting people out of jail but nothing as dramatic as saving somebody from the electric chair hours before an electrocution.

Why not?

Maybe he was just humble, I said in response to my own question.

When I backed out of the drive, he was idly pouring his iced tea into the inverted cone at the top of an anthill.

I drove out on the St. Martinville highway to the lime green duplex set back among pine trees where Della Landry had suddenly been thrust through a door into an envelope of pain that most of us can imagine only in nightmares. The killers had virtually destroyed the interior. The mattresses, pillows, and stuffed chairs were slashed open, dishes and books raked off the shelves, dresser drawers dumped on the floors, plaster and lathes stripped out of the walls with either a crowbar or claw hammer; even the top of the toilet tank was broken in half across the bowl.

Her most personal items from the bathroom's cabinets were strewn across the floor, cracked and ground into the imitation tile by heavy shoes. The sliding shower glass that extended across the tub had been shattered out of the frame. On the opposite side of the tub was a dried red streak that could have been painted there by a heavily soaked paintbrush.

When a homicide victim's life can be traced backward to a nether world of pickup bars, pimps, and nickel-and-dime hustlers and street dealers, the search for a likely perpetrator isn't a long one. But Della Landry was a social worker who had graduated in political science from LSU only three years ago; she attended a Catholic church in St. Martinville, came from a middle-class family in Slidell, taught a catechism class to the children of migrant farm workers.

She had a boyfriend in New Orleans who sometimes stayed with her on the weekends, but no one knew his name, and there seemed to be nothing remarkable about the relationship.

What could she have done, owned, or possessed that would invite such a violent intrusion into her young life?

The killers could have made a mistake, I thought, targeted the wrong person, come to the wrong address. Why not? Cops did it.

But the previous tenants in the duplex had been a husband and wife who operated a convenience store. The next-door neighbors were Social Security recipients. The rest of the semirural neighborhood was made up of ordinary lower-middle-income people who would never have enough money to buy a home of their own.

A small wire book stand by the television set had been knocked over on the carpet. The titles of the books were unexceptional and indicated nothing other than a general reading interest. But among the splay of pages was a small newspaper, titled *The Catholic Worker*, with a shoe print crushed across it.

Then for some reason my eyes settled not on the telephone, which had been pulled loose from the wall jack, but on the number pasted across the telephone's base.

I inserted the terminal back in the jack and dialed the department.

"Wally, would you go down to my office for me and look at a pink message slip stuck in the corner of my blotter?"

"Sure. Hey, I'm glad you called. The sheriff was looking for you."

"First things first, okay?"

"Hang on."

He put me on hold, then picked up the receiver on my desk.

"All right, Dave."

I asked him to read me the telephone number on the message slip. After he had finished, he said, "That's the number Sonny Marsallus left."

"It's also the number of the phone I'm using right now, Della Landry's."

"What's going on? Sonny decide to track his shit into Iberia Parish?"

"I think you've got your hand on it."

"Look, the sheriff wants you to head out by Spanish Lake. Sweet Pea Chaisson and a carload of his broads are causing a little hysteria in front of the convenience store."

"Then send a cruiser out there."

"It isn't a traffic situation." He began to laugh in a cigar-choked wheeze. "Sweet Pea's got his mother's body sticking out of the car trunk. See what you can do, Dave."

Chapter 3

Five miles up the old Lafayette highway that led past Spanish Lake, I saw the lights on emergency vehicles flashing in front of a convenience store and traffic backing up in both directions as people slowed to stare at the uniformed cops and paramedics who themselves seemed incredulous at the situation. I drove on the road's shoulder and pulled into the parking lot, where Sweet Pea and five of his hookers—three white, one black, one Asian—sat amidst a clutter of dirty shovels in a pink Cadillac convertible, their faces bright with sweat as the heat rose from the leather interior. A group of kids were trying to see through the legs of the adults who were gathered around the trunk of the car.

The coffin was oversize, an ax handle across, and had been made of wood and cloth and festooned with what had once been silk roses and angels with a one-foot-square glass viewing window in the lid. The sides were rotted out, the slats held in place by vinyl garbage bags and duct tape. Sweet Pea had wedged a piece of plywood under the bottom to keep it from collapsing and spilling out on the highway, but the head of the coffin protruded out over the bumper. The viewing glass had split cleanly across the middle, exposing the waxen and pinched faces of two corpses and nests of matted hair that had fountained against the coffin's sides.

A uniformed deputy grinned at me from behind his sunglasses.

"Sweet Pea said he's giving bargain rates on the broad in the box," he said.

"What's going on?" I said.

"Wally didn't tell you?"

"No, he was in a comic mood, too."

The smile went out of the deputy's face. "He says he's moving his relatives to another cemetery."

I walked to the driver's door. Sweet Pea squinted up at me against the late sun. His eyes were the strangest I had ever seen in a human being. There were webbed with skin in the corners, so that the eyeballs seem to peep out from slits like a baby bird's.

"I don't believe it," I said.

"Believe it," the woman next to him said, disgusted. Her pink shorts were grimed with dirt. She pulled out the top of her shirt and smelled herself.

"You think it's Mardi Gras?" I said.

"I don't got a right to move my stepmother?" Sweet Pea said. His few strands of hair were glued across his scalp.

"Who's in the coffin with her?"

His mouth made a wet silent O, as though he were thinking. Then he said, "Her first husband. They were a tight couple."

"Can we get out of the car and get something to eat?" the woman next to him said.

"It's better you stay where you are for a minute," I said.

"Robicheaux, cain't we talk reasonable here? It's hot. My ladies are uncomfortable."

"Don't call me by my last name."

"Excuse me, but you're not understanding the situation. My stepmother was buried on the Bertrand plantation 'cause that's where she growed up. I hear it's gonna be sold and I don't want some cocksucker pouring cement on top of my mother's grave. So I'm taking them back to Breaux Bridge. I don't need no permit for that."

He looked into my eyes and saw something there.

"I don't get it. I been rude, I did something to insult you?" he said.

"You're a pimp. You don't have a lot of fans around here."

He bounced the heels of his hands lightly on the steering wheel. He smiled at nothing, his white eyebrows heavy with sweat. He cleaned one ear with his little finger.

"We got to wait for the medical examiner?" he said.

"That's right."

"I don't want nobody having an accident on my seats. They drunk two cases of beer back at the grave," he said.

"Step over to my office with me," I said.

"Beg your pardon?" he said.

"Get out of the car."

He followed me into the shade on the lee side of the store. He wore white slacks and brown shoes and belt and a maroon silk shirt unbuttoned on his chest. His teeth looked small and sharp inside his tiny mouth.

"Why the hard-on?" he said.

"I don't like you."

"That's your problem."

"You got a beef with Sonny Boy Marsallus?"

"No. Why should I?"

"Because you think he's piecing into your action."

"You're on a pad for Marsallus?"

"A woman was beaten to death last night, Sweet Pea. How you'd like to spend tonight in the bag, then answer some questions for us in the morning?"

"The broad was Sonny's punch or something? Why 'front me about it?"

"Nine years ago I helped pull a girl out of the Industrial Canal. She'd been set on fire with gasoline. I heard that's how you made your bones with the Giacanos."

He removed a toothpick from his shirt pocket and put it in his mouth. He shook his head profoundly.

"Nothing around here ever changes. Say, you want a sno'ball?" he said.

"You're a clever man, Sweet Pea." I pulled my cuffs from my belt and turned him toward the cinder-block wall.

He waited calmly while I snipped them on each wrist, his chin tilted upward, his slitted eyes smiling at nothing.

"What's the charge?" he asked.

"Hauling trash without a permit. No offense meant."

"Wait a minute," he said. He flexed his knees,

grunted, and passed gas softly. "Boy, that's better. T'anks a lot, podna."

That evening my wife, Bootsie, and I boiled crawfish in a big black pot on the kitchen stove and shelled and ate them on the picnic table in the backyard with our adopted daughter, Alafair. Our house had been built of cypress and oak by my father, a trapper and derrick man, during the Depression, each beam and log notched and drilled and pegged, and the wood had hardened and grown dark with rainwater and smoke from stubble burning in the cane fields, and today a ball peen hammer would bounce off its exterior and ring in your palm. Down the tree-dotted slope in front of the house were the bayou and dock and bait shop that I operated with an elderly black man named Batist, and on the far side of the bayou was the swamp, filled with gum and willow trees and dead cypress that turned bloodred in the setting sun.

Alafair was almost fourteen now, far removed from the little Salvadoran girl whose bones had seemed as brittle and hollow as a bird's when I pulled her from a submerged plane out on the salt; nor was she any longer the round, hard-bodied Americanized child who read Curious George and Baby Squanto Indian books and wore a Donald Duck cap with a quacking bill and a Baby Orca T-shirt and red and white tennis shoes embossed with LEFT and RIGHT on each rubber toe. It seemed that one day she had simply stepped across a line, and the baby fat was gone, and her hips and young breasts had taken on the shape of a woman's. I still remember the morning, with a pang of the heart, when she asked that her father please not call her "little guy" and "Baby Squanto" anymore.

She wore her hair in bangs, but it grew to her shoulders now and was black and thick with a light chestnut shine in it. She snapped the tail off a crawfish, sucked the fat out of the head, and peeled the shell off the meat with her thumbnail.

"What's that book you were reading on the gallery, Dave?" she asked.

"A diary of sorts."

"Whose is it?"

"A guy named Sonny Boy."

"That's a grown man's name?" she asked.

"Marsallus?" Bootsie said. She stopped eating. Her hair was the color of honey, and she had brushed it up in swirls and pinned it on her head. "What are you doing with something of his?"

"I ran into him on Canal."

"He's back in New Orleans? Does he have a death wish?"

"If he does, someone else may have paid the price for it."

I saw the question in her eyes.

"The woman who was killed up on the St. Martin line," I said. "I think she was Sonny's girlfriend."

She bit down softly on the corner of her lip. "He's trying to involve you in something, isn't he?"

"Maybe."

"Not maybe. I knew him before you did, Dave. He's a manipulator."

"I never figured him out, I guess. Let's go into town and get some ice cream," I said.

"Don't let Sonny job you, Streak," she said.

I didn't want to argue with Bootsie's knowledge of the New Orleans mob. After she married her previous husband, she had found out he kept the books for the Giacano family and owned half of a vending machine company with them. She also discovered, when he and his mistress were shotgunned to death in the parking lot of Hialeah race track, that he had mortgaged her home on Camp Street, which she had brought free and clear to the marriage.

I didn't want to talk to Bootsie in front of Alafair about the contents of Sonny's notebook, either. Much of it made little sense to me—names that I didn't recognize, mention of a telephone tree, allusions to weapons drops and mules flying dope under U.S. coastal radar. In fact, the concern, the place names, seemed a decade out-of-date, the stuff of congressional inquiry during the mid-Reagan era.

But many of the entries were physical descriptions of events that were not characterized by ideology or after-the-fact considerations about legality or illegality:

The inside of the jail is cool and dark and smells of stone and stagnant water. The man in the corner says he's from Texas but speaks no English. He pried the heels off his boots with a fork and gave the guards seventy American dollars. Through the bars I can see the helicopters going in low across the canopy toward the village on the hillside, firing rockets all the way. I think the guards are going to shoot the man in the corner tomorrow morning. He keeps telling anyone who will listen he's only a marijuanista . . .

We found six cane cutters with their thumbs wired

behind them in a slough two klicks from the place where we picked up our ammunition. They'd had no connection with us. They had been executed with machetes while kneeling. We pulled out as the families were coming from the village . . .

Dysentery . . . water goes through me like a wet razor . . . burning with fever last night while the trees shook with rain . . . I wake in the morning to small-arms fire from the other side of an Indian pyramid that's gray and green and smoking with mist, my blanket crawling with spiders . . .

"What are you thinking about?" Bootsie said on our way back from the ice cream parlor.

"You're right about Sonny. He was born to the hustle."

"Yes?"

"I just never knew a grifter who deliberately turned his life into a living wound."

She looked at me curiously in the fading light.

I didn't go directly to the department in the morning. Instead, I drove out past Spanish Lake to the little community of Cade, which was made up primarily of dirt roads, the old S.P. rail tracks, the dilapidated, paintless shacks of black people, and the seemingly boundless acreage of the Bertrand family sugar plantation.

It had rained earlier that morning, and the new cane was pale green in the fields and egrets were picking insects out of the rows. I drove down a dirt lane past Bertha Fontenot's weathered cypress home, which had an orange tin roof and a tiny privy in back. A clump of banana trees grew thickly against her south wall, and petunias and impatiens bloomed out of coffee cans and rusted-out buckets all over her gallery. I drove past one more house, one that was painted, and parked by a grove of gum trees, the unofficial cemetery of the Negro families who had worked on the plantation since before the War Between the States.

The graves were no more than faint depressions among the drifting leaves, the occasional wooden cross or board marker inscribed with crude lettering and numbers knocked down and cracked apart by tractors and cane wagons, except for one yawning pit whose broken stone tablet lay half buried with fallen dirt at the bottom.

But even in the deep shade I could make out the name *Chaisson* cut into the surface.

"I can hep you with something?" a black man said behind me. He was tall, with a bladed face, eyes like bluefish scale, hair shaved close to the scalp, his skin the dull gold cast of worn saddle leather. He wore a grass-stained pink golf shirt, faded jeans, and running shoes without socks.

"Not really," I said.

"You ax Mr. Moleen you can come on the property?" he said.

"I'm Detective Dave Robicheaux with the sheriff's department," I said, and opened my badge holder in my palm. He nodded without replying, his face deliberately simple and empty of any emotion he thought I might read there. "Aren't you Bertie's nephew?"

"Yes, suh, that's right."

"Your name's Luke, you run the juke joint south of the highway?"

"Sometimes. I don't own it, though. You know lots of things." When he smiled his eyes became veiled. Behind him, I saw a young black woman watching us from the gallery. She wore white shorts and a flowered blouse, and her skin had the same gold cast as his. She walked with a cane, although I could see no infirmity in her legs.

"How many people do you think are buried in this grove?" I asked.

"They ain't been burying round here for a long time. I ain't sure it was even in here."

"Is that an armadillo hole we're looking at?"

"Miz Chaisson and her husband buried there. But that's the only marker I ever seen here."

"Maybe those depressions are all Indian graves. What do you think?"

"I grew up in town, suh. I wouldn't know nothing about it."

"You don't have to call me sir."

He nodded again, his eyes looking at nothing.

"You own your house, podna?" I said.

"Aint Bertie say she own it since her mother died. She let me and my sister stay there."

"She says she owns it, huh?"

"Mr. Moleen say different."

"Who do you believe?" I said, and smiled.

"It's what the people at the co'rthouse say. You want anything else, suh? I got to be about my work."

"Thanks for your time."

He walked off through the dappled light, his face

turned innocuously into the breeze blowing across the cane field. Had I been a cop too long? I asked myself. Had I come to dislike someone simply because he'd been up the road?

No, it was the disingenuousness, the hostility that had no handles on it, the use of one's race like the edge of an ax.

But why expect otherwise, I thought. We'd been good teachers.

Five minutes after I walked into my office, Helen Soileau came through the door with a file folder in her hand and sat with one haunch on the corner of my desk, her wide-set, unblinking pale eyes staring at my face.

"What is it?" I said.

"Guess who bailed out Sweet Pea Chaisson?"

I raised my eyebrows.

"Jason Darbonne, over in Lafayette. When did he start representing pimps?"

"Darbonne would hitch his mother to a dogsled if the price was right."

"Get this. The health officer wouldn't let Sweet Pea transport the coffin back to Breaux Bridge, so he got a guy to haul it for ten bucks in a garbage truck."

"What's the file folder?"

"You wanted to question Pissant again? Too bad. The Feds picked him up this morning . . . Hey, I thought that'd give your peaches a tug."

"Helen, could you give a little thought as to how you speak to people sometimes?"

"I'm not the problem. The problem is that black

four-eyed fuck at the jail who turned our man over to the FBI."

"What does the FBI want with a house creep?"

"Here's the paperwork," she said, and threw the folder on my desk. "If you go over to the lockup, tell that stack of whale shit to get his mind off copping somebody's pud, at least long enough to give us a phone call before he screws up an investigation."

"I'm serious, Helen . . . Why not cut people a little . . . Never mind . . . I'll take care of it."

After she left my office I went over to see the parish jailer. He was a three-hundred-pound bisexual with glasses as thick as Coke bottles and moles all over his neck.

"I didn't release him. The night man did," he said.

"This paperwork is shit, Kelso."

"Don't hurt my night man's feelings. He didn't get out of the eighth grade for nothing."

"You have a peculiar sense of humor. Roland Broussard was witness to a murder."

"So talk to the Feds. Maybe that's why they picked him up. Anyway, they just took him out on loan."

"Where's it say that? This handwriting looks like a drunk chicken walked across the page."

"You want anything else?" he asked, taking a wax paper-wrapped sandwich out of his desk drawer.

"Yeah, the prisoner back in our custody."

He nodded, bit into his sandwich, and opened the newspaper on his desk blotter.

"I promise you, my man, you'll be the first to know," he said, his eyes already deep in a sports story.

Chapter 4

AFTER YOU'RE A police officer for a while, you encounter certain temptations. They come to you as all seductions do, in increments, a teaspoon at a time, until you discover you made an irrevocable hard left turn down the road someplace and you wake up one morning in a moral wasteland with no idea who you are.

I'm not talking about going on a pad, ripping off dope from an evidence locker, or taking juice from dealers, either. Those temptations are not inherent in the job; they're in the person.

The big trade-off is in one's humanity. The discretionary power of a police officer is enormous, at least in the lower strata of society, where you spend most of your time. You start your career with the moral clarity of the youthful altruist, then gradually you begin to feel betrayed by those you supposedly protect and serve. You're not welcome in their part of town; you're lied to with regularity, excoriated, your cruiser Molotoved. The most venal bail bondsman can walk with immunity through neighborhoods where you'll be shot at by snipers.

You begin to believe there are those in our midst who are not part of the same gene pool. You think of them as subhuman, morally diseased, or, at best, as caricatures whom you treat in custody as you would humorous circus animals.

Then maybe you're the first to arrive on the scene after another cop has shot and killed a fleeing suspect. The summer night is hot and boiling with insects, the air already charged with a knowledge you don't want to accept. It was a simple B&E, a slashed screen in the back of a house; the dead man is a full-time bumbling loser known to every cop on the beat; the two wounds are three inches apart.

"He was running?" you say to the other cop, who's wired to the eyes.

"You goddamn right he was. He stopped and turned on me. Look, he had a piece."

The gun is in the weeds; it's blue-black, the grips wrapped with electrician's tape. The moon is down, the night so dark you wonder how anyone could see the weapon in the hand of a black suspect.

"I'm counting on you, kid," the other cop says. "Just tell people what you saw. *There's* the fucking gun. Right? It ain't a mushroom."

And you step across a line.

Don't sweat it, a sergeant and drinking buddy tells you later. It's just one more lowlife off the board. Most of these guys wouldn't make good bars of soap.

Then something happens that reminds you we all fell out of the same tree.

Imagine a man locked in a car trunk, his wrists bound behind him, his nose running from the dust and the thick oily smell of the spare tire. The car's brake lights go on, illuminating the interior of the trunk briefly, then the car turns on a rural road and gravel pings like rifle shot under the fenders. But something changes, a stroke of luck the bound man can't believe—the car bangs over a rut and the latch on the trunk springs loose from the lock, hooking just enough so that the trunk lid doesn't fly up in the driver's rearview mirror.

The air that blows through the opening smells of rain and wet trees and flowers; the man can hear hundreds of frogs croaking in unison. He readies himself, presses the sole of his tennis shoe against the latch, eases it free, then rolls over the trunk's lip, tumbles off the bumper, and bounces like a tire in the middle of the road. The breath goes out of his chest in a long wheeze, as though he had been dropped from a great height; rocks scour divots out of his face and grind red circles the size of silver dollars on his elbows.

Thirty yards up the car has skidded to a stop, the lid of the trunk flopping in the air. And the bound man splashes through the cattails into a slough by the side of the road, his legs tangling in dead hyacinth vines below the surface, the silt locking around his ankles like soft cement.

Ahead he can see the flooded stands of cypress and willow trees, the green layer of algae on the dead water, the shadows that envelop and protect him like a cloak. The hyacinth vines are like wire around his legs; he trips, falls on one knee. A brown cloud of mud mushrooms around him. He stumbles forward again, jerking at the clothesline that binds his wrists, his heart exploding in his chest.

His pursuers are directly behind him now; his back

twitches as though the skin has been stripped off with pliers. Then he wonders if the scream he hears is his own or that of a nutria out on the lake.

They fire only one round. It passes through him like a shaft of ice, right above the kidney. When he opens his eyes, he's on his back, stretched across a cushion of crushed willows on top of a sand spit, his legs in the water. The sound of the pistol report is still ringing in his ears. The man who wades toward him in silhouette is smoking a cigarette.

Not twice. It's not fair, Roland Broussard wants to say. *I got a meth problem. That's the only reason I was there. I'm a nobody guy, man. You don't need to do this.*

The man in silhouette takes another puff off his cigarette, pitches it out into the trees, perhaps moves out of the moon's glow so Roland's face will be better illuminated. Then he sights along the barrel and puts another round from the .357 Magnum right through Roland's eyebrow.

He walks with a heavy step back up the embankment, where a companion has waited for him as though he were watching the rerun of an old film.

Chapter 5

CLETE LISTENED, HIS powder blue porkpie hat slanted down on his forehead, his eyes roving out into the hall while I talked. He wore an immaculate pair of white tennis shorts and a print shirt covered with parakeets. The back of his neck and the tops of his immense arms were flaking with sunburn.

"Kidnapping a guy already in custody is pretty slick. Who do you figure these characters were?" he said, his eyes leaving two uniformed deputies on the other side of the glass.

"Guys who knew the drill, at least well enough to convince a night jailer they were FBI."

"The greaseballs?"

"Maybe."

"It's not their normal style. They don't like to stray into federal jurisdiction." He glanced through the glass partition into the hall again. "Why do I get the feeling I'm some kind of zoo exhibit?"

"It's your imagination," I said, my face flat.

"I bet." Then he winked and pointed at a deputy with one finger. The deputy looked down at some papers in his hand.

"Knock it off, Clete."

"Why'd you ask me down here?"

"I thought you'd like to go fishing."

He smiled. His face was round and pink, his green eyes lighted with a private sense of humor. A scar ran through part of his eyebrow and across the bridge of his nose, where he had been bashed with a pipe when he was a kid in the Irish Channel.

"Dave, I know what my old Homicide podjo is going to think before he thinks it."

"I've got two open murder cases. One of the victims may have been Sonny Boy Marsallus's girlfriend."

"Marsallus, huh?" he said, his face sobering.

"I tried to have him picked up by NOPD, but he went off the screen."

He drummed his fingers on the arm of the chair.

"Leave him off the screen," he said.

"What was he into down in the tropics?" I asked.

"A lot of grief."

Helen Soileau came through the door, without knocking, and dropped the crime scene report on my desk.

"You want to look it over and sign it?" she said. Her eyes went up and down Clete's body.

"Do y'all know each other?" I said.

"Only by reputation. Didn't he work for Sally Dio?" she said.

Clete fed a stick of gum in his mouth and looked at me.

"I'll go over the report in a few minutes, Helen," I said.

"We couldn't get a print off the cigarette butt, but the casts on the footprints and tire tracks look good," she said. "By the way, the .357 rounds were hollow-points."

"Thanks," I said.

Clete swiveled around in his chair and watched her go back out the door.

"Who's the muff-diver?" he said.

"Come on, Clete."

"One look at that broad is enough to drive you to a monastery."

It was a quarter to five.

"Do you want to pull your car around front and I'll meet you there?" I said.

He followed me in his old Cadillac convertible to the Henderson levee outside Breaux Bridge. We put my boat and outboard in the water and fished on the far side of a bay dotted with abandoned oil platforms and dead cypress trees. The rain was falling through shafts of sunlight in the west, and the rain looked like tunnels of spun glass and smoke rising into the sky.

Clete took a long-necked bottle of Dixie beer from the cooler and snapped off the top with his pocket-knife. The foam slid down the inside of the neck when he removed the bottle from his mouth. Then he drank again, his throat working a long time. His face looked tired, vaguely morose.

"Were you bothered by that crack Helen made about Sally Dio?"

"So I ran security for a greaseball. I also had two of his goons slam my hand in a car door. Sometime when you have a chance, tell the bride of Frankenstein what happened when Sal and his hired gumballs were flying friendly skies."

The plane had crashed and exploded in a fireball on a mountainside in western Montana. The National Transportation Safety Board said someone had poured sand in the gas tanks.

Clete finished his beer and blew out his breath. He pushed his hand down in the ice for another bottle.

"You okay, partner?" I said.

"I've never dealt real well with that bullshit I got involved with in Central America. Sometimes it comes back in the middle of the night, I mean worse than when I got back from Vietnam. It's like somebody striking a match on my stomach lining."

There were white lines at the corners of his eyes. He watched his red-and-white bobber move across the water in the shade of an oil platform, dip below the surface and rise quivering again; but he didn't pick up his rod.

"Maybe it's time for the short version of the Serenity Prayer. Sometimes you just have to say fuck it," I said.

"What's the worst day you had in 'Nam, I mean besides getting nailed by that Bouncing Betty?"

"A village chieftain called in the 105s on his own people."

"Sonny Boy and I hooked up with the same bunch of gunrunners. It was like an outdoor mental asylum down there. Half the time I didn't know if we were selling to the rebels or the government. I was so strung out on rum and dope and my own troubles I didn't care, either. Then one night we got to see what the government did when they wanted to put the fear of God in the Indians."

He pinched his mouth with his hand. His calluses made a dry sound like sandpaper against his whiskers. He took a breath and widened his eyes.

"They went into this one ville and killed everything in sight. Maybe four hundred people. There was an orphanage there, run by some Mennonites. They didn't spare anybody . . . all those kids . . . man."

He watched my face.

"You saw this?" I asked.

"I heard it, from maybe a half mile away. I'll never forget the sound of those people screaming. Then this captain walked us through the ville. The sonofabitch didn't give it a second thought."

He put a Lucky Strike in his mouth and tried to light it with a Zippo cupped in his hands. The flint scratched dryly and he took the cigarette back out of his mouth and closed his big hand on it.

"Let the past go, Cletus. Haven't you paid enough dues?" I said.

"You wanted to hear about Sonny Boy? Three weeks later we were with a different bunch of guys, I was so wiped out I still don't know who they were, Cubans maybe and some Belgians working both sides of the street. Anyway, we were on a trail and we walked right into an L-shaped ambush, M-60's, blookers, serious shit, they must have shredded twelve guys in the first ten seconds.

"Sonny was on point . . . I saw this . . . I wasn't hallucinating . . . Two guys next to me saw it, too . . ."

"What are you talking about?"

"He got nailed with an M-60. I saw dust jumping all over his clothes. I didn't imagine it. When he went down his shirt was soaked with blood. Three weeks later he shows up in a bar in Guatemala City. The rebels starting calling him the red angel. They said he couldn't die."

He took a long drink off the beer. The sunlight looked like a yellow flame inside the bottle.

"Okay, mon, maybe I fried my head down there," he said. "But I stay away from Sonny. I don't know how to describe it, it's like he's got death painted on his skin."

"It sounds like another one of Sonny's cons."

"There's nothing like somebody else telling you what you saw. You remember what an M-60 bouncing on a bungee cord could do to an entire ville? How about a guy who gets it from ten yards away? No, don't answer that, Dave. I don't think I can handle it."

In the silence I could hear the *whir* of automobile tires on the elevated highway that spanned the swamp. The setting sun looked like lakes of fire in the clouds, then a shower began to march across the bays and willow islands and dance in a yellow mist on the water around us. I pulled up the sash weight I used for an anchor, cranked the engine, and headed back for the levee. Clete opened another bottle of Dixie, then reached deep down in the crushed ice, found a can of Dr Pepper, and tossed it to me. "Sorry, Streak," he said, and smiled with his eyes.

But the apology would be mine to make.

* * *

That night I put on my gym shorts, running shoes, and a T-shirt, and drove out toward Spanish Lake and the little community of Cade. I can't explain why I decided to jog there rather than along the bayou, by my house, south of town. Maybe it was because the only common denominator in the case, so far, was a geographical one. For no reason I understood, Sonny Boy had mentioned a barracoon, built near the lake by Jean Lafitte, then Sweet Pea Chaisson, who could never be accused of familial sentiment, other than a violent one, had decided to exhume his adoptive mother's remains from the Bertrand plantation and transport them in a garbage truck back to Breaux Bridge. Both men operated in a neon and concrete world where people bought and sold each other daily and lived by the rules that govern piranha fish. What was their interest or involvement in a rural community of poor black people?

I parked my truck and jogged along a dirt road between sugarcane acreage, over the railroad tracks, past a dilapidated clapboard store and a row of shacks. Behind me, a compact white automobile turned off the highway, slowed so as not to blow dust in my face, and drove toward the lighted houses on the lake. I could see the silhouettes of two people talking to each other.

The breeze was warm and smelled of horses and night-blooming flowers, freshly turned soil, and smoke blowing off a stump fire hard by a pecan orchard. The tree trunks seemed alive with shadows and protean shapes in the firelight, as though, if you let imagination have its way, the residents from an earlier time had not yet accepted the inevitability of their departure.

I've often subscribed to the notion that perhaps history is not sequential; that all people, from all of history, live out their lives simultaneously, in different dimensions perhaps, occupying the same pieces of geography, unseen by one another, as if we are all part of one spiritual conception.

Attakapas Indians, Spanish colonists, slaves who dredged mud from the lake to make bricks for the homes of their masters, Louisiana's boys in butternut brown who refused to surrender after Appomattox, federal soldiers who blackened the sky with smoke from horizon to horizon—maybe they were all still out there, living just a breath away, like indistinct figures hiding inside an iridescent glare on the edge of our vision.

But the lights I saw in a distant grove of gum trees were not part of a metaphysical speculation. I could see them bouncing off tree trunks and hear the roar and grind of a large machine at the end of the dirt lane that ran past Bertie Fontenot's house.

I slowed to a walk, breathing deep in my chest, and wiped the sweat out of my eyes at the cattle guard and wisteria-grown arched gate that marked the entrance to the Bertrand property. The dirt lane was faintly haloed with humidity in the moonlight, the rain ditches boiling with insects. I began jogging toward the lights in the trees, the steady thud of my shoes like an intrusion on a nocturnal plantation landscape that had eluded the influences of the twentieth century.

Then I had the peculiar realization that I felt naked.

I had neither badge nor gun, and hence no identity other than that of jogger. It was a strange feeling to have, as well as to be forced into acknowledging simultaneously the ease with which my everyday official capacity allowed me to enter and exit any number of worlds where other people lived with an abiding trepidation.

The grinding sounds of the machine ceased and the headlights dimmed and then went off. I strained my eyes to see into the gum trees, then realized that the machine, a large oblong one with a cab and giant steel tracks, was parked beyond the trees in a field, its dozer blade glinting in the moonlight.

Bertie's house and the nephew's were dark. When I walked toward the grove I could see where the dozer blade had graded whole roadways through the trees, ripping up root systems, snapping off limbs, slashing pulpy divots out of the trunks, scooping out trenches and spreading the fill out into the cane field, churning and flattening and regrinding the soil and everything in it, until the entire ground area in and around the grove looked like it had been poured into an enormous bag and shaken out at a great height.

There was no one in sight.

I walked out onto the edge of the field by the earth mover. The moon was bright above the treetops and the new cane ruffled in the breeze. I picked up handfuls of dirt and sifted them through my fingers, touched the pieces of fractured bone, as tiny and brown as ancient teeth; strips of wood porous with rot and as weightless as balsa; the remains of a high button shoe, mashed flat by the machine's track.

The wind dropped and the air suddenly smelled of sour mud and humus and dead water beetles. The sky was a dirty black, the clouds like curds of smoke from an oil fire; sweat ran down my face and sides like angry insects. Who had done this, ripped a burial area apart, as though it had no more worth than a subterranean rat's nest?

I walked back down the dirt lane toward my truck. I saw the white compact car returning down the access road, slowing gradually. Suddenly, from a distance of perhaps forty yards, the person in the passenger's seat shined a handheld spotlight at me. The glare was blinding; I could see nothing except a circle of white red-rimmed heat aimed into my eyes.

No gun, no badge, I thought, a sweating late-middle-aged man trapped on a rural road like a deer caught in an automobile's headlights.

"I don't know who you are, but you take that light out of my eyes!" I shouted.

The car was completely stopped now, the engine idling. I could hear two people, men, talking to each other. Then I realized their concern had shifted from me to someone else. The spotlight went out, leaving my eyes filled with whorls of color, and the car shot forward toward my parked truck, where a man on foot was leaning through the driver's window.

He bolted down the far side of the railway, his body disappearing like a shadow into weeds and cattails. The white compact bounced over the train embankment, stopped momentarily, and the man in the passenger seat shined the spotlight out into the darkness. I used my T-shirt to wipe my eyes clear and tried to read the license plate, but someone had rubbed mud over the numbers.

Then the driver scorched a plume of oily dust out of the road and floored the compact back onto the highway.

I opened the driver's door to my truck. When the interior light flicked on, I saw curled on the seat, like a serpent whose back has been crushed with a car tire, a twisted length of rust-sheathed chain the color of dried blood. I picked it up, felt the delicate shell flake with its own weight against my palms. Attached to one end was a cylindrical iron cuff, hinged open like a mouth gaping in death.

I had seen one like it only in a museum. It was a leg iron, the kind used in the transportation and sale of African slaves.

Chapter 6

The next morning was Saturday. The dawn was gray and there were strips of mist in the oak and pecan trees when I walked down the slope to help Batist open up the dock and bait shop. The sun was still below the treeline in the swamp, and the trunks on the far side of the bayou were wet and black in the gloom. You could smell the fecund odor of bluegill and sun perch spawning back in the bays.

Batist was outside the bait shop, poking a broom handle into the pockets of rainwater that had collected in the canvas awning that extended on guy wires over the dock. I had never known his age, but he was an adult when I was a child, as black and solid as a woodstove, and today his stomach and chest were still as flat as boilerplate. He had farmed and trapped and fished commercially and worked on oyster boats all his life, and could carry an outboard motor down to the ramp in each hand as though they were stamped from plastic. He was illiterate and knew almost nothing of the world outside of Iberia Parish, but he was one of the bravest and most loyal men I ever knew.

He began wiping the dew off the spool tables, which we had inset with Cinzano umbrellas for the fishermen who came in at midday for the barbecue lunches that we sold for $5.95.

"You know why a nigger'd be setting in one of our boats this morning?" he asked.

"Batist, you need to forget that word."

"This is a *nigger* carry a razor and a gun. He ain't here to rent boats."

"Could you start over?"

"There's a high-yellow nigger wit' slacks on and shiny, pointy shoes," he said, tapping his finger in the air with each word as though I were obtuse. "He's setting out yonder in our boat, eating *boudin* out of a paper towel wit' his fingers. This is a nigger been in jail, carry a razor on a string round his neck. I ax what he t'inks he's doing. He look up at me and say, 'You clean up round here?'

"I say, 'Yeah, I clean trash out of the boat, and that mean you better get yo' worthless black ass down that road.'

"He say, 'I ain't come here to argue wit' you. Where Robicheaux at?'

"I say, 'He ain't here and that's all you got to know.' I say, '*Vas t'en, neg.*' That's it. We don't need them kind, Dave."

He used a half-mooned Clorox bottle to scoop the ashes out of the split oil barrel that we used for a barbecue pit. I waited for him to continue.

"What was his name?" I said. "What kind of car did he drive?"

"He didn't have no car, and I ain't ax him his name."

"Where'd he go?"

"Wherever people go when you run them down the road with a two-by-fo'."

"Batist, I don't think it's a good idea to treat people like that."

"One like that always work for the white man, Dave."

"I beg your pardon?"

"Everyt'ing he do make white people believe the rest of us ain't got the right to ax for mo' than we got."

It was one of those moments when I knew better than to contend with Batist's reasoning or experience.

"Somet'ing else I want to talk wit' you about," he said. "Look in yonder my shelves, my pig feet, my *graton*, tell me what you t'ink of that."

I opened the screen door to the shop but hated to look. The jar of pickled hogs' feet was smashed on the floor; half-eaten candy bars, hard-boiled eggs, and cracklings, called *graton* in Cajun French, were scattered on the counter. In the midst of it all, locked in a wire crab trap, Tripod, Alafair's three-legged coon, stared back at me.

I picked him up in my arms and carried him outside. He was a beautiful coon, with silver-tipped fur and black rings on his tail, a fat stomach and big paws that could turn doorknobs and twist tops off of jars.

"I'll send Alf down to clean it up," I said.

"It ain't right that coon keep messing up the shop, Dave."

"It looks to me like somebody left a window open."

"That's right. *Somebody.* 'Cause I closed every one of them."

I stopped.

"I didn't come down here last night, partner, if that's what you're saying."

He straightened up from a table, with the wiping rag in his hand. His face seemed to gather with a private concern. Two fishermen with a minnow bucket and a beer cooler stood by the door of the shop and looked at us impatiently.

"You wasn't down here last night, Dave?" he asked.

"No. What is it?"

He inserted his thumb and forefinger in the watch pocket of the bell-bottom dungarees he wore.

"This was on the windowsill this morning. I t'ought it was somet'ing you found on the flo'," he said, and placed the oblong piece of stamped metal in my hand. "What you call them t'ings?"

"A dog tag." I read the name on it, then read it again.

"What's wrong?" he said.

I felt my hand close on the tag, felt the edges bite into my palm.

"You know I cain't read, me. I didn't want to give you somet'ing bad, no."

"It's all right. Help those gentlemen there, will you? I'll be back down in a minute," I said.

"It ain't good you not tell me."

"It's the name of a man I was in the army with. It's some kind of coincidence. Don't worry about it."

But in his eyes I could see the self-imposed conviction that somehow his own ineptitude or lack of education had caused me injury.

"I ain't mad about that coon, Dave," he said. "Coon gonna be a coon. Tell Alafair it ain't nobody's fault."

I sat at the redwood table with a cup of coffee under the mimosa tree in the backyard, which was still cool and blue with shadow. The breeze ruffled the periwinkles and willows along the edge of the coulee, and two greenhead mallards, who stayed with us year-round, were skittering across the surface of the pond at the back of our property.

The stainless steel dog tag contained the name of Roy J. Bumgartner, his serial number, blood type, religion, and branch of service, the simple and pragmatic encapsulation of a human life that can be vertically inserted as neatly as a safety razor between the teeth and locked in place with one sharp blow to the chin.

I remembered him well, a nineteen-year-old warrant officer from Galveston, Texas, who had brought the slick in low out of the molten sun, the canopy and elephant grass flattening under the down draft while AK-47 rounds whanged off the ship's air-frame like tack hammers. Ten minutes later, the floor piled with wounded grunts, their foreheads painted with Mercurochromed *M*s to indicate the morphine that laced their hearts, we lifted off from the LZ and flew back through the same curtain of automatic weapons fire, the helicopter blades thropping, the windows pocking with holes like skin blisters snapping.

My body was as dry and dehydrated as a lizard's skin, all the moisture used up by the blood-expander the medic had given me during the night, the way spilled water evaporates off a hot stove. The same medic, a sweaty Italian kid from Staten Island, naked to the waist, held me in his arms now, and kept saying, as much to convince himself as me, *You're gonna make it, Loot . . . Say good-bye to Shitsville . . . You're going home alive in sixty-five . . . Bum's chauffeuring this baby right into Battalion Aid . . . They got refrigeration, Loot . . . Plasma . . . Don't put your hands down there . . . I mean it . . . Hey, somebody hold his goddamn hands.*

With the ship yawing and grooves shearing out of the rotary and black smoke from an electrical fire spiraling back through the interior, the rice paddies and earthen dikes and burned-out hooches streaking by below us, I stared at the back of the pilot's head as though my thoughts, which were like a scream inside my skull, could penetrate his: *You can do it, pappy, you can do it, pappy, you can do it, pappy.*

Then he turned and looked behind him, and I saw his thin blond face inside his helmet, the dry lump of chewing tobacco in his cheek, the red field dressing across one eye, the bloodshot and desperate energies in the other, and I knew, even before I saw the waves sliding onto the beach from the South China Sea, that we were going to make it, that no one this brave could perish.

But that conclusion was born out of political innocence and a soldier's naive belief that he would never be abandoned by his own government.

Bootsie brought me another cup of coffee and a bowl of Grape-Nuts with milk and blackberries in it. She wore a pair of faded jeans and a beige sleeveless shirt, and her face looked cool and fresh in the soft light.

"What's that?" she said.

"A dog tag that's thirty years old."

She touched the tag with the balls of her fingers, then turned it over.

"It belonged to a guy who disappeared into Laos," I said. "He never came back home. I think he's one of those who got written off by Nixon and Kissinger."

"I don't understand," she said.

"Batist found it on the windowsill in the bait shop this morning. It's thespian bullshit of some kind. Last night somebody put a rusted leg iron on the seat of my truck."

"Did you tell the sheriff?"

"I'll talk to him Monday."

I chewed a mouthful of Grape-Nuts and kept my face empty.

"Alafair's still asleep. You want to go back inside for a little while?"

"You bet."

A few minutes later we lay on top of the sheets in our bedroom. The curtains were gauzy and white with small roses printed on them, and they puffed in the breeze that blew through the azaleas and pecan trees in the side yard. Bootsie kissed like no woman I ever knew. Her face would come close to mine, her mouth parting, then she would angle her head slightly and touch her lips dryly against mine, remove them, her eyes never leaving mine; then she'd brush my lips with hers one more time, her fingernails making a slow circle in the back of my hair, her right hand moving down my stomach while her tongue slid across my teeth.

She made love without inhibition or self-consciousness, and never with stint or a harbored resentment. She sat on top of me, took me in her hand, and placed me deep inside her, her thighs widening, a wet murmur breaking from her throat. Then she propped herself on both arms so that her breasts hung close to my face, her breath coming faster now, her skin bright with a thin sheen of sweat. I felt her heat spreading into my loins, as though it were she who was controlling the moment for both of us. She leaned closer, gathering herself around me, her feet under my thighs, her face flushed and growing smaller and turning inward now, her hair damp against her skin like swirls of honey. In my mind's eye I saw a great hard-bodied tarpon, thick and stiff with life, glide through tunnels of pink coral and waving sea fans, then burst through a wave in strings of foam and light.

Afterward, she lay inside my arm and touched what seemed to me all the marks of my mortality and growing age—the white patch of hair on the side of my head, my mustache, now flecked with silver, the puckered indentation from a .38 round below my left collarbone, the gray scar, like a flattened earthworm, from a pungi stick, on my stomach, and the spray of arrow-shaped welts on my thigh where steel shards from a Bouncing Betty still lay embedded. Then she rolled against me and kissed me on the cheek.

"What's that for?" I said.

"Because you're the best, *cher*."

"You, too, Boots."

"But you're not telling me something."

"I have a bad feeling about this one."

She raised up on one elbow and looked into my face. Her bare hip looked sculpted, like pink marble, against the light outside.

"These two murders," I said. "We're not dealing with local dimwits."

"So?"

"It's an old problem, Boots. They come from places they've already ruined, and then it's our turn. By the time we figure out we're dealing with major leaguers, they've been through the clock shop with baseball bats."

"That's why we hire cops like you," she said, and tried to smile. When I didn't answer, she said, "We can't remove south Louisiana from the rest of the world, Dave."

"Maybe we should give it a try."

She lay against me and placed her hand on my heart. She smelled of shampoo and flowers and the milky heat in her skin. Outside, I could hear crows cawing angrily in a tree as the sun broke out of the clouds like a heliograph.

Chapter 7

It's probably safe to say the majority of them are self-deluded, uneducated, fearful of women, and defective physically. Their political knowledge, usually gathered from paramilitary magazines, has the moral dimensions of comic books. Some of them have been kicked out of the service on bad conduct and dishonorable discharges; others have neither the physical nor mental capacity to successfully complete traditional basic training in the U.S. Army. After they pay large sums of money to slap mosquitoes at a merc training camp in the piney woods of north Florida, they have themselves tattooed with death heads and grandiloquently toast one another, usually in peckerwood accents, with the classic Legionnaire's paean to spiritual nihilism, "*Vive la guerre, vive la mort.*"

Miami is full of them.

If you want to connect with them in the New Orleans area, you cross the river over to Algiers into a neighborhood of pawnshops and Vietnamese-owned grocery stores and low-rent bars, and visit Tommy Carrol's Gun & Surplus.

It was Sunday evening, and Helen Soileau and I were off the clock and out of our jurisdiction. Tommy Carrol, whom I had never met, was locking up his glass gun cases and about to close. He wore baggy camouflage trousers, polished combat boots, and a wide-necked bright yellow T-shirt, like bodybuilders wear. His shaved head reminded me of an alabaster bowling ball. He chewed and snapped his gum maniacally, his eyes flicking back and forth from his work to Helen and me as we walked in file between the stacks of survival gear, ammunition, inflatable rafts, knife display cases, and chained racks of bolt-action military rifles.

"So I'm stuck again with the goddamn kids, that's what you're saying?" Helen said over her shoulder to me. She wore tan slacks, lacquered straw sandals, and a flowered shirt hanging outside her belt. She sipped from a can of beer that was wrapped in a brown bag.

"Did I say that? Did I say that?" I said at her back.

"You need something?" Tommy Carrol said.

"Yeah, a couple of Excedrin," I said.

"Is there a problem here?" Tommy Carrol asked.

"I'm looking for Sonny Boy Marsallus," I said.

"Don't tell us the herpes outpatient clinic, either. We already been there," Helen said.

"Shut up, Helen," I said.

"Did I marry Mr. Goodwrench or not?" she said.

"What's going on?" Tommy asked, his gum snapping in his jaw.

"Doesn't Sonny hang in here?" I said.

"Sometimes. I mean he used to. Not anymore."

"Helen, why don't you go sit in the car?" I said.

"Because I don't feel like changing diapers on your goddamn kids."

"I've been out of the loop," I said to Tommy. "I'd like to get back to work."

"Doing what?"

"Peace Corps. Isn't this the sign-up place?" I said.

He arched his eyebrows and looked sideways. Then he made a tent on his chest with the fingers of one hand. His eyes were like blue marbles.

"It makes you feel better to jerk my Johnson, be my guest," he said. "But I'm closing up, I don't have any contact with Sonny, and I got nothing to do with other people's family troubles." He widened his eyes for emphasis.

"This is the guy knows all the mercs?" Helen said, and brayed at her own irony. She upended her beer can until it was empty. "I'm driving down to the store on the corner. If you're not there in five minutes, you can ride the goddamn bus home."

She let the glass door slam behind her. Tommy stared after her.

"For real, that's your wife?" he said, chewing his gum.

"Yeah."

"What's your experience? Maybe I can help."

"One tour in 'Nam. Some diddle-shit stuff with the tomato pickers."

He pushed a pencil and pad across the glass countertop.

"Write your name and number down there. I'll see what I can come up with."

"You can't hook me up with Sonny?"

"Like I say, I don't see him around, you know what

I mean?" His eyes were as bright as blue silk, locked on mine, a lump of cartilage working in his jaw.

"He's out of town and nobody's missing him?" I smiled at him.

"You summed it up."

"How about two guys who look like Mutt and Jeff?"

He began shaking his head noncommittally.

"The short guy's got a fire hydrant for a neck. Maybe he did some work for Idi Amin. Maybe Sonny Boy popped a cap on his brother," I said.

His eyes stayed fixed on mine, but I saw his hand tic on the countertop, heard his heavy ring click on the glass. He picked up the notepad from the countertop and tossed it on a littered desk behind him.

"You shouldn't job me, man," he said. His eyes were unblinking, his gum rolling on his teeth.

"You think I'm a cop?"

"You got it, Jack."

"You're right." I opened my badge holder on the countertop. "You know who the guy with the sawed-off neck is, don't you?"

He dropped his ring of keys in his pocket and called out to a man sweeping the wood floors in front, "Lock it up, Mack. I'm gonna see what the old woman's got for supper. The fun guy here is a cop. But you don't have to talk to him, you don't want." Then he spat his chewing gum neatly into a trash bag and clanged through a metal door into the back alley.

I went through the door after him. He began to walk rapidly toward his car, his keys ringing in the pocket of his camouflage trousers.

"Hold on, Tommy," I said.

Helen had parked her car by the end of the alley, next to a Dumpster and a stand of banana trees that grew along a brick wall. She got out of her car with her baton in her hand.

"Right there, motherfucker!" she said, breaking into a run. "Freeze! Did you hear me? I said freeze, goddamn it!"

But Tommy Carrol was not a good listener and tried to make his automobile. She whipped the baton behind his knee, and his leg folded under him as though she had severed a tendon. He crashed into the side of his car door, his knee held up before him with both hands, his mouth open as though he were trying to blow the fire out of a burn.

"Damn it, Helen," I said between my teeth.

"He shouldn't have run," she said. "Right, Tommy? You got nothing to hide, you don't need to run. Tell me I'm right, Tommy."

"Lay off him, Helen. I mean it." I helped him up by one arm, opened his car door, and sat him down in the seat. An elderly black woman, pulling a child's wagon, with a blue rag tired around her head, came off the side street and began rooting in the Dumpster.

"I'm going to file charges on you people," Tommy said.

"That's your right. Who's the short guy, Tommy?" I said.

"You know what? I'm gonna tell you. It's Emile Pogue. Send the mutt here after him. She'll make a great stuffed head."

I heard Helen move behind me, gravel scrape under her shoes.

"No," I said, and held up my hand in front of her.

Tommy kneaded the back of his leg with both hands. A thick blue vein pulsed in his shaved scalp.

"Here's something else to take with you, too," he said. "Emile didn't work for Idi Amin. Emile trained him at an Israeli jump school. You jack-offs don't have any idea of what you're fooling with, do you?"

Monday morning I went to the Iberia Parish Court House and began researching the records on the Bertrand plantation out by Cade. Bertie Fontenot maintained that Moleen Bertrand's grandfather had given a strip of land to several black tenants, her ancestors included, ninety-five years ago, but I could find no record of the transfer. Neither could the clerk of court. The early surveys of the Bertrand property were crude, in French arpents, and made use of coulees and dirt roads as boundaries; the last survey had been done ten years ago for an oil company, and the legal descriptions were clear and the unit designations now in acres. But no matter—there had been no apparent subdivision of the plantation granting Bertie and her neighbors title to the land on which they lived.

The secretary at Moleen's law office told me he had gone out to the country club to join his wife for lunch. I found them by the putting green, he on a wood bench, only enough bourbon in his glass to stain the water the color of oak, she in a short white pleated skirt and magenta blouse that crinkled with light, her bleached hair and deeply tanned and lined face a deceptive and electric illusion of middle-aged health down in the Sunbelt.

For Julia Bertrand was at the club every day, played a mean eighteen as well as game of bridge, was always charming, and was often the only woman remaining among the male crowd who stayed at the bar through supper time. Her capacity was awesome; she never slurred her words or used profane or coarse language; but her driver's license had been suspended twice, and years ago, before I was with the sheriff's department, a Negro child had been killed in a hit-and-run accident out in the parish. Julia Bertrand had been held briefly in custody. But later a witness changed his story, and the parents dropped charges and moved out of state.

She bent over the ball, the breeze ruffling her pleated skirt against her muscular thighs, and putted a ten-footer, *plunk*, neatly into the cup. From the wood bench she picked up her drink, which was filled with fruit and shaved ice and wrapped with a paper napkin and rubber band, and walked toward me with her hand extended. Her smile was dazzling, her tinted contacts a chemical blue-green.

"How are you, Dave? I hope we're not in trouble," she said. Her voice was husky and playful, her breath heavy with nicotine.

"Not with me. How you doing, Julia?"

"I'm afraid Dave's doing pro bono for Bertie Fontenot," Moleen said.

"Dave, not really?" she said.

"It's gone a little bit beyond that," I said. "Some peculiar things seem to be happening out at your plantation, Moleen."

"Oh?" he said.

"I went jogging on your place Friday night. I hope you don't mind."

"Anytime," he said.

"Somebody dropped a rusted leg iron on my truck seat."

"A leg iron? Well, that's interesting, isn't it?" Moleen said, and drank from his glass. His long legs were crossed, his eyes impossible to read behind his sunglasses.

"Somebody was running a dozer blade through that grove of gum trees at the end of Bertie Fontenot's lane. It looks to me like there might have been some old graves in there."

"I'm not quite sure what you're telling me or why, but I can tell you, with some degree of certainty, what *was* in there. My great-grandfather leased convicts as laborers after the Civil War. Supposedly there was a prison stockade right where those gum trees are today."

"No kidding?" I said.

"A bad chapter in the family history, I'm afraid."

"Oh, it was not. You liberals love collective guilt," Julia said.

"Why would somebody want to put a leg iron in my truck?"

"Search me." He took off his sunglasses, folded them on his knee, yawned, and looked at a distant, moss-hung oak by the fairway.

"It was probably just my night for strange memorabilia. Somebody left a dog tag on the windowsill of my bait shop. It belonged to a guy who flew a slick into a hot LZ when I was wounded."

"That's quite a story," he said.

He gazed down the fairway, seemingly uninterested in my conversation, but for just a moment there had been a brightening of color in his hazel eyes, a hidden thought working behind the iris like a busy insect.

"This guy got left behind in Laos," I said.

"You know what, Dave?" he said. "I wish I'd behaved badly toward people of color. Been a member of the Klan or a white citizens council, something like that. Then somehow this conversation would seem more warranted."

"Dave's not out here for any personal reason, Moleen," his wife said, smiling. "Are you, Dave?"

"Dave's a serious man. He doesn't expend his workday casually with the idle rich," Moleen said. He put a cigar in his mouth and picked a match out of a thin box from the Pontchartrain Hotel.

"Police officers ask questions, Moleen," I said.

"I'm sorry we have no answers for you."

"Thanks for your time. Say, your man Luke is stand-up, isn't he?"

"I beg your pardon?"

"Bertie Fontenot's nephew. He's loyal. I'd swear he was willing to see his sister and aunt and himself evicted rather than have you lose title to a strip of disputed land."

The skin of Moleen's forehead stretched against the bone. The humor and goodwill had gone out of his wife's face.

"What's he talking about, Moleen?" she said.

"I haven't any idea."

"What does that black man have to do with this?" she asked.

"Who knows? I believe Dave has a talent for manufacturing his own frame of reference."

"My, you certainly have managed to leave your mark on our morning," she said to me.

"A police investigation isn't preempted by a 'members only' sign at a country club," I said.

"Ah, now we get to it," Moleen said.

"You know a dude named Emile Pogue?" I said.

He took his cigar out of his mouth and laughed to himself.

"No, I don't," he said. "Good-bye, Dave. The matinee's over. Give our best to your wife. Let's bust some skeet before duck season."

He put his arm around his wife's waist and walked her toward the club dining room. She waved goodbye over her shoulder with her fingers, smiling like a little girl who did not want to offend.

Later that afternoon I went into Helen Soileau's office and sat down while she finished typing a page that was in her typewriter. Outside, the sky was blue, the azaleas and myrtle bushes in full bloom.

Finally, she turned and stared at me, waiting for me to speak first. Her pale adversarial eyes, as always, seemed to be weighing the choice between a momentary suspension of her ongoing anger with the world and verbal attack.

"I didn't get a chance to tell you yesterday, you'd make a great actress," I said.

She was silent, her expression flat and in abeyanc-,

as though my meaning had not quite swum into her ken.

"You had me convinced we were married," I said.

"What's on your mind?"

"I talked with a couple of guys I know at NOPD. Tommy Carrol isn't pressing charges. He's got a beef pending on an automatic weapons violation."

"That's the flash?"

"That's it."

She began leafing through some pages in a file folder as though I were not there.

"But I've got a personal problem about yesterday's events," I said.

"What might that be?" she said, not looking up from the folder.

"We need to take it out of overdrive, Helen."

She swiveled her chair toward me, her eyes as intense and certain as a drill instructor's.

"I've got two rules," she said. "Shitbags don't get treated like churchgoers, and somebody tries to take me, a civilian, or another cop down, he gets neutralized on the spot."

"Sometimes people get caught in their own syllogism."

"What?"

"Why let your own rules lock you in a corner?"

"You don't like working with me, Dave, take it to the old man."

"You're a good cop. But you're unrelenting. It's a mistake."

"You got anything else on your mind?"

"Nope."

"I ran this guy Emile Pogue all kinds of ways," she said, the door already closed on the previous subject. "There's no record on him."

"Hang on a minute." I went down to my office and came back. "Here's the diary and notebook Sonny Boy Marsallus gave me. If this is what Della Landry's killers were after, its importance is lost on me."

"What do you want me to do with it?"

"Read it or give it back, Helen, I don't care."

She dropped it in her desk drawer.

"You really got your nose out of joint because I took down that gun dealer?" she said.

"I was probably talking about myself."

"How about getting the corn fritters out of your mouth?"

"I've put down five guys in my career. They all dealt the play. But I still see them in my dreams. I wish I didn't."

"Try seeing their victims' faces for a change," she said, and bent back over the file folder on her desk.

The juke joint run by Luke Fontenot was across the railway tracks and down a dirt road that traversed green fields of sugarcane and eventually ended in a shell cul-de-sac by a coulee and a scattered stand of hackberry and oak trees. The juke joint was a rambling wood shell of a building on top of cinder blocks, the walls layered with a combination of Montgomery Ward brick and clapboard; the cracked and oxidized windows held together with pipe tape, still strung with Christmas lights and red and green crepe paper bells.

A rusted JAX sign, with stubs of broken neon tubing on it, hung above the front screen door.

In back were two small dented tin trailers with windows and doors that were both curtained.

Inside, the bar was made of wood planks that had been wrapped and thumbtacked with oilcloth. The air smelled of the cigarette smoke that drifted toward the huge window fan inset in the back wall, spilled beer, okra and shrimp boiling on a butane stove, rum and bourbon, and melted ice and collins mix congealing in the bottom of a drain bin.

All of the women in the bar were black or mulatto, but some of the men were white, unshaved, blue-collar, their expressions between a leer and a smile directed at one another, as though somehow their presence there was part of a collective and private joke, not to be taken seriously or held against them.

Luke Fontenot was loading long-necked bottles of beer in the cooler and didn't acknowledge me, although I was sure he saw me out of the corner of his eye. Instead, it was his sister, who had the same gold coloring as he, who walked on her cane across the duckboards and asked if she could help me. Her eyes were turquoise, her shiny black hair cut in a pageboy, except it was shaped and curled high up on the cheek, the way a 1920s Hollywood actress might have worn it.

"I think Luke wanted to see me," I said.

"He's tied up right now," she said.

"Tell him to untie himself."

"Why you want to be bothering him, Mr. Robicheaux? He cain't do anything about Aint Bertie's land problems."

"I'm sorry, I didn't get your name."

"Ruthie Jean."

"Maybe you've got things turned around, Ruthie Jean. I think Luke was out at my house at sunrise Saturday morning. Why don't you ask him?"

She walked with her cane toward the rear of the bar, and spoke to him while he kept lowering the bottles into the cooler, his face turning from side to side in case a hot bottle exploded in his face, her back turned toward me.

He wiped his hands on a towel and picked up an opened soft drink. When he drank from it he kept the left side of his face turned out of the light.

"I'm sorry Batist gave you a bad time out at my dock," I said.

"Everybody get cranky with age," he said.

"What's up, podna?"

"I need me a part-time job. I thought you might could use somebody at your shop."

"I should have known that. You walked fifteen miles from town, at dawn, to ask me about a job."

"I got a ride partway."

A white man in an oil field delivery uniform went out the back screen door with a black woman who wore cutoff Levi's and a T-shirt without a bra. She took his hand in hers before they went into one of the tin trailers. Luke's sister glanced at my face, then closed the wood door on the screen and began sweeping behind where the door had been.

"What happened to your face?" I asked Luke.

"It get rough in here sometime. I had to settle a couple of men down."

"One of them must have had a brick in his hand."

He leaned on his arms and took a breath through his nostrils. "What you want?" he said.

"Who dozered the cemetery by your house Friday night?"

"I done tole you, I don't know about no graves on that plantation. I grew up in town."

"Okay, partner. Here's my business card. I'll see you around."

He slipped it in his shirt pocket and began rinsing glasses in a tin sink.

"I ain't meant to be unpolite," he said. "Tell that to that old man work for you, too. I just ain't no hep in solving nobody's problems."

"I pulled your jacket, Luke. You're a hard man to read."

He raised his hand, palm outward, toward me.

"No more, suh," he said. "You want to ax me questions, come back with a warrant and carry me down to the jail."

When I got into my pickup the sky was steel gray, the air humid and close as a cotton glove. Raindrops were hitting in flat drops on the cane in the fields.

Ruthie Jean came through the side door and limped toward me. She rested one hand on my window jamb. She had full cheeks and a mole by her mouth; her teeth were white against her bright lipstick.

"You saw something out here you gonna use against him?" she said.

The curtains were blowing in the windows and doors of the tin trailers in back.

"I was never a vice cop," I said.

"Then why you out here giving him a bunch of truck?"

"Your brother's got a ten-year sheet for everything from concealed weapons to first-degree murder."

"You saw on there he stole something?"

"No."

"He hurt somebody didn't bother him first, didn't try cheat him out of his pay, didn't take out a gun on him at a bouree table?"

"Not to my knowledge."

"But y'all make it come out like you want."

"I'd say your brother's ahead of the game. If Moleen Bertrand hadn't pulled him out of the death house, with about three hours to spare, Luke would have been yesterday's toast."

I felt myself blink inside with the severity of my own words.

"Y'all always know, always got the smart word," she said.

"You're angry at the wrong person."

"When y'all cain't get at the people who really did something, y'all go down into the quarters, find the little people to get your hands on, put inside your reports and send up to Angola."

I started my truck engine. Her hand didn't move from the window jamb.

"I'm not telling the troot, no?" she said.

Her gold skin was smooth and damp in the blowing

mist, her hair thick and jet black and full of little lights.

"Who supplies your girls?" I said.

Her eyes roved over my face. "You're not very good at this, if you ax me," she said, and limped back toward the front door of the juke.

That afternoon, just before five, I received a call from Clete Purcel. I could hear seagulls squeaking in the background.

"Where are you?" I said.

"By the shrimp docks in Morgan City. You know where a cop's best information is, Streak? The lowly bail bondsman. In this case, with a fat little guy named Butterbean Reaux."

"Yeah, I know him."

"Good. Drive on down, noble mon. We'll drink some mash and talk some trash. Or I'll drink the mash while you talk to your buddy Sonny Boy Marsallus."

"You know where he is?"

"Right now, handcuffed to a D-ring in the backseat of my automobile. So much for all that brother-in-arms bullshit."

Chapter 8

Clete gave me directions in Morgan City, and an hour later I saw his battered Cadillac convertible parked under a solitary palm tree by an outdoor beer and hot dog stand not far from the docks. The sky was sealed with gray clouds, and the wind was blowing hard off the Gulf, capping the water all the way across the bay. Sonny sat in the backseat of the Cadillac, shirtless, a pair of blue suspenders notched into his white shoulders. His right wrist was extended downward, where it was cuffed to a D-shaped steel ring inset in the floor.

Clete was drinking a beer on a wood bench under the palm tree, his porkpie hat slanted over his forehead.

"You ought to try the hot dogs here," Clete said.

"You want to be up on a kidnapping charge?" I said.

"Hey, Sonny! You gonna dime me?" Clete yelled at the car. Then he looked back at me. "See, Sonny's stand-up. He's not complaining."

He brushed at a fleck of dried blood in one nostril.

"What happened?" I said.

"He'd rat-holed himself in a room over a pool hall, actually more like a pool hall and hot pillow joint. He said he wasn't coming with me. I started to hook him up and he unloaded on me. So I had to throw him down the stairs."

He rubbed the knuckles of his right hand unconsciously.

"Why do you have it in for him, Clete?"

"Because he was down in Bongo-Bongo Land for the same reasons as the rest of us. Except he pretends he's got some kind of blue fire radiating around his head or something."

I walked over to the car. Sonny's left eye was swollen almost shut. He grinned up at me. His sharkskin slacks were torn at the knee.

"How's the man, Streak?" he said.

"I wish you had come in on your own."

"Long story."

"It always is."

"You going to hold me?"

"Maybe." I turned toward Clete. "Give me your key," I called.

"Ask Sonny if I need rabies shots," he said, and pitched it at me.

"You're not going to get clever, are you?" I said to Sonny.

"With you guys? Are you kidding?"

"You're the consummate grifter, Sonny," I said, opened the door, and unlocked his wrist. Then I leveled my finger at his face. "Who were the guys who killed Della Landry?"

"I'm not sure."

"Don't you lie to me, Sonny."

"It could be any number of guys. It depends who they send in. You didn't lift any prints?"

"Don't worry about what we do or don't do. You just answer my questions. Who's *they*?"

"Dave, you're not going to understand this stuff."

"You're starting to piss me off, Sonny."

"I don't blame you."

"Get out of the car." I patted him down against the fender, then slipped my hand under his arm and turned him toward my truck.

"Where we going?" he said.

"You're a material witness. You're also an uncooperative material witness. That means we'll be keeping you for a while."

"Mistake."

"I'll live with it."

"Don't count on it, Dave. I'm not being cute, either."

"He's a sweetheart," Clete said from the bench. Then he rubbed the knuckles on his right hand and looked at them.

"Sorry I popped you, Cletus," Sonny said.

"In your ear, Sonny," Clete said.

We drove past boatyards then some shrimp boats that were knocking against the pilings in their berths. The air was warm and smelled like brass and dead fish.

"Can I stop by my room and pick up some things?" Sonny asked.

"No."

"Just a shirt."

"Nope."

"You're a hard man, Streak."

"That girl took your fall, Sonny. You want to look at her morgue pictures?"

He was quiet a long time, his face looking straight ahead at the rain striking the windshield.

"Did she suffer?" he said.

"They tore her apart. What do you think?"

His mouth was red against his white skin.

"They were after me, or maybe the notebook I gave you," he said.

"I've got it. You've written a potential best-seller and people are getting killed over it."

"Dave, you lock me up, those guys are going to get to me."

"That's the breaks, partner."

He was quiet again, his eyes focused inward.

"Are we talking about some kind of CIA involvement?" I said.

"Not directly. But you start sending the wrong stuff through the computer, through your fax machines, these guys will step right into the middle of your life. I guarantee it, Dave."

"How's the name Emile Pogue sit with you?" I said.

He let out his breath quietly. Under his suspenders his stomach was flat and corded with muscle.

"Another officer ran him all kinds of ways and came up empty," I said.

He rubbed the ball of his thumb across his lips. Then he said, "I didn't eat yet. What time they serve at the lockup?"

Try to read that.

* * *

Two hours later Clete called me at home. It was raining hard, the water sluicing off the gutters, and the back lawn was full of floating leaves.

"What'd you get out of him?" Clete said.

"Nothing." I could hear country music and people's voices in the background. "Where are you?"

"In a slop chute outside Morgan City. Dave, this guy bothers me. There's something not natural about him."

"He's a hustler. He's outrageous by nature."

"He doesn't get any older. He always looks the same."

I tried to remember Sonny's approximate age. I couldn't.

"There's something else," Clete said. "Where I hit him. There's a strawberry mark across the backs of my fingers. It's throbbing like I've got blood poisoning or something."

"Get out of the bar, Clete."

"You always know how to say it."

I couldn't sleep that night. The rain stopped and a heavy mist settled in the trees outside our bedroom window, and I could hear night-feeding bass flopping back in the swamp. I sat on the edge of the bed in my skivvies and looked at the curtains puffing in the breeze.

"What is it, Dave?" Bootsie said behind me in the dark.

"I had a bad dream, that's all."

"About what?" She put her hand on my spine.

"A captain I knew in Vietnam. He was a stubborn and inflexible man. He sent a bunch of guys across a rice field under a full moon. They didn't come back."

"It's been thirty years, Dave."

"The dream was about myself. I'm going into town. I'll call you later," I said.

I took two paper bags from the kitchen pantry, put a clean shirt in one of them, stopped by the bait shop, then drove up the dirt road through the tunnel of oak trees and over the drawbridge toward New Iberia.

It was still dark when I reached the parish jail. Kelso was drinking a cup of coffee and reading a comic book behind his desk. His face looked like a walrus's in the shadows from his desk lamp, the moles on his neck as big as raisins.

"I want to check Marsallus out," I said.

"Check him out? Like a book from the library, you're saying?"

"It's the middle of the night. Why make an issue out of everything?"

He stretched and yawned. His thick glasses were full of light. "The guy's a twenty-four kick-out, anyway, isn't he?"

"Maybe."

"I think you ought to take him to a shrink."

"What'd he do?"

"He's been having a conversation in his cell."

"So?"

"There ain't anybody else in it, Robicheaux."

"How about bringing him out, Kelso, then you can get back to your reading."

"Hey, Robicheaux, you take him to the wig mechanic, make an appointment for yourself, too."

A few minutes later Sonny and I got in my truck and drove down East Main. He was dressed in his sharkskin slacks and a jailhouse denim shirt. There were low pink clouds in the east now and the live oaks along the street were gray and hazy with mist.

"There's a shirt in that bag by the door," I said.

"What's this in the other one? You carrying around a junkyard, Dave?" He lifted the rusted chain and ankle cuff out of the bag.

I didn't answer his question. "I thought you might enjoy some takeout from Victor's rather than eat at the slam," I said, parking in front of a small cafeteria on Main across from the bayou. "You want to go get it?"

"You're not afraid I'll go out the back door?"

"There isn't one." I put eight one-dollar bills in his hand. "Make mine scrambled eggs, sausage, grits, and coffee."

I watched him walk inside, tucking my borrowed tropical shirt inside his rumpled slacks. He was grinning when he came back out and got in the truck.

"There *is* a back door, Streak. You didn't know that?" he said.

"Huh," I said, and drove us across the drawbridge, over the Teche, into City Park. The bayou was high and yellow with mud, and the wake from a tug with green and red running lights washed over the banks into the grass. We ate at a picnic table under a tree that was alive with mockingbirds.

"You ever see a leg iron like that before, Sonny?"

"Yeah, in the museum at Jackson Square."

"Why would you make it your business to know that Jean Lafitte operated a barracoon outside New Iberia?"

"Della told me. She was into stuff like that." Then he wiped his face with his hand. "It's already getting hot."

"I read your notebook. It doesn't seem to have any great illumination in it, Sonny."

"Maybe I'm a lousy writer."

"Why do these bozos want to kill people over your notebook?"

"They're called cleanup guys. They hose a guy and everything around him right off the planet."

"I'll put it to you, partner, that girl died a miserable death. You want to help me nail them or not?"

A pinched light came into his face. His hand tightened on the edge of the table. He looked out toward the bayou.

"I don't know who they were," he said. "Look, what I can tell you won't help. But you're a cop and you'll end up putting it in a federal computer. You might as well swallow a piece of broken glass."

I took Roy Bumgartner's dog tag out of my shirt pocket and laid it on the table beside Sonny's Styrofoam coffee cup.

"What's that mean to you?" I asked.

He stared at the name. "Nothing," he said.

"He flew a slick in Vietnam and disappeared in Laos. Somebody left this in my bait shop for me to find."

"The guy was an MIA or POW?"

"Yeah, and a friend of mine."

"There's a network, Dave, old-time intelligence guys, mercs, cowboys, shitheads, whatever you want to call them. They were mixed up with opium growers in the Golden Triangle. Some people believe that's why our guys were left behind over there. They knew too much about ties between narcotics and the American government."

I looked at him for a long time.

"What?" he said.

"You remind me of myself when I was on the grog, Sonny. I didn't trust anyone. So I seriously fucked up my life as well as other people's."

"Yeah, well, this breakfast has started to get expensive."

"I've got a few things to do in town. Can you take yourself back to the jail?"

"Take myself back to—"

"Yeah, check yourself in. Kelso's got a sense of humor. Tell him you heard the Iberia Parish lockup is run like the public library." I stuck my business card in his shirt pocket. "When you get tired of grandiose dog shit, give me a call."

I picked up my coffee cup and walked back toward my truck.

"Hey, Dave, this isn't right," he said behind me.

"You want to hang from a cross. Do it without me, partner," I said.

At one that afternoon I called Kelso at the lockup.

"Did Marsallus make it back there?" I asked.

"Yeah, we're putting in a special cell with a turnstile for him. You're a laugh a minute," he said.

"Kick him loose."

"You know what kind of paperwork you make for me?"

"You were right, Kelso, the prosecutor says we can't hold him. He wasn't a witness to anything. Sorry to inconvenience you."

"You know your problem, Robicheaux? You don't like doing the peon work like everybody else—filling out forms, punching clocks, going to coffee at ten A.M. instead of when you feel like it. So you're always figuring out ways to work a finger in somebody's crack."

"Anything else?"

"Yeah, keep that punk out of here."

"What's he done now?"

"Giving speeches to the wet-brains in the tank. I don't need that kind of shit in my jail. Wait a minute, I wrote the names down he was talking about to these guys. Who's Joe Hill and Woody Guthrie?"

"Guys from another era, Kelso."

"Yeah, well, two or three like your redheaded friend could have this town in flames. The wet-brains and stew-bums are all trying to talk and walk like him now, like they're all hipsters who grew up on Canal Street. It's fucking pathetic."

Two days later Helen Soileau called in sick. An hour later, the phone on my desk rang.

"Can you come out to my house?" she said.

"What is it?"

"Can you come out?"

"Yeah, if you want me to. Are you all right?"

"Hurry up, Dave."

I could hear her breath against the receiver, heated, dry, suddenly jerking in the back of her throat.

Chapter 9

SHE LIVED ALONE in a racially mixed neighborhood in a one-story frame house with a screened-in gallery that she had inherited from her mother. The house was Spartan and neat, with a new tin roof and a fresh coat of metallic gray paint, the cement steps and pilings whitewashed, the flower beds bursting with pink and blue hydrangeas in the shade of a chinaberry tree.

To my knowledge, she never entertained, joined a club, or attended a church. Once a year she left the area on a vacation; except for the sheriff, she never told anyone where she was going, and no one ever asked. Her only interest, other than law enforcement, seemed to lie in the care of animals.

She wore no makeup when she opened the door. Her eyes went past me, out to the street. Her face looked as hard and shiny as ceramic.

"Come inside," she said.

Her nine-millimeter automatic was in a checkered leather holster on the couch next to an eight-by-eleven manila envelope. The interior of the house was immaculate, slatted with sunlight, and smelled of burnt toast and coffee that had boiled over on the stove.

"You had me worried a little bit, Helen," I said.

"I had visitors during the night," she said.

"You mean a break-in?"

"They didn't come inside." Then her mouth twitched. She turned her face away and curled one finger at me.

I followed her through the kitchen and into the backyard, which was shaded by a neighbor's oak whose limbs grew across her fence. At the back of the lawn was a row of elevated screened pens where Helen kept rabbits, possums, armadillos, fighting cocks, or any kind of wounded or sick animal or bird that the humane society or neighborhood children brought her.

The tarps were pulled back on top of all the pens.

"It was warm with no rain in the forecast last night, so I left them uncovered," she said. "When I went out this morning, the tarps were down. That's when I saw that bucket on the ground."

I picked it up and smelled it. The inside was coated with a white powder. My head jerked back involuntarily from the odor, my nasal passages burning, as though a rubber band had snapped behind my eyes.

"They sprinkled it through the wire, then pulled the canvas down," she said.

The birds lay in lumps in the bottom of the pens, the way birds look after they've been shot in flight, their feathers puffing in the breeze. But the type of death the birds and animals died alike was more obvious in the stiffened bodies of the possums and coons. Their mouths were wide, their necks and spines twisted from convulsions, their claws extended as though they were defending themselves against invisible enemies.

"I'm sorry, Helen. It took a real sonofabitch to do something like this," I said.

"Two of them. Look at the footprints. One of them must wear lead shoes."

"Why didn't you call this in?"

Then once again I saw in her face the adversarial light and lack of faith in people that always characterized her dealings with others.

"I need some serious advice," she said. I could hear her breathing. Her right hand opened and closed at her side. There were drops of perspiration on her upper lip.

"Go ahead, Helen."

"I'll show you something that was under my door this morning," she said, and led the way back into her living room. She sat on her rattan couch and picked up the manila folder. The sunlight through the blinds made bright yellow stripes across her face. "Would you work with a queer?" she asked.

"What kind of question is that?"

"Answer it."

"What other people do in their private lives is none of my business."

"How about a bull or a switch-hitter?"

"I don't know where you're going with this, but it's not necessary."

Her hand was inserted in the envelope, her teeth biting on the corner of her lip. She pulled a large glossy black-and-white photograph out and handed it to me.

"It was taken two nights ago. The grain's bad because

he didn't use a flash. From the angle, I'd say it was shot through that side window."

I looked down at the photo and felt my throat color. She kept her eyes on the far wall.

"I don't think that's any big deal," I said. "Women kiss each other. It's how people show affection."

"You want to see the others?"

"Don't do this to yourself."

"Somebody already has."

"I'm not going to be party to an invasion of your private life, Helen. I respect you for what you are. These photographs don't change anything."

"You recognize the other woman?"

"No."

"She used to be a chicken for Sweet Pea Chaisson. I tried to help her get out of the life. Except we went a little bit beyond that."

"Who cares?"

"I've got to turn this stuff in, Dave."

"The hell you do."

She was silent, waiting.

"Do you have to prove you're an honest person?" I said. "And by doing so, cooperate with evil people in injuring yourself. That's not integrity, Helen, it's pride."

She returned the photo to the envelope, then studied the backs of her hands. Her fingers were thick and ringless, square on the ends.

"The only guy who comes to mind is that paramilitary fuck, what's his name, Tommy Carrol," she said.

"Maybe," I said. But I was already remembering Sonny Boy's warning.

"But why would he put this note on the envelope?" She turned it over so I could read the line someone had written with a felt pen—*Keep your mind on parking tickets, Muffy.* "Why the look?"

"Sonny Marsallus. He told me not to send anything on this guy Emile Pogue through the federal computer. All those informational requests had your name on them, Helen."

She nodded, then I saw her face cloud with an expression that I had seen too often, on too many people, over the years. Suddenly they realize they have been arbitrarily selected as the victim of an individual or a group about whom they have no knowledge and against whom they've committed no personal offense. It's a solitary moment, and it's never a good one.

I worked the envelope out from under her hands.

"We could do all kinds of doo-dah with these photos, and in all probability none of it would lead anywhere," I said. I slipped the photos facedown out of the envelope and walked with them into the kitchen. "So I'm making use of a Clete Purcel procedure here, which is, when the rules start working for the lowlifes, get a new set of rules."

I took a lucifer match from a box on the windowsill above the sink, scratched it on the striker, and held the flame to the corner of the photographs. The fire rippled and curled across the paper like water; I separated each sheet from the others to let the air and heat gather on the underside, the images, whatever they were, shrinking and disappearing into blackened cones while dirty strings of smoke drifted out the screen. Then I turned on the faucet and washed the ashes down the drain, wiped the sink clean with a paper towel and dropped it in the trash.

"You want to have some early lunch, then go to the office?" I said.

"Give me a minute to change." Then she said, "Thanks for what you did."

"Forget it."

"I'll say this only once," she said. "Men are kind to women for one of two reasons. Either they want inside the squeeze box or they have genuine balls and don't have to prove anything. When I said thank you, I meant it."

There are compliments you don't forget.

Before I drove away I put the stiffened body of one of the dead coons in a vinyl garbage sack and placed it in the bed of my truck.

The investigation had gone nowhere since the night of Della Landry's murder. I had made a mistake and listened to Sonny Boy's deprecation of the mob and his involvement with them. Sweet Pea Chaisson's name had surfaced again, and Sweet Pea didn't change toilet paper rolls without first seeking permission of the Giacano family. If the spaghetti heads had started to crash and burn back in the seventies, it was a secret to everyone except Sonny.

The heir to the old fat boy, Didoni Giacano, also known as Didi Gee, whose logo had been the blood-stained baseball bat that rode in the backseat of his Caddy convertible when he was a loan collector and who sometimes held down the hand of an adversary in an aquarium filled with piranhas, was his nephew, a businessman first, a gangster second, but with a bizarre talent for clicking psychotic episodes on and off at will—John Polycarp Giacano, also known as Johnny Carp and Polly Gee.

Friday morning I found him in his office out by a trash dump in Jefferson Parish. His eyes, nose, and guppy mouth were set unnaturally in the center of his face, compressed into an area the size of your palm. His high forehead was ridged and knurled even though he wasn't frowning. His hair was liquid black, waved on the top and sides, like plastic that had been melted, molded, and then cooled again.

When I knew him in the First District, he had been a minor soldier in the organization, a fight fixer, and a Shylock with jockies out at Jefferson Downs and the Fairgrounds. Supposedly, as a kid, he had been the wheelman on a couple of hundred-dollar hits with the Calucci brothers; but for all his criminal history, he'd only been down once, a one-year bit for possession of stolen food stamps in the late sixties, and he did the time in a minimum security federal facility, where he had weekend furloughs and golf and tennis privileges.

Johnny Carp was smart; he went with the flow and gave people what they wanted, didn't contend with the world or argue with the way things were. Celebrities had their picture taken with him. He lent money to cops with no vig and was never known to be rude. Those who saw his other side, his apologists maintained, had broken rules and earned their fate.

"You look great," he said, tilting back in his swivel chair. Through the window behind him, seagulls were wheeling and dipping over mountains of garbage that were being systematically spread and buried and packed down in the landfill by bulldozers.

"When did you get into the trash business, Johnny?"

"Oh, I'm just out here a couple of days a week to make sure the johns flush," he said. He wore a beige suit with thin brown stripes in it, a purple shirt and brown knit tie, and a small rose in his lapel. He winked. "Hey, I know you don't drink no more. Me, neither. I found a way around the problem. I ain't putting you on: Watch."

He opened a small icebox by the wall and took out an unopened quart bottle of milk. There were two inches of cream in the neck. Then he lifted a heavy black bottle of Scotch, with a red wax seal on it, from his bottom desk drawer. He poured four fingers into a thick water glass and added milk to it, smiling all the while. The Scotch ballooned and turned inside the milk and cream like soft licorice.

"I don't get drunk, I don't get ulcers, I don't get hangovers, it's great, Dave. You want a hit?"

"No thanks. You know why anybody would want to take down Sonny Boy Marsallus?"

"Maybe it's mental health week. You know, help out your neighborhood, kill your local lunatic. The guy's head glows in the dark."

"How about Sweet Pea Chaisson?"

"Clip Sonny? Sweet Pea's a marshmallow. Why you asking me this stuff, anyway?"

"You're the man, Johnny."

"Uncle Didi was the man. That's the old days we're talking about."

"You have a lot of people's respect, Johnny."

"Yeah? The day I go broke I start being toe jam again. You want to know about Marsallus? He came out of the womb with a hard-on."

"What's that mean?"

"He's read enough books to sound like he's somebody he ain't, but he's got sperm on the brain. He uses broads like Kleenex. Don't let that punk take you over the hurdles. He'd stand in line to fuck his mother . . . I say something wrong?"

"No," I said, my face blank.

He folded his hands, his elbows splayed, and leaned forward. "Serious," he said, "somebody's trying to whack out Sonny?"

"Maybe."

He looked sideways out the window, thinking, his coat bunched up on his neck. "It ain't anybody in the city. Look, Sonny wasn't never a threat to anybody's action, you understand what I'm saying? His problem is he thinks his shit don't stink. He floats above the ground the rest of us got to walk on."

"Well, it was good seeing you, Johnny."

"Yeah, always a pleasure."

I pulled on my earlobe as I got up to go.

"It's funny you'd tell me Sonny uses women badly. That was never his reputation," I said.

"People in the projects don't work. What do you think they do all day, why you think they have all them kids? He's a nickel-and-dime street mutt. The head he thinks with ain't on his shoulders. I'm getting through here?"

"See you around, Johnny."

He cocked one finger at me, drank from his glass of milk and Scotch, his compressed features almost disappearing behind his hand and wrist.

I don't remember the psychological term for it, but cops and prosecutors know the mechanism well. It involves unintended acknowledgment of guilt through the expression of denial. When Lee Harvey Oswald was in custody after the assassination of President Kennedy, he seemed to answer truthfully many of the questions asked him by cops and newsmen. But he consistently denied ownership of the 6.5 millimeter rifle found on the sixth floor of the Texas Book Depository, the one piece of physical evidence to which he was unquestionably and inextricably linked.

Della Landry had been murdered, in all probability, because of her association with Sonny. The first remark out of Johnny's mouth had been a slur about Sonny's misuse of women, as if to say, perhaps, that the fate of those who involved themselves with him was Sonny's responsibility and not anyone else's.

But maybe I was simply in another cul-de-sac, looking for meaning where there was none.

As I got into my truck three of Johnny Carp's hoods were standing by the back of his Lincoln. They wore slacks with knife creases, tasseled loafers, short-sleeve tropical shirts, gold chains on their necks, and lightly oiled boxed haircuts. But steroids had become fashionable with the mob, too, and their torsos and arms were thick with muscle like gnarled oak about to split the skin.

They were taking turns firing a .22 revolver at tin cans and the birds feeding along the dirt road that led between the trash heaps. They glanced at me briefly, then continued shooting.

"I'd like to drive out of here without getting shot," I said.

There was no response. One man broke open the revolver, shucked out the hulls, and began reloading. He looked at me meaningfully.

"Thanks, I appreciate it," I said.

I drove down the road, tapping my horn as cattle egrets on each side of me lifted into the air. In my rearview mirror I saw Johnny Carp walk out of his office and join his men, all of them looking at me now, I was sure, with the quiet and patient energies of creatures whose thoughts you never truly wish to know.

Friday night I went to the parish library and began to read about Jean Lafitte. Most of the material repeated in one form or another the traditional stories about the pirate who joined forces with Andrew Jackson to defeat the British at the Battle of New Orleans, the ships he robbed on the high seas, the gangs of cutthroats he lived with in Barataria and Galveston, his death somewhere in the Yucatán.

He had been considered a romantic and intriguing figure by New Orleans society, probably because none of them had been his victims. But also in the library was an article written by a local historian at the turn of the century that did not treat Lafitte as kindly. His crimes did not stop with piracy and murder. He had been a blackbirder and was transporting African slaves into the country after the prohibition of 1809. He sold his stolen goods as well as human cargo on the banks of the Teche.

Milton and Shakespeare both said lucidity and power lay in the world of dreams. For me, that has always meant that sleep and the unconscious can define what daylight and rationality cannot. That night, as a wind smelling of salt and wet sand and humus blew across the swamp, I dreamed of what Bayou Teche must have been like when the country was new, when the most severe tool or weapon was shaped from a stone, the forest floor covered with palmettos, the moss-hung canopy so thick and tall that in the suffused sunlight the trunks looked like towering gray columns in a Gothic cathedral.

In the dream the air was breathless, like steam caught under a glass bell, an autumnal yellow moon dissected with a single strip of black cloud overhead, and then I saw a long wood ship with furled masts being pulled up the bayou on ropes by Negroes who stumbled along the banks through the reeds and mud, their bodies rippling with sweat in the firelight. On the deck of the ship were their women and children, their cloth bundles gathered among them, their eyes peering ahead into the bayou's darkness, as though an explanation for their fear and misery were somehow at hand.

The auction was held under the oaks at the foot of the old Voorhies property. The Negroes did not speak English, French, or Spanish, so indigenous histories were created for them. The other property did not offer as great a problem. The gold and silver plate, the trunks filled with European fashions, the bejeweled necklaces and swords and scrolled flintlocks, all had belonged to people whose final histories were written in water somewhere in the Caribbean.

In a generation or two the banks of Spanish Lake and Bayou Teche would be lined with plantations, and people would eat off gold plate whose origins were only an interesting curiosity. The slaves who worked the sawmills, cane fields, and the salt domes out in the wetlands would speak the language and use the names of their owners, and the day when a large sailing ship appeared innocuously on a river in western Africa, amidst a green world of birds and hummocks, would become the stuff of oral legend, confused with biblical history and allegory, and finally forgotten.

I believed the dream. I remembered the oak trees at the foot of the Voorhies property, when lengths of mooring chain, driven with huge spikes into the trunks, grew in and out of the bark like calcified rust-sheathed serpents. Over the years, the chains had been drawn deeper into the heart of the tree, like orange-encrusted iron cysts in the midst of living tissue or perhaps unacknowledged and unforgiven sins.

At breakfast Saturday morning Bootsie said, "Oh, I forgot, Dave, Julia Bertrand called last night. She invited us out to their camp at Pecan Island next Saturday."

The kitchen window was open, and the sky was full of white clouds.

"What'd you tell her?" I said.

"I thought it was a nice idea. We don't see them often."

"You told her we'd come?"

"No, I didn't. I said I'd check to see if you had anything planned."

"How about we let this one slide?"

"They're nice people, Dave."

"There's something off-center out at Moleen's plantation."

"All right, I'll call her back." She tried to keep the disappointment out of her face.

"Maybe it's just me, Bootsie. I never got along well in that world."

"*That* world?"

"They think they're not accountable. Moleen always gives me the impression he lives in rarefied air."

"What are you talking about?"

"Nothing. Call Julia up and tell her we'll be out there."

"*Dave,*" she said, the exasperation climbing in her voice.

"Believe me, it's part of a game. So we'll check it out."

"I think this is a good morning to work in the garden," she said.

It rained hard that night, and when I fell asleep I thought I heard a motorboat pass by the dock. After the rain stopped, the air was damp and close and a layer of mist floated on the bayou as thick as cotton. Just after midnight the phone rang. I closed the bedroom door behind me and answered it in the living room. The house was dark and cool and water was dripping off the tin roof of the gallery.

"Mr. Robicheaux?" a man's voice said.

"Yeah. Who is this?"

"Jack."

"Jack?"

"You found a dog tag. We tried to get your friend out. You want to hear about it?" There was no accent, no emotional tone in the voice.

"What do you want, partner?"

"To explain some things you probably don't understand."

"Come to the office Monday. Don't call my house again, either."

"Look out your front window."

I pulled aside the curtain and stared out into the darkness. I could see nothing except the mist floating on the bayou and a smudged red glow from a gas flare on an oil rig out in the swamp. Then, out on the dock, a tall, angular man in raincoat and hat flicked on a flashlight and shined it upward into his face. He held a cellular phone to his ear and the skin of his face was white and deeply lined, like papier-mâché that has started to crack. Then the light clicked off again. I picked the phone back up.

"You're trespassing on my property. I want you off of it," I said.

"Walk down to the dock."

Don't fall into it, I thought.

"Put the light back on your face and keep your hands away from your sides," I said.

"That's acceptable."

"I'm going to hang up now. Then I'll be down in about two minutes."

"No. You don't break the connection."

I let the receiver clatter on the table and went back into the bedroom. I slipped on my khakis and loafers, and removed my holstered .45 automatic from the dresser drawer. Bootsie was sleeping with the pillow partially over her head. I closed the door quietly behind me, pulled back the slide on the .45 and chambered a round, eased the hammer back down, set the safety, then stuck the barrel inside the back of my belt.

I picked up the receiver.

"You still there, partner?" I said.

"Yes."

"Turn on your flashlight."

"What an excellent idea."

I went out the front door and down the slope through the trees. He had moved out on the dirt road now and I could see him more clearly. He was well over six feet, with arms that seemed too thin for the sleeves of his raincoat, wide shoulders, a face as grooved and webbed with lines as dried putty. His left coat pocket sagged with the weight of the cellular phone and his left hand now held the flashlight. His lips were purple in the beam of the flashlight, like the skin of a plum. His eyes watched me with the squinted focus of someone staring through smoke.

"Put your right hand behind your neck," I said.

"That's not dignified."

"Neither are jerk-off games involving the death of a brave soldier."

"Your friend could still be alive."

He raised his right hand, hooked it above his lapel, and let it rest there. I watched him and didn't answer.

"Sonny Marsallus is a traitor," he said.

"I think it's time we look at your identification."

"You don't listen well."

"You made a mistake coming here tonight."

"I don't think so. You have a distinguished war record. Marsallus doesn't. He's for sale."

"I want you to turn around, walk back to the dock, and place your hands on the rail . . . Just do it, partner. It's not up for debate."

But he didn't move. I could feel sweat running down my sides like ants, but the face of the man named Jack, who wore a hat and coat, was as dry as parchment. His eyes remained riveted on mine, like brown agate with threads of gold in them.

Then I heard a sound out in the shadows.

"Hey, Jack, what's shakin'?" a voice said.

Jack twisted his head sideways and stared out into the darkness.

"It's Sonny," the voice said. "Hey, Dave, watch out for ole Jack there. He carries a sawed-down twelve-gauge on a bungee rope in his right armpit. Peel back your raincoat, Jack, and let Dave have a peek."

But that was not in Jack's plan. He dropped the flashlight to the ground and bolted past me up the road. Then I saw Sonny move out from under the overhang of a live oak, a Smith & Wesson nine-millimeter gripped at an upward angle with both hands.

"Get out of the way, Dave!" he shouted.

"Are you crazy? Put that down!"

But Sonny swung wide of me and aimed with both arms stretched straight out in front of him. Then he began firing, *crack*, *crack*, *crack*, *crack*, fire leaping out of the barrel, the empty brass cartridges clinking on the road.

He picked up the flashlight the man named Jack had dropped and shined it down the road.

"Look at the ground, Dave, right by that hole in the bushes," he said. "I think Jack just sprung a leak." Then he called out into the darkness, "Hey, Jack, how's it feel?"

"Give me the gun, Sonny."

"Sorry, Streak . . . I'm sorry to do this to you, too . . . No, no, don't move. I'm just going to take your piece. Now, let's walk over here to the dock and hook up."

"You're going across the line, Sonny."

"There's just one line that counts, Dave, the one between the good guys and the shitbags." He worked a pair of open handcuffs from the back pocket of his blue jeans. "Put your hands on each side of the rail. You worried about procedure? That guy I just punched a drain hole in, dig this, you heard the Falangist joke down in Taco Tico country about the Flying Nun? This isn't a shuck, either. Some of the *junta* fucks in Argentina wanted a couple of nuns, human rights types, turned into object lessons. The guy who threw them out of a Huey at a thousand feet was our man Jack.

"See you around, Streak. I'll make sure you get your piece back."

Then he disappeared through the broken bushes where the wounded man had fled. I raked the chain on the cuffs against the dock railing while mosquitoes droned around my head and my eyes stung with sweat and humiliation at my own failure and ineptitude.

Chapter 10

AFTER I HAD gone down to the office Sunday morning and made my report, a mail clerk at the post office called the dispatcher and said that during the night someone had dropped an army-issue .45 automatic through a post office mail slot. The .45 had been wrapped in a paper bag with my name written on the outside.

It was hot and bright at noon, with a breeze blowing out of the south, and Clete Purcel walked with me along the dirt road to the spot where Sonny and the man named Jack had entered the brush and run down the bayou's bank toward the four corners. The blood on the leaves was coated with dust from the road.

"It looks like Sonny really cored a hole in the guy. He didn't show up at a hospital?"

"Not yet."

We walked through the brush and down to the bank. The deep imprints in the mud left by Sonny and the man named Jack were now crisscrossed with the shoe prints of the deputies who had followed Jack's blood trail to a break in the cattails where the bow of a flat-bottomed boat had been dragged onto the sand.

Clete squatted down heavily, slipped a piece of

cardboard under one knee, and looked back up the bank toward the dock. He wore a pair of baggy, elastic-waisted shorts with dancing zebras printed on them. He took off his porkpie hat and twirled it on his index finger.

"Did you ever see the sawed-down twelve?" he asked.

"No."

"You think he was carrying one?"

"I don't know, Clete."

"But you know a guy like that was carrying a piece of some kind? Right?"

We looked at each other.

"So the question is, why didn't he try to pop Sonny with it? He could have waited for him in the dark and parked one in his brisket," he said.

"Because he dropped it," I said. Then I said, "And why didn't anyone find it last night?"

He was spinning his hat on his finger now. His eyes were green and full of light.

"Because it fell in the water," he said, and lumbered to his feet.

It didn't take long. Seventy feet back down the bank, where the water eddied around a sunken and rotted pirogue that was green and fuzzy with moss, we saw the barrel of the twelve-gauge glinting wetly among the reeds and the wake from a passing boat. The barrel was sawed off at the pump and impacted with sand. The stock had been shaved and shaped with a wood rasp and honed into a pistol grip. A two-foot length of bungee cord, the kind you use to strap down luggage, was looped and screwed into the butt.

Clete shook the sand out of the barrel and jacked open the breech. Yellow water gushed out of the mechanism with the unfired shell. Then he jacked four more rounds out on the ground. I picked them up and they felt heavy and wet and filmed with grit in my palm.

"Our man doesn't use a sportsman's plug," Clete said. He looked at the shells in my hand. "Are those pumpkin balls?"

"Yeah, you don't see them anymore."

"He probably loads his own rounds. This guy's got the smell of a mechanic, Streak." He peeled a stick of gum with one hand and put it in his mouth, his eyes thoughtful. "I hate to say this, but maybe dick-brain saved your life."

Down by the dock a teenage kid was holding up a stringer of perch for a friend to see. He wore a bright-chrome-plated watchband on his wrist.

"You don't think this guy's a button man, he's mobbed-up?" Clete asked.

"I was thinking about Sonny . . . the handcuffs . . . the way he took me down."

Clete blew into the open breech of the shotgun, closed it, and snapped the firing pin on the empty chamber. He studied my face.

"Listen, Sonny's a walking hand-job. Stop thinking what you're thinking," he said.

"Then why are you thinking the same thing?"

"I'm not. A guy like Sonny isn't born, he's defecated into the world. I should have stuffed him down a toilet with a plumber's helper a long time ago."

"I've seen federal agents with the same kind of cuffs."

"This guy's no cop. You buy into his rebop and he'll piss in your shoe," he said, and put the shotgun hard into my hands.

Clete ate lunch with us, then I went down to the bait shop and picked up a Styrofoam cooler that I had filled with ice Friday afternoon. The corner of a black garbage bag protruded from under the lid. I walked back up the incline through the shade and set the cooler in the bed of my truck. Clete was picking up pecans from under the trees and cracking them in his hands.

"You want to take a ride to Breaux Bridge?" I asked.

"I thought we were going fishing," he said.

"I hear Sweet Pea Chaisson has rented a place out by the old seminary."

He smiled broadly.

We took the four-lane into Lafayette, then drove down the road toward Breaux Bridge, past Holy Rosary, the old Negro Catholic school, a graveyard with tombs above the ground, the Carmelite convent, and the seminary. Sweet Pea's rented house was a flat-roofed yellow brick building shielded by a hedge of dying azalea bushes. The lot next door was filled with old building materials and pieces of iron that were threaded with weeds and crisscrossed with morning glory vines.

No one was home. An elderly black man was cleaning up dog feces in the yard with a shovel.

"He taken the ladies to the restaurant down on

Cameron in Lafayette, down by the fo' corners," he said.

"Which restaurant?" I said.

"The one got smoke comin' out the back."

"It's a barbecue place?" I said.

"The man own it always burning garbage out there. You'll smell it befo' you see it."

We drove down Cameron through the black district in Lafayette. Up ahead was an area known as Four Corners, where no number of vice arrests ever seemed to get the hookers off of the sidewalks and out of the motels.

"There's his Caddy," Clete said, and pointed out the window. "Check this place, will you? His broads must have rubber stomach liners."

I parked in a dirt lot next to a wood frame building with paint that had blistered and curled into shapes like blown chicken feathers and with a desiccated privy and smoking incinerator in back.

"We're not only off your turf, big mon, we're in the heart of black town. You feel comfortable with this?" Clete said when we were outside the truck.

"The locals don't mind," I said.

"You checked in with them?"

"Not really."

He looked at me.

"Sweet Pea's a pro. It's not a big deal," I said.

I reached inside the Styrofoam cooler and pulled the vinyl garbage bag out. It swung heavily from my hand, dripping ice and water.

"What are you doing?" Clete said.

"I think Sweet Pea helped set up Helen Soileau."

"The muff-diver? That's the one who had her animals killed?"

"Give her a break, Clete."

"Excuse me. I mean the lady who thinks I'm spit on the sidewalk. What's in the bag?"

"Don't worry about it."

"I guess I asked for this." He spit his gum out with a thropping sound.

We went through the door. It was a cheerless place where you could stay on the downside of a drunk without making comparisons. The interior was dark, the floor covered with linoleum, the green walls lined with pale rectangles where pictures had once hung. People whose race would be hard to define were at the bar, in the booths, and at the pool table. They all looked expectantly at the glare of light from the opening front door, as though an interesting moment might be imminent in their lives.

"Man, that Sweet Pea can pick 'em, can't he? I wonder if they charge extra for the roaches in the mashed potatoes," Clete said.

In the light from the kitchen we could see Sweet Pea and another man sitting at a large table with four women. The other man was explaining something, his forearms propped on the edge of the table, his fingers moving in the air. The women looked bored, hungover, wrapped in their own skin.

"Do you make the dude with him?" Clete said close to my ear.

"No."

"That's Patsy Dapolito, they call him Patsy Dap,

Patsy Bones, Patsy the Baker. He's a button guy for Johnny Carp."

The man named Patsy Dapolito wore a tie and a starched collar buttoned tightly around his neck. His face was pinched-looking, the nose thin, sharp-edged, the mouth down-turned, the teeth showing as though he were breathing through them.

"Stay out of overdrive, Dave. Dapolito's a head-case," Clete said quietly.

"They all are."

"He baked another hood's bones in a wedding cake and sent it to a Teamster birthday party."

Sweet Pea sat at the head of the table, a bib tied around his neck. The table was covered with trays of boiled crawfish and beaded pitchers of draft beer. Sweet Pea snapped the tail off a crawfish, sucked the fat out of the head, then peeled the shell off the tail. He dipped the meat into a red sauce, put it in his mouth, and never looked up.

"Y'all get yoursef some plates, Mr. Robicheaux," he said. He wore cream-colored slacks and a bolo tie and a gray silk shirt that rippled with a metallic sheen. His mouth glistened as though it were painted with lip gloss.

I took the dead coon out of the bag by its hind feet. The body was leathery and stiff, the fur wet from the ice in the cooler. I swung it across the table right into Sweet Pea's tray. Crawfish shells and juice, beer, and coleslaw exploded all over his shirt and slacks.

He stared down at his clothes, the twisted body of the coon in the middle of his tray, then at me. But

Sweet Pea Chaisson didn't rattle easily. He wiped his cheek with the back of his wrist and started to speak.

"Shut up, Sweet Pea," Clete said.

Sweet Pea smiled, his webbed eyes squeezing shut.

"What I done to deserve this?" he said. "You ruin my dinner, you t'row dead animals at me, now I ain't even suppose to talk?"

I could hear the air-conditioning units humming in the windows, a solitary pool ball rolling across the linoleum floor.

"Your buddies tried to hurt a friend of mine, Sweet Pea," I said.

He wrapped a napkin around the coon's tail, then held the coon out at arm's length and dropped it.

"You don't want nothing to eat?" he asked.

"Fuck it," Clete said beside me, his voice low.

Then I saw the expression on the face of the man called Patsy Dap. It was a grin, as though he both appreciated and was bemused by the moment that was being created for all of us. I felt Clete's shoe nudge against mine, his fingers pull lightly on my arm.

But it was moving too fast now.

"What d' we got here, the crazy person hour, fucking clowns abusing people at Sunday dinner?" Dapolito said.

"Nobody's got a beef with you, Patsy," Clete said.

"What d' you call this, creating a fucking scene, slopping food on people, who the fuck is this guy?"

"We got no problem with you, Patsy. Accept my word on that," Clete said.

"Why's *he* looking at me like that?" Dapolito said.

"Hey, I don't like that. Why you pinning me, man? . . . . Hey . . ."

My gaze drifted back to Sweet Pea.

"Tell those two guys, you know who I'm talking about, not to bother my friend again. That's all I wanted to say," I said.

"Hey, I said why you fucking pinning me. You answer my question," Dapolito said

Then his hand shot up from under the table and bit like a vise into my scrotum.

I vaguely recall the screams of the women at the table and Clete locking his big arms around me and dragging me backward through a tangle of chairs. But I remember my palm curving around the handle of the pitcher, the heavy weight of it swinging in an arc, the glass exploding in strings of wet light; I remember it like red shards of memory that can rise from a drunken dream. Then Dapolito was on his knees, his face gathered in his hands, his scarlet fingers trembling as though he were weeping or hiding a shameful secret in the stunned silence of the room.

Chapter 11

"WHY'D YOU DO it, mon?" Clete said outside. We were standing between my truck and Sweet Pea's Cadillac convertible.

"He dealt it." I wiped the sweat off my face on my sleeve and tried to breathe evenly. My heart was beating against my rib cage. So far we had heard no sirens. Some of the restaurant's customers had come out the front door but none of them wanted to enter the parking lot.

"Okay . . . this is the way I see it," Clete said. "You had provocation, so you'll probably skate with the locals. Patsy Dap's another matter. We'll have to do a sit-down with Johnny Carp."

"Forget it."

"You just left monkey shit all over the ceiling. We're doing this one my way, Streak."

"It's not going to happen, Clete."

"Trust me, big mon," he said, lighting a cigarette. "What's keeping the locals?"

"It probably got called in as barroom bullshit in the black district," I said.

There was a whirring sound in my ears like wind blowing in seashells. I couldn't stop sweating. Clete propped his arm against the cloth top of Sweet Pea's car and glanced down into the backseat.

"Dave, look at this," he said.

"What?"

"On the floor. Under those newspapers. There's something on the carpet."

The exposed areas of the carpet, where people's feet had crumpled and bunched the newspaper, looked brushed and vacuumed, but there were stains like melted chocolate in the gray fabric that someone had not been able to remove.

"We took it this far. You got a slim-jim in your tool box?" Clete said.

"No."

"So he needs a new top anyway," he said, and snapped open a switchblade knife, plunged it into the cloth, and sawed a slit down the edge of the back window. He worked his arm deep inside the hole and popped open the door.

"Feel it," he said a moment later, stepping aside so I could place my hand on the back floor.

The stain had become sticky in the enclosed heat of the automobile. Hovering like a fog just above the rug was a thick, sweet smell that reminded me in a vague way of an odor in a battalion aid station.

"Somebody did some major bleeding back there," Clete said.

"Lock it up again."

"Wait a minute." He picked up a crumpled piece of paper that was stuck down in the crack of the leather seat and read the carbon writing on it. "It looks like Sweet Pea's got lead in his foot as well as his twanger. Ninety in a forty-five."

"Let's see it," I said.

He handed it to me. Then he looked at my face again.

"It means something?" he said.

"He got the ticket yesterday on a dirt road out by Cade. Why's he hanging around Cade?" In the distance I could hear a siren on an emergency vehicle, as though it were trying to find a hole through traffic at an intersection.

"Wait here. Everything's going to be copacetic," Clete said.

"Don't go back in there."

He walked fast across the lot, entered the side door of the restaurant, then came back out with his hand in one pocket.

"Why is it these dumb bastards always use the john to score? The owner's even got sandpaper glued on top of the toilet tank to keep the rag-noses from chopping up lines on it," he said.

He stood between my truck and the Cadillac and began working open a small rectangular cellophane-sealed container with two silhouetted lovers on it.

"You're one in a million, Cletus," I said.

He unrolled a condom, then removed a piece of broken talc from his pocket, crushed it into fragments and powder, poured it with his palm into the condom, and tied a knot in the latex at the top.

"There's nothing like keeping everybody's eye on the shitbags. By the way, they wrapped one of those roller towels from the towel machine around Patsy's head. Think of a dirty Q-Tip sitting in a chair," he said. He dropped the condom on the floor of the Cadillac with two empty crack vials and locked the door, just before an Acadian ambulance, followed by a Lafayette city police car, turned into the parking lot.

"Party time," he said. He crinkled his eyes at me and brushed his palms softly.

The sheriff had never been a police officer before his election to office, but he was a good administrator and his general decency and sense of fairness had gotten him through most of his early problems in handling both criminals and his own personnel. He had been a combat marine, an enlisted man, during the Korean War, which he would not discuss under any circumstances, and I always suspected his military experience was related to his sincere desire not to abuse the authority of his position.

When I sat down in his office the sun was yellow and bright outside the window, and an array of potted plants on his windowsill stood out in dark silhouette against the light. His cheeks were red and grained and woven with tiny blue veins, and he had the small round chin of the French with a cleft in it.

He reread my report with his elbows on the desk blotter and his knuckles propped against his brow.

"I don't need this on Monday morning," he said.

"It got out of hand."

"Out of hand? Let me make an observation, my friend. Clete Purcel has no business here. He causes trouble everywhere he goes."

"He tried to stop it, Sheriff. Besides, he knows Sonny Marsallus better than anyone in New Orleans."

"That's not an acceptable trade-off. What's this stuff about a dead coon?"

I cleared a tic out of my throat. "That's not in my report," I said.

"Last night I got a call at home from the Lafayette chief of police. Let's see, how did he put it? 'Would you tell your traveling clown to keep his circus act in his own parish?' You want to hear the rest of it?"

"Not really." Because I knew my straying into another jurisdiction, or even the beer pitcher smashed into Patsy Dapolito's face, was not what was on the sheriff's mind.

"What have you held back from me?" he said.

I looked at him blankly and didn't answer.

"You're not the only one who chooses what to file a report on and what not to, are you?" he asked.

"Excuse me?"

"Saturday I ran into a friend of mine with the humane society. He's a friend of Helen Soileau's. He mentioned a certain event he thought I already knew about."

The sheriff waited.

"I don't believe in using the truth to injure good people," I said.

"What gives you the right to make that kind of decision?"

My palms felt damp on the arms of the chair. I could feel a balloon of heat rising from my stomach into my throat.

"I never enjoyed the role of pin cushion," I said.

"You're being treated unfairly?"

I wiped my palms on my thighs and folded them

in my lap. I looked out the window at the fronds on a palm tree lifting in the breeze.

"Somebody killed all her animals. You knew about it but you didn't report it and you went after Sweet Pea Chaisson on your own," he said.

"Yes, sir, that's correct."

"Why?"

"Because some shitheads set her up for blackmail purposes."

He brushed at the corner of his eye with his fingertip.

"I have a feeling they didn't catch her in the sack with a boyfriend," he said.

"The subject's closed for me, Sheriff."

"Closed? Interesting. No, amazing." He swiveled his chair sideways, rocked back in it, pushing against his paunch with his stiffened fingers. "Maybe you ought to have a little more faith in the people you work for."

"She sent some inquiries through the federal computer. Somebody doesn't want her to pursue it," I said.

His eyes rested on the flowered teapot he used to water his plants, then they seemed to refocus on another concern. "I've got the FBI bugging me about Sonny Marsallus. What's their interest in a Canal Street gumball?"

"I don't know."

"They know a lot about him and I don't think it's off a rap sheet. Maybe he got loose from the witness protection program."

"Sonny's not a snitch," I said.

"Great character reference, Dave. I bet he took his grandmother to Mass, too."

I rose from the chair. "Are you going to tell Helen about our conversation?"

"I don't know. Probably not. Just don't try to take me over the hurdles again. Were you ever mixed up in army intelligence?"

"No, why?"

"This whole thing stinks of the federal government. Can you tell me why they have to track their shit into a town that's so small it used to be between two Burma-Shave signs?"

I sat back down. "I want to get a warrant to search Sweet Pea Chaisson's car."

"What for?"

"There's dried blood on the back floor."

"How do you know?"

"Clete and I were inside it . . . Clete salted the shaft but the Lafayette cops didn't find what they were supposed to."

"I don't believe what you're telling me."

"You said you wanted it straight."

"This is the last time we're going to have this kind of conversation, sir."

I picked up my mail and walked down to my office. Five minutes later the sheriff opened my door just far enough to lean his head in.

"You didn't skate after all," he said. "Sweet Pea's lawyer, what's his name, that greasebag from Lafayette, Jason Darbonne, just filed a harassment complaint against you and the department. Another thing, too,

Dave, just so we're clear on everything, I want this shit cleaned up and it'd better be damn soon."

I couldn't blame him for his anger. The case drawers in our building were filled with enough grief, mayhem, perversity, and institutional failure to match the quality of life in the worst Third World nations on earth. Like case histories at a welfare agency, a police file, once opened, never seemed to close. Instead, it grew generationally, the same family names appearing again and again, the charges and investigations marking the passage of one individual from birth to adolescence to adulthood to death, crime scene photo upon mug shot, yellowing page upon yellowing page, like layers of sedimentary accretion formed by sewage as it flows through a pipe.

Children aborted with coat hangers, born addicted to crack, scalded under hot faucets; teenage mothers with pipe cleaner legs living between detox, the welfare agency, and hooking on the street; high school kids who can let off a .44 Magnum point-blank into their classmates at a dance and seriously maintain they acted in self-defense because they heard firecrackers popping in the parking lot; armed robbers who upgrade their agenda to kicking ballpoint pens into the eardrums of their victims before they execute them in the back of a fast-food restaurant; and the strangest and most baffling phenomenon of all, the recidivist pedophiles who are repeatedly paroled until they not only sodomize but murder a small child.

At one time local AA meetings were made up largely of aging drunks like myself. Now kids who should be in middle school are brought to the meetings in vans from halfway houses. They're usually white, wear burr haircuts, floppy tennis shoes, and oversize baseball caps sideways on their heads and look like refugees from an Our Gang comedy, except, when it's their turn to talk, they speak in coonass blue-collar accents about jonesing for crack and getting UA-ed by probation officers. You have the feeling their odyssey is just beginning.

Our best efforts with any of it seem to do no good. In dark moments I sometimes believed we should simply export the whole criminal population to uninhabited areas of the earth and start over again.

But any honest cop will tell you that no form of vice exists without societal sanction of some kind. Also, the big players would still be with us—the mob and the gambling interests who feed on economic recession and greed in politicians and local businessmen, the oil industry, which fouls the oyster beds and trenches saltwater channels into a freshwater marsh, the chemical and waste management companies that treat Louisiana as an enormous outdoor toilet and transform lakes and even the aquifer into toxic soup.

They all came here by consent, using the word *jobs* as though it were part of a votive vocabulary. But the deception wasn't even necessary. There was always somebody for sale, waiting to take it on his knees, right down the throat and into the viscera, as long as the money was right.

The speeding ticket Clete had found in Sweet Pea's car had been written on the dirt road that led from the highway back to the juke joint operated by Luke and Ruthie Jean Fontenot. Before I left the office, I pulled the ten-year package we had on Luke.

He had been extricated from the death house while a convict barber was in the act of lathering and shaving his head, the state's final preparation for the moment when Luke would sit in an oak chair while men he didn't know screwed a metal cap down on his sweating pate and strapped his arms and shinbones so tightly into the wood that his own rigid configuration would seem part of the chair itself. The call had come from the governor's office after Moleen Bertrand had hand-delivered depositions from two witnesses who swore the victim, a white sharecropper, had brought a pistol out from under the bouree table. According to the witnesses, a wet-brain in the crowd had stolen the gun before the sheriff's deputies arrived.

Luke received not only a stay but eventually a new trial, and finally a hung jury and a prosecutorial decision to cut him loose. His debt to Moleen was a large one.

The morning was warm and humid and the breeze blew a fine dust out of the shell parking lot and powdered the leaves of the oak and hackberry trees that were clustered next to the juke joint. I drove through the empty lot and parked in the shady lee of the building. A trash fire was smoldering in a rusted oil barrel by one of the trailers. On the ground next to it, like a flattened snake with a broken back, was a long strip of crusted gauze. A black woman in purple shorts and an olive green V-neck sweater looked out the back screen and disappeared again. I kicked over the trash barrel, rolled it across the shells, and used a stick to pry apart a smoldering stack of newspaper and food-streaked paper plates, scorched *boudin* casings and pork rinds, until, at the bottom of the pile, I saw the glowing and blackened remains of bandages that dissolved into thread when I touched them with the stick.

I went through the screen door and sat at the empty bar. Motes of dust spun in the glare of light through the windows.

The woman had big arms and breasts, a figure like a duck, a thick and glistening black neck hung with imitation gold chains. She walked toward me in a pair of flip-flops, holding a cigarette with two fingers, palm upward, by the side of her face, her hoop earrings swinging on her lobes.

"You gonna tell me you the tax man, I bet," she said.

"Nope."

"You ain't the beer man."

"I'm not that either."

"Sorry, sugar, if you come down to check the jelly-roll. It's too early in the morning."

"I came down to see you," I said, and smiled.

"I knowed it soon as you come in."

"Is Luke here?"

"You see him?"

"How about Ruthie Jean?"

"They come in at night. What you gonna have?" she said, and folded her arms on the bar so that her breasts swelled like cantaloupes out of her sweater. A gold tooth glinted in the corner of her mouth. "If you big enough, you can have anything you want. You big, ain't you?"

"How about a Dr Pepper?" I watched her uncap a bottle and fill a glass with ice, her thought patterns, her true attitudes toward whites, the plan or absence of a plan that governed her day, her feelings for a lover or a child, the totality of her life, all of it a mystery, hidden behind a coy cynicism that was as implacable as ceramic.

"Y'all don't have a gun-shot white man in one of those trailers, do you?" I said, and drank out of my glass.

"Don't know nothing about guns."

"I don't blame you. Who bled all over those bandages?"

Her mouth was painted with purple lipstick. She pursed her lips into a large, thick button and hummed to herself. "Here's a red quarter. Can you put it in the jukebox for me?" she said. "It got fingernail polish on it so the jukebox man don't keep it when he picks up the coins."

I opened my badge holder on the bar.

"Do you mind if I look in your trailers?" I said.

"I thought I had me a new boyfriend. But you just being on the job, ain't you?"

"I think there might be an injured man back there. So that gives me the right to go in those trailers. You want to help me?"

She pressed her fingertip on a potato chip crumb on the bar, looked at it, and flicked it away.

"I give away my heart and a man wipe his feet on it every time," she said.

I went back outside. The windows in both trailers were open, the curtains blowing in the breeze, but the doors were padlocked. When I reentered the bar the woman was talking on the pay phone in back. She finished her conversation, her back to me, and hung up.

"Had to find me a new man," she said.

"Can I have the key?"

"Sure. Why you ain't ax? You know how to put it in? Cain't every man always get it in by hisself."

I unlocked and went inside the first trailer. It stunk of insecticide and moist garbage; roaches as fat as my thumb raced across the cracked linoleum. In the center of the floor was a double cot with a rubber air mattress on it and a tangled sheet spotted with gray stains. The small tin sink was full of empty beer cans, the drain stoppered with cigarette butts.

The second trailer was a different matter. The floor was mopped, the tiny bathroom and shower stall clean, the two trash cans empty. In the icebox was a gallon bottle of orange juice, a box of jelly doughnuts, a package of ground chuck steak. The sheets and pillowcases had been stripped from the mattress on the bed. I grabbed the mattress by one end and rolled it upside down on the springs. In the center of the rayon cover was a brown stain the size of a pie plate that looked like the source had pooled and soaked deep into the fabric.

I opened my Swiss Army knife and grooved a line of crusted flakes onto the blade and wiped them inside a Ziploc bag. I locked the trailer and started to get in my truck, then changed my mind and went back inside the bar. The woman was mopping out the women's rest room, her stomach swinging under her sweater.

"He was a tall white man with a face full of wrinkles," I said. "He probably doesn't like black people much, but he had at least one nine-millimeter round in him and wasn't going to argue when Sweet Pea drove him out here. How am I doing so far?"

"It ain't my bidness, baby."

"What's your name?"

"Glo. You treat me right, I light up. I light up your whole life."

"I don't think you mean harm to anyone, Glo. But that man, the one with the wrinkles in his face, like old wallpaper full of cracks, he's a special kind of guy, he thinks up things to do to people, anybody, you, me, maybe even some Catholic nuns, I was told he threw two of them from a helicopter at a high altitude. Was the man in the trailer that kind of guy?"

She propped the head of the mop in a bucket of dirty water and worked her Lucky Strikes out of her shorts. Her right eye looked bulbous and watery as she held the Zippo's flame to the cigarette. She exhaled, pressed the back of her wrist to her eye socket, then cleared her throat and spat something brown into the wastebasket.

She tilted her chin up at me, her face unmasked, suddenly real, for the first time. "That's the troot, what you saying about this guy?"

"As far as I know."

"I'm locking up now, sugar, gotta take my little

boy to the doctor today. There's a lot of grip going around."

"Here my business card, Glo."

But she walked away from me, her arms stiff at her sides, her hands extended at right angles, as though she were floating on currents of air, her mouth gathered into a silent pucker like a purple rose.

I drove across the cattle guard under the arched and wisteria-covered iron trellis at the entrance to the Bertrand plantation, down the dirt road to Ruthie Jean Fontenot's small white frame house, where I parked in the yard. The sun had gone behind a cloud, blanketing the fields with shadow, and the breeze felt moist and warm blowing across the tops of the cane.

Ruthie Jean opened her door on a night chain.

"What you want?" she said.

"Question and answer time."

"I'm not dressed."

"I'm not going away."

"Aren't you suppose to have a warrant or something?"

"No."

She made a face, closed the door hard, then walked into the back of the house. I waited ten minutes among the gum trees where the dirt had been bladed and packed smooth by the earthmover. I picked up the twisted tongue of an old shoe. It felt as dry and light as a desiccated leaf. I heard Ruthie Jean slip the night chain on the door.

Her small living room was cramped with rattan furniture that had come in a set. The andirons in the fireplace were stacked with stone logs, a blaze of scarlet cellophane pasted behind them to give the effect of flames. Ruthie Jean stood on her cane in a white dress with a lacy neckline, black pumps, and a red glass necklace. Her skin looked yellow and cool in the soft light.

"You look nice," I said, and instantly felt my cheeks burn at the license in my remark.

"What you want down here this time?"

Before I could answer, a phone rang in back. She walked back to the kitchen to answer it. On a shelf above the couch were a clutter of gilt-framed family photographs. In one of them Ruthie Jean was receiving a rolled certificate or diploma of some kind from a black man in a suit and tie. They were both smiling. She had no cane and was wearing a nurse's uniform. At the end of the shelf was a dust-free triangular empty space where another photograph must have been recently removed.

"Are you a nurse?" I asked when she came back in the room.

"I was a nurse's aide." Her eyes went flat.

"How long ago was that?"

"What you care?"

"Can I sit down, please?"

"Suit yourself."

"You have a phone," I said.

She looked at me with an incredulous expression.

"Your Aunt Bertie told me she didn't have a phone and I'd have to leave messages for her at the convenience store. But you live just next door. Why wouldn't she tell me to call you instead?"

"She and Luke don't get along." Her cheek twitched when she sat down on the couch. Behind her head was the shelf with the row of framed photographs on it.

"Because he's too close to Moleen Bertrand?" I said.

"Ax them."

"I want the white man named Jack," I said.

She looked at her nails, then at her watch.

"This guy's an assassin, Ruthie Jean. When he's not leaking blood in one of your trailers, he carries a cut-down twelve-gauge under his armpit."

She rolled her eyes, a whimsical pout on her mouth, and looked out the window at a bird on a tree branch, her eyelids fluttering. I felt my face pinch with a strange kind of anger that I didn't quite recognize.

"I don't understand you," I said. "You're attractive and intelligent, you graduated from a vo-tech program, you probably worked in hospitals. What are you doing with a bunch of lowlifes and white trash in a hot pillow joint?"

Her face blanched.

"Don't look injured. Sweet Pea Chaisson is supplying the girls at your club," I said. "Why are you letting these people use you?"

"What I'm suppose to do now, ax you to hep us, same man who say he doesn't need a warrant just 'cause he's down in the quarters?"

"I'm not the enemy, Ruthie Jean. You've got bad people in your life and they're going to mess you up in a serious way. I guarantee it."

"There's nothing y'all don't know," she said. But

her voice was thick now, tired, as though a stone bruise were throbbing deep inside a vulnerable place.

I started in again. "You're too smart to let a man like Sweet Pea or Jack run a game on you."

She looked back out the window, a hot light in her eyes.

"Jack's got a friend who's built like an icebox. Did you see a guy who looks like that?" I said.

"I been polite but I'm axing you to leave now."

"How do you think all this is going to end?"

"What you mean?"

"You think you can deal with these guys by yourself? When they leave town, they wipe everything off the blackboard. Maybe both you and your brother. Maybe Glo and your aunt, too. They call it a slop-shot."

"You pretend you're different from other policemen but you're not," she said. "You pretend so your words cut deeper and hurt people more."

I felt my lips part but no sound came out.

"I promise you, we'll nail this guy to the wall and I'll keep you out of it," I said finally, still off balance, my train of thought lost.

She leaned sideways on the couch, her hands tight on her cane, as though a sliver of pain were working its way up her spine into her eyes.

"I didn't mean to insult or hurt you," I said. I tried to organize my words. My eyes focused on the mole by her mouth and the soft curve of her hair against her cheek. She troubled me in a way that I didn't quite want to look at. "This man Jack is probably part of an international group of some kind. I'm not sure what it is, but I'm convinced they're here to do grave injury to us. By that I mean all of us, Ruthie Jean. White people, black people, it doesn't matter. To them another human being is just a bucket of guts sewn up in a sack of skin."

But it was no use. I didn't know what the man named Jack had told her, or perhaps had done to her, and I suspected his tools were many, but as was too often the case, I knew I was witnessing another instance when the fear that moral cretins could inculcate in their victims was far greater than any apprehension they might have about refusing to cooperate with a law enforcement agency.

I heard a car outside and got up and looked outside the window. Luke, in a 1970s gas guzzler, had driven just far enough up the lane to see my truck, then had dropped his car in reverse and floorboarded it back toward the entrance to the plantation, dirt rocketing off the tires like shards of flint.

"I'm beginning to feel like the personification of anthrax around here," I said.

"You what?"

"Nothing. I don't want to see y'all go down on a bad beef. I'm talking about aiding and abetting, Ruthie Jean."

She got up on her cane, her hand locking hard into the curved handle.

"I cain't sit long. I got to walk around, then do some exercises and lie down," she said.

"What happened to you?"

"I don't have any more to say."

"Okay, you do what you want. Here's my business card in case you or Luke feel like talking to me later," I said, weary of trying to break through her fear or layers of racial distrust that were generations in the making. And in the next few moments I was about to do something that would only add to them. "Could I have a glass of water?" I asked.

When she left the room I looked behind and under the couch. But in my heart I already knew where I was going to find it. When the perps are holding dope, stolen property, a gun that's been used in an armed robbery or murder, and they sniff the Man about to walk into their lives, they get as much geography as possible between them and it. But Ruthie Jean wasn't a perp, and when her kind want to conceal or protect something that is dear to them, they stand at the bridge or cover it with their person.

I lifted up the cushion she had rested her back against. The gilt-frame color photograph was propped against the bamboo supports and webbing of the couch.

I had never seen him with a suntan. He looked handsome, leaner, his blue air force cap set at an angle, his gold bars, pilot's sunglasses, unbuttoned collar, and boyish grin giving him the cavalier and romantic appearance of a World War II South Pacific aviator rather than a sixties intelligence officer who to my knowledge had never seen combat.

I heard her weight on a floor plank. She stood in the doorway, a glass of water in her hand, her face now empty of every defense, her secrets now the stuff cops talk about casually while they spit Red Man out car windows and watch black women cross the street at intersections.

"It must have fallen off the shelf," I said, my skin

flexing against my skull. I started to replace the photograph in the dust-free spot at the end of the shelf. But she dropped her cane to the floor, limped forward off balance, pulled the photo from my hand, and hurled the glass of water in my face.

At the front door I looked back at her, blotted the water out of my eyes on my sleeve, and started to say something, to leave a statement hovering in the air that would somehow redeem the moment; an apology for deceiving her, or perhaps even a verbal thorn because she'd both disturbed and bested me. But it was one of those times when you have to release others and yourself to our shared failure and inadequacy and not pretend that language can heal either.

I knew why the shame and anger burned in her eyes. I believe it had little to do with me. In a flowing calligraphy at the bottom of the photo he had written, "This was taken in some God-forsaken place whose name, fortunately, I forget—Always, Moleen." I wondered what a plantation black woman must feel when she realizes that her white lover, grandiose in his rhetoric, lacks the decency or integrity or courage or whatever quality it takes to write her name and personalize the photo he gives her.

Chapter 12

CLETE CALLED ME from his office the next day.

"I'll buy you dinner in Morgan City after work," he said.

"What are you up to, Clete?"

"I'm taking a day off from the colostomy bags. It's not a plot. Come on down and eat some crabs."

"Is Johnny Carp involved in this?"

"I know a couple of guys who used to mule dope out of Panama and Belize. They told me some interesting stuff about fuckhead."

"Who?"

"Marsallus. I don't want to tell you over the phone. There're clicking sounds on my line sometimes."

"You're tapped?"

"Remember when we had to smoke that greaser and his bodyguard in the back of their car? I know IAD had a tap on me then. Sounds just like it. You coming down?"

"Clete—"

"Lighten up."

He told me the name of the restaurant.

It was on the far side of Morgan City, just off the highway by a boat basin lined with docks, boat slips, and tin-roofed sheds that extended out over the water.

Clete was at a linen-covered table set with flowers by the window. On the horizon you could see rain falling out of the sunlight like a cloud of purple smoke. He had a small pitcher of draft beer and an ice-filmed schooner and plate of stuffed mushrooms in front of him. His face was glowing with alcohol and a fresh sunburn.

"Dig in, noble mon. I've got some fried soft-shells on the way," he said.

"What's the gen on Sonny?" I left my coat on to cover my .45.

"Oh, yeah," he said, as though he had forgotten the reason for our meeting. "These two mules, I know them because they're bondsmen now and handle a lot of the pukes dealing crack in the St. Bernard where I run down about three skips a week. They were flying reefer and coke out of Belize, which was some kind of stop-off place for a whole bunch of runs going in and out of Colombia and Panama. These guys say there were a lot of weird connections down there, CIA, military people, maybe some guys hooked into the White House. Anyway, they knew asswipe and say everybody had him made for DEA."

"'Asswipe' is Sonny Boy?"

His eyes fluttered. "No, I'm talking about a Maryknoll missionary. Come on, Dave, stop letting this guy job you. His parents should have been sterilized or given a lifetime supply of industrial-strength rubbers."

"You buy what these bondsmen say?"

"Not really. Marsallus never finished high school. The DEA hires college graduates, Notre Dame jocks with brains, not street mutts with tattoos and rap sheets."

"Then why'd you have me come down here?" I asked.

But even as his eyes were drifting toward the door of the restaurant, I already knew the answer. John Polycarp Giacano had just come through the carpeted foyer, a raincoat draped on his shoulders as a movie actor might wear it. He was talking to a man behind him whom I couldn't see.

"Wait in the car. It's all right," he said, his palms raised in a placating way. "Fix yourself a drink. Then we'll catch some more fish."

He slipped his coat off his shoulders and handed it to a waitress to hang up, never speaking, as though his intention should automatically be understood. He wore white boating shoes, pleated slacks that were the color of French vanilla ice cream, and a navy blue tropical shirt that was ablaze with big red flowers. He walked toward us, smiling, his close-set eyes, thick brows, nose, and mouth all gathered together like a facial caricature in the center of a cake.

"You shouldn't have done this, Clete," I said.

"It's got to be cleared up, Streak. Patsy Dap listens to only one man. Just let me do the talking and everything's going to be cool."

"How you doin', fellas?" Johnny Carp said, and sat down.

"What's the haps, John?" I said.

He picked up a stuffed mushroom with his fingers and plopped it in his mouth, his eyes smiling at me while he chewed.

"He asks me what's the haps," he said. "Dave, I love you, you fucking wild man."

"Glad you could make it, Johnny," Clete said.

"I love to fish," he said. "It don't matter redfish, gafftop, specs, white trout, it's the fresh air, the waves flopping against the boat, Dave, you're a fucking zonk, we ain't living in the days of the O.K. Corral no more, know what I'm saying?"

"I don't know what to tell you, Johnny," I said.

"Hey, Clete, get us some drinks over here, some snapper fingers, some oysters on the half shell, make sure they're fresh, I got to talk to this crazy guy," Johnny said.

"I don't think you do, John," I said.

"What's he saying, Clete?"

"Streak doesn't like to bother people with his trouble, that's all, Johnny."

"His trouble's my trouble. So let's work it out. I got a guy out in the car gonna have to have plastic surgery over in Houston. This is a guy nobody needs to have pissed off at him. I'm talking about a face looks like a basketball with stitches all over it. This guy couldn't get laid down at the Braille school. This ain't something you just blow out your ass because you happen to be a cop, Dave."

"You're a generous man with your time, Johnny," I said. "But I didn't ask for a sit-down."

"What, I'm here to play with my dick under the table?"

A family sitting close to us got up and left.

"Your man went across the line," I said.

"I think we got a problem with pride here, Dave. It ain't good."

"There're cops in New Orleans who would have blown out his candle, Johnny," I said.

"You ain't in New Orleans. You degraded the man. He works for me. I got to square it, I'm being upfront here."

"I don't think you're hearing me. I was off my turf. So your man's not down on an assault charge. End of subject, Johnny," I said.

"You're burning up a lot of goodwill, Dave. That's the oil makes all the wheels turn. You're educated, I ain't got to tell you that," Johnny said. "The guy I got out in the car never had your advantages, he don't operate on goodwill, he operates out of respect for me. I don't honor that respect, then I don't get it from nobody else, either."

"What do you think you're going to get here today?" I asked.

"I got an envelope with ten large in it. You give it to the guy for his hospital bill, just say you got no hard feelings. You ain't even got to say you're sorry. The money don't matter 'cause I'm paying his hospital bill anyway and he'll have to give me the ten back. So everybody wins, everybody feels better, and we don't have no problems later."

"Are you serious?" I said.

"I throw a net over a guy makes some people wake up with cold sweats, pump him full of Demerol so he don't kick out my fucking windows, just so I can get him off your back, you have the fucking nerve to ask me if I'm serious?"

He took a comb out of his shirt pocket and ran it through his hair, touching the waves with his fingers simultaneously, his knurled forehead furrowing as his eyes bored into my face. The teeth of his comb were bright with oil.

"Come on, Johnny, Dave's not trying to dis anybody. The situation just got out of control. It happens."

"He's not trying to *what*?" Johnny said.

"Dis anybody. He doesn't mean any disrespect."

"I know what it means, why you using nigger language to me?"

Clete eased out his breath and lifted his shirt off his collarbone with his thumb. "I got fried out in my boat today, Johnny," he said. "Sometimes I don't say things very well. I apologize."

"I accept your invitation to dinner, you talk to me like I'm a goddamn nigger?"

The waiter set down a Scotch and milk in front of Johnny, another pitcher of beer for Clete, an iced tea for me, and a round tray of freshly opened oysters flecked with ice. Johnny reached across the table and popped Clete on top of the hand.

"You deaf and dumb?" he said.

Clete's green eyes roved around the room, as though he were appraising the fishnets and ship's life preservers hung on the wall. He picked up a oyster, sucked it out of the shell, and winked at Johnny Carp.

"What the fuck's that supposed to mean?" Johnny said.

"You're a lot of fun, John," Clete said.

Johnny took a deep drink out of his Scotch and milk, his eyes like black marbles that had rolled together above the glass. He rubbed a knuckle hard across his mouth, then pursed his lips like a tropical fish staring out of an aquarium. "I'm asking you in a nice way, you're giving me some kind of queer-bait signals here, you're ridiculing me, you just being a wiseass 'cause we're in public, what?" he said.

"I'm saying this was a bad idea," Clete said. "Look, I was there. Patsy Dap violated my friend's person, you know what I'm saying? That's not acceptable anywhere, not with your people, not with ours. He got what he deserved. You don't see it that way, Johnny, it's because you're fifty-two cards short of a deck. And don't ever put your fucking hand on me again."

Five minutes later, under the porch, we watched Johnny Carp drive his Lincoln through the light rain toward the parking lot exit. He had rolled down the tinted windows to let in the cool air, and we could see Patsy Dapolito in the passenger seat, his face and shaved head like a bleached-out muskmelon laced with barbed wire.

"Hey, Patsy, it's an improvement. I ain't putting you on," Clete yelled.

"You're a terrific intermediary, Clete," I said.

"The Giacanos are scum, anyway. Blow it off. Come on, let's go out under the shed and throw a line in. Wow, feel that breeze," he said, inhaling deeply, his eyes filling with pleasure at the soft twilit perfection of the day.

* * *

Clete was probably the best investigative cop I ever knew, but he treated his relationships with the lowlifes like playful encounters with zoo creatures. As a result, his attitudes about them were often facile.

The Giacanos never did anything unless money and personal gain were involved. The family name had been linked repeatedly to both a presidential assassination and the murder of a famous civil rights leader, and although I believed them capable of committing either one or both of those crimes, I didn't see how the Giacanos could have benefited financially from them and for that reason alone doubted their involvement.

But Johnny didn't do a sit-down with a rural sheriff's detective to prevent a meltdown like Patsy Dapolito from getting off his leash. Dapolito was morally insane but not stupid. When his kind stopped taking orders and started carrying out personal vendettas, they were shredded into fish chum and sprinkled around Barataria Bay.

Johnny Carp'd had another agenda when he came down to Morgan City. I didn't know what it was, but I was sure of one thing—one way or another, Johnny had become a player in Iberia Parish.

Jason Darbonne was known as the best criminal lawyer in Lafayette. He had the hard, grizzled body of a weight lifter and daily handball player, with thick upper arms and tendons like ropes in his shoulders. But it was his peculiar bald head that you remembered; it had the shape and color of an egg that had been hard-boiled in brown tea, and because he had virtually no neck, the head seemed to perch on his high collar like Humpty-Dumpty's.

A cold front had gone through the area early Wednesday morning, and the air was brisk and sunny when I ran into him and Sweet Pea Chaisson on the courthouse steps.

"Hey, Dave," Sweet Pea said. "Wait a minute, I forgot. Is it your first name or your last name I ain't suppose to use?"

"What's your problem this morning?" I said.

"Don't talk to him," Darbonne said to Sweet Pea.

"I didn't even know y'all sliced up my top till I went through the car wash. The whole inside of my car got flooded. Then the female attendant picks up this rubber that floats out from under the seat. I felt like two cents."

"What's your point?" I said.

"I forgot to pay my State Farm. I'm gonna be out four t'ousand dollars. It ain't my way to go around suing people." He brushed off Darbonne's hand. "Just give me the money for the top and we'll forget it."

"You'll forget it? You're telling me I'm being sued?" I said.

"Yeah, I want my goddamn money. The inside of my car's ruined. It's like riding around inside a sponge."

I started inside the courthouse.

"What's the matter, there's something wrong with the words I use you don't understand?" he said.

His webbed, birdlike eyes focused earnestly on my face.

"I had nothing to do with damaging your car. Stay away from me, Sweet Pea," I said.

He pressed the few stands of hair on his head flat with the palm of his hand and squinted at me as though he were looking through a dense haze, his mouth flexing in disbelief. Darbonne put his hand on Sweet Pea's arm.

"Is that a threat, sir?" he asked.

"No, it's just a request."

"If you didn't do it, that fat fuck did," Sweet Pea said.

"I'll pass on your remarks to Purcel," I said.

"You're a public menace hiding behind a badge," Darbonne said. "If you come near my client again, you're going to wish your name was Job."

Two women and a man passing by turned and looked at us, then glanced away. Darbonne and Sweet Pea walked out to a white Chrysler parked by the curb. The sun reflected hotly off the tinted back window like a cluster of gold needles. Darbonne was poised by the driver's door, waiting for an opportunity to open it in the traffic, his nostrils dilating at something in the breeze.

I walked toward him, looked across the Chrysler's roof into his surprised face.

"When I was a patrolman in New Orleans, you were a prosecutor for the United States attorney's office," I said.

His hand was poised in midair, his sunglasses hanging from his fingers.

"What happened to you, sir?" I said.

He turned his face away from me and slipped his

sunglasses on his nose, but not before I saw a level of injury in his eyes that I had not anticipated.

Helen Soileau sat on the corner of my desk. She wore a pair of tan slacks and a pink short-sleeve shirt.

"I took Marsallus's diary home last night and read it till two this morning," she said. "He's pretty good with words."

"Sonny's not easy to put in one shoe box," I said. "Have you got all the paperwork on him?"

"Pretty much. None of it's very helpful, though. I got his family's welfare file if you want to look at it."

"What for?"

"No reason, really."

She picked up the folder from my blotter and began glancing through it.

"His mother was a prostitute?" she said.

"Yeah, she died of tuberculosis when he was a kid. His father was a blind man who sharpened knives and scissors on a grinder he used to wheel up and down Villere Street."

Helen put the folder down.

"In the diary he talks about some songwriters. He quotes a bunch of their lyrics," she said. "Joe Hill and Woody Guthrie. Is Woody Guthrie related to Arlo?"

"Woody was his dad. Woody and Joe Hill wrote songs about farm migrants, the early unions, that sort of thing."

"I don't get it," she said.

"What?"

"Marsallus, he's not a wiseguy. He doesn't think like one. The stuff in that diary, it bothers me."

"You mean the massacres in those villages?"

"Was that really going on down there?" she said.

"Everyone who was there tells the same story."

"Marsallus said something about the nature of memory that I couldn't stop thinking about. 'My cell partner told me today my head's like a bad neighborhood that I shouldn't go into by myself.' There was a time in my life when I was the same way. I just didn't know how to say it."

"I see," I said, focusing my eyes at a point middistance between us.

She bounced her fingertips on the file folder.

"You want to go to lunch?" I said.

"No, thanks. Say, where's the portable cluster fuck these days?"

"I beg your pardon?"

"Clete Purcel."

"Oh, he's around . . . Did you want me to tell him something?"

"I was just curious."

I nodded, my face empty. She stood up from the corner of the desk, straightened her shoulders and flattened her stomach, tucked her shirt under her gunbelt with her thumbs.

"You looking at something?" she said.

"Not me."

"I was too hard on the guy, that's all. I mean when he was in your office that time," she said.

"He's probably forgotten about it, Helen."

"Y'all go fishing a lot?"

"Once in a while. Would you like to join us?"

"I'm not much on it. But you're a cutie," she said, walked her fingers across my shoulders, and went out the door.

Moleen Bertrand's camp was located down in the wetlands on a chenier, a plateau of dry ground formed like a barrier island by the tides from water-pulverized seashells. Except for the site of his camp, a four-bedroom frame building with a tin roof and screened-in gallery, the chenier was pristine, the black topsoil bursting with mushrooms and buttercups and blue bonnets, no different than it had been when the first Spanish and French explorers came to Louisiana. The woods were parklike, the trees widely spaced, the branches and trunks hung and wrapped with vines that had the girth of boa constrictors, the moss-covered canopy of live oaks hundreds of feet above the ground, which was dotted with palmettos and layered with rotting pecan husks. At the edge of the chenier were bogs and alligator grass and blue herons lifting above the gum trees and acres of blooming hyacinths that were impassable with a boat, and, to the south, you could see the long, slate green, wind-capped roll of the Gulf and the lightning that danced over the water like electricity trapped in a steel box.

Moleen and his wife, Julia, were flawless hosts. Their guests were all congenial people, attorneys, the owner of a sugar mill, an executive from a hot sauce company, their wives and children. Moleen fixed drinks at a bar on the gallery, kept a huge ice chest filled with soda and imported beer, barbecued a pig on a spit under a tin shed and roasted trays of wild ducks from the freezer. We busted skeet with his shotguns; the children played volleyball and sailed Frisbees; the air smelled of wildflowers and salt spray and the hot brassy odor of a distant storm. It was a perfect spring day for friends to gather on an untouched strip of the Old South that somehow had eluded the twentieth century.

Except for the unnatural brightness and confidence in Julia's face, the wired click in her eyes when she did not assimilate words or meaning right away, and Moleen's ongoing anecdotal rhetoric that seemed intended to distract from his wife's affliction. Each time she returned to the bar she poured four fingers of Jack Daniel's into her glass, with no water or soda, added a half cup of ice, a teaspoon of sugar, and a sprig of mint. We were eating in the main room when she said, out of no apparent context, "Can any of y'all explain to me why this black congresswoman got away with refusing the Daughters of the Confederacy the renewal of their logo?"

"She didn't do it by herself," Moleen said quietly, and touched his lips with his napkin.

"They went along with her, but she was behind it. That's what I meant, Moleen. I think it's ridiculous," Julia said.

The other people at the table smiled, unsure of what was being said, perhaps faintly remembering a news article.

"Julia's talking about the Daughters of the Confederacy trying to renew the patent on their emblem," Moleen said. "The application was denied because the emblem has the Confederate flag on it."

"That woman's a demagogue. I don't know why people can't see that," Julia said.

"I think it's our fault," a woman down the table said, leaning out over her plate to speak. "We've let the Confederate flag become identified with all kinds of vile groups. I can't blame people of color for their feelings."

"I didn't say I blamed people of color," Julia said. "I was talking about this particular black woman."

"Julia makes a point," Moleen said. "The DOC's hardly a Fifth Column."

"Well, I think we should do something about it," Julia said. She drank from her glass, and the light intensified behind her chemical-green contact lenses.

"Oh, it gives them something to do in Washington," Moleen said.

"It's not a joke, Moleen," Julia said.

"Let me tell you something *she* did once," Moleen said, spreading his napkin and replacing it on his lap. "When she was a cheerleader at LSU. She and these other kids, they hooked up Mike the Tiger's empty cage to a pickup truck, with the back door flopping open, and drove all over nigger town on Saturday afternoon." He blew a laugh out of his mouth. "They'd stop in front of a bar or barbecue stand and say, 'Excuse me, we don't want to alarm anyone but have y'all seen a tiger around here?' There were darkies climbing trees all over Baton Rouge."

I stared at him.

"Don't tell that story. I didn't have anything to do with that," Julia said, obviously pleased at the account.

"It's a campus legend. People make too much about race today," he said.

"Moleen, that doesn't change what that woman has done. That's what I'm trying to say, which y'all don't seem to understand," she said.

"For God's sakes, Julia, let's change the subject," he said.

The table was quiet. Someone coughed, a knife scraped against a plate. The whites of Julia's eyes were threaded with tiny red veins, the lashes stuck together with mascara. I thought of a face painted on a windblown pink balloon that was quivering against its string, about to burst.

Later, outside, Moleen asked me to walk with him to the edge of the marsh, where his shotguns and skeet trap rested on top of a weathered picnic table. He wore laced boots, khaki trousers with snap pockets up and down the legs, a shooter's vest with twelve-gauge shells inserted in the cloth loops. He cracked open his double-barrel and plopped two shells in the chambers.

"Were you ever stationed in Thailand, Moleen?" I said.

"For a little while. Why do you ask?"

"A lot of intelligence people were there. I was just curious."

He scratched at the corner of his mouth with a fingernail. "You want to bust a couple?" he said.

"No thanks."

"You looked a little steely-eyed at the table."

I watched a nutria drop off a log and swim into a cluster of hyacinths.

"That little anecdote about Julia's cheerleading days bother you?" he asked.

"Maybe."

"Come on, Dave, I was talking about a college prank. It's innocent stuff."

"Not from you it isn't."

"You have an irritating habit. You're always suggesting an unstated conclusion for other people to guess at," he said. He waited. "Would you care to explain yourself, Dave?"

"The problem isn't mine to explain, sir." In the distance, out by the access road, I could see a heavyset man jogging in shorts and a T-shirt, a towel looped around his glistening neck.

"I think the role of human enigma would become kind of tiresome," he said. He raised his shotgun to his shoulder, tracked the flight of a seagull with it, then at the last second blew the head off a clump of pampas grass. He cracked open the breech, picked the empty casing out, and flung it smoking into the mud.

"I believe I'll go back inside," I said.

"I think you've made an unpleasant implication, Dave. I insist we clear it up."

"I went back out to your plantation this week. I'm not sure what's going on out there, but part of it has to do with Ruthie Jean Fontenot."

He looked into my eyes. "You want to spell that out?" he said.

"You know damn well what I'm talking about. If you want to hide a personal relationship, that's your business. But you're hiding something else, too,

Moleen, about that plantation. I just don't know what it is."

He fitted the shotgun's stock to his shoulder, fired at a nutria that was swimming behind a half-submerged log, and blew a pattern of bird shot all over the pond. The nutria ducked under the water and surfaced again but it was hurt and swimming erratically. Moleen snapped open the breech and flung the casing out into the water.

"I don't take kindly to people insulting me on my own property," he said.

"The insult is to that woman on the plantation. You didn't even have the decency to inscribe her name on the photograph you gave her."

"You're beyond your limits, my friend."

"And you're cruel to animals as well as to people. Fuck you," I said, and walked back toward the camp.

I found Bootsie on the gallery.

"We have to go," I said.

"*Dave,* we just ate."

"I already said our good-byes. I have some work to do at the dock."

"No! It's rude."

Three women drinking coffee nearby tried not to hear our conversation.

"Okay, I'm going to put on my gym shorts and tennis shoes and jog a couple of miles. Pick me up out on the road." She looked at me with a strangled expression on her face. "I'll explain it later."

We had come in Bootsie's Toyota. I unlocked the trunk, took out my running shoes and gym shorts, and changed in the lee of the car. Then I jogged across a glade full of buttercups, past a stand of persimmon trees that fringed the woods, and out onto the hard-packed dirt road that led off the chenier.

The wind was warm and the afternoon sky marbled with yellow and maroon clouds. I turned my face into the breeze, kept a steady pace for a quarter mile, then poured it on, the sweat popping on my forehead, the blood singing in my chest until Moleen Bertrand's words, his supercilious arrogance, became more and more distant in my mind.

I passed a clump of pecan trees that were in deep shadow, the ground under them thick with palmettos. Then in the corner of my vision I saw another jogger step out into the spangled light and fall in beside me.

I smelled him before I saw him. His odor was like a fog, gray, visceral, secreted out of glands that could have been transplanted from animals. His head was a tan cannonball, the shoulders ax-handle wide, the hips tapering down to a small butt that a woman could probably cover with both her hands. His T-shirt was rotted into cheesecloth, the armpits dark and sopping, the flat chest a nest of wet black hair.

His teeth were like tombstones when he grinned.

"You do it in bursts, don't you?" he said. His voice was low, full of grit, like a man with throat cancer. "Me, too."

His shoulder was inches away, the steady *pat-pat-pat-pat* of his tennis shoes in rhythm with mine, even the steady intake and exhalation of his breath now part of mine. He wrapped his towel over his head and knotted it under his chin.

"How you doin'?" I said.

"Great. You ever run on the grinder at Quantico?" He turned his face to me. The eyes were cavernous, like chunks of lead shot.

"No, I wasn't in the Corps," I said.

"I knew a guy looked like you. That's why I asked."

I didn't answer. Out over the salt a single-engine plane was flying out of the sun, its wings tilting and bouncing hard in the wind.

"Were you at Benning?" the man said.

"Nope."

"I know you from somewhere."

"I don't think so."

"Maybe it was Bragg. No, I remember you now. Saigon, sixty-five. Bring Cash Alley. You could get on the pipe and laid for twenty bucks. Fucking A, I never forget a face."

I slowed to a walk, breathing hard, my chest running with sweat. He slowed with me.

"What's the game, partner?" I said.

"It's a small club. No game. A guy with two Hearts is a charter member in my view." He pulled his towel off his head and mopped his face with it, then offered it to me. I saw Bootsie's Toyota headed down the road toward us.

I backed away from him, my eyes locked on his.

"You take it easy, now," I said.

"You too, chief. Try a liquid protein malt. It's like wrapping copper wire around your nuts, really puts an edge on your run."

I heard Bootsie brake behind me. I got in the passenger seat beside her. My bare back left a dark wet stain on the seat.

"Dave, put on your shirt," she said.

"Let's go."

"What's wrong?"

"Nothing."

She glanced in the rearview mirror. The man with the tan cannonball head was mopping the inside of his thighs with the towel.

"Yuck," she said. "*Who's* that?"

"I have a feeling I just met Mr. Emile Pogue," I answered.

Chapter 13

"THIS DOESN'T HAPPEN," the sheriff said, his hands on his hips, looking at the manila folders and papers on my floor, the prise marks where a screwdriver had sprung the locks on the drawers in my desk and file cabinet. "We have to investigate the burglary of our own department."

It was 8 A.M. Monday morning and raining hard outside. The sheriff had just come into the office. I'd been there since seven.

"What's missing?" he asked.

"Nothing that I can see. The files on Marsallus and Della Landry are all over the floor, but they didn't take anything."

"What about Helen's files?"

"She can't find her spare house key. She's going to have her locks changed today," I said.

He sat down in my swivel chair.

"Do you mind?" he said.

"Not at all." I began picking up the scattered papers and photographs from the floor and arranging them in their case folders.

He took a breath. "All right, Wally says the cleaning crew came in about eleven last night. They vacuumed, waxed the floors, dusted, did the rest rooms, and left around two A.M. He's sure it was the regular bunch."

"It probably was."

"Then who got in here?"

"My guess is somebody else wearing the same kind of uniform came in and picked the locks, probably right after the cleaning crew left. Nobody pays much attention to these guys, so the only people who might have recognized the impostors were gone."

The sheriff picked up my phone and punched a number.

"Come down to Dave's office a minute," he said into the receiver. After he hung up he leaned one elbow on the desk and pushed a thumb into the center of his forehead. "This makes me madder than hell. What's this country coming to?"

Wally opened my office door. He was a tall, fat man, with hypertension and a florid face and a shirt pocket full of cellophane-wrapped cigars. He was at the end of his shift and his eyes had circles under them.

"You're sure everybody on the cleaning crew was gone by two A.M.?" the sheriff said.

"Pretty sure. I mean after they went out the front door the hall down here was dark and I didn't hear nothing."

"Think about it, Wally. What time exactly did the last cleaning person leave?" the sheriff said.

"I told you, two A.M., or a minute or two one side or another of it."

"They all left together?" the sheriff said.

"The last guy out said good night at two A.M."

"Was it the last guy or the whole bunch?" I asked.

He fingered the cigars in his pocket and stared into space, his eyes trying to concentrate.

"I don't remember," he said.

"Did you know the guy who said good night?" I asked.

"He walked by me with a lunch pail and a thermos. A shooting came in two minutes earlier. That's how I knew the time. I wasn't thinking about the guy."

"Don't worry about it," I said.

Wally looked at the sheriff.

"It's not your fault, Wally. Thanks for your help," the sheriff said. A moment later he said to me, "What are these guys after?"

"They don't know that Marsallus gave me his notebook. But I bet they think we found a copy of it that they missed in Della Landry's house."

"What's in it, though? You said it reads like St. Augustine's *Confessions* among the banana trees."

"You got me. But it must be information they need rather than information they're trying to keep from us. You follow me?"

"No."

"If we have it, they know we've read it, maybe made copies of it ourselves. So that means the notebook contains something indispensable to them that makes sense only to themselves."

"This guy you met jogging yesterday, you think he's this mercenary, what's his name, Pogue?"

"He knew the year I was in Vietnam. He even knew how many times I'd been wounded."

The sheriff looked at the blowing rain and a mimosa branch flattening against the window.

"I see only one way through this," he said. "We find Marsallus again and charge him with shooting the man in front of your house. Then he can talk to us or take up soybean farming at Angola."

"We don't have a shooting victim."

"Find him."

"I need a warrant on Sweet Pea's Cadillac."

"You're not going to get it. Why aren't you sweating that black woman out at the Bertrand plantation on this?"

"That's a hard word," I said.

"She's involved, she's dirty. Sorry to offend your sensibilities."

"It's the way we've always done it," I said.

"Sir?"

The air-conditioning was turned up high, but the room was humid and close, like a wet cotton glove on the skin.

"Rounding up people who're vulnerable and turning dials on them. Should we kick a board up Moleen Bertrand's butt while we're at it? I think he's dirty, too. I just don't know how," I said.

"Do whatever you have to," the sheriff said. He stood up and straightened his back, his eyes empty.

But no urgency about Moleen, I thought.

He read it in my face.

"We have two open murder cases, one involving a victim kidnapped from our own jail," he said. "In part we have shit smeared on our faces because you and Purcel acted on your own and queered a solid investigative lead. Your remarks are genuinely testing my level of tolerance."

"If you want to stick it to Moleen, there's a way to do it," I said. The sheriff waited, his face narrow and cheerless. "Create some serious man-hours and reactivate the vehicular homicide file on his wife."

"You'd do that?" he asked.

"No, I wouldn't. But when you sweat people, that's the kind of furnace you kick open in their face, Sheriff. It's just easier when the name's not Bertrand."

"I don't have anything else to say to you, sir," he said, and walked out.

Sometimes you get lucky.

In this case it was a call from an elderly Creole man who had been fishing with a treble hook, using a steel bolt for weight and chicken guts for bait, in a slough down by Vermilion Bay.

Helen and I drove atop a levee through a long plain of flooded sawgrass and got there ahead of the divers and the medical examiner. It had stopped raining and the sun was high and white in the sky and water was dripping out of the cypress trees the elderly man had been fishing under.

"Where is it?" I asked him.

"All the way across, right past them cattails," he said. His skin was the color of dusty brick, his turquoise eyes dim with cataracts. "My line went bump, and I thought I hooked me a gar. I started to yank on it, then I knew it wasn't no gar. That's when I drove back up to the sto' and called y'all."

His throw line, which was stained dark green with

silt and algae, was tied to a cypress knee and stretched across the slough. It had disappeared beneath the surface by a cluster of lily pads and reeds.

Helen squatted down and hooked her index finger under it to feel the tension. The line was snagged on an object that was tugging in the current by the slough's mouth.

"Tell us again what you saw," she said.

"I done tole the man answered the phone," he said. "It come up out of the water. It liked to made my heart stop."

"You saw a hand?" I said.

"I didn't say that. It looked like a flipper. Or the foot on a big gator. But it wasn't no gator," he said.

"You didn't walk over to the other side?" Helen said.

"I ain't lost nothing there," he said.

"A flipper?" I said.

"It was like a stub, it didn't have no fingers, how else I'm gonna say it to y'all?" he said.

Helen and I walked around the end of the slough and back down the far side to the opening that gave onto a canal. The current in the canal was flowing southward into the bay as the tide went out. The sun's heat rose like steam from the water's surface and smelled of stagnant mud and dead vegetation.

Helen shoved a stick into the lily pads and moved something soft under it. A cloud of mud mushroomed to the surface. She poked the stick into the mud again, and this time she retrieved a taut web of monofilament fishing line that was looped through a corroded yellow chunk of pipe casing. She let it slide off the stick into the water again. Then an oval pie of wrinkled skin rolled against the surface and disappeared.

"Why do we always get the floaters?" she said.

"People here throw everything else in the water," I said.

"You ever see a shrink?"

"Not in a while, anyway," I said. In the distance I could see two emergency vehicles and a TV news van coming down the levee.

"I went to one in New Orleans. I was ready for him to ask me about my father playing with his weenie in front of the kids. Instead, he asked me why I wanted to be a homicide detective. I told him it's us against the bad guys, I want to make a difference, it bothers me when I pull a child's body out of a sewer pipe after a sex predator has gotten through with him. All the while he's smiling at me, with this face that looks like bread pudding with raisins all over it. I go, 'Look, Doc, the bad guys torture and rape and kill innocent people. If we don't send them in for fifty or seventy-five or ship them off for the Big Sleep, they come back for encores.'

"He keeps smiling at me. I go, 'The truth is I got tired of being a meter maid.' He thought that was pretty funny."

I waited for her to go on.

"That's the end of the story. I never went back," she said.

"Why not?"

"You know why."

"It still beats selling shoes," I said.

She combed her hair with a comb from the back

pocket of her Levi's. Her breasts stood out against her shirt like softballs.

"Fix your tie, cutie. You're about to be geek of the week on the evening news," she said.

"Helen, would you please stop that?"

"Lighten up, Streak."

"That's exactly what Clete Purcel says."

"Cluster fuck? No kidding?" she said, and grinned.

Twenty minutes later two divers, wearing wet suits and air tanks and surgical gloves over their hands, sawed loose the tangle of monofilament fish line that had been wrapped around and crisscrossed over the submerged body and threaded through a daisy chain of junkyard iron. They held the body by the arms and dragged it heavily onto the bank, the decomposed buttocks sliding through the reeds like a collapsed putty-colored balloon.

A young television newsman, his camera whirring, suddenly took his face away from his viewer and gagged.

"Excuse me," he said, embarrassed, his hand pinched over his mouth. Then he turned aside and vomited.

The divers laid the body front-down on a black plastic sheet. The backs of the thighs were pulsating with leeches. One of the divers walked away, took a cigarette from a uniformed deputy's mouth, and smoked it, his back turned toward us.

The pathologist was a tall white-haired man who wore a bow tie, suspenders, and a wide-brimmed straw hat with a thin black ribbon around the crown.

"I wonder why they didn't eviscerate him while they were at it," he said.

The body was nude. The fingers and thumbs of both hands had been snipped off cleanly at the joints, perhaps with bolt cutters. The head had been sawed off an inch above the collarbones.

Helen bit a hangnail off her thumb. "What do you think?" she said.

"Look at the size. How many guys that big end up as floaters?" I said.

Even in death and the gray stages of decomposition that take place under water in the tropics, the network of muscles in the shoulders and back and hips was that of a powerful, sinewy man, someone whose frame was wired together by years of calisthenics, humping ninety-pound packs in the bush, jolting against a parachute harness while the steel pot razors down on the nose.

I stretched a pair of white surgical gloves over my hands and knelt by the body. I tried to hold my breath, but the odor seemed to cling to my skin like damp wool, an all-enveloping hybrid stench that's like a salty tangle of seaweed and fish eggs drying on hot sand and pork gone green with putrefaction.

"You don't have to do that, Dave," the pathologist said. "I'll have him apart by five o'clock."

"I'm just checking for a bullet wound, Doc," I said.

I fitted both hands under the torso and flipped the body on its back.

"Oh shit," a newsman said.

"Maybe the guy was having a female implant put in," a uniformed deputy said.

"Shut up, asshole," Helen said.

There was a single wound above the groin area. It had been cored out by a fish eel, whose head was embedded deep in the flesh while the tail flipped in the air like a silver whip.

"You might look for a nine-millimeter, Doc," I said.

"You know this guy?" he asked.

"My guess is his name was Jack," I said.

Helen brushed at his thigh with a piece of folded cardboard. "Here's a tattoo his friends missed," she said.

It was a faded green, red, and gold Marine Corps globe and anchor imposed upon a cone-shaped open parachute.

"The poor dumb fuck didn't even know who he was on a skivvy run," Helen said.

Helen's therapist had asked her one of those questions for which an honest answer is seemingly disingenuous or so self-revealing that you don't wish to inhabit your own skin for a while.

My dreams seemed continuous, beginning with the first moments of sleep and ending at dawn, but the props and central characters always remained the same.

I stand at a brass-railed mahogany bar on a pink evening in the Philippines, the palm fronds in the courtyard waving slightly in the breeze. I knock back a shot glass of Beam and chase it with San Miguel on the side, rest my forearms on the coolness of the wood and wait for the rush, which, like an old friend, never disappoints, which always lasers straight to the nerve endings at the base of the brain and fills the glands and loins and the sealed corridors of memory with light and finally gives ease to the constricted and fearful heart.

For a while.

The bartender's face is pale yellow, the skin tight against the skull, the skin stretched into cat's whiskers, the mouth a stitched slit. The evening air is filled with the rustle of bead curtains and the silky whisper of the Oriental women who move through them; redolent with the thick, sweet smell of opium, like honey and brown sugar burned in a spoon, and the smoky scent of whiskey aged in charcoal barrels, the black cherries and sliced oranges and limes that you squeeze between your back teeth with an almost sexual pleasure, as though somehow they connect you with tropical gardens rather than places under the earth.

The dream always ends in the same way, but I never know if the scene is emblematic or an accurate recall of events that took place during a blackout. I see myself lifted from a floor by men with no faces who pitch me through a door into a stone-paved alley that reverberates with a clatter of metal cans and crones who scavenge through garbage. A pimp and a whore rifle my pockets while I stare up at them, as helpless as if my spine were severed; my hands are cuffed behind me in a chair in a Third World police station while I shake with delirium tremens and sweat as big as flattened marbles slides down my face.

When I wake from the dream my breath shudders in my throat, the air in the room seems poisoned with exhaled and rebreathed alcohol, and I sit on the edge of my bed and begin to rework the first three steps of the AA recovery program. But there are other images in my mind now, more disturbing than the ones from my sleep. It's like a red bubble rising out of a heated place just beyond the limits of vision; then it bursts in the back of the brain and I can see tracers lacing the night like strips of barroom neon and taste the bitterness of cordite on my tongue. The rush is just like the whiskey that cauterizes memory and transforms electrified tigers into figures trapped harmlessly inside oil and canvas.

My shield and my 1911-model army-issue .45 automatic sit on top of my dresser in the moonlight. I think it's not an accident they found their way into my life.

An hour after I got home that evening the phone rang in the kitchen.

"We dug out two rounds," the medical examiner said. "One of them's in good shape. But I'd say both are either nine-millimeter or .38 caliber."

"Two?" I said.

"There was a second entry wound below the right armpit. It did the most damage. It flattened against something and toppled before it entered the chest cavity. Anyway, it pierced both his lungs. You still think this was the guy out at your house?"

"Yeah, the guy was carrying a cut-down twelve-gauge under his right arm. One of the rounds probably deflected off it."

"I suspect he was wrapped awful tight, then."

"I don't understand," I said.

"He jacked a lot of adrenaline into his heart before he got hit. Otherwise, I don't know how he made it out of there. Anyway, tomorrow we'll see if we can match his blood to the specimens you gave me from Cade and the bushes in front of your house."

"Thanks for your help, Doc."

"Keep me posted on this one, will you?"

"Sure."

"I wasn't passing on an idle thought about the adrenaline in this man's heart. I've read medical papers about the deaths of royalty who were executed during the French Revolution. Sometimes they were told if the headsman's blow was off the mark and they were able to get up and run, their lives would be spared. Some of them actually rose headless from the block and ran several yards before they collapsed."

"Pretty grim stuff."

"You're missing my point. I believe the man I took apart today was absolutely terrified. What could put that level of fear in a soldier of fortune?"

Not bad, podna, I thought.

After supper I sat on the gallery and watched Alafair currying her Appaloosa, whose name was Tex, out in the railed lot by the shed we had built for him. Tripod was off his chain and sitting on top of the rabbit hutch, his tail hanging down the side of the wire like a ringed banner. My neighbor had moved out of his house and put it up for sale, but each evening he returned to turn on his soak hoses and water sprinklers, filling the air with an iridescent mist that drifted across his hydrangeas onto our lawn. The sun had descended into a flattened red orb on the western horizon, and in the scarlet wash of the afterglow the flooded tree trunks in the swamp seemed suffused with firelight, and you could see an empty rowboat tied up in the black stillness of the bayou's far bank, the wood as dry and white as bone.

Bertie Fontenot's dinged and virtually paintless pickup truck bounced through the ruts in the road and turned into our drive. She got out, slammed the truck door, and labored up the incline, her elephantine hips rolling inside her print-cotton dress, her big lacquered straw bag with the plastic flowers on it gripped under her arm like an ammunition box.

"What you done about my title?" she said.

"Nothing."

"That's all you got to say?"

"You don't seem to accept my word, Bertie. So I've given up explaining myself."

She looked away at the horse lot.

"I seen you at Ruthie Jean's house. I thought maybe you was working on my title," she said.

"A murder investigation."

"Ruthie Jean don't know nothing about a murder. What you talking about?"

"You want to sit down, Bertie?"

"You finally axed," she said.

I helped her up the steps into the swing. She wrapped one hand around the support chain and pushed herself back and forth in a slowly oscillating arc.

"This is a nice place for your li'l girl to grow up in, ain't it?" she said.

"Yes, it is."

"How long your family own this?"

"The land was part of my grandfather's farm. My father built the house in nineteen thirty."

"How'd you like it if somebody just took it away from you, say you ain't got no proof it was part of your gran'daddy's farm? Run a dozer through the walls and scrape away the ground just like none of y'all was ever here?"

"You've got to give me some time, Bertie. I'm doing the best I can."

She snapped open the big clasp on her bag and reached inside.

"You don't believe Moleen after some treasure on our land, so I brought you something," she said. "I dug these out of my li'l garden early this spring."

One at a time she removed a series of thin eight- or nine-inch objects individually wrapped in tissue paper and bound with rubber bands. Then she rolled the rubber bands off one and peeled back the paper and flattened it against the swing.

"What you think of that?" she said.

The spoon was black as a scorched pot with tarnish, but she had obviously rubbed the metal smooth and free of dirt with rags so you could clearly see the coat of arms and the letter *S* embossed on the flanged head of the handle.

"That's pretty impressive," I said. "How deep was this in the soil?"

"From my elbow to the tip of my finger."

"Have you shown this to anybody else?"

"No, and I ain't going to. Not till I get a piece of paper that say that's my land."

"There's an antique gun and coin store in New Orleans, Cohen's, it's on Royal Street. Can I take one of these spoons there if I don't tell them where I got it?"

"You give me your word on that?"

"Yes, ma'am."

"How long that gonna take?" she said, fanning herself with a flowered handkerchief.

Chapter 14

I CHECKED OUT of the office early Tuesday afternoon and drove across the Atchafalaya Basin through Baton Rouge into New Orleans. I went first to Cohen's on Royal, whose collection of antique guns and coins and Civil War ordnance could match a museum's, then I met Clete at his office on St. Ann and we walked through Jackson Square to a small Italian restaurant down from Tujague's on Decatur.

We sat in back at a table with a checkered cloth and ordered, then Clete went to the bar and came back with a shot glass of bourbon and a schooner of draft. He lowered the shot into the schooner with his fingertips and watched it slide and clink down the side to the bottom, the whiskey corkscrewing upward in an amber cloud.

"Why don't you pour some liquid Drāno in there while you're at it?" I said.

He took a deep hit and wiped his mouth with his hand.

"I had to pull a bail jumper out of a motel on the Airline Highway this afternoon. He had both his kids with him. I got to lose this PI gig," he said.

"You did it when you had your shield."

"It doesn't work the same way, mon. Bondsmen

dime one guy just to bring in another. The shitbags are just money on the hoof." He took another drink from his boilermaker and the light began to change in his eyes. "Your ME matched up the blood on the floater?" he asked.

"Yeah, it's the guy named Jack. We got the media to sit on the story, though."

He reached across the table and pulled the tissue-paper-wrapped spoon given me by Bertie Fontenot from my shirt pocket. He worked the paper off the embossed tip of the handle.

"What'd they tell you at Cohen's?" he said.

"It's eighteenth-century silverware, probably cast in Spain or France."

He rubbed the ball of his thumb on the coat of arms, then stuck the spoon back in my pocket.

"This came off the Bertrand plantation, you say?" he said.

"Yep."

"I think you're pissing up a flagpole, Streak."

"Thanks."

"You don't see it."

"See what?"

"I think you've got a hard-on for this guy Bertrand."

"He keeps showing up in the case. What am I supposed to do?"

"That's not it. He's the guy whose shit don't flush."

"He's dirty."

"So is the planet. Your problem is Marsallus and the mercs and maybe Johnny Carp. You got to keep the lines simple, mon."

"What do you hear about Patsy Dapolito?" I said, to change the subject.

"I thought I told you. He's in jail in Houston. He told the plastic surgeon he'd put his eye out if he messed up the job."

"The ME said the guy named Jack was probably terrified when he caught the two nine-millimeters."

"You mean terrified of Sonny Boy?" he said.

"That's the way I'd read it."

"There's another side to that guy, Streak. I saw him make a couple of captured army dudes, I mean they were real greaseballs, guys with children's blood splattered on their boots, so they probably had it coming, but you don't get something like that out of your memory easy—he made them scoop out a grave in the middle of a trail with pie plates and kneel on the edge, then from six inches he blew their brains all over the bushes with a .44 Magnum."

Clete shook the image out of his face, then held up his empty shot glass at the bartender.

He'd had six boilermakers by the time we finished dinner. He started to order another round. His throat was red and grained, as though it were wind chafed.

"Let's get some coffee and beignets at the Cafe du Monde," I said.

"I don't feel like it."

"Yeah, you do."

"Ole Streak, swinging through town like a wrecking ball, pretending everything's under control. But I love you anyway, motherfucker," he said.

We walked under the colonnade of the French

Market, then had coffee and pastry at the outdoor tables. Across the street, in Jackson Square, the sidewalk artists were still set up along the walkway, and at the end of the piked fence that surrounds the park you could see a gut-bucket string band playing adjacent to the cathedral. I walked with Clete back to his office and sat with him on the edge of a stone well in the courtyard while he told me a long-winded story about riding with his father on the father's milk delivery route in the Garden District; then the lavender sky began to darken and swallows spun out of the shadows and when the lights in the upstairs apartments came on I could see the alcohol gradually go out of Clete's eyes, and I shook hands with him and drove back to New Iberia.

When I got home from the office the next afternoon, Alafair was sitting in the swing on the gallery, snapping beans in a pot. Her face was scratched, and there were grass and mud stains on her Levi's.

"You look like you rode Tex through a briar patch, Alf," I said.

"I fell down the coulee."

"How'd you do that?" I leaned against the rail and a post on the gallery.

"A dog got after Tripod. I ran over in Mr. LeBlanc's yard and tripped on the bank. I fell in a bunch of stickers."

"The coulee's pretty steep over there."

"That's what that man said."

"Which man?"

"The one who got me out. He climbed down the

side and got all muddy. He might buy Mr. LeBlanc's house."

I looked over into the neighbor's yard. A realtor I knew from town had just walked from the far side of the house with a clipboard in his hand. He was pointing at some features in the upstairs area, talking over his shoulder, when my eyes locked on the man behind him.

"Did this man say anything to you?" I said.

"He said I should be careful. Then he got Tripod out of the willow tree."

"Where's Bootsie?" I said.

"She had to go to the store. Is something wrong, Dave?"

"No. Excuse me a minute."

I went inside and called the dispatcher for a cruiser. Then I went back out on the gallery.

"I'm going next door. But you stay on the gallery, understand?" I said.

"He didn't do anything wrong, Dave."

I walked across the grass toward my neighbor's property and the man with miniature buttocks and ax-handle shoulders and chunks of lead for eyes.

He was dressed in a pale blue summer sports coat, an open-collar white shirt with ballpoint pens in the pocket, gray slacks, shined brown wingtips that were caked with mud around the soles; except for the stains on his clothes, he could have been a working man on his way to a fine evening at the track.

The realtor turned and looked at me.

"Oh hello, Dave," he said. "I was just showing Mr. Pogue the property here."

"I'd like to thank the gentleman for helping my daughter out of the coulee," I said.

"It was my pleasure," the man with the buckshot eyes said, his mouth grinning, his head nodding.

"Mr. Andrepont, could I talk with him in private a minute?" I said.

"I beg your pardon?" he said.

"It'll take just a minute. Thank you," I said.

"I see, well, let me know when you're finished, sir." He walked toward his car, averting his eyes to hide the anger in them.

"You're Emile Pogue," I said.

"Why not?" The voice sounded like it came from rusted pipe.

"You get around a lot. Exercising out at Pecan Island, showing up at the house next door. What's your interest, Mr. Pogue?"

"I'm retired, I like the weather, I like the price on this house."

"Why is it I think you're full of shit?"

"Be fucked if I know." He grinned.

"I'd like to ask a favor of you, take a ride down to our jail with me, we had a little problem there."

"I was planning on having an early dinner with a lady friend," he said.

"Change it to candlelight. Put your hands behind your head, please."

"You got to have a warrant, don't you, chief?"

"I'm not big on protocol. Turn around."

When he laced his fingers behind his neck his muscles almost split his coat. I rotated his left hand counterclockwise to the center of his back and pushed it into a pressure position between his shoulder blades. His upper arm had the tension and resistance of a wagon spring.

"Move your right hand higher, no, no, up behind your ear, Mr. Pogue. That's right," I said.

I cuffed his right wrist and moved it clockwise to his spine and then hooked it up to his left. I could see the cruiser coming up the road under the oak trees. I walked him down the sloping lawn to meet it, past the realtor, who stared at us open-mouthed.

"Is it true Sonny Marsallus popped a cap on your brother?" I said.

"Sounds like you left your grits on the stove too long," he answered.

I rode in the back of the cruiser with him to the department, then took him down to my office and hooked him to the D-ring inset in the floor. I called the sheriff and Kelso, the jailer, at their homes. When I hung up the phone, Pogue was staring at me, his eyes taking my measure, one shoulder pulled lopsided by the D-ring. He gave off a peculiar smell, like testosterone in his sweat.

"We're going to have to wait a little bit," I said.

"For what?"

I took out my time sheet from my desk drawer and began filling it in. We'd had a power failure earlier and the air-conditioning had been off for two hours.

"Wait for what?" he said.

I heard him shift in his chair, the handcuff clink against the steel D-ring. Five minutes later, he said,

"What's this, Psy Ops down in Bumfuck?" His sports coat was rumpled, his face slick with heat.

I put away my time sheet and opened a yellow legal pad on my desk blotter. I uncapped my fountain pen and tapped it idly on the pad. Then I wrote on several lines.

"You were an instructor at an Israeli jump school?" I said.

"Maybe. Thirty years in, a lot of different gigs."

"Looks like you managed to stay off the computer."

He worked his wrist inside the cuff.

"I'm maxing out here on this situation, chief," he said.

"Don't call me that again."

"You ever fish with a Dupont special, blow fish up into the trees? You cut to the chase, that's how it gets done. Who you think runs this country?"

"Why don't you clear that up for me?"

"You're a smart guy. Don't make like you ain't."

"I see. You and your friends do?"

He smiled painfully. "You got you a good routine. I bet the locals dig it."

Through my window I saw the sheriff, Kelso, and the night man from the jail out in the hall. They were watching Emile Pogue. Kelso's eyes were distorted to the size of oysters behind his thick glasses. He and the night man shook their heads.

"We selling tickets? What's going on?" Pogue said.

"You ever work CID or get attached to a federal law enforcement agency?" I said.

"No."

"Somebody with insider experience kidnapped a

man out of our jail. They murdered him out at Lake Martin."

His laugh was like the cough of a furnace deep under a tenement building.

"Don't tell me, the black guy looking out of the fishbowl has got to be the jailer," he said.

Kelso and the night man went down the hall. The sheriff opened my door and put his head inside.

"See me on your way out, Dave," he said, and closed the door again.

"It doesn't look like you're our man," I said.

"I got no beef, long as we get this thing finished . . . What you writing there?"

"Not much. Just a speculation or two." I propped the legal pad on the edge of the desk and looked down at it. "How's this sound? You probably enlisted when you were a kid, volunteered for a lot of elite units, then got into some dirty stuff over in 'Nam, the Phoenix Program maybe, going into Charlie's ville at night, slitting his throat in his sleep, painting his face yellow for his wife to find in the morning, you know the drill."

He laughed again, then pinched the front of his shirt with his fingers and shook it to cool himself. I could see the lead fillings in his molars, a web of saliva in his mouth.

"Then maybe you went into poppy farming with the Hmongs over in Laos. Is that a possibility, Emile?"

"You like cold beer? At the White Rose they had it so cold it'd make your throat ache. You could get ice-cold beer and a blow job at the same time, that's no jive. You had to be up for it, though, know what I'm saying?"

"You should have gone out to Washington State," I said.

"I'm a little slow this evening, you got to clue me."

"That's where your kind end up, right, either in a root cellar in the Cascades or fucking up other people's lives in Third World countries. You shouldn't have come here, Emile." I tore off the page on my legal pad, which contained a list of items I needed for the bait shop and couldn't afford, and threw it in the wastebasket. Then I unlocked his cuffed wrist from the D-ring.

He rose from the chair and his nostrils flared.

"I feel like I'm wrapped in stink," he said.

"If you need a ride, a deputy will take you wherever you want," I said.

"Thanks, I'll get a cab. Can I use your john? I got to wash up."

I pointed toward the men's room, then I said, "Let me ask a favor of you, Emile."

"You got it."

"You're a pro. Don't come through the wrong man's perimeter."

"The house next to yours? Who the fuck wants to live on a ditch full of mosquitoes?"

He went down the hall and pushed through the men's room door. The light from inside framed him like a simian creature caught in the pop of a flashbulb.

I worked open the window to rid the office of the peculiar odor that Pogue left behind, like the smell of a warm gym that's been closed for days. Then I called home and went inside the men's room. It was usually clean and squared away, but around one basin soap and water were splashed on the mirror and walls and crumpled paper towels were scattered all over the floor. I walked down the darkened hall to the sheriff's office.

"Where's Pogue?" he said.

"Gone."

"Gone? I asked you to see me before—"

"That's not what you said."

"I was going to put a tail on the guy. I just called the FBI in Lafayette."

"It's a waste of time."

"Would you care to explain that?" he said.

"His kind don't disappear on you. I wish they would."

"What are you talking about, Dave?"

"He's evil incarnate, Sheriff."

Bootsie and Alafair and I had a cold supper of chicken salad sandwiches, bean salad, and mint tea on the redwood table in the backyard. The new cane in my neighbor's field was pale green and waving in the sun's afterglow; he had opened the lock in his irrigation canal and you could smell the heavy, wet odor of the water inching through the rows.

"Oh, I forgot, Dave. A man named Sonny called while you were gone," Alafair said. She had showered and put on makeup and baby powder on her neck and a dark pair of blue jeans and a lavender blouse with primroses sewn on the sleeves.

"What'd he have to say?"

"Nothing. He said he'd call back."

"He didn't leave a number?"

"I asked him to. He said he was at a pay phone."

Bootsie watched my face.

"Where you going tonight?" I said to Alafair.

"To study. At the library."

"You're going fifteen miles to study?" I said.

"Danny's picking me up."

"Danny who? How old is this kid?"

"Danny Bordelon, and he's sixteen years old, Dave," she said.

"Great," I said. I looked at Bootsie.

"What's the big deal?" Alafair said.

"It's a school night," I said.

"That's why we're going to the library," she said.

Bootsie put her hand on my knee. After Alafair finished eating she went inside, then said good-bye through the window screen and waited on the gallery with her book bag.

"Ease up, skipper," Bootsie said.

"Why'd you call me that?" I said.

"I don't know. It just came to mind."

"I see."

"I won't do it," she said.

"I'm sorry. It's fine," I said. But I could still hear that name on the lips of my dead wife, Annie, calling to me from the bed on which she was murdered.

"What's troubling you, Dave?" Bootsie said.

"It's Marsallus. We sat on the story about the body we pulled out of the slough by Vermilion Bay. It was the guy Sonny parked a couple of rounds in."

She waited.

"He doesn't know we've got a murder charge against him. I might have to set him up, the same guy who possibly saved my life."

Later, Bootsie drove to Red Lerille's Health and Racquet Club in Lafayette and I tried to find things to do that would take me away from the house and Sonny's call. Instead, I turned on the light in the tree, spread a cloth over the redwood table, and cleaned and oiled an AR-15 rifle I had bought from the sheriff and a Beretta nine-millimeter that Clete had given me for my birthday. But the humidity haloed the light bulb and my eyes burned with fatigue from the day. I couldn't concentrate and lost screws and springs in the folds of the cloth and finally gave it up just as the phone rang in the kitchen.

"Was that your kid I talked to?" Sonny said.

"Yes."

"She sounds like a nice kid."

I could hear traffic and the clang of a streetcar in the background.

"What's up?" I said.

"I thought I ought to check in. Something wrong?"

"Not with me."

"I heard about what you did to Patsy Dap," he said.

"Are you in New Orleans?"

"Sure. Look, I heard Patsy got out of jail in Houston and he's back in town. The guy's got the thinking processes of a squirrel with rabies."

"I need to talk with you, Sonny."

"Go ahead."

"No, in person. We've got to work some stuff out."

"You put me in the bag once, Dave."

"I kicked you loose, too."

He was silent. I could hear the streetcar clanging on the neutral ground.

"I'll be in the Pearl at ten o'clock in the morning," I said. "Be there or stay away, Sonny. It's up to you."

"You got something on Della's murder?"

"How can I, unless you help me?"

"I eat breakfast at Annette's on Dauphine," he said.

I rose early in the morning and helped Batist open up the shop, fire the barbecue pit, and bail the boats that had filled with rainwater during the night. The sky was clear, a soft blue, the wind cool and sweet smelling out of the south, and I tried to keep my mind empty, the way you do before having surgery or entering into situations that you know you'll never successfully rationalize.

He looked good at the table in Annette's, with a fresh haircut, in a lavender shirt and brown suit with dark stripes in it, eating a full breakfast of scrambled eggs with bloodred catsup and sausage patties and grits off a thick white plate; he even smiled, his jaw full of food, when Helen and I came through the entrance with a murder warrant and a First District NOPD homicide cop behind us.

He kept chewing, his eyes smiling, while I shook him down against the wall and pulled the nine-millimeter Smith & Wesson from the back of his belt and hooked up each of his wrists.

Then he said, "Excuse me, I almost choked on my food there. Don't worry about this, Streak. A Judas goat has got to do its job."

Chapter 15

THURSDAY MORNING JULIA Bertrand walked into my office, her tan face glowing with purpose. She sat down without asking, as though we were both there by a prearranged understanding.

"Could I help you, Julia?"

"I have a complaint," she said, smiling prettily, her back erect, her hands uncertain.

"What might that be?"

"It's prostitution, if you ask me. Out by Cade, I'm talking about." One hand fluttered on her thigh, then remained motionless.

"By Cade?"

"I drove our maid home yesterday. She lives on the dirt road by this bar. You know the one I'm talking about."

"I think I do, Julia."

"There were white men walking with these black women back to these trailers."

When I didn't respond, she said, "Dave, I'm not a prude. But this *is* our community."

"Two doors down, there're a couple of guys inside you can talk to."

"I suspect one of them is the same gentleman I spoke to earlier. He could hardly contain his yawn."

"Some people believe it's better to know where the players are rather than spread them all over the community," I said.

"The maid told me a black woman named Ruthie Jean Fontenot brings the prostitutes to that nightclub, or whatever you want to call it."

I looked at her, at the manic, pinched energy in her face and the bleached hair spiked on the ends, the eyes bright with either residual booze or black speed, and I didn't doubt that the Furies waited for Julia each morning inside her dresser mirror.

"I'll ask someone to look into it," I said.

"How kind."

"Have I done something to offend you?"

"Of course not. You're a sweetie, Dave. I just wish I'd had a chance with you before Bootsie came along."

"It's always good to see you, Julia."

A few minutes later I watched through the window as she got into her yellow convertible and roared out into the traffic, her morning temporarily in place, as though reporting a crippled black woman to a rural sheriff's office had purged the earth of a great evil.

I had a cup of coffee, opened my mail, and went to the lockup. Kelso was chewing on a soda straw and reading from a folder opened on his desk. At the top of a page I could see Sonny's name.

"Robicheaux, my man, work out something, get his bail reduced, go the bail yourself, let him box up worms out at your dock, he don't belong here," Kelso said.

"That's the way it shakes out sometimes, Kelso."

"I got him in isolation like you asked, I'm even taking his food from my house to his cell. So what's he tell me? He wants to go back in main pop."

"Bad idea."

"He says it don't matter where I put him, his ticket's run out, he don't like small places. He wants to go back into main pop or he ain't gonna eat his food."

"You've dealt with problem inmates before."

"Here's the rest of it. My night man, he didn't make this cat Pogue, right, but now he says maybe he saw him around the jail earlier, maybe with some other guys. I go, 'Why the fuck didn't you tell me this?' So now he says he don't remember anything, and besides that, his wife calls him in sick. I never had a hit in my jail, Robicheaux. You get this cocksucker out of here."

I checked my weapon with Kelso, and a uniformed guard pulled the levers on a sliding barred door that gave onto a corridor of individual cells. The guard walked me past three empty cells to the last one on the row and let me in.

Sonny sat on the edge of his bunk in his skivvies, one bare foot pulled up on the thin mattress. His body looked hard and white, the scars on his rib cage and chest like a network of dried purple lesions.

I lowered the bunk from the opposite wall on its chain and sat down.

"You want to square with me?" I said.

"If you're here for absolution, I don't have the right collar for it," he said.

"Who says I need it?"

"You work for the Man, Dave. You know how things really are, but you still work for the Man."

"I'm going to be hard on you, Sonny. I think that girl in St. Martinville is dead because of you, so how about getting your nose out of the air for a while?"

He put both his feet on the concrete floor and picked up an apple from a paper plate that contained two uneaten sandwiches and a scoop of potato salad.

"You want it? Kelso brought it from his house," he said.

"You're really going on a hunger strike?"

He shrugged, let his eyes rove over the graffiti on the walls, looked at a cross somebody had scorched on the ceiling with a cigarette lighter. "You're not a bad guy, Streak," he said.

"Help us. Maybe I can get you some slack."

"Hey, how about some prune-o? The sweep-up slipped me some." He looked at the expression on my face. "I got nothing I can help you with. That's what you don't hear."

"What's in the notebook?"

He looked at me for a beat, considering his words, perhaps already dismissing their value. "How close are the next-door neighbors?" he said.

"The next three cells are empty."

"I did a gig with the DEA, not because they liked me, they just thought my city library card meant I probably had two or three brain cells more than the pipeheads and rag-noses they usually hire for their scut work. Anyway, considering the environment, it's not the kind of press I need, know what I'm saying?"

"Come on, Sonny."

"Down in the tropics, the cocaine trail always leads back to guns. I met guys who'd been in Laos, the Golden Triangle, guys who'd helped process opium into heroin in Hong Kong. Then I started hearing stories about POW's who'd gotten written off by the government.

"I was carrying this shitload of guilt, so I thought I could trade it off by involving myself with these MIA-POW families. I helped put together this telephone tree, with all kinds of people on it who I didn't even know. I didn't realize some of them were probably ex-intelligence guys who'd been mixed up with these opium growers in Laos. You with me?"

"Yeah, I think so," I said.

"Their consciences bothered them and they started telling the families about what went on over there. I was making out a death list and didn't know it. At least that's the best I can figure it. I burned the Xerox copy. Do the same with the original, Dave, before more people get hurt."

"Guilt about what?" I said.

"I used people—Indians, peasant girls, people who'd always gotten the dirty end of the stick, anyway."

He brushed at the top of his bare thigh.

"We walked into an ambush. I had a flak vest on. Everybody around me got chewed up," he said.

"Sometimes a guy feels guilt when the guy next to him catches the bus. That's just the way it is, Sonny."

"I was hit twice. When I went down, a half dozen other guys got shredded into horse meat right on top of me. Later, the Indians thought I had religious powers or I was an archangel or something. I played it for all it was worth, Streak. Look, my whole life I peddled my ass and ran games on people. Guys like me don't see a burst of light and change their hustle."

He reached under the top of the mattress and took out a jar and unscrewed the cap. The smell was like soft fruit that had been mixed with lighter fluid and left in a sealed container on a radiator. After he drank from the jar the skin of his face seemed to flex against his skull.

"You called me a Judas goat. I have a hard time accepting that, Sonny."

"Yeah, I don't like this cell too much, either."

"You think I led you down the slaughter chute?"

"No, not really," he said.

I nodded, but I couldn't look at his face. We both knew that had he not phoned me at the house to warn me about Patsy Dap, he might be riding on a breezy streetcar down St. Charles Avenue.

"I'll tell you something else, Dave," he said. "I've whacked out five guys since I left the tropics. Jack and Pogue's brother were just two knots on the string."

"You have a peculiar way of expiating your sins."

"I don't want to hurt your feelings, for a roach you're a stand-up guy, but go write some parking tickets, or shuffle some papers, or take some of the Rotary boys out to supper and let them work your dork under the table. I'm probably going down for the big bounce. Don't drag your bullshit into my cell, Streak. This is one place where it's truly an insult."

I hit on the bars with the side of my fist and called for the turnkey to open up. When I looked back at him, the cartilage working in my jaw, he was picking at a callus on his foot. The tattoo of the blue Madonna on his right shoulder, with needles of orange light emanating from it, looked like a painting on polished moonstone. I started to speak again, but he turned his eyes away from me.

Rufus Arceneaux had been a tech sergeant in the Marine Corps at age twenty-three. In the ten years he had been with the department he had gone from uniform to plainclothes and back to uniform again. He was a tall, raw-boned man, with a long nose and blond crewcut hair, whose polished gunbelt and holster fitted against his trim body as though it had been welded there. Rufus wore dark-tinted pilot's sunglasses and seldom smiled, but you always had the sense that his hidden eyes were watching you, taking your inventory, a suppressed sneer tugging at his mouth as soon as your back was turned.

It was Friday morning when Luke Fontenot called and told me his sister, Ruthie Jean, was in jail and that Rufus had been the arresting officer.

I walked down to his office and went inside without knocking. He was talking on the phone, one leg propped across an opened desk drawer. He glanced sideways at me, then returned to his conversation. I waited for him to finish. But he didn't.

His mouth dropped open when I tore the receiver out of his hand and hung it up in the cradle.

"What the hell you think you're doing, Robicheaux?"

"You busted Ruthie Fontenot for procuring?"

"So what?"

"You're intruding in a homicide investigation."

"Tough shit. That place is crawling with nigger whores. It should have been cleaned out a long time ago."

"You think Julia Bertrand is going to get you promoted?"

"Get the fuck out of my office."

I leveled my finger at him. "She'd better be kicked loose by five o'clock this afternoon. Don't underestimate your situation, Rufus."

"*Fuck* you," he said as I went out the door.

I talked with the sheriff and the prosecutor's office. Rufus had done his job well; he used another deputy as a witness to the sting, paid a prostitute at the juke to go in back, waited until she in turn passed the money to Ruthie Jean at the bar, and busted and Mirandized both the hooker and Ruthie Jean on the spot.

At eleven o'clock I got a surprise phone call.

"What can you do?" Moleen said.

"I don't know. Maybe nothing," I said.

"She's not a procurer. What kind of crazy ideas do y'all operate on down there?"

"She took the money, she put it in the cash register."

"You know what goes on in those places. She can't sanitize every dollar that goes through her hands."

"You're getting on the wrong person's case, Moleen."

"Yeah?"

I didn't speak. I could almost hear his anger building on the other end of the line.

"Goddamn it, you stop jerking me around, Dave."

"Your wife was in here yesterday. I explained to her I didn't take vice complaints. I think she found the right person, though."

"Are you telling me . . ." He couldn't get the sentence out.

"The arresting officer was Rufus Arceneaux. Talk to him, Moleen. In the meantime, you want to do some good, go her bail."

"You self-righteous sonofabitch."

"Thanks for your call," I said, and hung up.

At noon, as I was leaving the building for lunch, I saw Luke Fontenot's paintless, smoking, 1970s gas-guzzler, its ruptured muffler roaring against the pavement, swing out of the traffic toward the curb.

He leaned down so he could see me through the passenger's window.

"I ain't gone hide no more," he said. "I got to talk. When you gone be back?"

"Talk about what?"

"He ain't want the baby. That's where it all gone bad, even before I had to shoot that man 'cause he was bad-mouthing my sister and blackmailing Mr. Moleen at the same time."

I opened the car door and got in beside him.

"How about I buy us both a po'-boy?" I said.

Chapter 16

THIS IS HOW Luke told it to me, or as best as I can reconstruct it.

The Bertrand family had always been absentee landowners and had left the general care of the plantation to an overseer named Noah Wirtz, a sharecropper from the Red River parishes who could pass or not pass for a person of color, whichever the situation required. Other than a few teachers at the rural elementary school, Ruthie Jean, at age eleven, had little immediate contact with white adults, until that smoky winter morning when Moleen came to the plantation with his college friends from Springhill to shoot doves.

He had been kneeling by the coulee's edge, his double-barrel propped against the trunk of a leafless sycamore, pouring a cup of coffee from his thermos while his dog hunted for the birds Moleen had just downed in the cane stubble, when he turned around and saw her watching him.

Her pigtails were tied with rubber bands, her plump body lost in a man's mackinaw.

"Why, good heavens, you gave me a start," he said, although she knew it wasn't true. He winked at her. "My friends and I are all out of coffee. Can you go ask your mama to fill this up?"

She took the thermos and wet cup from his hands, her eyes fascinated with his handsome face and the lifeless birds that he had charmed out of the sky into his canvas game pouch.

"Wait a minute," he said, and slipped his thumb in his watch pocket and put a silver dollar in her palm. The ends of his slender fingers brushed her skin. She had not known a coin could be that heavy and big. "That's for Christmas. Now, run along and tell your mama the coffee's for Mr. Moleen."

She didn't see him again for six years, then on a cold New Year's afternoon she heard guns popping on the far side of the cane field, out by the treeline, and when she went out on the gallery she saw four men walking abreast through the frozen stubble, while a frenzy of birds leaped into the air in front of them and tried to find invisibility against a pitiless blue sky.

The hunters unloaded canvas chairs, a cooler, a collapsible grill from the bed of a pickup, and drank whiskey and cooked two-inch bloodred steaks on a wood fire that whipped in the wind like a torn handkerchief. When the one named Moleen saw her from across the field and asked her to bring water, she went quickly into the kitchen and filled a plastic pitcher, her heart beating in her breast for a reason she didn't understand.

The faces of the hunters were red with windburn and bourbon, their eyes playful, their conversation roaming between the depth of drilling wells and the remembered adrenaline surge in the glands when they led a throbbing covey with ventilated-rib sights and, one-two-three-four-five, turned each bird into a broken smudge against the winter sun. She filled their glasses, now aware that her sense of alarm was not only baseless but vain, that their eyes never really took note of her, other than a glance to ensure the water didn't spill over their outstretched wrists.

But as she walked away, she heard a pause, a silence so loud that her ears popped, then the register dropped in one man's voice, and the muscles in her back seemed to gather and constrict inside her dress, as though the coarseness, the undisguised connotation of the remark had the power to shrink her in physical as well as emotional stature.

"It's all pink inside, Moleen."

She kept her eyes straight ahead, focused on the gallery where her aunt and brother were husking and shelling pecans in a bucket, where the Christmas lights were still strung under the eaves, where her two cats played in a water oak that stood as stark against the winter light as a cluster of broken fingers.

She expected to hear the hunters laugh. Instead, there was silence again, and in the wind blowing at her back she clearly heard the voice of the man named Moleen:

"You've had too much to drink, sir. Regardless, I won't abide that kind of discourtesy toward a woman on my property."

She never forgot that moment.

He came back from the service long after the other soldiers had returned. He never explained why, or told anyone exactly where he had been. But he had the quiet detachment of someone who has lived close to death, or perhaps of one who has watched the erosion of the only identity he ever had. He often sat alone in his car by the grove of gum trees, the doors open to catch the evening breeze, while he smoked a cigar in the drone of cicadas and stared at the molten sun descending over the cane fields.

One time Ruthie Jean opened an old issue of *Life* magazine and saw a picture taken in Indochina of a valley filled with green elephant grass and a sun like a red wafer slipping into the watery horizon. She walked with it to Moleen's car, almost as though she had picklocked his thoughts, and placed it in his hand and looked him directly in the face, as if to say the debt for the silver dollar and the rebuke of the drunken hunter was not being repaid but openly acknowledged as the bond between them that race and social station had made improbable.

He knew it, too. Whatever sin he had carried back from the Orient, blood that could not be rinsed from his dreams, a shameful and unspoken memory he seemed to see re-created in the fire of Western skies, he knew she looked into him and saw it there and didn't condemn him for it and instead by her very proximity told him he was still the same young man who was kind to a child on a hunter's dawn and who had struck dumb a peer whose words had the power to flay the soul.

The first time it happened was back beyond the treeline, toward the lake, in a cypress shack that had once been part of the old slave quarters and was later used as a corn crib. The two of them pulled the backseat out of his car and carried it inside, their bodies still hot from their first caresses only moments earlier. They undressed without speaking, their private fears etched in their faces, and when he found himself nude before she was, he couldn't wait, either out of need or embarrassment, and began kissing her shoulders and neck and then the tops of her breasts while she was still attempting to unsnap her bra.

She had never been with a white man before, and he felt strangely gentle and tender between her thighs, and when they came at the same time, she kissed his wet hair and pressed her palms into the small of his back and kept her stomach and womb tight against him until the last violent shudder in his muscles seemed to exorcise the succubus that fed at his heart.

He bought her a gold watch with sapphires set in the obsidian face, sent her gift certificates for clothes at Maison Blanche in New Orleans, and then one day an envelope with a plane ticket to Veracruz, money, and directions to a hotel farther down the coast.

Their rooms adjoined. Moleen said the owners of the hotel were traditional people whom he respected and to whom he did not want to lie by saying they were married.

The rented boat he took her out on was as white and gleaming as porcelain, with outriggers, fighting chairs, and a flying bridge. He would tie leader with the care and concentration of a weaver, bait the feathered spoons, then fling them into the boat's wake, his grin full of confidence and expectation. The curls of hair on his chest and shoulders looked like bleached corn silk against his tan skin.

On the first morning he showed her how to steer

the boat and read the instrument panel. The day was boiling, the Gulf emerald green with patches of blue in it like clouds of ink, and while she stood at the wheel, her palms on the spokes, the engines throbbing through the deck, she felt his hands on her shoulders, her sides and hips, her breasts and stomach, then his mouth was buried in the swirls of her hair and she could feel his hardness grow against her.

They made love on an air mattress, their bodies breaking out with sweat, the boat rolling under them, the sky above them spinning with light and the cry of gulls. She came before he did, and then moments later she came again, something she had never done with another man.

Later, he fixed vodka and collins mix and cracked ice in two glasses, wrapped them in napkins with rubber bands, and they sat in their bathing suits in the fighting chairs and trolled across a coral reef whose crest was covered with undulating purple and orange sea fans.

She went below to use the rest room. When she came back up into the cabin, she saw another fishing boat off their port bow. A man and woman on the stern were waving at Moleen. He put his binoculars on them, then rose from his chair and came inside the cabin.

"Who's that?" she said.

"I don't know. They probably think we're someone else," he said.

He took the wheel and eased the throttle forward. She watched the other boat drop behind them, the two figures on the stern staring motionlessly after them. She picked up the binoculars from the top of the instrument panel and focused them on the lettering on the boat's hull.

Later, she would not remember the boat's name, but the words designating its home port, *Morgan City, Louisiana*, filled her with a bitter knowledge that trysts among palm trees, or even the naked hunger that he would bring again and again to the plantation, on his knees in the corn crib, his hands clenching the backs of her thighs, would never efface.

Noah Wirtz was a lean, short man, with skin that looked like it had been singed by a gunpowder flash. He wore a black, short-billed leather cap, even in summer, and always smiled, as though the situation around him was fraught with humor that only he saw. He lived in a frame house at the head of the road with his wife, a fundamentalist Sunday school teacher from Mississippi who walked on a wooden leg. The black people on the plantation said, "Mr. Noah know how to make the eagle scream." He and his wife spent nothing on movies, vacations, automobiles, liquor, outboard boats, pickup trucks, shotguns, even food that would make their fare better than the cornbread, greens, bulk rice and red beans, buffalo fish, carp, and low-grade meat most of the blacks ate. Every spare nickel from his meager salary went into the small grocery store they bought in Cade, and the profits from the store went into farm machinery, which he began to lease to sugar growers in Iberia and St. Martin parishes.

It was a sweltering August night, the trees threaded

with the electric patterns of fireflies, when Moleen discovered the potential of his overseer. He and Ruthie Jean had met in the shack beyond the treeline, and just as he had risen from her, his body dripping and limp, her fingers sliding away from his hips, he heard dry leaves breaking, a stick cracking, a heavy, audibly breathing presence moving through the undergrowth outside.

He put on his khakis, pulled his polo shirt on over his head, and ran out into the heated air and the aching drone of cicadas. Through the tree trunks, on the edge of the field, he saw Noah Wirtz getting into his battered flatbed truck, the points of his cowboy boots curled up into snouts on his feet, the armpits of his long-sleeved denim shirt looped with sweat.

"You! Wirtz!" Moleen shouted. "You hold up there!"

"Yes, sir?" Wirtz smiled from under his leather cap, his skin as dark as if it had been smoked in a fire.

"What are you doing out here?"

"Cleaning up the trash the niggers throwed on the ground at lunchtime."

"I don't see any trash."

"That's 'cause I buried hit. You want me to haul hit back to my house?" His seamed face was as merry as an elf's.

They looked at each other in the fading light.

"Have a good evening, cap'n," Wirtz said, and spit a stream of Red Man before he got into the cab of his truck.

Moleen walked back through the trees to the shack. Even in the soft yellow afterglow through the canopy he knew, without looking, what he would find below the unshuttered and gaping shack window. The heels of the boots had bitten through the dry leaves into the wet underlayer, with the sharp and razored precision of a cleft-footed satyr.

The blackmail began later, after Moleen's marriage to Julia, but it was not overt, and never a difficult yoke to bear; in fact, it was so seemingly benign that after a while Moleen convinced himself that better it be Wirtz, who did what he was told, who was obsequious and contemptible (who sometimes even played the role of pimp and ensured their trysts would not be disturbed), than someone who was either more cunning or less predictable.

Moleen gave him a useless tractor that would have rusted into the weeds otherwise; a smoked ham at Christmas and Thanksgiving; venison and ducks when he had too much for his own freezer; the use of five acres that had to be cleared and harrowed first.

Ironically, the denouement of their arrangement came not because of Wirtz's avarice but because of his growing confidence that he no longer needed Moleen. He began selling liquor in his grocery store and lending money to black field hands and housemaids, on which they made five-percent interest payments one Saturday night a month until the principal was liquidated.

His farm machinery filled a rented tin shed up Bayou Teche.

Moleen heard the story first as rumor, then from the mouth of the sixteen-year-old girl who said Wirtz came to her house for his laundry when the parents were gone, then, after paying her and hanging the broomstick hung with his ironed shirts across the back of his truck cab, had gone back in the kitchen, not speaking, his eyes locked on the girl's, his breath now covering her face like a fog, and had clenched one of her wrists in his hand and simultaneously unzipped his overalls.

Moleen drove straight from the girl's house to Wirtz's and didn't even bother to cut the engine or close the door of his Buick behind him before he strode through the unpainted picket gate and up the narrow path lined with petunias to the gallery, where Wirtz, his face cool and serene in the shade, was eating from a box of Oreo cookies, his leather cap suspended on a nail above his head.

"The girl's too scared and ashamed to bring charges against you, but I want you off my property. In fact, I want you out of the parish," Moleen said.

"Out of the parish, huh?" Wirtz said, and smiled so broadly his eyes were slits.

"Why in God's name I hired some white trash like you I'll never know," Moleen said.

"White trash, huh? You hear this, cap'n. Befo' I'd put mine in that nigger, I'd cut hit off and feed hit to the dog."

"Clean your house out. I want you gone by nightfall."

Moleen started toward his car.

"You're a piece of work, Bertrand. You fuck down and marry up and don't give hit a second thought," Wirtz said. He bit down softly on a cookie.

The blood climbed into Moleen's neck. He leaned inside the open door of the Buick, pulled the keys, and unlocked the trunk.

Noah Wirtz stared at him impassively, brushing his hands with a sound like emery paper, as Moleen came toward him with the horse quirt. He barely turned his face when the leather rod whipped through the air and sliced across his cheek.

"You ever speak to me like that again, I'll take your life," Moleen said.

Wirtz pressed his palm to the welt, then opened and closed his mouth. His eyes seemed to study a thought inches in front of his face, then reject it. He laced his fingers together and cracked his knuckles between his knees.

"I got me a contract," he said. "Till the cane's in, I got a job and I got this house. You're trespassing, cap'n. Get your automobile off my turnaround."

"The shooting," I said to Luke, as he sat across from me at a picnic table under the pavilion in the park.

"I don't want to talk about that," he said. He tried to light a cigarette, but the match was damp with his own perspiration and wouldn't ignite against the striker. "They was gonna electrocute me. I still wake up in the middle of the night, I got the sheets tangled all over me, I can feel that man drawing his razor across my scalp."

"Tell me what happened in that saloon, Luke."

"He said it in front of all them men, about a woman ain't done anything to him, ain't ever hurt anybody."

"Who?"

"Noah Wirtz, he talk about her at the bouree table like ain't even niggers gonna take up for her."

"Said what, Luke?"

" 'That bitch got a pumpkin up her dress, and I know the name of the shithog put it there.' That's what he say, Mr. Dave, looking me right in the eyes, a li'l smile on his mouth."

Then he described that winter night in the saloon, almost incoherently, as though a few seconds in his life had been absorbed through his senses in so violent a fashion that he now believed the death he had been spared was in reality the only means he would ever have to purge and kill forever the memory that came aborning every night in his sleep.

It's the first Saturday of the month, and the bar and tables are crowded with blacks, mulattos, redbones, and people who look white but never define themselves as such. The air smells of expectorated chewing tobacco and snuff, animal musk, oily wood, chemically treated sawdust, overcooked okra, smoke, and unwashed hair. The video poker machines line an unadorned fiberboard wall like a magical neon-lit instrument panel that can transport the player into an electronic galaxy of wealth and power. But the big money is at the round, felt-covered bouree table, where you can lose it all—the groceries, the rent on a pitiful shack, the installment on the gas-guzzler, the weekly payment for the burial insurance collector, even the food stamps you can discount and turn into instant capital.

The man at the table with the cash is Noah Wirtz, and he takes markers in the form of bad checks, which he holds in lieu of payment on his loans and which he can turn over to the sheriff's office if the borrower defaults. Sometimes he uses a shill in the game, a hired man who baits a loser or a drunk and goads him into losing more, since bouree is a game in which great loss almost always follows recklessness and impetuosity.

Wirtz consoles, buys a drink for those who have lost all their wages, says, "Come see me at the store in the morning. We'll work something out." He knows how far to press down on a nerve, when to give it release. Until tonight, the cane harvest in, the contract with Bertrand finished, when perhaps his own anger, the quiet residual rage of his kind (and that had always been the word used to describe his social class), passed down like an ugly heirloom from one generation to the next, begins to throb like the blow of a whip delivered contemptuously across the face, and the name Moleen Bertrand and the world he represents to Wirtz and which Wirtz despises and envies becomes more important than the money he has amassed through stint and self-denial and debasing himself to the servile level of the blacks with whom he competes.

"What you got to say about it, Luke?" Wirtz says.

Luke's eyes can't focus, nor can he make the right words come out of his throat. His face contains the empty and deceptive intensity of a scorched cake pan.

"A certain white man didn't have to pull you off hit to get to hit hisself, did he?" Wirtz says.

Luke's one-inch nickel-plated .38 revolver, with no trigger guard and electrician's tape holding the handles together, is one step above scrap metal. But its power and short-range accuracy are phenomenal. The single steel-jacketed round he squeezes off splinters through the table-

top and felt cover and enters Wirtz's chin as though a red hole were punched there with a cold chisel.

Wirtz stumbles through the washroom door, a crushed fedora squeezed against the wound, his mouth a scarlet flower that wishes to beg for help or mercy or perhaps even forgiveness but that can only make unintelligible sounds that seem to have no human correspondent. He curls into a ball behind the toilet tank, his knees drawn up in front of him, his eyes pleading, his hands trembling on the fedora.

Luke pulls the trigger and the hammer snaps dryly on a defective cartridge. This time he cocks the hammer, feels the spring and cylinder and cogs lock into place, but the rage has gone, like a bird with hooked talons that has suddenly freed itself from its own prey and flown away, and he drops the pistol in the toilet bowl and walks into the larger room and the collective stare of people who realize they never really knew Luke Fontenot.

But the man he leaves behind closes and opens his eyes one more time, then expels a red bubble of saliva from his mouth and stares sightlessly at an obscene word scrawled in pencil on the wall.

"What happened to Wirtz's gun?" I said. "Moleen found witnesses who saw Wirtz pull a gun."

"Mr. Moleen got money. You got money, you find anybody, anything you need."

"I see," I said. It was starting to sprinkle on the bayou. A mother opened an umbrella over her child, and the two of them ran for the cover of the trees. "You mentioned a baby," I said.

"I done tole you, he ain't want it." Then his face

became indescribably sad, unmasked, devoid of any defense or agenda. "What they call that, 'trimester,' yeah, that's it, third trimester, she went did it wit' some man in Beaumont, cut up the baby inside her, cut her up, leave her walking on a cane, leave her with that baby crying in her head."

He cleaned off his place and walked in the rain toward his car.

Chapter 17

After Luke dropped me off at the department, I found a phone message from Clete Purcel in my mailbox. I called him at his office in New Orleans.

"You still got Marsallus in the bag?" he said.

"Yeah, he's on a hunger strike now."

"The word's out Johnny Carp doesn't want anybody writing his bond."

"I was right, then. Johnny's been after him from the jump."

"He's probably already got somebody inside, or he'll get a local guy to bail him out. Any way you cut it, I think Sonny's floated into deep shit."

"How do you figure Johnny's stake?" I said.

"Something to do with money. I hear his toilet seats are inset with gold pesos. He owned a lot with a thirty-foot Indian mound on it and sold it for landfill. It's a great life, isn't it, mon?"

Later, I gazed through the window at a rainbow arching across the sky into a bank of steel-colored clouds that were hung with wisps of rain. Sonny Boy was trussed and tagged and on the conveyor belt, like a pig about to be gutted, and the man who had kicked the machinery into gear was a police officer.

I crumpled up a letter inviting me to speak to the Rotary Club and threw it against the wall.

Moleen's law office was in a refurbished white-columned Victorian home, shaded by oaks, down the street from the Shadows on East Main.

I had to wait a half hour to see him. When the door opened, rather, when it burst back on its hinges, Julia Bertrand came through it as though she were emerging from the dry heat of a bake oven.

"Why, Dave," she said, her makeup stretching on her features as though it had been painted there by a blind man. "It's so appropriate for you to be here. You fellows can kick the war around. Moleen has all this guilt but he never got to kill anybody. How unfair of the gods."

She brushed past me before I could answer.

I picked up the paper bag by my feet and closed Moleen's office door behind me. He sat behind a huge, dark red oak desk, his knitted brown tie pulled loose at the throat. His face was flushed, as though he had a fever.

"How's life, Moleen?"

"What do you want?"

"She's still in jail."

He bit his thumbnail.

"Moleen?"

"I can't do anything."

"She lives on your plantation. Bail her out. Nobody'll question your motivation."

"Where the hell do you get off talking to me like that?" he said.

I sat down without being asked. I set the paper bag containing the leg iron on his desk. The manacle yawned out of the bag like a rusty mouth.

"Luke owned up to putting this in my truck. He said he doesn't care if I tell you about it or not."

"I think you should see a therapist. I don't mean that unkindly, either," he said.

"Luke's pretty sharp for a guy who didn't finish high school. He read a story in a magazine about a construction site that was shut down because there was an Indian mound on it. He thought he'd given me the means to put you out of business, whatever it is."

"It's been a long day, Dave."

"Is it a gambling casino?"

"Good-bye."

"That's why you got rid of the cemetery."

"Is there anything else you want to say before you leave?"

"Yeah. It's quarter to five on Friday afternoon and she's still in jail."

He looked at me distractedly, breathing with his mouth open, his chest sunken, his stomach protruding over his belt like a roll of bread dough. When I got up to go, three buttons were flashing hot pink on his telephone, as though disembodied and cacophonous voices were waiting to converge and shout at him simultaneously.

After supper that night I put on my gym shorts and running shoes and did three miles along the dirt road by the bayou, then I did three sets of military presses, dead lifts, and arm curls with my barbells in the backyard. The western sky was streaked with fire, the air warm and close and alive with insects. I tried to rethink the day, the week, the month, my involvement with Sonny Boy Marsallus and Ruthie Jean and Luke and Bertie Fontenot and Moleen Bertrand, until each of my thoughts was like a snapping dog.

"What's bothering you, Dave?" Alafair said behind me.

"I didn't see you there, Alf."

She held Tripod on her shoulder. He tilted his head at me and yawned.

"Why you worrying?" she asked.

"A guy's in jail I don't think belongs there."

"Why's he in there then?"

"It's that fellow Marsallus."

"The one who shot the—"

"That's right. The guy who was looking out for me. Actually, looking out for all of us."

"Oh," she said, and sat down on the bench, her hand motionless on Tripod's back, an unspoken question in the middle of her face.

"The man he shot died, Alf," I said. "So Sonny's down on a homicide beef. Things don't always work out right."

Her eyes avoided mine. I could smell my own odor, hear my breathing in the stillness.

"It's not something I had a choice about, little guy," I said.

"You said you wouldn't call me that."

"I'm sorry."

"It's all right," she said, then picked up Tripod in her arms and walked away.

"Alafair?"

She didn't answer.

I put on a T-shirt without showering and began hoeing weeds out of the vegetable garden by the coulee. The air was humid and mauve colored and filled with angry birds.

"Time for an iced tea break," Bootsie said.

"I'll be inside in a minute."

"Cool your jets, Streak."

"What's with Alf?"

"You're her father. She associates you with perfection."

I chipped at the weeds with the corner of the hoe. The shaft felt hard and dry and full of sharp edges in my hands.

"Moleen's the problem, Dave. Not Sonny," Bootsie said.

"What?"

"You think he's a hypocrite because he left the black woman in jail. Now maybe you're wondering about yourself and Sonny Boy."

I looked up at her, squinted through the sweat in my eyes. I wanted to keep thudding the hoe into the dirt, let her words go by me as though they were illogical and unworthy of recognition. But there was a sick feeling in my stomach.

I propped my hands on the hoe handle, blotted my eyes on my forearm.

"I'm a police officer," I said. "I can't revise what

happened. Sonny killed a man, Boots. He says he's killed others."

"Then put it out of your mind," she said, and went back inside the house.

Across the fence in my neighbor's field, I saw an owl swoop low out of the sun's last red light and, in a flurry of wings, trap and then scissor a field mouse in its beak. I could hear the mouse's voice squeaking helplessly as the owl flew into the sun.

Saturday morning I worked until noon at the bait shop, counting change twice to get it right, feigning interest in conversations I hardly heard. Then I put a Dr Pepper and two bottles of beer in a paper bag, with two ham and onion sandwiches, called the sheriff, and asked him to meet me up the road by the four corners.

He walked down the bank in a pair of floppy khaki shorts with zipper pockets, a white straw cowboy hat, and a denim shirt with the sleeves cut off at the armpits. He carried a spinning rod that looked like it belonged to a child.

"Beautiful day for it," he said, lifting his face in the breeze.

The boat dipped heavily when he got into the bow. The tops of his arms were red with sunburn and unusually big for a man who did administrative work.

I took us through a narrow channel into the swamp, cut the engine, and let the boat drift on its wake into a small black lagoon surrounded with flooded cypress. A deserted cabin, built on pilings, was set back in the trees. A rowboat that was grayish blue with rot was tied to the porch and half-submerged in the water.

The sheriff bit into a ham sandwich. "I got to admit this beats hitting golf balls in sand traps," he said.

But he was an intelligent and perceptive man whose weekend humor served poorly the concern in his eyes.

Then I said it all, the way as a child I took my confused and labored thoughts into the confessional and tried to explain what both my vocabulary and loneliness made unexplainable. Except now, in order to undo a wrong, I was—

He said the word for me.

"Lying, Dave. We've never had that problem between us. I have a hard time dealing with this, podna."

"The guy's grandiose, he's a huckster, he's got electrodes in his temples. But he's down on the wrong beef."

"I don't give a goddamn what he is. You're violating your oath as a police officer. You're walking on the edges of perjury as well."

I looked into the diffused green and yellow light on the rim of the lagoon. "The eye remembers after the fact sometimes," I said.

"You saw the cut-down twelve-gauge under the guy's coat? You felt you were in danger?"

"I'll put my revised statement in your mailbox this afternoon."

"You missed your calling over in Vietnam. You remember those monks who used to set themselves on fire? You were born for it, Dave."

"Marsallus doesn't belong in prison. At least not for popping the guy in front of my house."

The sheriff set his fishing rod across his thighs and pulled up the anchor without my asking him. He stared into the water and the black silt that swirled out of the bottom, then wiped his face with his hand as though he were temporarily erasing an inevitable conclusion from his thoughts.

Monday morning I was suspended from the department without pay.

Monday night I drove out to the Bertrand plantation and returned the spoon Bertie Fontenot had given me. She fanned herself with a ragged magazine in the swing, her breasts hanging like watermelons inside her cotton dress.

"It's the right time period, but I don't think pirates buried those spoons in your garden," I said.

"They growed there with my radish seeds?"

"The *S* on those spoons makes me think they're from the Segura plantation on the lake. During the Civil War, a lot of people buried their silverware and coins to keep them from the Yankees, Bertie."

"They should have buried themselves while they was at it."

I looked at the lights inside the house next door. Two shadows moved across the shades.

"A lawyer come down from Lafayette and got her out of jail this morning," she said.

"Which lawyer?"

"I ain't ax his name. I seen him out here with

Moleen once. The one look like he got grease on his bald head."

"Jason Darbonne."

"I'm going inside now. The mosquitoes is eating me up." She paused in the square of light the door made, the white ends of her hair shiny with oil. "They gonna run us off, ain't they?"

I had a half dozen answers, but all of them would have been self-serving and ultimately demeaning. So I simply said good night and walked to my truck by the grove of gum trees.

The moon was down, and in the darkness the waving cane looked like a sea of grass on the ocean's floor. In my mind's eye I saw the stubble burning in the late fall, the smoke roiling out of the fire in sulphurous yellow plumes, and I wanted to believe that all those nameless people who may have lain buried in the field—African and West Indian slaves, convicts leased from the penitentiary, Negro laborers whose lives were used up for someone else's profit—would rise with the smoke and force us to acknowledge their humanity and its inextricable involvement and kinship with our own.

But they were dead, their teeth scattered by plowshares, their bones ground by harrow and dozer blade into detritus, and all the fury and mire that had constricted their hearts and tolled their days were now reduced to a chip of vertebrae tangled in the roots of a sugarcane stalk.

Chapter 18

Sonny Boy was sprung and I was now the full-time operator of a bait shop and boat-rental business that, on a good year, cleared fifteen thousand dollars.

He found me at Red Lerille's Gym in Lafayette.

"Jail wasn't that bad on you, Sonny. You look sharp," I said.

"Get out of my face with that patronizing attitude, Dave." He chewed gum and wore a tailored gray suit with zoot slacks and a blue suede belt and a T-shirt.

"I'm off the case, off the job, out of your problems, Sonny."

I'd forgotten my speed bag gloves at home, but I began working the bag anyway, creating a circular motion with each fist, throbbing the bag harder and harder against the circular board it was suspended from.

"Who appointed you my caretaker?" he asked.

I skinned my knuckles on the bag, hit it harder, faster. He grabbed it with both hands.

"Lose the attitude. I'm talking to you. Who the fuck says you got to quit your job because of me?" he said.

"I didn't quit, I'm suspended. The big problem

here is somebody pulled you down from your cross and you can't stand it."

"I got certain beliefs and I don't like that kind of talk, Dave."

I opened and closed my palms at my sides. My knuckles stung, my wrists pounded with blood. The gym echoed with the smack of gloves on leather, the ring of basketballs against the hardwood floor. Sonny's face was inches from mine, his breath hot on my skin.

"Would you step back, please? I don't want to hit you with the bag," I said.

"I don't let anybody take my bounce, Dave."

"That's copacetic, Sonny. I can relate to it. Hey, I don't want to offend you, but you're not supposed to be in here with street shoes on. They mark up the floors."

"You can be a wiseass all you want, Dave. Emile Pogue is a guy who once put a flamethrower down a spider hole full of civilians. You think you're on suspension? In whose world?"

He walked across the gym floor, through a group of sweating basketball players who looked like their muscles were pumped full of hardening concrete.

I hit the speed bag one more time and felt a strip of skin flay back off my knuckle.

It rained hard the next morning. Lightning struck in the field behind my house and my neighbor's cows had bunched in the coulee and were lowing inside the sound of the rain. I read the paper on the gallery, then went back inside to answer the phone.

"You got to hear me, Dave," Sonny said. "Once

they take me out, it'll be your turn, then the woman cop, what's-her-name, Helen Soileau, then maybe Purcel, then maybe your wife. They don't leave loose ends."

"All right, Sonny, you made your point."

"Another thing, this is personal, I'm no guy on a cross. In medieval times, I would have been one of those guys selling pigs' bones for saints' relics. The reality is I got innocent people's blood on my hands."

"I don't know what to tell you, partner."

"I'm not going away, Dave. You'll see me around."

"That's what I'm afraid of," I said. He didn't answer. For some reason I imagined him on a long, empty beach where the waves were lashed by wind but made no sound. "Good-bye, Sonny," I said, and replaced the receiver in the cradle.

An hour later the thunder had stopped and the rain was falling steadily on the gallery's tin roof. Clete's chartreuse Cadillac convertible, with fins and grillwork like a torn mouth, bounced through the chuckholes in the road and turned into my drive. He ran through the puddles under the trees, his keys and change jingling in his slacks, one hand pressed on top of his porkpie hat.

"They gave you the deep six, huh, big mon?" he said. He sat in the swing and wiped his face on his sleeve.

"Who told you?"

"Helen."

"You're on a first-name basis now?"

"She met me at my office last night. She doesn't

like seeing her partner get reamed. I don't either." He looked at his watch.

"Don't put your hand in it, Clete."

"You afraid your ole podjo's going to leave gorilla shit on the furniture?"

I made a pocket of air in my cheek.

"You want to go partners in my agency?" he said. "Hey, I need the company. I'm a grunt for Wee Willie Bimstine and Nig Rosewater. My temp's an ex-nun. My best friends are mutts in the city prison. The desk sergeant at First District wouldn't spit in my mouth."

"Thanks, anyway, Cletus. I don't want to move back to New Orleans."

"We'll open a branch here in New Iberia. Leave it to me, I'll set it up."

Several nightmarish visions floated before my eyes. Clete looked at his watch. "You got anything to eat?" he said.

"Help yourself."

He walked through the house to the kitchen and came back on the gallery with a bowl of Grape-Nuts and a tall glass of coffee and hot milk. His teeth made a grinding sound while he ate. His eyes glanced at his watch again.

"Who you expecting?" I said.

"I'm meeting Helen in town. She's photocopying Sonny's diary for me."

"Bad idea."

He stopped chewing and his face stretched as tight as pig hide. He raised his spoon at me.

"Nobody fucks my podjo, pardon the word in your house," he said.

* * *

I felt like the soldier who enlists at the outset of a war, then discovers, after his energies and blood lust have waned, that there is no separate peace, that he's a participant until the last worthless shot is fired on the last worthless day. Sonny was right. There are no administrative suspensions, no more so than when pistol flares burst overhead and flood the world with a ghostly white light and you turn into the skeletal, barkless shape of a tree.

When the rain stopped and the sky began to clear and gradually turn blue again, I took Alafair's pirogue and rowed it into the swamp. The stands of cypress were bright green and dripping with rainwater, and under the overhang every dead log and gray sand spit was covered with nutrias.

I slid the pirogue into a cove and ate a ham and onion sandwich and drank from a cold jar of sun tea.

Oftentimes when you work a case and the players and events seem larger than life, you leapfrog across what at first seems the minuscule stuff of police procedural novels. Details at a crime scene seldom solve crimes. The army of miscreants whose detritus we constantly process through computers and forensic laboratories usually close their own files by shooting themselves and one another, OD-ing on contaminated drugs, getting dosed with AIDS or busted in the commission of another crime, or perhaps turning over a liquor store where the owner had tired of being cleaned out and introduces the robber to Messieurs Smith & Wesson.

Several years ago the wire services reported rumors that Jimmy Hoffa's body had been entombed in concrete under the goal posts of a football stadium. Each time someone kicked the extra point, Hoffa's old colleagues would shout, "This one's for you, Jimmy!"

It makes a good story. I doubt that it's true. The mob isn't given to poetics.

A New Orleans hit man, who admitted to murdering people for as little as three hundred dollars, told me Hoffa was ground up into fish chum and thrown by the bucket-load off the stern of a cabin cruiser, then the deck and gunnels hosed and wiped down a pristine white, all within sight of Miami Beach.

I believed him.

The body of the man named Jack had probably been mutilated by a professional, or at least the directions to do so had been given by one. But sinking the body with a tangle of fish line and scrap iron on the edge of a navigable channel had all the marks of an amateur, and probably a lazy one at that, or we would have never found it.

I called Helen at the department.

"What's ruthless, lazy, and stupid all over?" I asked.

"The guy taking your calls?"

"What?" I said.

"The old man assigned your open cases to Rufus Arceneaux."

"Forget Rufus. We missed something when we pulled the floater out. He was tied up with scrap iron and fish line."

"I'm not following you."

"Let me try again. What's perverse, is not above anything, looks like a ghoul anyway, and would screw up a wet dream?"

"Sweet Pea Chaisson," she said.

"Clete and I went to his house on the Breaux Bridge road before we had that run-in with him and Patsy Dap in Lafayette. I remember a bunch of building materials in the lot next door—building materials or maybe junk from a pipe yard."

"Pretty good, Streak."

"It's enough for a warrant," I said.

"Then we toss his Caddy and maybe match the blood on the rug to the scraping you took from the trailer behind the juke. Dave, square your beef with the old man. I can't partner with Rufus."

"It's not my call."

"You heard Patsy Dap's in town?"

"No."

"Nobody told you?" she said.

"No."

"He got stopped for speeding on East Main yesterday. The city cop made him and called us. I'm sorry, I thought somebody told you."

"Where is he now?"

"Who knows? Wherever disfigured paranoids hang out."

"Keep me informed on the warrant, will you?" I said.

"You're a good cop, Dave. You get your butt back here."

"You're the best, Helen."

I walked down to the dock. The air was hot and

still and down the road someone was running a Weed Eater that had the nerve-searing pitch of a dentist's instrument. So Patsy Dapolito was in New Iberia and no one had bothered to tell me, I thought. But why not? We did it all the time. We cut loose rapists, pedophiles, and murderers on minimum bail, even on their own recognizance, and seldom notified the victims or the witnesses to their crimes.

Ask anyone who's been there. Or, better yet, ask the victims or survivors about the feelings they have when they encounter the source of their misery on the street, in the fresh air, in the flow of everyday traffic and normal life, and they realize the degree of seriousness with which society treats the nature of their injury. It's a moment no one forgets easily.

My thoughts were bitter and useless.

I knew the origins of my self-indulgence, too. I couldn't get the word *disfigured* out of my mind. I tried to imagine the images that flashed through Patsy Dap's brain when he saw his face reflected in the mirror.

I helped Batist fill the coolers with beer and soda and scoop the ashes out of the barbecue pit, then I sat in the warm shade at one of the spool tables with a glass of iced tea and thought about Clete's offer.

Chapter 19

The next morning I drove out to the Bertrand plantation to talk to Ruthie Jean, but no one was at home. I walked next door to Bertie's and knocked on the screen. When she didn't answer, I went around the side and saw her get up heavily from where she had been sitting on the edge of the porch. Her stomach swelled out between her purple stretch pants and oversize white T-shirt. She unhooked a sickle from the dirt and began slicing away the dead leaves from the banana trees that grew in an impacted clump against the side wall of the house.

I had the impression, however, she had been doing something else before she saw me.

"I'm worried about Ruthie Jean, Bertie," I said. "I think she nursed a man named Jack who died in the trailer behind the juke. She probably heard and saw things other people don't want her to talk about."

"You done already tole her that."

"She's not a good listener."

"There's two kinds of trouble. What *might* happen, and what done *already* happen. White folks worry about *might*. It ain't the same for everybody, no."

"You lost me."

"It ain't hard to do," she said. She ripped a tangle

of brown leaves onto the ground, then lopped a stalk cleanly across the middle. The cut oozed with green water.

On the planks of the porch I saw a square of red flannel cloth, with a torn root and a tablespoon of dirt in the middle. I saw Bertie watch me out of the corner of her eye as I walked closer to the piece of flannel. Among the grains of dirt were strands of hair, what looked like a shirt button, and a bright needle with blood on it.

"I'm going to take a guess—dirt from a grave, root of a poison oak, and a needle for a mess of grief," I said.

She whacked and lopped the dead stalks and flung the debris behind her.

"Did you get Moleen's hair and shirt button out of the shack by the treeline?" I asked.

"I ain't in this world to criticize. But you come out here and you don't do no good. You pretend like you know, but you playing games. It ain't no fun for us."

"You think putting a gris-gris on Moleen is going to solve your problems?"

"The reason I put it on *him* is 'cause she ain't left nothing out here so I can put it on *her.*"

"Who?"

"Julia Bertrand." She almost spit out the words. "She already been out here once this morning. With that man work down the hall from you. Ruthie Jean ain't got her house no more. How you like that?"

I blew out my breath.

"I didn't know," I said.

She tossed the sickle in the flower bed.

"That's my point," she said, and went in her house.

A few minutes later, almost as though Bertie had planned Julia appearance's as part of my ongoing education about the realities of life on a corporate plantation, I saw Julia's red Porsche turn off the highway and drive down the dirt road toward me. Rufus Arceneaux sat next to her in a navy blue suit that looked like pressed cardboard on his body.

When she stopped next to me, her window down, her face cheerful, I tried to be pleasant and seem unknowing, to mask the embarrassment I felt for her and the level of vindictiveness to which she had devoted herself.

"Bertie doesn't have you digging holes after pirate's treasure, does she, Dave?" she said.

"She told me something disturbing," I said, my voice bland, as though she and I were both concerned about the ill fortune of a third party. "It looks like Ruthie Jean and Luke are being evicted."

"We need the house for a tenant family. Ruthie Jean and Luke don't work on the plantation, nor do they pay rent. I'm sorry, but they'll have to find a new situation."

I nodded, my face blank. I felt my fingers tapping on the steering wheel. I cut my engine.

"You already dropped the dime on her and had her locked up. Isn't that enough?" I said.

"Whatever do you mean?" she said.

I opened my door partway to let the breeze into the truck's cab. I felt my pulse beating in my neck, words forming that I knew I shouldn't speak.

"With y'all's background and education, with all

Moleen's money, can't you be a little forgiving, a little generous with people who have virtually nothing?" I said.

Rufus bent down in the passenger's seat so I could see his face through the window. He had taken off his pilot's sunglasses, and his eyes looked pale green and lidless, the pupils as black and small as a lizard's, the narrow bridge of his nose pinched with two pink indentations.

"You're operating without your shield, Dave. That's something IA doesn't need to hear about," he said.

She placed her hand on his arm without looking at him.

"Dave, just so you understand something, my husband is a charming man and a wonderful litigator who also happens to be a financial idiot," she said. "He has no money. If he did, he'd invest it in ski resorts in Bangladesh. Is Ruthie Jean home now?"

Her eyes fixed pleasantly on mine with her question. Her lipsticked smile looked like crooked red lines drawn on parchment.

I dropped the truck into low and drove under the wisteria-hung iron trellis of the Bertrand plantation, wondering, almost in awe, at the potential of the human family.

That afternoon Batist called me from the phone in the bait shop.

"Dave, there's a man out on the dock don't belong here," he said.

"What's wrong with him?"

"I ax him if he want a boat. He says, 'Give me a

beer and a sandwich.' An hour later he's sitting at the table under the umbrella, smoking a cigarette, he ain't eat the sandwich, he ain't drunk the beer. I ax him if there's anyt'ing wrong with the food. He says, 'It's fine. Bring me another beer.' I say, 'You ain't drunk that one.' He says, 'It's got a bug in it. You got the afternoon paper here?' I say, 'No, I ain't got the paper.' He says, 'How about some magazines?' "

"I'll be down in a minute," I said.

"I ought to brought him a paper bag."

"What d' you mean?"

"To put over his head. He looks like somebody took a sharp spoon and stuck it real deep all over his face."

"Stay in the bait shop, Batist. You understand me? Don't go near this man."

I hung up, without waiting for him to reply, called the department for a cruiser, took my .45 out of the dresser drawer, stuck it through the back of my belt, and hung my shirt over it. As I walked down the slope through the broken light under the pecan and oak trees, I could see a strange drama being played out among the spool tables on the dock. Fishermen who had just come in were drinking beer and eating smoked sausage and *boudin* under the umbrellas, their faces focused among themselves and on their conversations about big-mouth bass and goggle-eye perch, but in their midst, by himself, smoking a cigarette with the concentrated intensity of an angry man hitting on a reefer, was Patsy Dapolito, his mouth hooked downward at the corners, his face like a clay sculpture someone had mutilated with a string knife.

I remembered a scene an old-time gunbull had once pointed out to me on the yard, inside the Block, at Angola Penitentiary. Inmates stripped to the waist, their apelike torsos wrapped with tattoos, were clanking iron, throwing the shotput, and ripping into heavy bags with blows that could eviscerate an elephant. In the center of the lawn was a tiny, balding, middle-aged man in steel-rimmed spectacles, squatting on his haunches, chewing gum furiously, his jaws freezing momentarily, the eyes lighting, then the jaws moving again with a renewed snapping energy. When a football bounced close to the squatting man, a huge black inmate asked permission before he approached to pick it up. The squatting man said nothing and the football remained where it was.

"Forget about them big 'uns," the gunbull told me. "That little fart yonder killed another convict while he had waist and leg chains on. I won't tell you how he done it, since you ain't eat lunch yet."

I looked down at Patsy Dapolito's ruined face. His pale eyes, which were round like an outraged doll's, clicked upward into mine.

"You made a mistake coming here," I said.

"Sit down. You want a beer?" he said. He picked up a bottle cap from the tabletop and threw it against the screen of the bait shop. "Hey, you! Colored guy! Bring us a couple more beers out here!"

I stared at him with my mouth open. Batist's head appeared at the screen, then went away.

"You've pulled some wiring loose, partner," I said.

"What, I don't got a right to drink a beer in a public place?"

"I want you out of here."

"Let's take a ride in a boat. I ain't never seen a swamp. You got swamp tours?" he said.

"*Adios*, Patsy."

"Hey, I don't like that. I'm talking here."

I had already turned to walk away. His hand clenched on my forearm, bit into the tendons, pulled me off balance into the table.

"Show some courtesy, act decent for a change," he said.

"You need some help, Dave?" a heavyset man with tobacco in his jaw said at the next table.

"It's all right," I said. People were staring now. My .45 protruded from under my shirt. I sat down on a chair, my arms on top of the spool table. "Listen to me, Patsy. A sheriff's cruiser is on its way. Right now, you got no beef with the locals. As far as I see it, you and I are slick, too. Walk away from this."

His teeth were charcoal colored and thin on the ends, almost as though they had been filed. His short, light brown hair looked like a wig on a mannequin. His eyes held on mine. "I got business to do," he said.

"Not with me."

"With you."

The fishermen at the other tables began to drift off toward their cars and pickup trucks and boat trailers.

"I want part of the action," he said.

"What action?"

"The deal at the plantation. I don't care what it is, I want in on it. You're on a pad for Johnny Carp. That means you're getting pieced off on this deal."

"A pad for—"

"Or you'd be dead. I know Johnny. He don't let nobody skate unless it's for money."

"You're a confused man, Patsy."

He pinched his nose, blew air through the nostrils, looked about at the sky, the overhang of the trees, a cloud of dust drifting from a passing pickup through a cane brake. "Look, there's guys ain't even from the city in on this deal, military guys think they're big shit because they cooled out a few gooks and tomato pickers. I did a grown man with a shank when I was eleven years old. You say I'm lying, check my jacket."

"It's Johnny you want to bring down, isn't it?" I said.

He kept huffing puffs of air through his nostrils, then he pulled a wadded handkerchief from his pocket and blew his nose in it.

"Johnny don't show it, but he's a drunk," Dapolito said. "A drunk don't look after anybody but himself. Otherwise you'd be fish bait, motherfucker."

I walked out to meet the cruiser sent by the dispatcher. The deputy was a big redbone named Cecil Aguillard whose face contained a muddy light people chose not to dwell upon.

"You t'ink he's carrying?" Cecil said.

"Not unless he has an ankle holster."

"What he's done?"

"Nothing so far," I said.

He walked down the dock ahead of me, his gunbelt, holster, and baton creaking on his hips like saddle leather. The umbrella over Patsy's head tilted and swelled in the wind. Cecil pushed it at an angle so he could look down into his face.

"Time to go," Cecil said.

Patsy was hunkered down over the tabletop, scowling into a state fish and game magazine. He made me think of a recalcitrant child in a school desk who was not going to let a nun's authority overwhelm him.

"Dave don't want you here," Cecil said.

"I ain't done nothing." His shoulders were hunched, his hands clenched into fists on the edges of the magazine, his eyes flicking about the dock.

Cecil looked at me and nodded his head toward the bait shop. I followed him.

"Clear everybody out of here, Dave, I'll take care of it," he said.

"It won't work on this guy."

"It'll work."

"No, he'll be back. Thanks for coming out, Cecil. I'll call you later if I have to."

"It ain't smart, Dave. You turn your back on his kind, he'll have your liver flopping on the flo'."

I watched Cecil drive down the road in the deepening shadows, then I helped Batist seine the dead shiners out of our bait tanks and hose down the boats we had rented that day. Patsy Dapolito still sat at his table, smoking cigarettes, popping the pages in his magazine, wiping bugs and mosquitoes from in front of his face.

The sun had dipped behind my house, and the tops of the cypress in the swamp had turned a grayish pink in the afterglow.

"We're closing up, Patsy," I said.

"Then close it up," he said.

"We've got a joke out here. This fellow woke up on his houseboat and heard two mosquitoes talking about him. One said, 'Let's take him outside and eat him.' The other one said, 'We'd better not. The big ones will carry him off for themselves.' "

"I don't get it," he said.

"Have a good one," I said, and walked up the slope to the house.

Two hours later it was dark. I used the switch inside the house to turn on the string of lights over the dock. Patsy Dapolito still sat at his table, the Cinzano umbrella furled above his head. His hard, white body seem to glow with electrified humidity.

Later, Bootsie and Alafair pulled into the drive, the car loaded with bags of groceries they had bought in Lafayette.

"Dave, there's a man sitting on the dock," Bootsie said.

"It's Patsy Dap," I said.

"The man you—" she began.

"That's the one."

"I can't believe it. He's on our *dock*?"

"He's not going to do anything," I said.

"He's not going to have a chance to. Not if I have anything to do with it," she said.

"I think Johnny Giacano's cut him loose. That's why he's here, not because of me. He couldn't think his way out of a wet paper bag, much less rejection by the only form of authority he's ever respected."

But she wasn't buying it.

"I'll get rid of him," I said.

"How?"

"Sometimes you've got to make their souls wince."

"Dave?"

I carried a sack of groceries inside, then wrapped both my .45 and nine-millimeter Beretta inside a towel, took a tube of first-aid cream from the medicine cabinet, and walked down to the dock. Patsy's elbows were splayed on the table, his face pale and luminous with heat and perspiration. The tide was out and the current was dead in the bayou. Patsy worked a thumbnail between his teeth and stared at me.

"Put some of this stuff on those mosquito bites," I said.

He surprised me. He filled both palms with white cream and rubbed it into his forearms and on his face and neck, his round chin pointed up in the air.

I unfolded the towel on the table. His eyes dropped to the pistols, then looked up at me.

"What, you got cold pieces for sale?" he said.

I released the magazine from the butt of each automatic so he could see the top round, inserted it again, chambered the round, set the safety, and placed both weapons butt to butt in the center of the table. Then I sat down across from him, my eyes stinging with salt. Up the slope, I could see Bootsie under the light on the gallery.

"If you want to square what I did to you, now's the time," I said. "Otherwise, I'm going to mop up the dock with you."

He smiled and screwed a fresh cigarette in his mouth, crumpled up the empty pack. "I always heard you were a drunk. That ain't your problem. You're fucking stupid, man," he said.

"Oh?"

"I want to make somebody dead, I don't even have to get out of bed. Don't try to shine me off, worm man. Tell Johnny and those military asswipes they piece me off or I leave hair on the walls."

He walked on the balls of his feet toward his automobile, lifting his arm to smell himself again.

Sometimes they don't wince.

Chapter 20

Even inside the dream I know I'm experiencing what a psychologist once told me is a world destruction fantasy. But my knowledge that it is only a dream does no good; I cannot extricate myself from it.

As a child I saw the sun turn black against a cobalt sky and sink forever beyond the earth's rim. Years later the images would change and I'd revisit my brief time as a new colonial, see Victor Charles, in black pajamas, sliding on his stomach through a rice paddy, a French bolt-action rifle strapped across his back; two GI's eating C-rations in the shade of banyan trees after machine-gunning a farmer's water buffalo just for meanness' sake; three of our wounded after they'd been skinned and hung in trees like sides of meat by NVA.

In my dream tonight I can see the Louisiana coastline from a great height, as alluvial and new as it must have been after Jehovah hung the archer's bow in the sky and drew the waters back over the earth's edges, the rivers and bayous and wetlands shimmering like foil under the moon. But it's a view that will not hold at the center, because now I realize the cold light of the moon is actually the fire from chemical plants and oil refineries along the Mississippi, the shook foil of a dead Jesuit poet nothing more than industrial mercury systemically injected into the earth's veins. The roadways and ditches are blown with litter, the canals a depository for rubber tires, beer cans, vinyl sacks of raw garbage thrown from pickup trucks. A fish's gills are orange with fungus.

I wake from the dream and sit alone in the kitchen. I can hear thunder out of the Gulf and Tripod pulling his chain along the clothesline. Through the window my neighbor's freshly cut lawn smells like corn silk and milk. I sit on the back steps until the trees turn gray with the false dawn, then I go back inside and fall asleep just as the first raindrops *ping* against the blades of the window fan.

At noon Bootsie and I were eating lunch in the kitchen when Ruthie Jean Fontenot called.

"Moleen's at Dot's in St. Martinville. You know where that's at, I'm talking about in the black section?" she said.

"I'm not his keeper, Ruthie Jean."

"You can get him out."

"Get him out yourself."

"Some secrets suppose to stay secret. You know the rules about certain things that go on between white and black people."

"Wrong man to call," I said.

"The man owns the place is a friend of Luke's. He said Moleen's got a li'l pistol stuck down inside his coat. The man doesn't want to call the police unless he has to."

"Forget Moleen and take care of yourself, Ruthie Jean. He's not worth—"

She hung up. I sat down at the table and started eating again. Bootsie watched my face.

"Moleen's a grown man," I said. "He's also a hypocritical sonofabitch."

"He got her out of jail," Bootsie said.

"He paid somebody else to do it. Which is Moleen's style. Three cushion shots."

"Too harsh, Streak," she said.

I drank out of my iced tea, sucked on a sprig of mint, finally squeezed my temples between my fingers.

"See you before five," I said.

"Watch your ass, kiddo," she said.

I took the old road into St. Martinville, along Bayou Teche and through cane fields and pastureland where egrets stood like spectators on the backs of grazing cows. Dot's was a ramshackle bar toward the end of the main artery that traversed the black district and eventually bled into the square where Evangeline was buried with her lover behind the old French church. Ironically, the bar's geographical location, set like a way station between two worlds, was similar to the peculiar mix of blood and genes in the clientele—octoroons and quadroons, redbones, and people who were coal black but whose children sometimes had straw-colored curly hair.

Moleen sat in the gloom, at the far end of the bar, on a patched, fingernail-polish-red vinyl stool, his seersucker coat tight across his hunched shoulders, one oxblood loafer twisted indifferently inside an aluminum rung on the stool. I could smell his unwashed odor three feet away.

"She's worried about you," I said, and sat down next to him.

He drank from a glass of bourbon and melted ice, pushed two one-dollar bills out of his change toward the bartender.

"You want a drink?" he said.

I didn't answer. I peeled back the edge of his coat with one finger. He glared at me.

"A .25 caliber derringer. That's dumb, Moleen," I said. "One of those is like bird shit hitting a brick."

He pointed at his empty glass for the bartender. A deformed mulatto man with a shoe-shine box came through the front door in a burst of hot sunlight, let the door slam hard behind him, vibrating the glass and venetian blinds. His face was moronic, his mouth a wet drool, his arms like gnarled oak roots that were half the length they should have been. I looked away from him.

"You want your shoes shined?" Moleen said, a smile playing at the corner of his mouth.

"I think a remark like that is unworthy of you," I said.

"I wasn't being humorous. His great-grandfather and mine were the same gentleman. If you think he's an eyeful, you should meet his mother. Hang around. She comes in about seven."

"I can't stop you from fucking up your life, Moleen, but as a law officer, I want you to hand over your piece."

"Take it. I've never fired a shot in anger, anyway."

I slipped it from inside his belt, cracked open the breech below the lip of the bar.

"It's empty," I said.

"Oh, yeah," he said absently, and took two steel-jacketed rounds from his coat pocket and dropped them in my palm. "They're going to take your friend Marsallus out."

"Who?"

He tilted the glass to his mouth. His eyes were red along the rims, his face unshaved and shiny with a damp sweat.

"What's the worst thing you saw in Vietnam, Dave?" he asked.

"It's yesterday's box score."

"You ever leave your own people behind, sell them out, scratch their names off a list at a peace conference, lie to their families?"

"Quit sticking thumbtacks in your head. Go public with it."

"It *is* public, for God's sakes. Nobody cares."

"Why do these guys want to kill Sonny?"

"He's a one-man firing squad. He gets them in his sights and they tend to dissolve in a red mist."

"A good woman cares for you, Moleen. A guy could have worse problems," I said.

"Which woman?"

"See you around, partner. Don't let them get behind you." I started to get up.

"You're always the wiseguy, Dave. Try this. Ruthie Jean got her Aunt Bertie to file suit against the plantation. They retained a little sawed-off ACLU lawyer from New Orleans who can tie us up in court for years."

"Sounds like a smart move."

"Glad you think so. I know some gentlemen who probably won't agree with you. After they take Marsallus off the board, you may get to meet a few of them."

"I already have. They're just not that impressive a crowd," I said, got up off the stool, and collided into the deformed man. His wood shoe-shine box tumbled out of his hands; brushes, cans of wax and saddle soap, bottles of liquid polish clattered and rolled across the floor. His eyes had the panicked, veined intensity of hard-boiled eggs. He slobbered and made a moaning sound in his throat as he tried to pick up a cracked bottle of liquid polish that was bleeding into a black pool in the wood. But his torso was top-heavy, his arms too short and uncoordinated, and he stared helplessly at the dripping polish on his fingers as the bottle rolled farther from his grasp and left a trail of black curlicues across the floor.

I got down on my knees and began putting his things back in the box.

"I'm sorry, partner. We'll go down to the store and replace whatever I broke here. It's going to be okay," I said.

His expression was opaque, his tongue thick as a wet biscuit on his teeth. He tried to make words, but they had no more definition than a man clearing a phlegmy obstruction from his throat.

I saw Moleen grinning at me.

"Racial empathy can be a sticky business, can't it, laddie?" he said.

I wanted to wipe him off the stool.

The anger, the inability to accept, would not go out of Bootsie's words. There were pale discolorations like melted pieces of ice in her cheeks. I couldn't blame her.

"Dave, she's only thirteen years old. She could have killed someone," she said.

"But she didn't. She didn't chamber the round, either," I said.

"That seems poor consolation."

"I'll lock up all the guns," I said.

It was eleven Friday night and we were in the kitchen. I had turned on the floodlight in the mimosa tree in the backyard. Alafair was in her room with the door closed.

I took another run at it.

"I know it's my fault. I left the Beretta where she could find it," I said. "But what if this guy had tried to come through the door or window?"

She washed a cup in hot water with her hands. Her skin was red under the tap. Her back looked stiff and hard against her shirt.

"You want to install a burglar alarm system?" I said.

"Yes!"

"I'll call somebody in the morning," I said, and went into the backyard, where I sat for a long time at the picnic table and stared listlessly at the shadows of the mimosa tree shifting back and forth on the grass. It was not a good night to be locked up with your own thoughts, but I knew of nowhere else to take them.

In the morning I drove to New Iberia with Alafair to pick up an outboard engine from the freight agent at the train depot.

"You shouldn't have messed with the gun, Alf," I said.

"I'd already called 911. What was I supposed to do next? Wait for him to kick the door in?" She looked straight ahead, her eyes dancing.

"I couldn't find any footprints."

"I don't care. I saw him. He was out there in the trees. Tripod got scared and started running on his chain."

"It wasn't the guy who got Tripod out of the coulee?"

"He was thinner. A car went by and his skin looked real white."

"Did he have red hair?"

"I don't know. It was only a second."

"Maybe it's time we learn how to use a pistol properly," I said.

"Why's everybody mad at me? It's not fair, Dave."

"I'm not mad at you, little guy . . . Sorry . . . Bootsie isn't, either. It's just—"

"Yes, she is. Don't lie about it. It makes it worse."

"That's pretty strong, Alf."

"Why'd y'all leave me alone, then? What am I supposed to do if bad people come around the house?" Her voice grew in intensity, then it broke like a stick snapping and she began to cry.

We were on East Main in front of the Shadows. I pulled into the shade of the oaks, behind a charter bus full of elderly tourists. The bus's diesel engine throbbed off the cement.

"I screwed up. I won't do it again," I said.

But she kept crying, with both of her hands over her face.

"Look, maybe I won't go back with the department. I'm tired of being a punching bag for other people. I'm tired of the family taking my fall, too."

She took her hands from her face and looked out the side window for a long time. She kept sniffing and touching at her eyes with the backs of her wrists. When she turned straight in the seat again, her eyes were round and dry, as though someone had popped a flashbulb in front of them.

"It's not true," she said.

"What isn't?"

"You'll always be a cop, Dave. Always."

Her voice was older than her years, removed from both of us, prescient with a joyless knowledge about the nature of adult promises.

By Sunday morning I still hadn't put the matter to rest. I woke early and tapped on Alafair's door.

"Yes?"

"It's Dave. You got a second?"

"Wait." I heard her bare feet on the floor. "Okay."

Her shelves were filled with stuffed animals, the walls covered with posters featuring cats of all kinds. Alafair had propped a pillow behind her head and pulled up her knees so that they made a tent under the sheet. The curtains puffed in the breeze and the screen hung loose from the latch.

I sat in the chair by her homework desk.

"I was upset for another reason yesterday, one that's hard to explain," I said. "You didn't do anything wrong, Alf. I did."

"You already said that."

"Listen. When you kill another human being, no matter how necessary it might seem at the time, something goes out of your life forever. I never want that to happen to you. I still have dreams about the war, I have them about men I ran up against as a police officer. Their faces don't go underground with them."

Her eyes blinked and went away from mine.

I saw the sheet ruffle and hump at the foot of the bed. It should have been a humorous moment, but it wasn't.

"Let's get this guy out of here so we can talk," I said, and lifted Tripod from under the sheet. He hung heavily from my hands and churned his paws in the air as I walked to the window.

"He'll run down to the dock again," she said, as if she could open a door out of our conversation.

"Batist can handle it," I said, and dropped Tripod into the yard.

I sat back down. It was sunny and blue outside. In a short while we would be driving to Mass at St. Peter's in New Iberia, then we'd have lunch at Victor's on Main. I didn't want to address the question in her eyes.

Her hands were pinched together on top of her

knees. She looked at a poster of two calico kittens on the far wall.

"How many people, Dave, how many did you—"

"You never let yourself see a number in your mind, Alf. The day you do, the day it comes out of your mouth, that's the day you start being someone else," I said.

Sonny Boy called the bait shop at three o'clock that afternoon.

"You've got a serious hearing problem," I said. "I want you out of my life. Don't come around my house anymore, you understand? You want to be a guardian angel, go to New York, put on a red beret, and buy a lot of subway tokens."

"What do you mean come around your house?" he said. I could hear waves breaking against rocks or a jetty, then the sound of a door on a telephone booth closing.

"Friday night," I said.

"I was in New Orleans," he said.

"Don't give me that, Sonny."

"I'm telling you the truth."

"My daughter saw a guy in the trees. It wasn't Emile Pogue, it wasn't Patsy Dap, Patsy wants to do business and screw Johnny Carp, that leaves you." But my words sounded hollow even to myself.

"They got lots of guys working for them, Streak, a lot of them in Florida. They get gooned-up like over-the-hill jarheads on a skivvy run, blow into town, give a guy a fatal accident, and catch the red-eye back to Tampa the same night."

I could hear myself breathing against the receiver. Outside the screen window, the sunlight's reflection on the bayou was like a sliver of glass in the eye.

"Why'd you call?" I said.

"A rag-nose used to work for Johnny Carp told me Johnny's in on a deal to get some land by a train track. He said he heard Johnny tell a guy on the phone the land's got to be by a train track. That's the key."

"To what?" I said.

"I don't know. You ought to see the rag-nose. He's got nostrils that look like tunnels going straight into his brain. The real reason I called, if my string runs out, like I bounce back treys and boxcars, know what I'm saying, I wanted to tell you I'm sorry for the trouble I caused other people."

"Come on, Sonny, you got your ticket punched a long time ago. You'll be standing on Canal with a glass of champagne when they drive Johnny's hearse by . . . Sonny?"

I heard the phone booth door rachet back violently on its hinges, the receiver clattering back and forth on its cord, then, almost lost in the crash of waves against rocks or a jetty, a sound like a string of firecrackers popping.

Chapter 21

Early Monday morning the sheriff called and asked me to come to the department. I thought it was about Sonny. It wasn't.

He was scraping out the bowl of his pipe over the wastebasket with a penknife when I walked into his office.

"Sit down," he said. He wiped the blade of the penknife on a piece of paper and folded it against the heel of his hand. "This is a bad day, my friend . . . I wish I could tell you it's just a matter of IAD finding against you."

I waited.

"You know the route," he said. "It's the kind of deal usually gets a guy a letter of reprimand in his jacket or a suspension." He wadded up the piece of paper and tried to wipe the pipe's ashes out of his palm. "This one's different."

"Too many times across the line?"

"The problem is you're a police officer who doesn't like rules. You kept yourself on the job while you were officially suspended, didn't you?"

In my mind's eye I saw Rufus Arceneaux's face leaning across the seat inside Julia's automobile, the green eyes lighted with ambition and long-held grievance.

"There's something you're not saying, Sheriff."

"I couldn't cover for you anymore, Dave. I told them about you and Purcel salting Sweet Pea's Caddy and queering the warrant."

"I'm fired?"

"You can submit your resignation. It needs to be on my desk by five."

I bounced my palms on my thighs.

"About queering the warrant," I said. "I made the connection between the scrap iron on the floater's body and a junk pile next to Sweet Pea's house. How'd that play out?"

"I'm afraid it's not your concern any longer."

It was a windy day outside, and I could see the flag snapping and popping on the steel pole without making any sound.

"I'll box up my stuff," I said.

"I'm sorry about this," he said.

I nodded and opened the door to leave.

"Are you going to have that letter on my desk?" he asked.

"I don't think so," I said.

On the way down the hall I picked up my mail and messages, found an empty cardboard box in a custodian's closet, unlocked my office door, and went inside.

It was all that quick, as though a loud train had gone past me, slamming across switches, baking the track with its own heat, creating a tunnel of sound and energy so intense that the rails seem to reshape like bronze licorice under the wheels; then silence that's like hands clapped across the eardrums, a field of weeds that smell of dust and creosote, a lighted club car disappearing across the prairie.

Or simply a man walking through glass doors into a sun-drenched parking lot, a box on his shoulder, and no one taking particular notice.

An electrical storm struck New Iberia that afternoon, and I sent Batist home and shut down the dock and watched a twenty-four-hour news station on the television set that I kept on top of the soda and lunch meat cooler. A lorry carrying three white men had gone into the black homelands of South Africa and had been shot up by black militia of some kind. The footage was stunning. One white man was already dead, crumpled over the steering wheel, his face pushed into a lopsided expression by the horn button; the two other men lay wounded on the pavement. One had propped his back against the tire and had his hands up, but he never spoke. The other man was on his stomach and having trouble raising his head so he could speak to the soldiers whose legs surrounded him. He was a large man, with a wild red beard, a broad nose, and coarse-grained skin, and he could hardly contain the rage in his throat.

"Will you call a fucking ambulance?" he said in a British accent. "My friend's hurt. Did you hear me? We need the *fucking* ambulance. How do I say it to you? Call the fucking hospital for an ambulance . . . Oh you have, have you? Well, *thank* you very much. Thank you fucking bloody very much."

The militia shot him and his friend. Later, the replay of the tape did not show the bearded man getting in the face of his executioners. Instead, the newscaster said the victims had begged for their lives. That last line was repeated over and over throughout the afternoon. I kept waiting for it to be corrected. It never was, not to my knowledge. A brave man's death was revised downward to a shameful and humiliating one, either for categorical or dramatic purposes. The truth had become an early casualty.

What's the point?

I didn't know myself.

The thunder finally stopped and the rain roared on the tin roof and drenched the dock and spool tables and blew through the screens in a fine mist. I waited for it to slack off, then I locked up the bait shop and ran up the slope with a raincoat over my head and told Bootsie of the change in our circumstances.

That evening, which was unseasonably cool and marked by strange lights in the sky, Helen Soileau came out to the house and sat with me on the front steps, her thick forearms propped on her thighs like a ballplayer in a dugout, and told me the story about Sonny's phone call within earshot of waves bursting against a coastline.

The two shooters were pros, probably ex-military men, not the much-inflated contract wiseguys who undid their victims through treachery and had to press the muzzle into the hairline to ensure they didn't miss. They had him triangulated from forty yards out, with either AR-15's or .223 carbines. Had the target been anyone else, he would have been hurled backward, matted with shards of glass, and made to dance on invisible wires inside the phone booth. But one of the shooters probably blew it, shifted his sling to box the side of Sonny's face more tightly in his sights, to lock cartilage and jawbone and the almost feminine mouth, which made soundless words the shooter hated without even hearing them, lock them all into a narrow iron rectangle that would splinter into torn watermelon with the slightest pull of the shooter's finger.

But the inverted boat hull he was aiming across dented and made a thunking sound when he shifted the sling, and suddenly Sonny was on rock 'n' roll, his heart bursting with adrenaline, springing from the booth, his shoulders hunched, zigzagging through the boatyard, his hips swiveling like a football quarterback evading tacklers, his skin twitching as though someone had touched a hot match to it.

A witness down by the collapsed pier said Sonny seemed painted with magic. He raced between cinderblock tool shops and dry-docked shrimp boats that were eaten with rot, while the shooters tried to lock down on him again and whanged rounds off a welding truck, blew glass out of a watchman's hut, dissected the yawning door of a junked Coca-Cola machine, and stitched a row of bleeding holes across a corrugated tin paint shed.

Sonny bolted down the sandy slope to the riverbank and poured it on. But for some unexplainable reason he ran for the beach, the wheeling of gulls and other winged creatures, rather than back up the river to higher ground, and the sand became wetter and wetter under his feet, until his shoes sank up to the ankles in porridge.

Then they nailed him.

One shooter, a thick-bodied, truncated man, with knots of muscle through his back and skin-tight cutoffs rolled into his genitals, came over the riverbank in a breath-wheezing run, his rifle at port arms, and fired and fired until the breech locked open and shell casings littered the sand like broken gold teeth.

Sonny's Hawaiian shirt jumped and puffed as though carrion birds were pecking at it. His gait broke, his torso twisted momentarily, and he became a man ingesting a chunk of angle iron. But a long time ago, perhaps back in the Iberville welfare project, Sonny had learned the fate of those who go down in front of their adversaries' booted feet. He seemed to right himself, his face concentrating with a fragile inner balance, forcing a composed and single thought in front of his eyes; then he stumbled toward the surf and the crumpled pier that rang with the cries of frightened birds.

He waded through the breakers, his destroyed shirt billowing out into the tide like wings. The shooters fired twice more, wide and high, the rounds toppling and skipping across the water. But Sonny had become his own denouement. He struggled forward into the undertow, staining the world of fish and crabs and eels and stingrays with his blood, then simply stepped off into the depths, his red hair floating briefly beneath a wave like a windblown flower.

"You handling this, Dave?" Helen said.

"Sure."

"He always lived on the edge. It was his way."

"Yeah, I know what you mean," I said. My voice seemed outside of my skin, my words spoken by someone else. After a while I said, "Who pulled the body out?"

"They didn't find it." I could feel her eyes moving on the side of my face. "Forget it, Dave. He didn't make it. The Fed I talked to said the blood spore looked like dogs had been chewing on him."

I felt my teeth scrape against one another. "What was he doing in Mississippi?"

"The beach is full of casinos and greaseballs. Maybe he was tying another knot on his string. The Fed I talked to got pretty vague when I asked him the same thing."

I bounced my forehead on my thumbs, looked at the sky that was metallic and burned-looking and flickering with lights. Helen stood up with her car keys in her hand.

"He pissed you off, he dragged his shit into your life, but you took his fall, anyway. Don't you dare put this on your conscience," she said. She aimed her index finger at me.

She walked toward her car, then stopped and turned.

"Did you hear me?" she said.

"Sure."

Her eyes fixed on mine, then her breasts rose and she walked through the wet leaves and pools of water to the drive, her shoulders squared with a moral certitude that I could only envy.

* * *

I woke at four in the morning and sat on the edge of the bed. I couldn't remember the details of the dream I'd just had, but in the center of my mind was an ugly and inescapable thought, like an angry man walking toward you in a darkened, wood-floored hallway.

We'd had him in custody. Then Johnny Giacano had put out the word he didn't want Sonny bailed out.

Question: What was the best way to make sure I heard what Johnny wanted?

Answer: Feed the information to Clete Purcel.

Had Johnny sucked me in?

I didn't know.

I couldn't accept Sonny's death. People like Sonny didn't die. They stayed high on their own rebop, heard Charlie Parker's riffs in the friction of the spheres, thrived without sunlight in the neon glaze of Canal and St. Charles, fashioned sonnets out of street language, and proved to the rest of us that you could live with the full-tilt boogie in your heart and glide above the murderous fastenings of triviality.

They didn't find a body, I told myself. The sea always gives back its dead, and they didn't find Sonny's body.

You're dead when they unzip the bag, pry your dog tag out of your teeth, and drain your fluids through a grate in the bottom of a stainless steel trough. *That's* dead.

I lay back on the pillow with my forearm across my eyes and fell asleep. I dreamed I saw Sonny rise like Triton from the sea, his body covered with fish scales, a wreathed horn in his hand, already transforming into a creature of air and spun light.

The next afternoon Batist answered the phone in the bait shop, then handed me the receiver. The weather was hot and muggy, and I pressed a sweating can of Dr Pepper against my cheek and sat on a counter stool with the phone against my ear.

"Robicheaux?" the voice said.

There was no mistaking the thick, whiskey-and-cigarette-seared rasp, the words that rose like ash inside a chimney.

"Yes," I said, and swallowed something stale and bitter in my throat.

"You must have run your thumb up somebody's hole. You got eighty-sixed out of your own department?"

"What's on your mind, Pogue?"

"I think you're not a bad dude. We need local guys to make it work. You want to piece off Purcel, it's copacetic with us."

"Make what work? Who's us?"

"The whole fucking planet. Get with the program, ace."

"I don't know what the program is."

He laughed, his voice wheezing as though there were pinholes in his lungs.

"I like you, motherfucker," he said. "I told them to cut you in. I'd rather see you front points for us than y'all's resident cunt, what's the name, Bertrand?"

"Moleen?"

"Got to get the locals humping for you. Ever light up a ville with Zippo tracks? Something about the stink of fried duck shit really gets their attention."

The phone receiver was warm and moist against my ear. Someone slammed the screen door behind me like the crack of a rifle.

"You were one of the shooters," I said.

"The Marsallus gig? He took out some good men. He had it coming."

"You fucked it up."

I heard him shift the phone in his hand, his breath fan the mouthpiece in a dry, heated exhalation.

"Fucked it up, huh?"

"The Feds didn't find a body. I think Sonny'll be back to piss on your grave," I said.

"You listen—" A nail caught in his throat and he began again. "We busted his wheels, ace. I saw the bone buckle. That punk's down in the slime where he belongs."

"He shows up when you don't expect him. Your buddy Jack got capped before he knew what hit him. Think about it," I said, and hung up the receiver.

I hoped I left him with razors turning in his viscera.

Chapter 22

AT NOON TUESDAY a city cop picked up Ruthie Jean outside a restaurant on Main Street and took her to the city jail, where she was booked for disturbing the peace and disorderly conduct. He even cuffed her, put his hand hard inside her arm before he sat her down in the back of the cruiser and threw her cane across her lap and slammed the door to indicate his sympathies to anyone watching. I heard the story from a half dozen people, all of whom told it with a sense of genteel dismay, but I suspected they were secretly pleased, as small-town people are, when the sins of another are exposed and they no longer have to be complicit in hiding them.

People at first thought she was simply drunk, then they saw the feverish shine in the eyes, like someone still staring into the flame held to a crack pipe. An elderly woman who lived by Spanish Lake recognized and tried to counsel her, shushing her, patting her shoulders, trying to turn her away from Julia Bertrand, who had just parked her red Porsche at the curb in front of the Shadows and was walking cheerfully toward the restaurant, her mental fortifications in place, her long tan riding skirt whipping against her legs.

"Oh, it's all right," she said to the other white woman. "Ruthie Jean's upset about a tenant problem Moleen had to settle on the plantation. Now, you go on about your business, Ruthie Jean, and don't be bothering people. You want me to call somebody to drive you home?"

"You put me off the plantation, Julia. When you cut the balloon loose, it goes where it wants."

"I'd appreciate it if you didn't address me by my first name."

"You cain't hide from your thoughts. Not when he touches you in the dark, under the sheets, his eyes shut, and you know where his hand's been on me, you know he's thinking of me and that's why he does it to you with his eyes shut, he hurries it so he doesn't have to think about who he's doing it with, about how he's making a lie for both y'all, just like he hepped make my baby and kept pretending I could have it without a husband and live on the plantation like colored folks are suppose to do, like his ancestors did to us, like there wasn't any sin on the child, 'cause the child got Bertrand blood in him."

"How dare you!"

"You cain't run away when you see that li'l boy in your headlights, either, see the fright in his li'l face, hear his voice speaking to you through the dirt they packed in his mouth. Liquor and drugs cain't keep a spirit in the grave. That li'l boy, his name was John Wesley, he sits on the floor by your nightstand and whispers all the secrets he learned down in the ground, all the things he didn't get to do, the questions he got about his momma and daddy and why they aren't there to take care of him or bring him things on his birthday 'cause your father run them out of the parish."

"If you come close to me again, I'm going to slap your face."

Julia crossed the street against the light, her waxed calves flashing like scissors.

But Ruthie Jean followed her, into the restaurant, through the linen-covered tables, past the framed charcoal sketches and pastel paintings of rural Louisiana on the walls, into an interior dining room that should have been an enclave for Julia but had become a cul-de-sac.

Julia sat erectly in her chair, her menu held tightly in her fingers, a bitter thought clenched in her face. When Ruthie Jean took a chair at the next table, Julia began to laugh. It was a braying, disconnected sound, ongoing, like furniture falling down stairs.

"Is anything wrong, Miss Julia?" the owner asked.

"I thought this was a private dining room. It is a private dining room, isn't it?"

"Sometimes. When people reserve it for banquets and club meetings," he answered.

"I'd like another table. Over there. By the window."

"You bet. Are you sure everything's all right, Miss Julia?"

"Are you blind, sir?"

The owner held the chair for her at a table whose linen glowed in the sunlight. Now Ruthie Jean approached both of them, her dark eyes as bright as glass.

"John Wesley was buried in the rain in a casket

made of papier-mâché and kite sticks," she said. "It's rotted away, eaten up with worms now, and that's how come he can visit in your room at night, sit right by your pillow and draw a picture in the air of the thing that got bounced up under your car and lost inside that sound that doesn't ever go out of your head."

"You're a vicious, cunning, ungrateful nigra, Ruthie Jean. You can end in an asylum. Mark my word," Julia said.

Someone was punching numbers on a telephone in the background.

"You cain't do nothing to stop Moleen from coming 'round my house again," Ruthie Jean said. "But I don't want him anymore. In Mexico one time he put a flower on my stomach and put his mouth on my nipples and put himself inside me and said I was all the food he'd ever need. Except he stole my nipples from my baby. That's 'cause y'all's kind of white people don't know how to love anything outside of what y'all need."

After Ruthie Jean had been taken away in the cruiser, her soft black hair like the wig on a mannequin in the rear window, Julia sat numbed and motionless at the table in the deserted dining room; her lips were bloodless, her makeup dry and flaking from her facial hair, as though parched by an inner heat. One thumb kept digging into her cuticles, cutting half-moons into her knuckles, massaging a nest of thoughts that crawled through her veins like spiders.

She smiled and rose from the chair to meet her

husband, who had just hurried from his law office down the street.

"Moleen, you dear," she said. "How good of you to come. Is something bothering you? Oh, what shall we do, dear boy?"

She used one sharpened fingernail to draw vertical red lines in the skin under his eyes, as though she were imprinting tears on a clown.

At dusk that same evening Clete Purcel's rust-eaten Caddy, with its mildewed and tattered top folded back at a twisted angle, throbbed into the drive and died like a sick animal.

He wore his porkpie hat and a tropical shirt with tiny purple seahorses printed all over it. He was eating an oyster po'-boy sandwich with one hand, tuning the radio with the other.

"Take a ride with me," he said.

"What's up?"

"I need to talk, that's all."

"Turn the radio down," I said.

"Hey, you listen to Dr. Boogie and the *Bon Ton Soul Train?*"

"No."

He started the engine again and kept feeding it the gas while the Caddy's gutted muffler vibrated and rattled against the frame.

"Okay!" I said, above the noise, and got in beside him. A few minutes later we were approaching the drawbridge. "Do you realize you always end up driving the same kind of cars greaseballs do?" I said.

"That's because I buy them off greaseballs. I'm lucky I can afford greaseball hand-me-downs."

I waited for him to get to it. We turned into New Iberia, then headed out toward Spanish Lake. He bit down softly on his thumbnail, his face reflective and cool in the wind.

"I heard about Sonny. The guy didn't deserve to die like that," he said. We were on the old two-lane road now. The azaleas and purple wisteria along the roadside were still in bloom and you could see the lake through the trees. Clete's voice was hoarse, down in his throat. "Something else bothers me, too." He turned and looked at me. "I told you, when I hit Sonny, I got a red bruise on my knuckles, it looked like strawberry juice under the skin, it wouldn't go away?"

He shook his head, without waiting for me to answer.

"I was always pissed off at Sonny, I can't even tell you why. When I heard he got clipped, I felt really bad the way I treated him. I was in the can at Tujague's last night, washing my hands, and that strawberry bruise was gone."

He held up the back of his hand in the sun's red glow off the dashboard.

"This stuff's in your mind, Clete."

"Give me some credit, mon. My hand throbbed all the time. Now it doesn't. I think Johnny Carp used both of us to set up the whack."

He turned left off the two-lane, drove past a collapsed three-story house that had been a gambling club in the sixties, then followed a dirt road to a woods where people had dumped raw garbage and mattresses and stuffed chairs in the weeds. Clete backed the Caddy into the gloom of the trees. The sun was below the horizon now, the air thick with birds.

"What are you doing?" I said.

"Helen Soileau got the warrant on Sweet Pea's house. Guess what? He'd ripped the carpet out of his Caddy."

The radio was off now, and when he cut the engine I heard movement in the trunk, a shift of weight, the scrape of shoe leather against metal.

"This is a mistake," I said.

"Watch the show. He's a geek. Geeks get off on being the center of attention."

Clete took a can of beer from the Styrofoam cooler in the backseat and popped the trunk. Sweet Pea Chaisson's long body was curled between the tire wells, his webbed eyes glistening in the enclosed heat, his tin-colored silk shirt swampy with sweat. He climbed out over the bumper, his small mouth compressed as though he were sucking a mint.

"Hey, Dave. What's the word, babe?" he said.

Clete shoved him backward across a log, onto the ground.

"Streak lost his shield, Sweet Pea. We're operating on different rules now. Bad time to be a wiseass, know what I'm saying?" Clete said.

Sweet Pea inserted his little finger into an empty space in his teeth, then looked at the blood on the tip of it and spit in the weeds. He grinned up at Clete.

"I got to go to the bat'room," he said.

"Do it in your clothes," Clete said. Then to me,

"I found our man behind a colored juke joint. He was beating the shit out of one of his chippies with a rolled newspaper."

"That was my wife," Sweet Pea said.

Clete pitched the can of beer into his lap.

"Rinse your mouth out. Your breath's bad," he said.

"T'anks, Purcel," Sweet Pea said, ripped the tab, and drank deeply from the can. His face was covered with pinpoints of sweat and dirt. "Where we at?" He looked off into the purple haze above the cane fields. "Oh yeah, my mother's grave was right across them railway tracks."

"Who put the whack on Sonny?" Clete said.

"I live in Breaux Bridge now. A crawfish getting run over on the highway is big news there. How do I know?"

Sweet Pea tipped the beer can to his mouth. Clete kicked it into his face. Sweet Pea's lips were suddenly bright red, his eyebrows dripping with beer foam, his face quivering with the force of the blow. But not one sound came from his throat. I pushed Clete away from him.

"No more," I said.

"Take a walk down the road. Enjoy the evening. Stroll back in ten minutes," he said. His blue-black .38 one-inch hung from his right hand.

"We take him back to wherever you got him. That's the way it is, Cletus."

"You're screwing it up, Streak."

Behind me, I heard Sweet Pea stirring in the weeds, getting to his feet.

"Stay where you are, Sweet Pea," I said.

He sat on a log with his head between his legs and let the blood and saliva drain out of his mouth. When he looked up at me again, his face was changed.

"You're a pair of white clowns playing big shit out in the wood," he said. His sharp, tiny teeth looked like they were stained with Mercurochrome.

Clete stepped toward him. I put my hand on his chest.

"What the fuck y'all know?" Sweet Pea said. "Y'all ever hear there's a glow hanging over the ground at night on the Bertrand place? Where all them convicts was killed and buried in their chains. You t'ink you shit vanilla ice cream?"

"You're not making much sense, Sweet Pea," I said.

"The juke where I bring my broads, how's it stay open? It's Bertrand's."

"That's not true, partner. I've seen the deeds on all the land around here."

"It's part of a con . . . a consor . . . something . . . what do you call it?" he said.

"Consortium."

"Yeah," he said. "Hey, Purcel, you look like you need an enema. Why don't you shove that gun up your ass?"

Clete took a Lucky Strike out of his pocket and lit it. Then he pulled a strand of tobacco off his lip and dropped it in the air. The lighted windows of the Amtrak streamed by on the train tracks across the cane field. Sweet Pea sat on the log and looked at the train and scratched his cheek as though we were no longer there.

"You got a lot of luck, Sweet Pea," I said.

"Yeah? Tell your wife I got an opening. For an older broad like that, I'll make an exception, too. Just straight dates, no sixty-nines," he said.

I dream that night of people who live in caves under the sea. Their arms and shoulders are sheathed in silver feathers; their abalone skins dance with fiery sparks.

I once knew a helicopter pilot from Morgan City whose Jolly Green took an RPG right through the door. He had been loaded with ammunition and wounded civilians, and when they crashed in the middle of a river, most of the civilians burned to death or drowned. He became psychotic after the war and used to weigh and sink plastic statues of Jesus all over the waterways of southern Louisiana. He maintained that the earth was wrapped with water, that a bayou in the Atchafalaya Basin was an artery that led to a flooded rice plain in the Mekong Delta, that somehow the presence of a plastic statue could console those whose drowned voices still spoke to him from the silt-encrusted wreckage of his helicopter.

When he hung himself, the wire service story made much of his psychiatric history. But in my own life I had come to believe in water people and voices that can speak through the rain. I wondered if Sonny would speak to me.

It was a blue-gold morning, the sky clear, the wind balmy out of the south, when the sheriff parked his cruiser by the boat ramp and walked down the dock. I was shirtless, sanding dried fish scales out of the guardrail, the sun warm on my back, the day almost perfect. I didn't want to hear about someone else's troubles, their guilt, or even an apology for wrongs real or imagined.

"We've got Patsy Dapolito in lockup," he said.

"That seems like a good place for him."

"He says somebody stole the tip he left in the motel restaurant. He made quite a scene. Scared the shit out of everybody in the place. This guy is probably as close to Freddy Kruger as New Iberia will ever get."

I drew the sandpaper along the grain of the wood and brushed the dust out into the sunlight.

"It doesn't concern you anymore, huh?" the sheriff said.

"Not unless he comes around here."

"I wish I could tell you it's that easy, Dave."

I started sanding again, my eyes on his.

"The FBI called yesterday. They thought you were still with us." He shrugged off the discomfort of his own remark. "They've got a tap on some of Johnny Carp's people. Your name came up in a conversation."

"I'm not a player anymore, Sheriff. Maybe it's time you and the Feds got the word out."

"The greaseballs think you know something you shouldn't. Or you're trying to queer their action over here."

"They're wrong."

"One of them said, 'Let the Rambo fucks take care of it.' They laughed, and another guy said, 'Yeah, let 'em send in Charlie.' Does that mean something to you?"

"Yeah, it does. I was fired. Y'all clean up your own mess."

"I don't think anger will help us, Dave."

"When a drunk gets eighty-sixed out of a bar, he's not supposed to buy drinks for the people still inside. You want a cup of coffee, Sheriff?"

Clete came by at noon, drank a beer under the awning on the dock, then insisted I drive into New Iberia with him.

"I've got to work," I said.

"That's my point," he said, crushing his beer can, his porkpie hat cocked over his scarred eyebrow, his face full of fun.

We drove down East Main, past the old Burke home and the Steamboat House, into the shade of live oaks, past the city library and the stone grotto dedicated to Christ's mother, which was the only remnant of the old Catholic elementary school and which in antebellum days had been the home of George Washington Cable, past the law offices of Moleen Bertrand and the Shadows into the full sunlight and practicality of the business district.

Clete parked by the side of a small office on the corner. The backs of the buildings were old, redbrick, still marked with nineteenth-century lettering. Fifty yards away a tugboat moved down Bayou Teche toward the drawbridge.

Two men in tennis shoes who were too slight to be professional movers were carrying furniture from a U-Haul van into the office.

"Clete?" I said.

"Your licenses will be a breeze. Till we get the paperwork done, I'll put you down as my associate or some bullshit like that."

"You should have asked before you did this."

"I did. You weren't listening," he said.

"Who're these guys?"

"Uh, a package deal from Nig Rosewater Bail Bonds. Nig owes me for a couple of skips I ran down, in fact, it was these two guys right here, and the guys owe Nig for their bonds, so Nig threw in some furniture and everybody wins."

"Clete, I really appreciate this but—"

"It's a done deal, big mon. Tell the guys where you want your desk and file cabinets. Make sure they don't walk out of here with any keys, either." He looked at his watch, then glanced up the street. "Here she comes. Look, take my car back to your house when you get finished, okay? Helen's taking me to lunch."

He saw the look in my eyes.

"So she bats from both sides of the plate. Who's perfect?" he said.

The two of them drove away, waving out the windows as I stood on the sidewalk between Clete's junker Caddy and an office window that had already been lettered with the words ROBICHEAUX, PURCEL, AND ASSOCIATES INVESTIGATIVE AGENCY.

At twilight I drove out to the Bertrand plantation and parked by the grove of gum trees. I didn't have permission to be there, and didn't care. I had wanted to believe my involvement with Sonny Boy, Julia and Moleen, Luke and Ruthie Jean and Bertie Fontenot was over. But I knew better. Even Sweet Pea Chaisson did.

This piece of land was our original sin, except we had found no baptismal rite to expunge it from our lives. That green-purple field of new cane was rooted in rib cage and eye socket. But what of the others whose lives had begun here and ended in other places? The ones who became prostitutes in cribs on Hopkins Street in New Iberia and Jane's Alley in New Orleans, sliced their hands open with oyster knives, laid bare their shin bones with the cane sickle, learned the twelve-string blues on the Red Hat gang and in the camps at Angola with Leadbelly and Hogman Matthew Maxey, were virtually cooked alive in the cast-iron sweatboxes of Camp A, and rode Jim Crow trains North, as in a biblical exodus, to southside Chicago and the magic of 1925 Harlem, where they filled the air with the music of the South and the smell of cornbread and greens and pork chops fixed in sweet potatoes, as though they were still willing to forgive if we would only acknowledge their capacity for forgiveness.

Tolstoy asked how much land did a man need.

Just enough to let him feel the pull of the earth on his ankles and the claim it lays on the quick as well as the dead.

Chapter 23

EVEN THOUGH MY name was on the window, I didn't go to the office and, in fact, didn't formally accept the partnership, even though Bootsie and I needed the income.

Not until three days later, when Clete called the bait shop.

"Check this. Johnny Carp says he wants another sit-down. Eleven o'clock, our office," he said.

"Tell him to stay out of town."

"Not smart, big mon."

"Don't try to negotiate with these guys."

"The guy's rattled about something."

"Who cares?" I said.

"Wake up, Dave. You got no radar anymore. You read the street while you got the chance or it eats you."

I waited until almost eleven, then drove into New Iberia. John Polycarp Giacano's white stretch limo with the charcoal-tinted windows was double-parked in front of the office. A back window was partially lowered and two women with bleached hair and Frankenstein makeup were smoking on the backseat, looking straight ahead, bored, oblivious to each other. Three of Johnny's crew, wearing shades and boxed haircuts, stood on the sidewalk, looking up and down the street as though they were Secret Service agents.

I parked around the corner and walked back to the front door. One of them looked at me from behind his glasses, his expression flat, his hands folded in front of him. He chewed on a paper match in the corner of his mouth, nodding, stepping back to let me pass.

"Is that you, Frankie?" I said.

"Yeah. How you doing, Mr. Robicheaux?" he answered.

"I thought you were away for a while."

"This broad's conscience started bothering her and she changed her testimony. What're you gonna do?" He shrugged his shoulders as though a great metaphysical mystery had been placed on them.

"It might be a good idea to move the limo, Frankie."

"Yeah, I was just going to tell the chauffeur that. Thanks."

"When did Charlie start working with you guys?" I asked.

He held the tips of his fingers in the air, touched his cheek, gestured with his fingers again.

"Who?" he said. His mouth pursed into a small O the size of a Life Saver.

Inside the office, Clete sat behind an army-surplus metal desk, his hands hooked behind his neck. Johnny Carp sat across from him, his arms and legs set at stiff angles, his eyes filled with a black light, his knurled brow like ridges on a washboard. He wore a yellow shirt with the purple letter *G* embroidered on the pocket and a gray suit with dark stripes in it, a yellow handkerchief in the pocket. His shoes were dug into the floor like a man about to leap from a building.

"Dave, help me convince Johnny of something here," Clete said. He smiled good-naturedly.

"What's happening, Johnny?" I said, and sat down on the edge of another metal desk.

"You guys tried to cowboy Patsy Bones," he said.

"Wrong," I said.

"Somebody put a nine-millimeter round six inches from his head. He thinks it come from me," Johnny said.

"I can see that would be a problem," I said.

"Don't crack wise with me, Dave."

"I always treated you with respect, Johnny. But I'm out of the game now. You've got the wrong guy."

"Hear what I'm saying." His close-set eyes and mouth and nose seemed to shrink into an even smaller area in the center of his face. "Don't try to scam us. You want something, you got a hard-on, bring it to the table. But you lay off this voodoo bullshit or whatever it is. I'm talking about Sonny here."

I looked at Clete. He shook his head and turned up his palms.

"You've lost me, Johnny," I said.

"A hooker says she saw him going by on the street-car. Last night Frankie and Marco out there swear either him or his twin brother was walking into Louis Armstrong Park. What white person goes into Louis Armstrong Park at night? Then my wife tells me a redheaded guy was standing in our side yard, looking through our window." A smile tugged at the corner of his mouth. "What, y'all hire an actor or something?" Then his eyes clicked away from mine.

"Nope," I said.

He wiped the front of his teeth with his index finger, rubbed it dry on his knee. His gaze roved around the room.

"This place is a shithole," he said.

"Sonny's dead," Clete said. "You put the whack out, you ought to know, John."

"You're a Magazine Street mick, Purcel, it ain't your fault you always got your foot up your own ass, so I don't take offense," Johnny said. "But, Dave, you got a brain. I'm asking you, no, I'm begging you, if you guys are trying to cowboy Patsy, or fuck with me, or fuck with anybody in my crew, stop it now. I'm in legitimate business. We put a lot of the old ways behind us, but don't provoke me."

His words were those of a man in control. But I could smell a peculiar odor on his breath, like sour baby formula laced with booze.

"It's not us," I said.

"The guy was a disease. Nobody else cared about him," he said.

"Sonny was stand-up, Johnny. He took his own bounce and he didn't need Scotch and milk and a couple of chippies to get him through the morning," I said.

Clete lit a cigarette with his Zippo, his broad shoulders hunched, seemingly unconcerned about the drift of the conversation, but through the smoke his eyes were fastened on Johnny's neck.

"You've developed a bad mouth, Dave. I'm here

for accommodation, you don't want to listen, fuck you. Just don't try to run no games on me," Johnny said.

"The problem's inside you, John. It's not with me or Clete."

"You got an office and some furniture Nig Rosewater couldn't give away in colored town and you're a shrink now?"

"You've got blood on your hands. It doesn't wash off easily," I said.

He rose from his chair, slipped two twenty-dollar bills out of his wallet, and laid them on Clete's desk. "Y'all go up the street, have a nice lunch," he said, and walked out into the sunlight.

Clete tipped his cigarette ashes in the tray. Then he scratched his eyebrow with his thumbnail, as though he didn't know which thought in his head to express first. "You nailed him on that stuff about his chippies. He pays them a hundred bucks to blow him so he won't get AIDS," he said. He tilted back in his swivel chair and stared at the wall. "I can't believe this, the first person in our office is a psychotic greaseball." He mashed out his cigarette and went outside with the two twenties wadded in his fist.

He caught the limo just as it was leaving the curb and knocked with his ring on the charcoal-tinted glass. Johnny Carp was bent forward on the seat when he rolled down the window, a smear of milk on his mouth.

"Hey, John, give this to your broads for their oral hygiene," Clete said, and bounced the bills like soiled green Kleenex off Johnny Carp's face.

* * *

I cut the engine on the outboard and Alafair and I drift on the wake into a sandbar, then walk toward a line of willow and cypress trees. The sun is white, straight overhead, in a blue, cloudless sky. Behind the lacy movement of the trees, in a trapped pool of water, is the rusted, purple outline of a wrecked tow barge. I set up a cardboard box at the end of the sandbar, walk back to the boat, and unzip the carrying case from the Beretta nine-millimeter.

Once again, I show her the safeties and how the trigger mechanism disengages from the hammer, let her work the slide; then I take it from her and slip an empty magazine into the butt.

"Okay, what's the rule, Alf?" I say.

"Never assume a gun is unloaded. But never assume it's loaded, either."

"You've got it. Do you remember how to clear the action?"

She pushes the release button on the butt, drops the magazine, works the slide twice, then peers into the empty chamber.

"Terrific," I say.

This time I give her a loaded magazine. I stand behind her while she chambers a round and takes aim with both hands. She fires once and throws sand in the air by the side of the cardboard box.

"Aim a little higher and to your right, Alf."

She misses twice and the rounds *whang* into the barge back in the trees. But the next round leaves a hole the size of a pencil in the cardboard. She starts to lower the pistol.

"Keep shooting till you're empty, Alf."

The Beretta spits the empty casings into the sunlight, *pow, pow, pow,* each report echoes across the water. The breech locks open; a tongue of cotton white smoke rises from the chamber. The box is tilted sideways now, its clean surfaces peppered with black holes.

When Alafair smiles at me, I wonder if I have given away a knowledge that should never belong to a child.

She wants to reload.

It rained in the predawn hours this morning and the trees in the swamp were gray and shaggy with mist. Then the sun rose out of the steam and broke against the seal of clouds like a flattened rose.

I drop into the office on Main, a sojourner, still not quite accepting the reality of being a fired cop. The door is open to let in the clean smell of the rain tumbling out of the sunlight.

Clete is hooking paper clips in a chain on his desk blotter. I can feel his eyes flicking back and forth between his preoccupation and the side of my face.

"When you chase skips, you've got latitude no cop does," he says. "You can cross state lines, bust in doors without a warrant, pick up one perp to squeeze another. The Supreme Court will get a hand on it eventually, but right now it's kind of like being on point in a free-fire zone."

He knows I'm not listening, but he continues anyway.

"We'll have a secretary in here tomorrow. I'm transferring some of the business from the New Orleans office. It just takes a while to make things come together," he says.

I nod absently, try to avoid looking at my watch.

"You bother me, big mon," he says.

"Don't start it, Clete."

"It's not Sonny's death. It's not getting canned from your department, either. Even though that's what you want me to think."

"I'm not up to it." I splay my fingers in the air.

"The big problem is one that won't go away, Dave. You can't accept change. That's why you always got a firestorm inside you, that's why you ripped up Patsy Dap. You got to ease up, noble mon. You don't have a shield anymore. You smoke the wrong dude, you go down on a murder beef. Take it from a cat who's been there."

"I think I'll go back to the bait shop now," I say.

"Yeah, I guess you better."

"I apologize for my attitude. You've been a real friend about this partnership."

"No big deal. My business in New Orleans is going down the drain, anyway."

Outside, the rain is blowing in the sunlight. When I look back through the office window, Clete is drinking coffee, staring at nothing, alone in the silence, a new, virtually unused white telephone on his army surplus desk.

I feel a pain in my chest and go back inside the office. Together, we walk down Main to Victor's for lunch.

* * *

Johnny Carp had made a pilgrimage to New Iberia, his second attempt at reconciliation. He was a mercurial headcase, a functioning drunk, a physiological caricature, a libidinous nightmare whose sexual habits you tried never to think about, but, most important, Johnny, like all drunks, was driven by a self-centered fear that made his kind see blood in tap water and dead men walking out of the surf.

I called Helen Soileau at the sheriff's department.

"What's the deal on Patsy Dapolito?" I asked.

"He has a rental dump by a pipeyard on the Jeanerette Road. Somebody popped one right through his bedroom window."

"It was a nine-millimeter?"

"Or a .38. It was pretty beat up. Why?"

"Johnny Carp thinks Sonny was the shooter."

"Big reach from the salt." She paused. "Sorry," she said.

"Sonny's nine-millimeter is still in Possessions, isn't it?" I said.

"I hate to admit this, but I asked that question myself. No."

"What happened to it?"

"We didn't charge him with carrying a concealed weapon because we busted him in Orleans Parish. So when he skated on the murder beef, he was home free and got his nine back. A Smith & Wesson, right?"

"What's the status on Dapolito?"

"We painted his doorknobs with roach paste so he can't go outside. Come on, Dave, what status? Even New Orleans doesn't know how to deal with this guy.

We get three or four calls a day on him. He took a leak in the washbasin at Mulate's."

"Thanks for your help, Helen."

"It's not right what the old man did. I told him what I thought, too."

"You shouldn't take my weight."

She was quiet, as if she was deciding something, perhaps a choice about trust, which was always Helen's most difficult moment.

"I've got an awful feeling, Streak. It's like somebody put out a cigarette on my stomach lining. I get up in the morning with it."

"Feeling about what?"

"They tore Della Landry apart with their bare hands. They took down Sonny Marsallus in broad daylight. You watch your butt, you understand me?"

"Don't worry about me."

I heard her hand clench and squeak on the receiver.

"I'm not explaining myself well," she said. "When I dropped those two perps, I saw my face on theirs. That's how I feel now. Do you understand what I'm talking about?"

I told her it was her imagination, to get away from that kind of thinking. I told her Batist was waiting for me down at the dock.

My answer was not an honest one.

Later, I sat in the backyard and tried to convince myself that my evasiveness was based on concern for a friend. A physician turns his eyes into meaningless glass, shows no expression when he listens through a stethoscope, I told myself. But that wasn't it. Her fear, whether for me or herself, had made me angry.

When you buy into premonitions, you jinx yourself and everyone around you. Ask anyone who's smelled its vinegar reek in the man next to him.

I remembered a helicopter hovering against a fiery red ball that could have been heated in a devil's forge, its blades thropping monotonously, the red dust and plumes from smoke grenades swirling into the air. But for those of us who lay on poncho liners, our wounds sealed with crusted field dressings and our own dried fluids, the dust was forming itself into an enormous, animate shape—domed, slack-jawed, leering, the nose a jagged hole cut in bone, a death's head that ballooned larger and larger above the clearing and called our names through the churning of the blades, the din of voices on the ground, the popping of small-arms fire that was now part of somebody else's war, just like the watery sound of a human voice speaking into an electric fan.

And if you did not shut out the syllables of your name, or if you looked into the face of the man next to you and allowed the peculiar light in his eyes to steal into your own, your soul could take flight from your breast as quickly as a dog tag being snipped onto a wire ring.

The sheriff called me early the next morning.

"I can't just deal you out, Dave. You need to be told this," he said.

"What?"

"Sweet Pea and a black woman. We're not sure who she is yet."

"Could you start over?" I said.

During the night a farmer had seen a cone of fire burning in an oak grove out by Cade. The heat was so intense the trees were scaled and baked into black stone. After the firemen covered the Cadillac with foam and stared through the smoke still billowing off the exploded tires, they made out the carbonized remains of two figures sitting erectly on the springs of the front seat, their lipless mouths wide with secrets that had risen like ash into the scorched air.

"The pathologist says double-ought bucks," the sheriff said.

But he knew that was not the information I was waiting for.

"Sweet Pea had on a locket with his mother's name engraved on it," he said. Then he said, "I don't have any idea who she is, Dave. Look, I've already tried to find Ruthie Jean. She's disappeared. What else can I tell you? I don't like making this damn phone call."

I guess you don't, I thought.

Chapter 24

I CALLED CLETE at the small house he had rented by City Park and asked him to meet me at the office on Main. When I got there the newly hired secretary was hanging a curtain on the front window. She was a short, thick-bodied blond woman, with orange rouge on her cheeks and a pleasant smile.

"Clete didn't get here yet?" I said.

"He went for some coffee. Are you Mr. Robicheaux?"

"Yes. How do you do? I'm sorry, I didn't get your name."

"Terry Serrett. It's nice to know you, Mr. Robicheaux."

"You're not from New Iberia, are you?"

"No, I grew up in Opelousas."

"I see. Well, it's nice meeting you," I said.

Through the window I saw Clete crossing the street with a box of doughnuts and three sealed paper cups of coffee. I met him at the door.

"Let's take it with us," I said.

He drove with one hand and ate with the other on the way out to Cade. The top was down and his sandy hair was blowing on his forehead.

"How are you going to pay a secretary?" I said.

"She works for five bucks an hour."

"That's five bucks more than we're making," I said.

He shook his head and smiled to himself.

"What's the joke?" I asked.

"We're going out to see where Sweet Pea Chaisson got turned into a human candle."

"Yeah?"

"Are we on somebody's clock? Am I a dumb shit who's missed something?"

"You want to go back?"

He set his coffee cup in a wire ring that was attached to his dashboard and tried to put on his porkpie hat without losing it in the wind.

"You think they're wiping the slate clean?" he said.

"Their object lessons tend to be in Technicolor."

"Why the black woman?"

"Wrong place, wrong time, maybe. Unless the dead woman is Ruthie Jean Fontenot."

"I don't get it. Black people keep showing up in the middle of all this bullshit. Let's face it, mon. Ripping off the food stamp brigade isn't exactly the big score for these guys."

"It's land."

"For what?"

I didn't have an answer.

We drove down a gravel road through sugar and cattle acreage, then turned into an empty field where a section of barbed wire fence had been knocked flat. The weeds in the field were crisscrossed with tire tracks, and in the distance I could see the oak grove and a bright yellow strand of crime scene tape jittering in the wind.

Clete parked by the trees and we got out and walked into the shade. The fire-gutted, lopsided shell of Sweet Pea's convertible was covered with magpies. I picked up a rock and sailed it into the frame; they rose in an angry clatter through the leafless branches overhead.

Clete fanned the air in front of his face.

"I don't think the ME got everything off the springs," he said.

"Look at this," I said. "There's glass blown into the backseat and a partial pattern on top of the door." I inserted my little finger into a ragged hole at the top of the passenger door, then looked at the ground for empty shell casings. There weren't any.

"What a way to get it," Clete said.

"You can see the angle of fire," I said. "Look at the holes in the paneling just behind the driver's seat." I aimed over the top of my extended arm and stepped backward several feet. "Somebody stood just about where I'm standing now and fired right into their faces."

"I don't see Sweet Pea letting himself get set up like this," Clete said.

"Somebody he trusted got in the backseat. Another car followed. Then the dice were out of the cup."

"I got to get out of this smell," Clete said. He walked back into the sunlight, spit in the weeds, and wiped his eyes on his forearm.

"You all right?" I said.

"In 'Nam I saw a tank burn. The guys inside

couldn't get out. I don't like remembering it, that's all."

I nodded.

"So I probably signed Sweet Pea's death warrant when I put him in the trunk of my car," he said. "But that's the breaks, right? One more piece of shit scrubbed off the planet." With his shoe he rubbed the place where he had spit.

"You blaming yourself for the woman?" I asked.

He didn't have time to answer. We heard a car on the gravel road. It slowed, then turned through the downed fence and rolled across the field, the weeds rattling and flattening under the bumper.

"I know that guy, what's his name, he thinks we should be buddies because we were both in the Crotch," Clete said.

"Rufus Arceneaux," I said.

"Oh, oh, he doesn't look like he wants to be friends anymore."

Rufus cut the engine and got out of the car. He wore tight blue jeans and a faded yellow polo shirt and his pilot's sunglasses, with his badge and holster clipped on a western belt. A small black boy of about ten, in an Astros baseball cap and oversize T-shirt, sat in the backseat. The windows were rolled up to keep the air-conditioning inside the car. But the engine was off now and the doors were shut.

"What the hell do you think you're doing?" Rufus said.

"The sheriff called me this morning," I said.

"He told you to come out here?"

"Not exactly."

"Then you'd better get out of here."

"Did y'all find out who the broad was?" Clete said.

"It's not your business, pal," Rufus said.

"*Pal.* Terrific," Clete said. "Who's the kid? He looks like he's about to melt."

"Did y'all find any shell casings?" I said, and opened the back door to Rufus's car and brought the little boy outside. There was a dark, inverted V in his blue jeans where he had wet his pants.

"I don't know what it is with you, Robicheaux," Rufus said. "But, to be honest, I'd like to beat the living shit out of you."

"What are you doing with the boy?" I said.

"His mother didn't come home. I'm taking him to the shelter. Now, y'all get the fuck out of here."

I squatted down on my haunches and looked into the little boy's face. His upper lip was beaded with sweat.

"Where do you live, podna?" I asked.

"In the trailer, up yonder on the road."

"What's your mama's name?"

"Gloria Dumaine. They call her 'Glo' where she work."

"Does she work at the juke?" I said.

"Yes, suh. That's where she gone last night. She ain't been back."

I stood erect and put my fingers lightly on Rufus's arm, turned him toward the trees. I saw the skin stretch tight at the corners of his eyes.

"Walk over here with me," I said.

"What . . ."

"I know his mother," I said. "She knew something

about the decapitated floater we pulled out of the slough in Vermilion Parish. I think she was in the car with Sweet Pea."

He removed his sunglasses, his eyes looking from the burned Caddy to the little boy. His mouth was a tight seam, hooked downward at the corners, his expression wary, as though a trap were being set for him.

"Take the little boy to the shelter. I'll call the sheriff and tell him what I told you," I said.

"I'll handle it from here," he said.

I walked over to Clete's convertible and got inside.

"Let's hit it," I said.

As we drove across the field toward the gravel road, I looked back toward the oak grove. Rufus was squatting on his haunches, smoking a cigarette, staring at the scorched hulk in the trees, a man whose keen vision could snap the twine off Gordian knots. The little boy stood unnoticed and unattended in the sunlight, like a black peg tamped into the weeds, one hand trying to hide the wetness in his jeans.

They had killed Sweet Pea and Gloria. Who was next? I didn't want to think about it.

I drove to the office on Main with Clete, then walked down to Moleen Bertrand's law offices across from the Shadows. His secretary told me he had gone home for lunch. I drove across the drawbridge, past the old graystone convent, which was now closed and awaiting the wrecking ball, and followed the winding drive through City Park to Moleen's deep, oak-shaded lawn and rambling white house on Bayou Teche.

Julia was spading weeds out of a rosebed by the driveway, a conical straw hat on her head. She looked up and smiled at me as I drove by. Her shoulders were tan and covered with freckles and the skin above her halter looked dry and coarse in the sunlight. Behind her, balanced in the St. Augustine grass, was a tall highball glass wrapped with a napkin and rubber band.

Moleen was eating a tuna fish sandwich on a paper plate inside the Plexiglas-enclosed back porch. He looked rested, composed, his eyes clear, almost serene. Outside, blue hydrangeas bloomed as big as cantaloupes against the glass.

"I'm sorry to bother you at home," I said.

"It's no bother. Sit down. What can I do for you? You want something to eat?"

"You're looking good."

"I'm glad you approve."

"I'm not here to give you a bad time, Moleen."

"Thank you."

"Did you hear about a guy named Sweet Pea Chaisson getting whacked out by Cade?"

"I'm afraid not."

"A black woman died with him."

He nodded, the sandwich in his mouth. His eyes were flat. Against the far wall was a mahogany-and-glass case full of shotguns and bolt-action rifles.

"Call it off," I said.

"What?"

"I think you have influence with certain people."

"I have influence over no one, my friend."

"Where's Ruthie Jean?"

"You're abusing my hospitality, sir."

"Give it up, Moleen. Change your life. Get away from these guys while there's time."

His eyes dropped to his plate; the ball of one finger worked at the corner of his mouth. When he looked at me again, I could see a nakedness in his face, a thought translating into words, a swelling in the voice box, the lips parting as though he were about to step across a line and clasp someone's extended hand.

Then it disappeared.

"Thanks for dropping by," he said.

"Yeah, you bet, Moleen. I don't think you picked up on my purpose, though."

"I didn't?" he said, wiping his chin with a linen napkin, his white shirt as crinkly and fresh as if he had just put it on.

"I have a feeling me and Clete Purcel might be on somebody's list. Don't let me be right."

He looked at something outside, a butterfly hovering in a warm air current against the glass.

"Read *Faust*, Moleen. Pride's a pile of shit," I said.

"I was never theologically inclined."

"See you," I said, and walked out into the humidity and the acrid reek of the chemical fertilizer Julia was feverishly working into her rosebushes.

But my conversation with him was not over. Two hours later he called me at the bait shop.

"I don't want to see you or your friend harmed. That's God's honest truth," he said.

"Then tell me what you're into."

"Dave, take the scales off your eyes. We don't serve flags or nations anymore. It's all business today. The ethos of Robert E. Lee is as dead as the world we grew up in."

"Speak for yourself."

He slammed the receiver down.

It was hot and dry that night, and through the bedroom I could see veins of heat lightning crawl and flicker through the clouds high above the swamp. Bootsie woke and turned toward me. The window fan made revolving shadows on her face and shoulders.

"Can't you sleep?" she said.

"I'm sorry, I didn't mean to wake you."

"Are you worried about our finances?"

"Not really. We're doing okay."

She placed one arm across my side.

"The department did you wrong, Dave. Accept it and let it go. We don't need them. What do you call that in AA?"

"Working the Third Step. But that's not it, Boots. I think Johnny Giacano or these military guys are starting to take people off the board."

"They'd better not try it around here," she said.

I looked into her face. It was calm, without anger or any display of self-manufactured feeling. Then she said, "If one of those sonsofbitches tries to harm anyone in this family, he's going to think the wrath of God walked into his life."

I started to smile, then looked at the expression in her eyes and thought better of it.

"I believe you, kiddo," I said.

"Kiddo, yourself," she answered.

She tilted her head slightly on the pillow and moved

her fingers on my hip. I kissed her mouth, then her eyes and hair and ran my hands down her back.

Bootsie never did anything in half measures. She closed the door that gave onto the hallway—in case Alafair got up from bed and went into the kitchen for a drink of water—then pulled off her nightgown and stepped out of her panties in front of the window. She had the smoothest complexion of any woman I'd ever known, and in the spinning shadows of the window fan's blades the curves and surfaces of her body looked like those of a perfectly formed statue coming to life against a shattering of primordial light.

I moved on top of her and she hooked her legs inside mine and pressed her palms into the small of my back, buried her mouth in my neck, ran her fingers up my spine into my hair, rolled her rump in a slow circle as her breath grew louder in my ear and her words became a single, heart-twisting syllable: "Dave . . . Dave . . . Dave . . . oh Dave . . ."

It started to rain outside, unexpectedly, the water sluicing hard off the roof, splaying in front of the window fan. The wind-stiffened branches of the oak tree seemed to drip with a wet light, and I felt Bootsie lock her arms around my rib cage and draw me deeper inside her, into coral caves beneath the sea where there was neither thought nor fear, only an encompassing undulating current that rose and fell as warmly as her breast.

I had wired my house with a burglar alarm system that I couldn't afford and had taught my thirteen-year-old daughter how to use a weapon that could turn an intruder into potted meat product.

I also had dragged my insomnia and worry into the nocturnal world of my wife.

Who was becoming the prisoner of fear? Or, better put, who was allowing himself to become a spectator while others wrote his script?

Early Saturday morning Clete took one of my outboards down the bayou, with his spinning rod and a carton of red wigglers, and came back with a stringer of bream and sun perch that he lifted out of his cooler like a heavy, gold-green ice-slick chain. He knelt on the planks in the lee of the bait shop and began cleaning them in a pan of bloody water, neatly half-mooning the heads off at the gills.

"You should have gone out with me," he said.

"That's like inviting the postman for a long walk on his day off," I said.

He put an unlit cigarette in his mouth and smiled. The fish blood on his fingers made tiny prints on the cigarette paper.

"You look sharp, big mon. How about I take y'all to Possum's for lunch?" he said.

"Not today . . . I'm going to New Orleans in a few minutes. I told Bootsie you might hang around a little bit."

He got to his feet and washed his hands under a faucet by the rail.

"What are you up to, Streak?"

"I'm tired of living in a bull's-eye."

"Who's going to cover your back, mon?" he said, drying his hands on a rag.

"Thanks for watching the house," I said, and walked back up the dock to my truck. When I looked in the rearview mirror, he was leaning against the dock rail, his face shadowed by his hat, one hand propped on his hip. The wind was hot blowing across the swamp and smelled of beached gars and humus drying in the sunlight. Just as I started my truck, the shadows of large birds streaked across the surface of the bayou. I looked into the sky and saw a circle of buzzards descending out of their pattern into the cypress, their wings clattering for balance just before they lighted on their prey.

There are a lot of ways to see New Orleans. At the right time of day the Quarter is wonderful. A streetcar ride up St. Charles Avenue through the Garden District, past Audubon Park and Tulane, is wonderful anytime. Or you can try it another way, which I don't recommend.

Those who feed at the bottom of the food chain—the hookers, pimps, credit card double-billers, Murphy artists, stalls and street dips—usually work out of bars and strip joints and do a relatively minor amount of damage. They're given to the classical hustle and con and purloined purse rather than to physical injury.

One rung up are the street dealers. Not all of them, but most, are black, young, dumb, and carry a Jones themselves. The rock they deal in the projects almost guarantees drug-induced psychosis; anything else they sell has been stepped on so many times you might as well try to get high huffing baby laxative or fixing with powdered milk.

In another category are people who simply deal in criminal finance. They're usually white, older, have few arrests and own legitimate businesses of some kind. They fence stolen property, operate chop shops, and wash stolen and counterfeit money, which sells for ten to twenty cents on the dollar, depending on its origins or quality.

Then there is the edge of the Quarter, where, if you're drunk or truly unlucky, you can wander out of a controlled and cosmetic libertine environment into a piece of moral moonscape—Louis Armstrong Park or the St. Louis cemeteries will do just fine—where kids will shoot a woman through the face at point-blank range for amounts of money you could pry out of a parking meter with a screwdriver. The murders receive national attention when the victim is a foreign tourist. Otherwise, they go on with unremarkable regularity, to the point that Louisiana now has the highest murder rate per capita in the United States.

Those at the top of the chain—dealers who form the liaison between Colombia and the wetlands, casino operators who front points for a Mafia-owned amusement company in Chicago—seldom do time or even have their names publicly connected with the forces they serve. They own newspaper people and literally employ the governor's children. Floating casino owners with state legislators on a pad work their shuck on morning television shows like good-natured Rotarians; Mafiosi who some think conspired to kill John Kennedy tend their roses and dine unnoticed in downtown restaurants.

It's not exaggeration.

I took the tour, thinking I could find information in the streets of New Orleans that had eluded me at home, and came up empty. But what should I have expected? Back alley hypes, graduates of City Prison, and prostitutes with AIDS (one of whom, with a haunted look in her eyes, asked me if the stories were true about this place called Lourdes) were people whose idea of a successful scam was to drill holes in their electric meters and pour honey inside so ants would foul and retard the mechanism or, more indicatively of the fear that defined their lives, wondered daily if the Mexican tar and water they watched bubbling in a heated spoon was not indeed the keyhole to the abyss where all the hungry gargoyles and grinding sounds of their childhoods awaited them.

It rained at dusk and I sat under the pavilion at the Cafe du Monde and ate a plate of beignets with powdered sugar and drank coffee *au lait*. I was tired and wet and there was a hum, a pinging sound in my head, the way your eardrums feel when you've stayed under water too long at a depth beyond your tolerance. St. Louis Cathedral and the park in Jackson Square were gray in the rain, and a cold mist was blowing under the eaves of the pavilion. A young college couple with a portable stereo crossed against the light and ran breathlessly out of the rain into the cafe and sat at a table next to me. They ordered, and the boy peeled the cellophane off a musical tape and stuck it in his machine.

Anybody who grew up in south Louisiana during the fifties would remember those songs: "Big Blue Diamond," "Shirley Jean," "Lawdy Miss Clawdy," "I Need Somebody Bad Tonight," "Mathilda," "Betty and Dupree," and "I Got the Rockin' Pneumonia and the Boogie Woogie Flu."

I hadn't realized I was staring.

"You like those songs?" the boy said.

"Sure, you bet," I said. "They're hard to beat."

"We bought them over on the corner. It's great stuff," he said.

"I saw those guys. Cookie and the Cupcakes, Lloyd Price, Warren Storm. They used to play around here."

They smiled and nodded, as though they were familiar with all those names, too, then tried to return to their own conversation without seeming impolite. I felt suddenly old and foolish.

I wanted to drive back home, mark off the day, forget all the faces I had looked into, erase the seared voices that could have been those of William Blake's lost souls on Lower Thames Street.

But I knew what I had to do. I was no longer a cop. My family was at risk as long as Johnny Carp thought I was a threat to one of his enterprises. I had told Moleen pride was a pile of shit. I wondered how good I would be at accepting my own admonition.

I walked back toward Esplanade, got in my truck, and headed up the entrance ramp to I-10 and Jefferson Parish. I thought I saw a chartreuse Cadillac convertible in my rearview mirror; then it disappeared in a swirl of rain.

The Giacano family had successfully controlled New Orleans for many reasons, one of which was the fact that they loved the appearance of normalcy and lived in upper-middle-class homes that didn't draw attention to their wealth. Johnny's limo stayed in a garage downtown; when he drove home from work, it was in his Lincoln. Johnny knew if there was one emotion that could overcome fear—which he instilled in his enemies with regularity—it was envy.

When whites began to flee New Orleans for Jefferson Parish and Metairie, the political base of David Duke, Johnny went with them. He joined any club he could buy his way into, pushed a basket around in the supermarket on Saturday mornings, played softball in the neighborhood park, and on Saturday nights threw huge dinners, where the tables with checkered cloths groaned with platters of pasta, sausage, meatballs, and baked lasagna, at a working-class Italian restaurant by the lake.

It was a strange evening. The rain was blowing harder now, and the swells in the lake were dark green and dimpled with rain, the causeway haloed with mist and electric lights all the way across the water to Covington, but the late sun had broken free of the clouds on the horizon and filled the western sky with a red glow like flames inside oil smoke.

It was a happy, crowded place, with wide verandas and high windows, private banquet rooms, a long railed bar, potted palms and plush maroon sofas by the cash register. I took off my seersucker coat in the men's room, dried my hair and face with paper towels, straightened my tie, tried to brush the powdered sugar from the Cafe du Monde off my charcoal shirt, then combed my hair and looked in the mirror. I didn't want to go back outside; I didn't want to say the words I would have to say. I had to look away from my own reflection.

Johnny was entertaining in a back room, with lacquered pine paneling and windows that gave onto the lake and the lighted sailboats that rocked in the swells. He was at the bar, in fine form, dressed in tailored, pegged gray slacks, tasseled loafers, plum-colored socks, a bright yellow dress shirt with bloodred cuff links as big as cherries. His marcelled hair gleamed like liquid plastic, his teeth were pink with wine. The hood at the door was in a jovial mood, too, and when I said, "I got no piece, I got no shield, Max," he smiled and answered, "I know that, Mr. Robicheaux. Johnny seen you outside. He wants you come on in and have a good time."

I ordered a Dr Pepper and drank it five feet from where Johnny was holding a conversation with a half dozen people. My presence never registered in his face while he grinned and beamed and told a joke, rocking on the balls of his feet, his lips pursed as he neared the conclusion of his story, a clutch of fifty-dollar bills folded in a fan between his ringed fingers.

Again, I could hear a peculiar creaking sound in my head, like the weight of a streetcar pinging through steel track. I looked out the rain-streaked side window and thought I saw Clete Purcel staring back at me. When I blinked and widened my eyes, he was gone.

I finished my Dr Pepper and ordered another. I kept looking directly into Johnny's face. Finally I said it, gave recognition to his power, acknowledged my dependence on his mood and the enormous control he had over the lives of others: "Johnny, I need a minute of your time."

"Sure, Dave," he said, and moved toward me along the bar, pointed toward his Manhattan glass for the bartender. "How you doin'? You didn't bring that Irish ape, did you? Hey, just kidding. Purcel don't bother me. You ever know his mother? She was a wet-brain, used to sell out of her pants when her old man run off. Ask anybody in the Channel."

"Can we talk somewhere?" I said.

"This is good." Two of his hoods stood behind him, eating out of paper plates, salami and salad hanging off their lips. Their steroid-pumped upper arms had the diameter and symmetry of telephone poles inside their sports coats. "Don't be shy. What's the problem?"

"No problem. That's what I'm saying, Johnny. I'm no threat to you guys."

"What am I listening to here? I ever said you were a problem?" He turned to his men, a mock incredulous look on his face.

"My daughter saw a guy hanging around our house, Johnny. You think I have information, which I don't. They pulled my shield, I'm out of the game, I don't care what you guys do. I'm asking you to stay away from me and my family."

"You hear this crazy guy?" he said to his hoods.

Then to me, "Eat some dinner, drink some wine, you got my word, anybody bother you with anything, you bring it to me."

"I appreciate your attitude, Johnny," I said.

My palms felt damp, thick, hard to fold at my sides. I was sweating inside my shirt. I swallowed and looked away from the smile on his face.

"I accused you of something that was in the imagination. I'm sorry about that," he said. His men were grinning now.

"Excuse me?" I said.

"A redheaded guy, looked like Sonny Boy Marsallus, out at my house, walking around downtown, I asked you and Purcel if you'd hired an actor, remember?" he said.

I nodded.

"There he is," he said, and pointed to a man in a white jacket busing a table. "He's Sonny's cousin, a retard or something, I got him a job here. He looks just like him, except his brains probably run out his nose."

"He looks like a stuffed head," one of Johnny's men said.

"He'd make a great doorstop," the other man said.

"Why was he at your house?" I said. The skin of my face burned and my voice felt weak in my throat.

"He was looking for a job. He'd been out there with Sonny once. Now he's making six bucks an hour and tips cleaning slops. So I done a good one for Sonny."

One of the men behind Johnny gargled with his drink.

"Salt water's good for the throat," he said to me. "Take a glass-bottom boat ride, Robicheaux, ask Sonny if that ain't true."

Johnny stripped a folded fifty out of the fan in his hand and dropped it on my forearm.

"Get something nice for your daughter," he said. "You done the right thing here tonight." He reached out with one hand and adjusted the knot in my tie.

I saw the balloon of red-black color well up behind my eyes, heard a sound like wet newspaper ripping in my head, saw the startled and fearful look in his face just before I hooked him above the mouth, hard, snapping my shoulder into it, his nose flattening, his upper lip splitting against his teeth. I caught him again on the way down, behind the ear, then brought my knee into his face and knocked his head into the bar.

I kept waiting for his men to reach inside their coats, to pinion my arms, but they didn't move. My breath was heaving in my chest, my hands were locked on the lip of the bar, like a man aboard ship during a gale, and I was doing something that seemed to have no connection with me. He fought to get up, and I saw my shoe bite into his chin, his ear, his raised forearm, his rib cage, I felt Johnny Carp cracking apart like eggshell under my feet.

"Mother of God, that's enough, Dave!" I heard Clete shout behind me. Then I felt his huge arm knock me backward, away from Johnny's body, which was curled in an embryonic position next to the brass bar rail, his yellow shirt streaked with saliva and blood, his fists clenched on his head.

Then Clete laced his fingers under my arm, a paper

bag crushed against the contour of his palm, and drew me back toward the door with him, a pistol-grip, sawed-down double-barrel twelve-gauge pointed at Johnny's men. The only sound in the room was the service door to the kitchen flipping back and forth on its hinges. The faces of the diners were as expressionless as candle wax, as though any movement of their own would propel them into a terrible flame. I felt Clete push me out into the darkness and the cold odor of an impending electric storm that invaded the trees like a fog. He shoved the sawed-down twelve-gauge into the paper bag and threw it on the seat of his convertible.

"Oh Dave," he said. "Noble mon . . ." He shook his head and started his car without finishing his sentence, his eyes hollow and lustrous with a dark knowledge, as though he had just seen the future.

Chapter 25

BY MONDAY MORNING nothing had happened. No knock at the door from New Orleans plainclothes, no warrant cut. To my knowledge, not even an investigation in progress.

The sky was clear and blue, windless, the day warm, the sun as bright as a shattered mirror on the bayou's surface. After the early fishermen had left the dock and I had started the fire in the barbecue pit for the lunches Batist and I would sell later, I called Clete at the office on Main.

"You need me for anything?" I said.

"Not really. It's pretty quiet."

"I'm going to work at the dock today."

"He's coming, Dave."

"I know."

The priest sits next to me on the weathered planks of the bleachers by the baseball diamond at New Iberia High. The school building is abandoned, the windows broken by rocks, pocked with BB holes. The priest is a tall, gray, crewcut man who used to be a submarine pitcher for the Pelicans back in the days of the Evangeline League and later became an early member of Martin Luther King's Southern Christian Leadership

Conference. Today he belongs to the same AA group I do.

"Did you go to the restaurant with that purpose in mind?" he asks.

"No."

"Then it wasn't done with forethought. It was an impetuous act. That's the nature of anger."

It's dusk and the owner of the pawn and gun shop on the corner rattles the glass in his door when he slams and locks it. Two black kids in ball caps gaze through the barred window at the pistols on display.

"Dave?"

"I tried to kill him."

"That's a bit more serious," he says.

The black kids cross the street against the red light and pass close to the bleachers, in the shadows, oblivious to our presence. One picks up a rock, sails it clattering through a tree next to the school building. I hear a faint tinkle of glass inside.

"Because of your friend, what was his name, Sonny Boy?" the priest says.

"I think he put the hit on Sonny. I can't prove it, though."

His hands are long and slender, with liver spots on the backs. His skin makes a dry sound when he rubs one hand on top of the other.

"What bothers you more than anything else in the world, Dave?"

"I beg your pardon?"

"Vietnam? The death of your wife Annie? Revisiting the booze in your dreams?"

When I don't reply, he lifts one hand, gestures at

the diamond, the ruined school building that's become softly molded inside the fading twilight. A torn kite, caught by its string on an iron fire escape, flaps impotently against a wall.

"It's all this, isn't it?" he says. "We're still standing in the same space where we grew up but we don't recognize it anymore. It's like other people own it now."

"How did you know?"

"You want absolution for what you did to this guy?"

"Yes."

"Dave, when we say the Serenity Prayer about acceptance, we have to mean it. I can absolve sins but I can't set either one of us free from the nature of time."

"It has nothing to do with time. It's what we've allowed them to do—all of them, the dope traffickers, the industrialists, the politicians. We gave it up without even a fight."

"I'm all out of words," he says, and lays his hand on my shoulder. It has the weightlessness of an old man's. He looks at the empty diamond with a private thought in his eyes, one that he knows his listener is not ready to hear.

"Come on down to the office and talk to somebody for me, will you?" Clete said when I answered the phone early the next morning. Then he told me who.

"I don't want to talk to him," I said.

"You're going to enjoy this. I guarantee it."

Twenty minutes later I parked my truck in front

of the office. Through the window I could see Patsy Dapolito sitting in a wood chair next to my desk, his brow furrowed as he stared down at the BB game that he tilted back and forth in his hands. His face looked like stitched pink rubber molded against bone.

I walked inside and sat behind my desk. The new secretary looked up and smiled, then went back to typing a letter.

"Tell Dave what's on your mind, get his thoughts on it," Clete said to the back of Patsy's head.

"You guys hire operatives. Maybe we can work something out," Patsy said.

"Like work for us, you mean?" I asked.

"Nobody catches any flies on you. I can see that," he answered, and tilted more BB's into the tiny holes of his game.

Clete widened his eyes and puffed air in his cheeks to suppress the humor in his face.

"We're not hiring right now, Patsy. Thanks, anyway," I said.

"Who tried to peel your box?" he said.

Clete and I looked at each other.

"You didn't know your place got creeped?" He laughed, then pointed with his thumb to the safe. "You can punch 'em, peel 'em, or burn 'em. The guy tried to do this one was a fish. He should have gone through the dial."

Clete got up from his desk and rubbed his fingers along the prised edge of the safe, then went to the front and back doors.

"How'd the guy get in?" he said to me, his face blank.

"It's called a lock pick, Purcel," Patsy said.

"There're no scratches," Clete said to me.

"Maybe the safe was already damaged when you got it from Nig," I said. But Clete was already shaking his head.

Patsy lit a cigarette, held it upward in the cone of his fingers, blew smoke around it as though he were creating an artwork in the air.

"There's a hit on me. I got a proposition," he said.

"Tell me who Charlie is," I said.

"Charlie? What the fuck you talking about?"

"Would you watch your language, please," I said.

"Language? That's what's you guys got on your mind, I use bad language?" he said.

"You're a beaut, Patsy," I said.

"Yeah? Well, fuck you. The hit's coming from Johnny Carp. You stomped the shit out of him, Robicheaux; Purcel bounced money off his face. That gives all of us a mutual interest, you get my drift?"

"Thanks for coming by," I said.

He stood up, ground his cigarette out in an ashtray, stabbing it into the ceramic as though he were working an angry thought out of his mind.

"Marsallus ever wash up on the shore?" he said.

"No, why?" I said.

"No reason. I wish I'd been there for it. It was time somebody broke that mutt's legs."

"Get out," I said.

When he walked past the secretary, he drew his finger, like a line of ice water, across the back of her neck.

* * *

When I closed the bait shop that night and walked up the dock toward the house, I saw Luke Fontenot waiting for me in the shadows of the oaks that overhung the road. He wore a pair of pink slacks, a braided cloth belt, a black shirt with the collar turned up on the neck. He flipped a toothpick out onto the road.

"What's up, partner?" I said.

"Come out to the plantation wit' me."

"Nope."

"Ruthie Jean and me want to bring all this to an end."

"What are you saying?"

"Moleen Bertrand gonna fix it so it come out right for everybody."

"I'm afraid I'm not one of his fans, Luke."

"Talk to my Aint Bertie. If it come from you, she gonna listen." I could hear the strain, like twisted wire, in his throat.

"To what? No, don't tell me. Somebody's going to give y'all a lot of money. Sounds great. Except Bertie's one of those rare people who's not for sale and just wants her little house and garden and the strip Moleen's grandfather gave y'all's family."

"You ain't got to the part that counts most."

He rubbed a mosquito bite on his neck, looked hotly into my face.

"Moleen and Ruthie Jean?" I said.

"That's what it always been about, Mr. Dave. But if it don't go right, if Aint Bertie gonna act old and stubborn . . . There's some bad white people gonna be out there. I'm between Ruthie Jean and that old woman. What I'm gonna do?"

I followed him in my truck out to the Bertrand plantation. The sky was freckled with birds, the air heavy with smoke from a trash fire, full of dust blowing out of the fields. The grove of gum trees at the end of the road thrashed in black-green silhouette against the dying sun. While he told me a story of reconciliation and promise I sat with Luke on the tiny gallery of the house from which he and Ruthie Jean had been evicted, and I wondered if our most redeeming quality, our willingness to forgive, was not also the instrument most often used to lay bare and destroy the heart.

Moleen had found Luke first, then Ruthie Jean, the latter in a motel in a peculiar area of north Lafayette where Creoles and blacks and white people seemed to traverse one another's worlds without ever identifying with any one of them. He spent the first night with her in the motel, a low-rent 1940s cluster of stucco boxes that had once been called the Truman Courts. While he made love to her, she lay with her head propped up on pillows, her hands lightly touching his shoulders, her gaze pointed at the wall, neither encouraging nor dissuading his passion, which seemed as insatiable as it was unrequited.

Then in the middle of the night he sat naked on the side of the bed, his skin so white it almost glowed, his forearms on his thighs, his confession of betrayal and hypocrisy so spontaneous and devoid of ulterior motive that she knew she would have to forgive whatever injury he had done her or otherwise his sin would become her own.

She rose to her knees, pressed him back on the pillow, then mounted him and kissed his face and throat, made love to him almost as though he were a child.

When the light broke against the window curtains in the morning and she heard the sound of diesel trucks outside, car doors slamming, people talking loudly because they didn't care if others slept or not, all the hot, busy noise of another day in the wrong part of town, she could feel the nocturnal intimacy of their time together slipping away from her, and she knew he would shower soon, drink coffee with her, be fond, even affectionate, while the attention in his eyes wandered, then begin to refocus on the world that awaited him with all the guarantees of his race and position as soon as he left the motel.

But instead he drove them to Galveston, where they ate lunch at a hotel restaurant on the beach, rented a boat and fished for speckled trout in the deep drop-off beyond the third sandbar, walked barefoot along the edge of the surf by the old World War I fort at sunset, and on a whim flew to Monterrey to watch a bullfight the next afternoon.

By the time they returned to Lafayette, Ruthie Jean believed her life had turned a corner she had not thought possible.

"He's leaving his wife?" I said.

"He give his word. He cain't stay with Miss Julia no more," Luke said.

I didn't say anything for a long time.

"You're a smart man, Luke. Where's he going to take his law practice?"

"He sell the property, they ain't gonna have to worry."

"I see."

I had an indescribably sad feeling inside that I could not translate into words. Then I saw Ruthie Jean come out of Bertie's house and walk on her cane toward us. She looked beautiful. Her hair was brushed in thick swirls that curved on her high cheekbones, and the low-cut white knit dress she wore showed every undulation in her body. When she recognized me in the gloom, she went through the back door of the house.

"Are y'all staying here now?" I asked Luke.

"Yes, suh."

"But it was Julia Bertrand who evicted y'all, wasn't it?"

He studied the grove of gum trees at the end of the road.

"So it must be with her knowledge y'all are back here. Does that make sense to you?" I said.

"Talk to Aint Bertie, Mr. Dave."

"I have too much respect for her. No offense meant. I'll see you, Luke."

"Moleen Bertrand gonna keep his word."

When I started my truck he was standing alone in his yard, a jail-wise hustler, pulled from the maw of our legal killing apparatus, who grieved over his elderly aunt and put his trust in white people, whom a behaviorist would expect him to fear and loathe.

I wondered why historians had to look to the

Roman arena for the seeming inexhaustible reservoirs of faith that can exist in the human soul.

The next evening, after I had closed the bait shop and dock, I put on my running shoes and gym shorts and worked out with my weights in the backyard. I did three sets of curls, dead lifts, and military presses, then jogged through the tunnel of trees by the bayou's edge. The sky was the color of gunmetal, the sun a crack of fire on the western horizon. I came out of the trees, the wind in my face, and headed for the drawbridge.

For some reason I wasn't even surprised when he came out of the shadows and fell in next to me, his tennis shoes powdering the dust in sync with mine, the granite head hunched down on his oily shoulders as though the neck had been surgically removed, his evenly measured breath warm with the smell of beer and tobacco.

"I saw you working out on the speed bag at Red Lerille's Gym," he said. "The trick's to do it without gloves." He held out his square, blunt hands, his words bouncing up and down in his throat. "I used to wrap mine with gauze soaked in lye water. Puts a sheath of callus on the outside like dry fish scale. The problem today is, some faggot cuts his hand on the bag, then you skin your hand on the same bag and you got AIDS, that's what these cocksuckers are doing to the country."

"What's your problem, Pogue?"

"You gonna dime me?"

"I'm not a cop anymore, remember?"

"So the bar's open," he said, and pointed toward a brown Nissan parked by the side of the road.

"I'm tied up."

"I got the cooler on the backseat. Take a break, chief. Nobody's after your cherry," he said.

Up ahead I could see the drawbridge and the bridge tender inside his little lighted house. Emile Pogue tugged his cooler out onto the road, stuck his corded forearm down into the water and melting ice, and pulled out two bottles of Coors.

"No, thanks," I said.

He twisted off the cap on one bottle and drank it half-empty. His torso looked as taut and knurled as the skin on a pumpkin, crisscrossed with stitched scars, webbed with sinew like huge cat's whiskers above the rib cage. He worked his arms through a sleeveless, olive green shirt.

"You don't like me?" he said.

"No."

He pinched his nostrils, flexed his lips back on his gums, looked up and down the road.

"Here's the deal," he said. "You put a stop to what's happening, I'll rat-fuck any greaseball you want, then I'm gone."

"Stop what?"

"That demented guy, the one looks like a dildo you scrambled, Patsy Dapolito, he thinks Johnny Carp's got a hit on him. It ain't coming from Johnny, though." His breath was like a slap, his body aura-ed with a fog of dried sweat and testosterone. He tapped me on the chest with his finger. "Look at me when I'm talking to you. Sonny killed my brother. So I had a personal and legitimate hard-on for the guy."

"I hear you."

"But that ain't why Sonny's back."

I stared at him, open-mouthed. His eyes had the dead quality of ball bearings. He breathed loudly through his nose.

"Back?" I said.

"Get you some Q-Tips, open up the wax. Don't tell me what I seen. Look, chief, till you been down in the bush with the Indians, done a few mushrooms with these fuckers, I'm talking about on a stone altar where their ancestors used to tear out people's hearts, don't knock what somebody else tells you he sees."

"You lost me."

"I saw him at a camp I use out in the Atchafalaya. I looked out in the trees, inside all this hanging moss, there was a swarm of moths or butterflies, except they were on fire, then they formed a big cluster in the shape of a guy, and the guy walked right through the trunk of a tree into the water. It was Sonny Marsallus, he was burning like hundreds of little tongues of flame under the water. I ain't the only one seen it, either."

His hand was squeezed like a huge paw around his beer bottle, his mouth an expressionless slit.

"I think we're talking about an overload of acid or steroids, Emile," I said.

"You get word to Sonny," he said. "That Mennonite's words . . . they were a curse. I'm saying maybe I'm damned. I need time to get out of it."

His breath was rife with funk, his eyes jittering, riveted on mine.

"What Mennonite?" I said.

Sometimes you pull aside the veil and look into the Pit. What follows is my best reconstruction of his words.

Chapter 26

I HAD THIRTY guys strung out on the trail in the dark. It sounded like a traveling junkyard. I stopped them at the river, told the translator, Look, we got a problem here, two more klicks we're in Pinkville South, know what I'm saying, we go in, make our statement, then boogie on back across the river, the beer is five hours colder and we let the dudes from Amnesty International count up the score. In and out, that's the rhythm, none of our people get hurt, even the volunteers we took out of the last ville don't need to walk through any toe-poppers.

I'm talking to guys here who think the manual of arms is a Nicaraguan baseball player.

Look, ace, you got to understand, I didn't target the ville, it targeted itself. They were giving food to the people who were killing us. We warned them, we warned the American priest running the orphanage. Nobody listened. I didn't have no grief with the Mennonite broad. I saw her in the city once, I tipped my hat to her. I admired her. She was a homely little Dutch wisp of a thing working in a shithole most people wouldn't take time to spit on. The trouble came from a couple of liaison guys, officers who spent some time at a special school for greasers at Benning, listen, chief, I was an adviser, got me, I didn't get paid for interfering, you see these guys walk a dude into a tin shed that's got a metal bed frame in it, they close the door behind them, you'll hear the sounds way out in the jungle and pretend it's just monkeys shrieking.

Ellos! they'd yell when we came into the ville, and then try to hide. That was our name. As far as these poor bastards knew, I could have been Pancho Villa or Stonewall Jackson. Look, it got out of control. We were supposed to set up a perimeter, search for weapons, take one guy out in particular, this labor organizer, one object lesson, that's all, they used to call it a Christmas tree, a few ornaments hanging off the branches in the morning, you with me, but the guy runs inside the church and the priest starts yelling at our people out on the steps, and *pop pop pop*, what was I supposed to do, man? Suddenly I got a feeding frenzy on my hands.

You got to look at the overview to see my problem. It's in a cup of mountains, with nobody to see what's going on. That can be a big temptation. In the center of the ville is this stucco church with three little bell towers on it. The priest looks like a pool of black paint poured down the steps. The streets run off in all directions, like spokes on a wheel, and the guys did the priest are scared and start popping anybody in sight. Before I know it, they're down all the spokes, deep in the ville, the circus tent's on fire and I'm *one* fucking guy.

Geese and chickens are exploding out of the yards, pigs squealing, women screaming, people getting pulled into the street by their hair. She comes around a corner, like she's walking against a wind and it takes everything in her to keep walking toward the sounds that make most people cover their ears and hide. I ain't ever going to forget the look in her face, she had these ice blue eyes and hair like white corn silk and blood on her blouse, like it was thrown from an ink pen, but she saw it all, man, just like that whole street and the dead people in it zoomed right through her eyes onto a piece of film. The problem got made right there.

I pushed her hard. She had bones like a bird, you could hold her up against a candle and count them with your finger, I bet, and her face was a little pale triangle and I knew why she was a religious woman and I shoved her again. "This is an accident. It's ending now. You haul your butt out of here, Dutchie," I said.

I squeezed her arm, twisted her in the other direction, scraped her against the wall and saw the pain jump in her face. But they're hard to handle when they're light; they don't have any weight you can use against them. She pulled out of my hands, slipped past me, even cut me with her nails so she could keep looking at the things she wasn't supposed to see, that were going to mess all of us up. Her lips moved but I couldn't understand the words, the air between the buildings was sliced with muzzle flashes, like red scratches against the dark, and you could see empty shell casings shuttering across the lamplight in the windows. Then I heard the blades on the Huey before I felt the downdraft wash over us, and I watched it set down in a field at the end of this stone street and the two officers from the special school at Benning waiting for me, their cigars glowing inside the door, and I didn't have any doubt how it was going to go.

They said it in Spanish, then in English. Then in Spanish and English together. "It is sad, truly. But this one from Holland is *communista*. She is also very *serio*, with friends in the left-wing press. *Entiende, Señor Pogue?*"

It wasn't a new kind of gig. You throw a dozen bodies out at high altitudes. Sometimes they come right through a roof. Maybe it saves lives down the line. But she was alive when they brought her onboard. Look, chief, I wasn't controlling any of it. My choices were I finish the mission, clean up these guys' shit and not think about what's down below, because the sun was over the ridges now and you could see the tile roof of the church and the body of the labor organizer hanging against the wall and Indians running around like an ants' nest that's been stepped on, or stay behind and wait for some seriously pissed-off rebels to come back into the ville and see what we'd done.

Two guys tried to lift her up and throw her out, but she fought with them. So they started hitting her, both of them, then kicking her with their boots. I couldn't take it, man. It was like somebody opened a furnace door next to my head. This stuff had to end. She knew it, too, she saw it in my eyes even before I picked her up by her shoulders, almost like I was saving her, her hands resting on my cheeks, all the while staring into my eyes, even while I was carrying her to the door, even when she was framed against the sky, like she was inside a painting, her hair whipping in the wind, her face jerking back toward the valley floor and what was waiting for her, no stopping any of it now, chief, and I could see white lines in her scalp and taste the dryness and fear on her breath, but her lips were moving again while I squeezed her arms tighter and moved her farther out into a place where nobody had to make decisions anymore, her eyes like holes full of blue sky, and this time I didn't need to hear the words, I could read them on her mouth, they hung there in front of me even while the wind tore her out of my hands and she became just a speck racing toward the earth: *You must change your way.*

Chapter 27

CLETE AND I had breakfast the next morning at Victor's on Main. It was cool inside, and the overhead fans made shadows on the stamped tin ceiling.

"What'd he do then?" Clete said.

"Got in his car and drove away."

"He confesses to a murder, tells you he sees flames burning under the water, then just drives away?"

"No, he repeated the Mennonite woman's words, then said, 'How's that for a mind-fuck, chief?' "

The restaurant was almost empty, and a black woman was putting fresh flowers on the tables. Clete folded and unfolded his palms, bit down on the corner of his lip.

"You think Sonny's back?" I asked.

"*Back* from what? You don't come *back*. You're either alive or you're dead."

"What set you off?"

"Nothing."

"Look, somebody took a shot at Patsy Dap. Maybe with a nine-millimeter. Pogue says it didn't come from Johnny Carp," I said.

His green eyes lingered on mine.

"You didn't?" I said.

"You said it a long time ago. They're all headcases. The object is to point them at each other," he said.

"You can't orchestrate the behavior of psychopaths. What's the matter with you?"

"I did it when I had a few beers. I told you, nobody fucks my podjo." He rolled his fork back and forth on the tablecloth, clicking it hard into the wood.

"What's worrying you?" I said.

"Pogue's a pro, he's got ice water in his veins. When's the last time a guy like that told you a dead man's trying to cap him?"

I went to a noon AA meeting and tried to turn over my problems to my Higher Power. I wasn't doing a good job of it. I had stomped and degraded Johnny Giacano in front of his crew, his friends and family. Were I still a police officer, I would have a marginal chance of getting away with it. But because of my new status, there was no question about the choices Johnny had before him. He would either redeem himself in an unmistakable, dramatic way or be cannibalized by his underlings.

As assassins, the Mafia has no peer. Their experience and sophistication go back to the Napoleonic wars; the level of physical violence imposed on their victims is usually grotesque and far beyond any practical need; the conviction rate of their button men is a joke.

The hit itself almost always comes about in an insidious fashion. The assassin is trusted, always has access, extends an invitation for a quiet dinner with friends, an evening at the track, a fishing trip out on the salt. The victim never suspects the gravity of his situation until, in the blink of an eye, he's looking into a face that's branded with an ageless design, lighted with energies that are not easily satiated.

I went to two meetings a day every day that week. When I got home Friday evening, Luke Fontenot was waiting for me in the bait shop.

He sat at a table in the corner, in the gloom, a cup of coffee in front of him. Batist was mopping down the counter when I came in. He looked back at me and shrugged, then dropped his rag in a bucket and went outside and lit a cigar on the dock.

"Aint Bertie got rid of her lawyer and signed a quit . . . what d' you call it?" Luke said.

"A quitclaim?"

"Yeah, that's it."

He looked smaller in the weak light through the screened windows. His hair grew in small ringlets on the back of his neck.

"They give her twenty-five t'ousand dollars," he said.

"Does she feel okay with that?"

"She don't want nothing to happen to me or Ruthie Jean."

His eyes didn't meet mine. His face was empty, his mouth audibly dry when he spoke, like that of a person who's just experienced a moment for which he has little preparation.

"That lawyer from Lafayette, the one use to work for Sweet Pea Chaisson, Jason Darbonne, and some men from New Orleans come out to the place last night," he said. "They was standing by the gum trees, where the graves use to be, pointing out toward the train track. I went outside and ax them what they want. They say we got to be gone in thirty days, that strip of houses ain't gonna be nothing but broken bo'rds and tore-up water pipe.

"I tole them I ain't heard Moleen Bertrand tell me that, and the last I heard Moleen Bertrand own this plantation.

"One of them men from New Orleans say, 'We was gonna copy you on all the documents, boy, but we didn't have your address.'

"I said, 'Moleen Bertrand tole my aunt she can stay on long as she likes.'

"They didn't even hear me. They went on talking like I wasn't there, talking about pouring a foundation, cutting roads down to the train track, doing something with electric transformers. Then one guy stops the others and looks at me. 'Here's twenty dollars. Go down to the sto' and get us some cold beer. Keep a six-pack for yourself.'

"You know what I said? 'I ain't got my car.' That's all the words I could find, like I didn't have no other kind of words, except to make an excuse for not running their errands.

"So the guy say, 'Then go on in the house. You got no bidness out here.'

"I said, 'Moleen Bertrand done already talked to Aint Bertie. Y'all wasn't there, so maybe y'all don't know about it.'

"Then the same guy, he walked real close to me, right up in my face, he was a big, blond guy with hair tonic on and muscles about to bust out of his shirt, he say, like we was the only two people on the earth and he knew exactly who he was talking to, he say, 'Listen, you dumb nigger, you open your mouth again and you're gonna crawl back up those steps on your hands and knees.' "

Luke raised his coffee cup, then set it back down without drinking from it. He looked through the screen window at the line of cypress trees across the bayou, at the sky above it that was like a crimson-streaked ink wash. His face had the lifeless quality of tallow.

"But that's not it, is it?" I asked.

"What ain't?"

"You've known white men like that before. You were stand-up even in the death house, Luke."

"I called Moleen Bertrand at his office this morning. His secretary say he's in conference. I waited till eleven o'clock and called again. This time she say let me get your number. At three o'clock he still ain't called back. The next time I tried, she say he done gone for the day. I axed if he gone home. She waited a long time, then she say, No, he playing racquetball over in Lafayette.

"I knew where he play at. I was going in the front door when him and three other men was coming out, carrying canvas bags on their shoulders, their hair wet and combed, all of them smiling and stepping aside to let a lady pass.

"Moleen Bertrand shook hands with me and gone right on by. Just like that. Just like I was some black guy maybe he seen around once in a while."

I got up from the table and turned on the string

of lights over the dock. I heard Batist folding up the Cinzano umbrellas over the spool tables. Luke opened and closed his hand on a fifty-cent piece in his palm. Its edges left a circular print almost like an incision in his gold skin. I sat back down across from him.

"I don't think Moleen is in control of his life," I said.

"He saved me from the electric chair. Didn't have nothing to gain for it, either. How come he start lying now?"

"He's involved with evil men, Luke. Get away from him."

"I ain't worried about me."

"I know you're not," I said. Then I said, "Where is she?"

"Out at the house, packing her new clothes, talking about some place in the Islands they're going to, pretending everything all right with Aint Bertie, pretending he fixing to come by anytime now."

"I wish I had an answer for you."

"I ain't ax you for one. I just wanted you to know something befo'hand. It ain't gonna end like Moleen want it to."

"You'd better explain that."

"You don't know Ruthie Jean, suh. Nobody do. Specially not Moleen Bertrand."

He went out the screen door and walked down the dock under the string of light bulbs. I picked up the fifty-cent piece he had left for the coffee. It felt warm and moist from the pressure of his hand.

* * *

Saturday morning I was reading the newspaper on the front steps when Helen Soileau's cruiser came up the dirt road and turned in my drive. She closed the car door behind her and walked through the shade like a soldier on a mission, her dark blue slacks and starched white shirt, badge and black gunbelt and spit-shined black shoes and nickel-plated revolver as unmistakable a martial warning as the flat stare and the thick upper arms that rolled like a man's.

"Who's the in-your-face bitch-woman at your office?" she said.

"Beg your pardon?"

"You heard me, the one with the mouth on her."

"Clete hired her. She didn't strike me that way, though."

"Well, tell her to pull the splinters out of her ass or learn how to talk on the telephone."

"How's life?" I said, hoping the subject would change.

"I'm working a double homicide with Rufus Arceneaux. I never quite appreciated the expression 'dirt sandwich' before."

"It sounds like you really got a jump start on the day. You want breakfast?"

She hooked one thumb in her gunbelt and thought about it. Then she winked. "You're a sweetie," she said.

I fixed coffee and hot milk and bowls of Grape-Nuts and blueberries for us on the picnic table in the backyard.

"There's something weird going on with Fart, Barf, and Itch," she said. "The RAC in New Orleans called me yesterday and asked if I'd heard anything about Sonny Boy Marsallus. I said, 'Yeah, he's dead.' He says, 'We think that, too, but his body's never washed up. The tide was coming in when he got it.'

"I say, 'Think?'

"This guy is a real comedian. He says, 'You remember that army-surplus character you bent out of round with your baton? Guy with a haircut like a white bowling ball, always chewing gum, Tommy Carrol? Somebody found him working late in his store last night and fried his mush.'

" 'Sorry, I don't remember a baton,' I say.

"He thought that was real funny. He says, 'Tommy Carrol did more than sell khaki underwear. He was mixed up with Noriega and some dope operations in Panama. After the ME dug him out of the ashes and opened him up, he found a nine-millimeter slug in what was left of his brain.'

"I knew what was coming but I go, 'So?'

"He says, 'I want to see if we got a match with the rounds from Marsallus's Smith & Wesson. Y'all still have those in your evidence locker, don't you?'

"I say, Sure, no problem, glad to do it. But guess who the department just hired to catalog evidence? Kelso's little brother threw them out.

"I called the comedian back and told him he was out of luck, then asked why he thought Marsallus could be involved. It was strange, he was quiet a long time, then he said, 'I guess I'd like to believe Sonny's not dead. I met him years ago in Guatemala City. He was a good guy.' "

"He's heard something," I said. "Those ex-military guys believe Sonny's still out there." I told her about my encounter with Emile Pogue by the drawbridge.

"Why do they want the Bertrand plantation?" she said.

"One day the country is going to bottom out and get rid of the dope trade. The smart ones are putting their money somewhere else."

"In what?"

"You got me," I said.

"Come back with the department."

"The sheriff's the man."

She grinned and didn't reply.

"What's that mean?" I said.

"He needs you. With guys like Rufus and Kelso and his brother on the payroll, give me a break. Stop thinking with your penis, Dave." She put a spoonful of cereal and milk in her mouth.

That evening I drove past Spanish Lake and bought a Dr Pepper at a convenience store by the four corners in Cade and drank it in the cab of my truck. It had rained hard that afternoon, and the air was bright and clear and the sugarcane on the Bertrand acreage rippled in the wind like prairie grass.

I was convinced this was where the story would end, one way or another, just as it had started here when Jean Lafitte and his blackbirders had sailed up Bayou Teche under a veiled moon with their cargo of human grief.

Moleen didn't see it. His kind seldom did. They hanged Nat Turner and tanned his skin for wallets, and used their educations to feign a pragmatic cynicism and float above the hot toil of the poor whose fate they saw as unrelated to their own lives. The consequence was they passed down their conceit and arrogance like genetic heirlooms.

I wondered what it would be like to step through a window in time, into another era, into an age of belief, and march alongside Granny Lee's boys, most of them barefoot and emaciated as scarecrows, so devoted to their concept of honor and their bonnie blue flag they deliberately chose not to foresee the moment when their lives would be scattered by grapeshot like wildflowers blown from their stems.

As I finished my cold drink, I looked again at the red-tinged light on the fields and wondered if history might not be waiting to have its way with all of us.

Chapter 28

Most people think it's a romantic and intriguing business. The imagination calls to mind the wonderful radio shows of the forties, featuring private investigators who were as gallant as their female clients were beautiful and cunning.

The reality is otherwise.

When I went into the office Monday morning Clete was talking to two men in their twenties who were slumped forward in their metal chairs, tipping their cigarette ashes on the floor, looking at their watches, at the secretary, at the door. One of them had three slender blue teardrops tattooed by the corner of his eye; the second man was blade-faced, his skin the color and texture of the rind on a smoked ham.

"So you guys got your bus tickets, your money for lunch, all the paperwork in case anybody stops you," Clete said, his voice neutral, his eyes empty. "But y'all check in with Nig soon as you arrive in New Orleans. We're clear on that, right?"

"What if Nig ain't in?" the man with the teardrops said.

"He's in," Clete said.

"What if he ain't?"

"Let me try it another way," Clete said. He popped

a crick out of his neck, laced his fingers on his desk blotter, stared through the front window rather than address his listener. "You're probably going to skate, even though you raped a two-year-old girl. Primarily because the child is too young to testify and the mother, who is your girlfriend, was too wiped out on acid to remember what happened. But the big factor here is Nig wrote your bond because you're willing to dime your brother, who skipped his court appearance and hung Nig out to dry for a hundred large.

"What does that all mean to a mainline con and graduate of Camp J like yourself? It means we don't have bars on the windows anymore. It also means you report in to Nig, you stay at the flop he's got rented for you, or I hunt your skinny, worthless ass down with a baseball bat." Clete opened his palm, held it out in the air. "Are we're connecting here?"

The man with the teardrops studied his shoes, worked an incisor tooth against his lip, his eyes slitted with private thoughts.

"How about you, Troyce? Are you squared away on this?" Clete said to the second man.

"Sure." He drew in on his cigarette, and you could hear the fire gather heat and crawl up the dry paper.

"If the woman you branded stands up, Nig will continue your bond on the appeal. But you got to get UA-ed every day. Don't come back to the halfway house with dirty urine, you okay with that, Troyce?" Clete said.

"She's not gonna stand up."

"You boys need to catch your bus, check out the

countryside between here and New Orleans," Clete said.

The blade-faced man rose from his chair, offered his hand to Clete. Clete took it, looked at nothing when he shook it. Later, he went into the lavatory and came back out, drying his hands hard with a paper towel, his breath loud in his nose. He wadded up the towel and flipped it sideways toward the wastebasket, the unshaved back of his neck stippled with roses, as swollen against his collar as a fireplug.

An hour later I was walking toward my truck when Helen Soileau angled her cruiser out of the traffic and pulled to the curb. She leaned over and popped open the passenger door.

"Get in," she said.

"What's wrong?"

"The old man had a heart attack. He got up to fix a sandwich at four this morning, the next thing his wife heard him crash across the kitchen table."

"How bad is it?"

"They had to use the electric paddles. They almost didn't get him back."

I looked through the windshield at the quiet flow of traffic on the street, the people gazing in shop windows, and felt, almost with a sense of shame, my unacknowledged and harbored resentment lift like a film of ash from a dead coal. "Where is he now?" I asked.

"Iberia General . . . Hold on, that's not where we're going. He wants us to interview a guy in a county lockup in east Texas."

"Us?"

"You got it, sweet cakes."

"I need to talk with him, Helen."

"Later, after we get back. This time we're doing it his way. Come on, shake it, you're on the clock, Streak."

The county prison was an old, white brick two-story building just across the Sabine River, north of Orange, Texas. From the second-story reception room Helen and I could look down onto the exercise yard, the outside brick wall spiraled with razor wire, and the surrounding fields that were a shimmering violent green from the spring rains. Two guards in khaki uniforms without guns crossed the yard and unlocked a cast-iron, slitted door that bled rust from the jamb, and snipped waist and leg chains on a barefoot leviathan of a man in jailhouse whites named Jerry Jeff Hooker who trudged between them as though a cannonball were hung from his scrotum.

When the two guards, both of them narrow-eyed and cheerless piney woods crackers, brought him into the reception room and sat him down in front of a scarred wood table in front of us and slipped another chain around his belly and locked it behind the chair, which was bolted to the floor, I said it would be all right if they waited outside.

"Tell that to the nigger trusty whose arm he busted backward on a toilet bowl," one of them said, and took up his position five feet behind Hooker.

"You want to run it by us, Jerry Jeff?" I said.

His skin was as pale as dough, his massive arms

scrolled with green dragons, his pale blond eyebrows ridged like a Neanderthal's.

"I was the wheelman on the Marsallus hit," he said. "I testify against Emile Pogue, I walk on the vehicular homicide."

"Wheelman?" I said.

"I drove. Emile chopped him."

"Witnesses say there were two shooters," Helen said.

"There was only one," he said.

"We have trouble buying your statement, Jerry Jeff," I said.

"That's your problem," he said.

"You're copping to a murder beef," Helen said.

"Marsallus ain't dead."

I felt my heart quicken. He looked at my face, as though seeing it for the first time.

"He was still flopping around in the waves when we left," he said. "A guy in New Orleans, Tommy Carrol, got clipped the other night with a nine-Mike. That's Marsallus's trademark."

"You a military man?" I said.

"Four-F," he answered. He tried to straighten himself in his chains. His breath wheezed in his chest. "Listen, these people here say I got to do a minimum two-bit in the Walls."

"That doesn't sound bad for a guy who went through a red light drunk and killed a seventy-year-old woman," I said.

"That's at Huntsville, my man, with the Mexican Mafia and the Black Guerrilla Liberation Army. For white bread it's the Aryan Brotherhood or lockdown. Fuck that."

Helen and I let our eyes meet.

"You're jailwise but you got no sheet. In fact, there's no jacket of any kind on you anywhere," I said.

"Who gives a shit?" he said.

"Who put out the hit?" I asked.

"Give me a piece of paper and a pencil," he answered.

I placed my notebook and felt pen in front of him and looked at one of the guards. He shook his head.

"We need this, sir," I said.

He snuffed down in his nose and unlocked Hooker's right wrist from the waist chain, then stepped back with his palm centered on the butt of his baton. Hooker bent over the pad and in a surprisingly fluid calligraphy wrote a single sentence, *You give me the name of the donkey you want and I'll pin the tail on him.*

"Bad choice of words," I said, tearing the page from the pad.

"Emile used a .223 carbine. He had Marsallus trapped in a phone booth but he blew it," he said.

"You'll rat-out Pogue to beat a two-year bounce?" I said.

His free hand rolled into a big fist, the veins in his wrist cording with blood, as though he were pumping a small rubber ball.

"I'm in the first stage of AIDS. I don't want to do it inside," he said. "What's it gonna be?"

"We'll think about it," Helen said.

His nose was starting to run. He wiped it on the back of his wrist and laughed to himself.

"What's funny?" I said.

"Think about it? That's a kick. I'd do more than *think*, Muffy," he said, his blue eyes threaded with light as they roved over her face.

"You killed my animals and birds," she said.

He twisted his neck until he could see the guard behind him. "Hey, Abner, get me a snot rag or walk me back to my cell," he said.

The sheriff was in the Intensive Care unit when Helen and I visited him at Iberia General in the morning. Tubes dripped into his veins, fed oxygen into his nose; a shaft of sunlight cut across his forearm and seemed to mock the grayness of his skin. He looked not only stricken but also somehow diminished in size, shrunken skeletally, the eyes hollow and focused on concerns that floated inches from his face, like weevil worms.

I sat close to his bed and could smell an odor similar to withered flowers on his breath.

"Tell me about Hooker," he whispered.

"It's time to let other people worry about these guys, skipper," I said.

"Tell me."

I did, as briefly and simply as possible.

"Say the last part again," he said.

"He used the term 'nine-Mike' for a nine-millimeter," I said. " 'Mike' is part of the old military alphabet. This guy came out of the same cookie cutter as Emile Pogue and the guy named Jack."

He closed and opened his eyes, wet his lips to speak again. He tilted his head until his eyes were looking directly into mine. He was unshaved, and there were red and blue veins, like tiny pieces of thread, in the hollows of his cheeks.

"Last night I saw star shells bursting over a snowfield filled with dead Chinese," he said. "A scavenger was pulling their pockets inside out."

"It was just a dream," I said.

"Not just a dream, Dave."

I heard Helen rise from her chair, felt her hand touch my shoulder.

"We should go," she said.

"I was wrong. But so were you," he said.

"No, the fault was mine, Sheriff, not yours," I said.

"I squared it with the prosecutor's office. Don't let anybody tell you different."

He lifted his hand off the sheet. It felt small and lifeless inside mine.

But I didn't go back to the office the next day. Instead, Batist and I took my boat all the way down Bayou Teche, through the vast green splendor of the wetlands, where blue herons and cranes glided above the flooded gum trees and the rusted wrecks of oil barges, into West Cote Blanche Bay and the Gulf beyond, while a squall churned like glazed smoke across the early sun.

My father, Aldous, was an old-time oil field roughneck who worked the night tower on the monkey board high above the drill platform and the sliding black waves of the Gulf of Mexico. The company was operating without a blowout preventer on the wellhead, and when the bit punched into a natural gas dome unexpectedly, the casing geysered out of the hole under thousands of pounds of pressure, a spark danced off a steel surface, and the sky blossomed with a flame that people could see from Morgan City to Cypremort Point.

My father clipped his safety belt onto the Geronimo wire and jumped into the darkness, but the derrick folded in upon itself, like coat hanger wire melting in a furnace, taking my father and nineteen other men with it.

I knew the spot by heart; I could even feel his presence, see him in my mind's eye, deep below the waves, his tin hat cocked at an angle, grinning, his denim work clothes undulating in the tidal current, one thumb hooked in the air, telling me never to be afraid. Twice a year, on All Saints' Day and the anniversary of his death, I came here and cut the engines, let the boat drift back across the wreckage of the rig and quarterboat, which was now shaggy with green moss, and listened to the water's slap against the hull, the cry of seagulls, as though somehow his voice was still trapped here, waiting to be heard, like a soft whisper blowing in the foam off the waves.

He loved children and flowers and women and charcoal-filtered bourbon and fighting in bars, and he carried the pain of my mother's infidelity like a stone bruise and never let anyone see it in his eyes. But once on a duck hunting trip, after he got drunk and tried to acknowledge his failure toward me and my mother, he said, "Dave, don't never let yourself be alone," and

I saw another dimension in my father, one of isolation and loneliness, that neither of us would have sufficient years to address again.

The water was reddish brown, the swells dented with rain rings. I walked to the stern with a clutch of yellow roses and threw them into the sun and watched a capping wave break them apart and scatter their petals through the swell.

Never alone, Al, I said under my breath, then went back into the cabin with Batist and hit it hard for home.

That night I had an old visitor, the vestiges of malaria that lived like mosquito eggs in my blood. I woke at midnight to the rumble of distant thunder, felt the chill on my skin and heard the rain tinking on the blades of the window fan, and thought a storm was about to burst over the wetlands to the south. An hour later my teeth were knocking together and I could hear mosquitoes droning around my ears and face, although none were there. I wanted to hide under piles of blankets even though my sheet and pillow were already damp with sweat, my mouth as dry as an ashtray.

I knew it would pass; it always did. I just had to wait and, with luck, I would wake depleted in the morning, as cool and empty as if I had been eviscerated and washed out with a hose.

Sometimes during those nocturnal hours I saw an electrified tiger who paced back and forth like a kaleidoscopic orange light behind a row of trees, hung with snakes whose emerald bodies were as supple and thick as an elephant's trunk.

But I knew these images were born as much out of my past alcoholic life as they were from a systemic return to the Philippines, just another dry drunk, really, part of the *guignol* that a faceless puppeteer in the mind put on periodically.

But tonight was different.

At first I seemed to see him only inside my head. He walked out of the swamp, his upper torso naked, with seaweed clinging to his ankles like serpents, his skin as bloodless as marble, his hair the same brightness and metamorphic shape as fire.

The storm burst over the swamp and I could see the pecan and oak trees flickering whitely in the yard, the tin roof on the bait shop leaping out of the darkness, wrenching against the joists in the wind. The barometer and the temperature seemed to drop in seconds, as though all the air were being sucked out of our bedroom, drawn backward through the curtains, into the trees, until I knew, when I opened my eyes, I would be inside a place as cold as water that had never been penetrated by sunlight, as inaccessible as the drop-off beyond the continental shelf.

What's the haps, Streak? he said.

You know how it is, you get deep in Indian country and you always think somebody's got iron sights on your back, I replied.

How about that Emile Pogue? Isn't he a pistol?

Why'd you play their game, Sonny? Why didn't you work with me?

Your heart gets in the way of your head, Dave. You've got a way of wheeling the Trojan horse through the gates.

What's that mean?

They want my journal. After they get it, somebody close to you will snap one into your brain pan.

Rough way to put it.

He picked my hand up by the wrist, drew it toward his rib cage.

Put your thumb in the hole, Dave. That's the exit wound. Emile caught me four times through the back.

I apologize, Sonny. I let you down.

Lose the guilt. I knew the score when I smoked Emile's brother.

We should have kept you in lockdown. You'd be alive now.

Who says I'm not? Stay on that old-time R and B, Streak. Don't stray where angels fear to tread. Hey, that's just a joke.

Wait, I said.

When I reached out to touch him, my eyes opened as though I had been slapped. I was standing in front of the window fan, whose blades were spinning in the mist that blew into the room. My hand was extended, lifeless, as though it were suspended in water. The yard was empty, the trees swollen with wind.

The sheriff had dreamed of star shells popping above the frozen white hills of North Korea. I had lied and sought to dispel his fear, as we always do when we see death painted on someone's face.

Now I tried to dispel my own.

At my foot was a solitary strand of brown seaweed.

Chapter 29

I SLEPT UNTIL seven, then showered, dressed, and ate breakfast in the kitchen. I could feel the day slowly come into focus, the predictable world of blue skies and wind blowing through the screens and of voices on the dock gradually becoming more real than the experience of the night before.

I told myself the gargoyles don't do well in sunlight.

Vanity, vanity.

Involuntarily I kept touching my wrist, as though I could still feel Sonny's damp fingers clamped around it.

"Were you walking around last night?" Bootsie said.

"A little touch of the mosquito."

"You have anxiety about going back, Dave?"

"No, it's going to be just fine."

She leaned over the back of my chair, folded her arms under my neck, and kissed me behind the ear. Her shampoo smelled like strawberries.

"Try to come home early this afternoon," she said.

"What's up?"

"You never can tell," she said.

Then she pressed her cheek against mine and patted her hand on my chest.

A half hour later Clete Purcel sat across from me in my office at the department.

"A strand of seaweed?" he said.

"Yep."

"Dave, you were out on the Gulf yesterday. You tracked it into the house."

"Yeah, that's probably what happened," I said, and averted my eyes.

"I don't like this voodoo stuff, mon. We keep the lines simple. You got your shield back. It's time to stick it to Pogue and the greaseballs . . . Are you listening?"

"The problem's not coming from outside. It was already here."

"This guy Bertrand again?"

"He's the linchpin, Clete. If he hadn't provided the opportunity, none of these others guys would be here."

"He's a marshmallow. I saw him in the grocery the other day. His old lady was talking to him like he was the bag boy."

"That doesn't sound right."

"Maybe he has a secret life as a human poodle. Anyway, I got to deedee. Just keep gliding on that old-time R and B, noble mon."

"What did you say?"

"Oh, that's just something Sonny Boy was always saying down in Guatemala," he said, his eyes crinkling at the corners. "I never thought I'd say this, but I miss that guy . . . What's wrong?"

I spent the next two hours doing paperwork and trying to update my case files, half of which I had to recover from Rufus Arceneaux's office.

"I got no hard feelings," he said as I was about to go back out the door.

"Neither do I, Rufus," I said.

"We gonna work that double homicide at Cade together?" he said.

"No," I said, and closed his door behind me.

I cleared off my desk, then covered it with all the case material I had on Johnny Giacano, Patsy Dapolito, Sweet Pea Chaisson, Emile Pogue, Sonny Boy Marsallus, the man named Jack whose decapitated body we pulled out of the slough, even Luke Fontenot—faxs, mug shots, crime scene photographs, National Crime Information Center printouts (the one on Dapolito was my favorite; while in federal custody at Marion he had tried to bite the nose off the prison psychologist).

What was missing?

A file on Moleen Bertrand.

It existed somewhere, in the Pentagon or at Langley, Virginia, but I would never have access to it. Neither, in all probability, would the FBI.

But there was another clerical conduit into the Bertrand home, a case file I should have looked at a long time ago.

Julia Bertrand's.

Helen Soileau and I spent the next hour sorting through manila folders and string-tied brown envelopes in a storage room that was stacked from the floor to the ceiling with cardboard boxes. Many were water damaged and tore loose at the bottom when you picked them up.

But we found it.

Halloween of 1983, on a dirt road between two cane fields out in Cade. Three black children, dressed in costumes, carrying trick or treat bags and jack-o'-lanterns, are walking with their grandfather toward the next house on the road. A blue Buick turns off the highway, fishtails in the dirt, scours a cloud of dust into the air. The grandfather hears the engine roar, dry clods of dirt rattling like rocks under the fenders, the tires throbbing across the baked ruts. The headlights spear through him and the children, flare into the cattails in the ditches; the grandfather believes the driver will slow, surely, pull wide toward the other side of the road, somehow abort what cannot be happening.

Instead, the driver accelerates even faster. The Buick flies by in a suck of air, a mushrooming cloud of sound and dust and exhaust fumes. The grandfather tries to close his ears as his grandchild disappears under the Buick's bumper, sees a still-lighted and grinning jack-o'-lantern tumble crazily into the darkness.

I worked through lunch, read and reread the file and all the spiral notebook pages penciled by the original investigator.

Helen came back from lunch at 1 P.M. She leaned on her knuckles on top of my desk and stared at the glossy black-and-white photos taken at the scene. "Poor kid," she said.

The original accident report was brown and stiff on the edges from water seepage, the ink almost illegible, but you could still make out the name of the deputy who had signed it.

"Check it out," I said, and inverted the page so Helen could read it.

"Rufus?"

"It gets more interesting," I said, turning through the pages. "A plainclothes named Mitchell was assigned the investigation. The grandfather remembered three numbers off the license plate, and the plainclothes made a match with Julia's Buick. Julia admitted she was driving her car out by Cade on Halloween night, but there was no apparent physical damage to link the car to the accident scene. The real hitch is in the old man's statement, though."

"What?"

"He said the driver was a man."

She rubbed the corner of her mouth with one finger, her eyes narrowing.

"The investigator, this guy Mitchell, was confused, too," I said. "His last note says, 'Something sucks about this.' "

"Mitchell was a good cop. I remember, it was about eighty-three he went to work for the Feds," she said.

"Guess who replaced him on the case?" I said.

She studied my face. "You're kidding?" she said.

"Our man Rufus again. Tell me, why would a cop who investigated a woman for hit-and-run vehicular homicide end up as her friend and confidant inside the department?"

"Dave, this really stinks."

"That's not all. Later the grandfather said he didn't have on his glasses and wasn't sure about the numbers on the license plate. End of investigation."

"You want to haul that sonofabitch in here?"

"Which one?" I said.

"Rufus. Who'd you think I meant?"

"Moleen Bertrand."

He wasn't at his office. I drove to his home on Bayou Teche. A crew of black yardmen were mowing the huge lawn in front, raking leaves under the oaks, pruning back the banana trees until they were virtual stubs. I parked by the side garage and knocked. No one seemed to be inside. The speedboat was in the boathouse, snugged down under a tarp, wobbling in the bladed gold light off the water's surface.

"If you looking for Mr. Moleen, he's out at Cade," one of the black men said.

"Where's Miss Julia?" I asked.

"Ain't seen her."

"Y'all look like you're working hard."

"Mr. Moleen say do it right. He ain't gonna be around for a while."

I took the old highway out to Spanish Lake, past the restored antebellum homes on the shore and the enormous moss-strung oak trees that rippled in the breeze off the water. Then I turned down the corrugated dirt lane, under the rusted iron trellis, into the Bertrand plantation. Whoever Moleen's business partners were, they had been busy.

Bulldozers had cut swaths through the sugarcane, flattened old corn cribs and stables, splintered wild persimmon trees into torn root systems that lay exposed like pink tubers in the graded soil. I saw Moleen on horseback by the treeline, watching a group of land surveyors drive wood stakes and flagged laths in what appeared to be a roadway that led toward the train tracks.

I drove across the field, through the flattened cane, and got out of my truck. The sun was white in the sky, the air layered with dust. Moleen wore riding pants and boots and military spurs, a blue polo shirt, a bandanna knotted wetly around his neck, a short-brimmed straw hat with a tropical band. His right hand was curled around a quirt, his face dilated in the heat that rose from the ground.

"A hot day for it," I said.

"I hadn't noticed," he said.

A man operating a bulldozer shifted into reverse, made a turn by the treeline, and snapped a hackberry off at ground level like a celery stalk.

"I hate looking up at a man on horseback, Moleen," I said.

"How about just saying what's on your mind?"

"After all these years, I finally figured you out."

"With you, it always has to be an unpleasant moment. Why is that, sir?" he said, dismounting. He led his horse into the shade of the trees, turned to face me, a line of clear sweat sliding down his temple. Behind him, in the shadows, was the corn crib, strung with the scales of dead morning glory vines, where he and Ruthie Jean had begun their love affair years ago.

"I think Julia took your weight, Moleen." He looked back at me, uncomprehending. "When the child was run down, on Halloween night in eighty-three. You were the driver, not she."

"I think you've lost your sanity, my friend."

"It was a slick scam," I said. "A successful lie always

has an element of truth in it. In that way, the other side can never figure out what's true and what's deception. Julia admitted to having driven the car that night, but y'all knew the witness said the driver was a man. So what appeared to be her honesty threw his account into question."

"I think you need counseling. I genuinely mean that, Dave."

"Then you got to Rufus Arceneaux and he twisted some screws on the witness. That's why you've never dumped your wife. She could get you disbarred, even sent up the road."

His eyebrows were heavy with sweat, his knuckles white as slivers of ice on the quirt.

"I don't believe I can find adequate words to express my feelings about a man like you," he said.

"Clean the peanut brittle out of your mouth. That child's death is on your soul."

"Your problem is your own, sir. You don't respect the class you were born into. You look into the mirror and always see what you came from. I feel sorry for you."

He waited, the quirt poised at his side.

"You're not worth punching out, Moleen," I said.

I turned and walked back out into the field toward my truck, into the hot sunlight and the smell of diesel and the drift of dust from the machines that were chewing up the Bertrand plantation. My ears were ringing, my throat constricted as though someone had spit in my mouth. I heard Moleen's saddle creak as he mounted his horse. He sawed the reins and used his spurs hard at the same time, wheeling his horse and cantering toward the survey crew.

I couldn't let it go.

I walked after him through the destroyed cane, laced my hand inside the horse's bridle, felt it try to rear against my weight. The survey crew, men whose skin was as dark as chewing tobacco, paused in their work with chaining pins and transit and metal tapes, grinning good-naturedly, unsure of what was taking place.

Moleen wasn't prepared for an audience.

"If you're planning on a trip, I hope it's with Ruthie Jean," I said.

He tried to jerk the horse's head free. I tightened my fingers inside the leather.

"Cops don't prevent crimes, they solve them after the fact," I said. "In this case, I'm creating an exception. Don't take either her or Luke Fontenot for granted because they're black. The person who kills you is the one at your throat before you ever know it."

He raised his quirt. I flung the bridle from my hand, slapped his horse, and spooked it sideways among the surveyors.

I glanced back at him before I got into my truck. He was reining and soothing his horse, turning in a circle, his skin filmed with sweat and the dust that rose around him like a vortex, his face dark with shame and embarrassment.

But it was no victory. I was convinced Moleen had sold us out, was bringing some new form of evil into our lives, and there was nothing I could do about it.

* * *

An hour later I was in the Iberia Parish building permit office. All the applications for construction permits on Moleen's property had been filed by Jason Darbonne. The blueprints had the clean, rectangular lines that you associate with a high school drafting class; but they were also general in nature, and the interior seemed to be nothing more than a huge concrete pad, an empty shell, a question mark without function or purpose.

"What's the name of the company?" I asked the engineer.

"Blue Sky Electric," he said.

"What do they do?"

"They work on electrical transformers or something," he answered.

In small letters, in one corner of the blueprint, was the word *incinerator*.

"These plans have all the specifics of a blimp hangar," I said.

He shrugged his shoulders.

"What's the problem?" he said.

"I wish I knew."

Late that evening Bootsie looked out the kitchen screen into the backyard.

"Clete Purcel's sitting at our picnic table," she said.

I went out the back door. Clete sat with his back to the house, hunched over a six-pack of Budweiser, an opened can in one hand, a Lucky Strike in the other. He wore elastic-waisted white tennis shorts, flip-flops, and a starched short-sleeve print shirt. By his foot was a cardboard box with tape across the top. The sun had dropped below my neighbor's treeline, and the sugarcane field behind my house was covered with a purple haze.

"What are you doing out here?" I asked.

"Figuring out how I should tell you something."

I sat down across from him. His green eyes were filled with an indolent, alcoholic shine. My foot accidentally hit the cardboard box under the table.

"You look like you made an early pit stop today," I said.

"You remember those two geeks I put on the bus, the brander and the child rapist? I called Nig to see if they got there all right. Guess what? The brander's back in custody. He got to the victim and beat the living shit out of her. Of course, he asks Nig to write another bond for him. Nig tells him the guy is past his envelope, the guy's a flight risk, he's going down for sure this time, and, besides, even Nig can't stomach this barf bag any longer.

"So the barf bag gets cute, tells Nig, 'Write the bond, I'll give up the guy's gonna do Purcel's buddy, what's-his-face, Robicheaux.'

"Nig asks the barf bag who put him inside a whack on a cop, and the barf bag says, get this for lowlife class distinction, Patsy Dap used to piece off five-hundred-buck hits to him in the projects because Patsy thinks it's beneath him to do colored dope dealers."

Clete drank from his beer can, looked at me over the tops of his fingers.

"Patsy's working for Johnny Carp again?" I said.

"It makes sense, mon. Patsy's a stir bug. Johnny

puts Patsy back in the jar and takes you out at the same time."

"They don't hit cops."

"Dave, you rubbed shit in John Giacano's face in front of everybody he respects. You broke his nose and four of his ribs. A paramedic had to pry his bridge out of his throat. I didn't tell you everything the barf bucket said, either . . .

"The word is Johnny wants it in pieces, like the Giacanos did it to Tommy Fig, remember, they processed him into pork roasts and strung them from the ceiling fan in his own butcher shop, then had a big eggnog party while Tommy went spinning around in the air, except Johnny wants it to go down even worse, longer, on videotape, with an audio . . ."

Clete collapsed the aluminum beer can slowly in his huge hand, his eyes glancing away from mine uncertainly.

"Look, I need to be off the record here," he said.

"About what?"

"I'm serious, Streak. When you operate with your shield you think too much like these Rotary cocksuckers . . . Excuse my language."

"Will you just say it, Clete?"

He lifted the cardboard box from under the table, tore the tape, reached down inside the flaps.

"This afternoon I creeped the dump Patsy rents out on the Jeanerette Road," he said. "Don't worry, he was in a motel with his chippy at Four Corners in Lafayette. Dig this, big mon, a Tec-9, ventilated barrel, twenty-five-round nine-millimeter magazine, courtesy of an arms dealer in Miami who can provide them on the spot so the Jamaicans and the Cuban crazies don't have to wait on the mailman."

He worked the action, snapped the firing pin on the empty chamber. "It's got a 'hell trigger' these guys out in Colorado make. You can fire bursts with it almost as fast as a machine gun. Fits neatly under a raincoat. Great for schoolyards and late-night convenience- store visits . . . Here's a set of Smith & Wesson handcuffs, state of the art, solid steel, spring-loaded. Aren't you glad to know a guy like Patsy can buy these at any police supply store . . ."

He put his hand back in the box and I saw his face change, his mouth form a seamed, crooked line, the scar through his eyebrow tighten against the bone. His hand was fitted through the handle of a stubby, cylindrical metal object shaped like a coffeepot.

"The receipt was stuck to the bottom, Dave. He bought it yesterday. Patsy Bones with a blowtorch? Put yourself inside his head—"

Through the kitchen window I could see Bootsie and Alafair washing dishes, talking to each other, the breeze from the attic fan blowing the curtains by the sides of their lighted faces.

Clete scratched his cheek with four fingers, like a zoo creature in a cage, his eyes waiting.

Chapter 30

IT WAS MIDMORNING, the sun hazy through the oak trees that shaded the cluster of trailers and cottages where Patsy Dapolito lived east of town. Helen and I were parked in my truck behind a tin shed that had already started to creak with heat, watching Patsy shoot baskets in a dirt clearing by the side of a garage. His sockless ankles and white legs were layered with scar tissue and filmed with dust, his gym shorts knotted around his genitals like a drenched swimsuit, his T-shirt contoured against his hard body like wet Kleenex.

He whanged one more shot off the hoop, then dribbled the ball—*bing, bing, bing*—toward the door to his cottage. I got out of the truck, moved in fast behind him, and pushed him hard through the door. When he turned around, his mouth hooked like a cornered predator's, my .45 was pointed in the middle of his face.

"Oh, you again," he said.

I shoved him into a wood chair. My hand came away damp from his T-shirt.

The floor was littered with movie and wrestling and UFO magazines, hamburger containers, empty Kentucky Fried Chicken buckets, dozens of beer and soda cans.

Helen came through the door with Clete's cardboard box hanging from her hand. She looked around the room.

"I think it needs a trough inset in the floor," she said.

"This my get-out-of-Shitsville roust?" he said.

Helen gathered up his basketball, bounced it on the linoleum floor twice—*bing, bing*—then two-handed it off his forehead and caught the rebound between her palms. His head jerked, as though a thin wire had snapped behind his eyes, then he stared at her, with that bemused, inverted grin, the mouth turned downward at the corners, the teeth barely showing in a wet line above the lip.

"Your place got creeped, Patsy. We're returning your goods," I said. I replaced my .45 in my clip-on holster and one at a time removed the Tec-9, the handcuffs, and the blowtorch from the cardboard box and set them on his breakfast table. He fingered the half-moon scars and divots on his face, watched me as though I were a strange shadow moving about on a surreal landscape that only he saw.

"The contract you took from Johnny is already sour, Patsy," I said. "There's a guy willing to give you up."

"It must have been lard-ass that got in my place. He helped himself to the beer and potato salad in my icebox," Patsy said. There was a red spot, like a small apple, in the middle of his forehead.

"You going to do me?" I said.

He picked at the calluses on his palm, looked up

at me, breathed over the top of his teeth, his eyes smiling.

Helen caromed the ball off his head again.

"Hey!" he said, swatting the air, his face knotting. "Lay off that!"

I reached back down in the cardboard box and retrieved a manila folder that was almost three inches thick. I pulled out a chair and sat in it, spread the folder on one thigh.

"You did a nickel on Camp J, you've gone out max-time twice, we're not going to insult you by treating you like a fish. I'm talking about the consequences of harming a police officer," I said.

He crinkled his nose, looked at a spot three inches in front of his eyes. The shape of his head reminded me of a darning sock.

"But there's some weird stuff in your jacket, Patsy," I said. "You got picked up in a porno theater in New York once. The owner was connected to a child prostitution ring. You remember that gig?"

His eyes lifted into mine.

"When you were thirty-eight you went down for statutory rape. She was fourteen, Patsy. Then way back here . . ." I turned to the front of the folder, looked down at a page. "It says here you got busted for abducting a little girl from a playground. The father wouldn't stand up so you walked. You see a pattern here?"

His hands shifted into his lap, his fingers netting together. Helen and I stared at him silently. His eyes blinked, looked back and forth between us, his nostrils whitening, as though he were breathing air off a block of ice.

"What?" he said. *"What?"*

"You're a button man, all right, but you're a pedophile first," I said.

He churned the edges of his tennis shoes on the floor, his ankles bent sideways, his shoulders pinched forward, his neck hunched. I could hear him breathing, smell an odor like soiled cat litter that rose from his armpits. He started to speak.

"Here's the rest of it, Patsy. Your mother set fire to you in your crib," I said.

His pale eyes stared back at me as though they had no lids. His mouth looked like a deformed keyhole in his face.

"You try to do me, all this becomes public knowledge," I said. "Anytime you're around Four Corners, you'll be picked up as a sex predator. We'll put you with every open molestation case we have, we'll make sure NOPD Vice gets in on it, too."

"They'll have your picture in the T and A joints on Bourbon, Patsy," Helen said.

"They made that up about my mother. There was a fire in the project," he said.

"Yeah, she set it. That's why she died in the insane asylum," I said.

"The message is, you're a geek. You start some shit, we'll finish it. You still think this is just a roust in Bumfuck?" Helen said, stepping toward him, her arms pumped.

When we left him, he was still seated in the chair, his head canted to one side, his mouth indented like a collapsed football bladder, his ankles folded almost flat with the floor, his eyes staring into tunnels and secret rooms that only Patsy Dapolito knew about.

Smoke 'em or bust 'em, make their puds shrivel up and hide, Clete used to say. But how do you take pride in wrapping razor wire around the soul of a man who in all probability was detested before he left the womb?

It rained after sunset, and the mist floated like smoke out of the cypress in the swamp. The air was cool when I closed up the bait shop, and I could hear bass flopping back in the bays. Through the screen I saw Alafair walking Tripod on his chain down the dock, while his nose sniffed at the dried blood and fish scales baked into the planks.

She came through the door, eased it back on the spring so it wouldn't slam, sat on a counter stool, and lifted Tripod into her lap. She had put on a fresh pair of blue jeans, a flowered cowboy shirt, and had tied her hair in back with a blue ribbon. But her face looked empty, her brown eyes remote with thoughts she couldn't resolve.

"What's the trouble, Alf?" I said.

"It's gonna make you mad."

"Let's find out."

"A bunch of us were up by the bar, you know, Goula's, the other side of the drawbridge."

"A bunch of you?"

"We were in Danny Bordelon's pickup truck. They wanted to get some beer." She watched my face.

"Danny had his brother's ID card. He went inside the bar and got it."

"I see."

"They were going to drink it down the road."

"What happened?"

"Are you going to be mad at Danny?"

"He shouldn't be buying beer for you guys."

"I got out of the truck and walked. I was scared. They were mixing it with something called 'Ever Clear,' it's like pure grain alcohol or something."

"Danny didn't try to take you home?"

"No." She dropped her eyes to the floor.

"So we leave Danny alone in the future. You did the right thing, Alafair."

"That's not all that happened, Dave . . . It started to rain and the wind was blowing real hard out of the swamp. A car came up the road with its lights on. The man who got Tripod out of the coulee, the man you handcuffed, he rolled down his window and said he'd take me home . . ."

"Did you get in the—"

"No. The way he looked at me, it was sickening. His eyes went all over me, like they were full of dirty thoughts and he didn't care if I knew it or not."

I sat on the stool next to her, put my hand on her back.

"Tell me what happened, Alf," I said.

"I told him I didn't want a ride. I kept walking toward the house. The rain was stinging my face and he kept backing up with me, telling me to get in, he was a friend of yours, I was gonna catch cold if I didn't get in."

"You didn't do anything wrong, Alf. Do you understand me?"

"He started to open his door, Dave. Then this other man came out of nowhere. He had red hair and a black rain hat on with rain pouring off it, and he walked like he was hurt. He said, 'I don't want it to go down in front of a kid, Emile. Time for you to boogie.'

"The man in the car turned white, Dave. He stepped on the gas and threw mud and water all over us. You could see sparks gashing off his bumper when he crossed the drawbridge."

I looked out the window into the darkness, tried to clear an obstruction, like a fish bone, in my throat.

"Have you ever seen the man in the raincoat before?" I said.

"It was hard to see his face in the rain. It was pale, like it didn't have any blood . . . He said, 'You shouldn't be out here by yourself.' He walked with me till we could see the lights on the dock. Then I turned around and he was gone."

I took Tripod out of her lap and set him on the counter, then bent over her and hugged her against my chest, pressed my cheek against the top of her head.

"You're not mad?" she said.

"Of course not."

Her eyes crinkled at the corners when she looked up at me. I smiled emptily, lest she sense the fear that hovered like a vapor around my heart.

* * *

The next morning the sun rose yellow and hot into a bone white sky. There was no wind, and the trees and flowers in my yard were coated with humidity. At 9 A.M. I glanced through my office window and saw Luke Fontenot park his car on the street and walk toward the entrance of the sheriff's department, his rose-colored shirt peppered with sweat. Just before he went through the door, he rubbed his mouth unconsciously.

When he sat down in the metal chair in front of my desk, he kept glancing sideways through the glass at the uniformed deputies who passed in the corridor.

"It's all right, Luke," I said.

"I been in custody here. For killing a white man, back when things was a li'l different. You believe in the gris-gris, Mr. Dave?"

"No."

"Aint Bertie do. She put the gris-gris on Moleen Bertrand, now she say she cain't get it off."

"That stuff's superstition, partner."

"Come out to the cafe where she work."

"Bertie can take care of herself."

"I ain't worried about that old woman. It's Ruthie Jean. Suh, ain't it time you listen a li'l bit to what black folks got to say?"

Bertie Fontenot worked off and on in a black-owned clapboard cafe up Bayou Teche in Loreauville. She sat under a tarp extended on poles behind the building, next to a worktable and two stainless steel cauldrons that bubbled on a portable butane burner. The surrounding fields were glazed with sunlight, the shade under the tarp as stifling as a wool blanket on your skin.

Through the back screen I could hear the jukebox playing, *I searched for you all night in vain, baby. But you was hid out wit' another man.*

"Tell him," Luke said.

"What for? Some people always know what they know," she said.

She lifted her mammoth weight out of the chair and poured a wood basket filled with artichokes, whole onions, corn on the cob, and peeled potatoes into the cauldrons. Then she began feeding links of sausage into the steam, her eyes watering in the evaporation of salt and cayenne pepper. Stacked on the table were three swollen gunnysacks that moved and creaked with live crawfish.

"Aint Bertie, he took off from his work to come up here," Luke said.

She wiped the perspiration off her neck with a tiny handkerchief and walked to her pickup truck, which was parked by an abandoned and partially collapsed privy, and came back into the shade with an old leather handbag drawn together at the top by a leather boot lace. She put her hand inside and removed a clutch of pig bones. They looked like long pieces of animal teeth against her coppery palm.

"It don't matter when or where I t'row them, they come up the same," she said. "I ain't got no power over what's gonna happen. I gone along with Ruthie Jean, even though I knowed it was wrong. Now I cain't undo any of it."

She cast the bones from her hand onto the plank table. They seemed to bounce off the wood as lightly as sewing needles.

"See, all the sharp points is at the center," she said. "Moleen Bertrand dragging a chain I cain't take off. For something he done right here, it's got to do wit' a child, out on a dirt road, in the dark, when Moleen was drunk. There's a bunch of other spirits following him around, too, soldiers in uniforms that ain't nothing but rags now. Every morning he wake up, they sitting all around his room."

"You told me you were worried about Ruthie Jean," I said to Luke.

"She's in a rooming house in New Orleans, off Magazine by the river. Waiting for Moleen to get his bidness things together, take her to the Islands," he said.

"Some people give they heart one time, keep believing when they ain't suppose to believe no more," Bertie said. She unfolded the curved blade of a banana knife from its case, pulled a gunnysack filled with crawfish across the table toward her. "Moleen gonna die. Except there's two bones in the middle of the circle. Somebody going wit' him."

"Maybe Moleen thinks New Orleans is a better place for her right now. Maybe he's going to keep his word," I said.

"You wasn't listening, Mr. Dave," Luke said. "We ain't tole you Moleen Bertrand sent her to New Orleans. It was a police officer, he come down here at night, carried her on down to the airport in Lafayette."

"Excuse me?" I said.

"You got him right down the hall from you, Mr. White Trash himself, Rufus Arceneaux, same man run errands for Julia Bertrand," she said.

She ripped the sack along the seam with her banana knife, then shucked it empty into the cauldron, where the crawfish stiffened with shock, as though they had been struck with electricity, and then roiled up dead in the churning froth.

That night the air was breathless, moonlit, filled with birds, stale with dust and the heat of the day that lingered in the baked wood and tin roofing of the house. It was long after midnight when the phone rang in the kitchen.

"You got the wrong signal, ace," the voice said.

"Pogue?"

"Your little girl misunderstood."

"No, you did. I told you not to come through the wrong man's perimeter."

"I was there to help. They got a mechanic on you."

"Come anywhere near my house, I'm going to take you off at the neck."

"Don't hang up . . ." I could hear his breath rise and fall against the receiver. "The Dutchie don't let me alone. I think I got only one way out. I cool out the hitter, I don't let nobody hurt your family. The problem is, I got no idea who they sent in. I need time, man, that's what you fucking don't hear."

"Do you know what 'roid-induced psychosis is?" I said.

"No."

"Too many injections in the butt. Then you drink

a few beers and the snakes put on a special floor show. Don't call here again."

"You got cement around your head? I ain't a bad guy. We went into Laos twice to get your friend back. You know anybody else who gave a shit about him?"

"You frightened my daughter. One way or another, that's going to get squared, Emile."

"*Me?* Marsallus was there. She didn't tell you?"

"Your wheelman, Jerry Jeff Hooker, is in custody. He gave you up. Come in and maybe we can get you into a federal hospital."

"I could smell Marsallus's breath, it was like the stink when you pop a body bag. The Dutchie turned him loose on me. Laos, Guatemala, colored town out there on the highway, it's all part of the same geography. Hell don't have boundaries, man. Don't you understand that?"

The phone was silent a long time. In the moonlight I saw an owl sink its razored beak into a wood rabbit in my neighbor's field. Then Emile Pogue quietly hung up.

Chapter 31

THE SHERIFF HAD been moved out of Intensive Care into an ordinary room at Iberia General, one that was filled with flowers and slatted sunlight. But his new environment was a deception. His whiskers were white against his flaccid skin, and his eyes had a peculiar cast in them, what we used to call the thousand-yard stare, as though he could not quite detach himself from old events that were still aborning for him on frozen hilltops that rang with bugles.

"Can you hand me my orange juice, please?" he said.

I lifted the glass straw to his lips, watched him draw the juice and melting ice into his mouth.

"I dreamed about roses under the snow. But then I saw they weren't roses. They were drops of blood where we marched out of the Chosin. It's funny how your dreams mix up things," he said.

"It's better to let old wars go, skipper."

"New Iberia is a good place."

"It sure is."

"We need to get these bastards out of here, Dave," he said.

"We will."

"Your daughter ID-ed Marsallus from his mug shot?"

"I shouldn't have told you that story," I said.

"They couldn't pull him across the Styx. That's a good story to hear . . . Dave?"

"Yes?"

"I never told this to anyone except a marine chaplain. I sent three North Korean POW's to the rear once with a BAR man who escorted them as far as one hill. In my heart I knew better, because the BAR man was one of those rare guys who enjoyed what he did . . ."

I tried to interrupt, but he raised two fingers off the sheet to silence me.

"That's why I always sit on you, always try to keep the net over all of us . . . so we don't take people off behind a hill."

"That's a good way to be," I said.

"You don't understand. It's the rules get us killed sometimes. You got too many bad people circling you."

His voice became weaker, and I saw the light in his eyes change, his chest swell, as he breathed more deeply.

"I'd better go now. I'll see you tomorrow," I said.

"Don't leave yet." His hand moved across my wrist. "I don't want to fall asleep. During the day I dream about trench rats. It was twenty below and they'd eat their way inside the dead. That's how they live, Dave . . . By eating their way inside us."

I went home for lunch, then walked down to the dock to talk to Alafair, who had just gotten out of school for the summer. Sitting under an umbrella at one of the spool tables was Terry Serrett, Clete's secretary. She wore pale blue shorts and a halter and her skin looked as white as a fish's belly. She read a magazine behind a pair of dark glasses while she idly rubbed suntan lotion on her thighs. When she heard my footsteps, she looked up at me and smiled. Her cheeks were roughed with orange circles like makeup on a circus clown.

"You're not working today?" I said.

"There's not much to do, I'm afraid. It looks like Clete is going to move back to New Orleans in a couple of weeks."

"Can I bring you something?"

"Well, no, but . . . Can you sit down a moment?"

"Sure."

The wind was warm off the water, and I was sweating inside my shirt even in the umbrella's shade.

"Clete's told me a little bit about this man Sonny Marsallus," she said. "Is it true he knows something about POW's in Southeast Asia?"

"It's hard to say, Ms. Serrett."

"It's Terry . . . We think my brother got left behind in Cambodia. But the government denies he was even there."

"Sonny was never in the service. Anything he . . . knew was conjecture, probably."

"Oh . . . I got the impression he had evidence of some kind."

Her sunglasses were tinted almost black, and the rest of her face was like an orange and white mask.

"I'm sorry about your brother," I said.

"Well, I hope I haven't bothered you," she said, and touched my elbow softly.

"No, not at all."

"I guess I'd better go before I burn up in this sun."

"It's a hot one," I said.

I watched her walk up the dock on her flats toward her car, a drawstring beach bag hanging from her wrist. The line of soft fat that protruded from her waistband was already pink with sunburn.

I went inside the bait shop. Alafair was stocking lunch meat and cold drinks in the wall cooler.

"Hi, Dave," she said. "Who was that lady?"

"Clete's secretary."

She made a face.

"What's wrong?" I said.

She looked out the window screen. "Where's Batist?" she said.

"Out on the ramp."

"She was sitting inside a half hour ago, smoking one cigarette after another, smelling the whole place up. Batist gave me his Pepsi because he had to go put some man's boat in. After he went out, she said, 'Better bring that over here, honey.'

"I didn't know what she meant. I walked over to her table and she took the can out of my hand and got a bunch of napkins out of the holder and started wiping the top. She said, 'You shouldn't drink after other people.' Then she put it back in my hand and said, 'There . . . Maybe now you won't have to scrub your gums with disinfectant. But I'd still pour it down the drain if I were you.'

"What's she doing here, Dave?"

* * *

Rufus Arceneaux lived in a wood frame house on Bayou Teche just outside St. Martinville. He had a gas light in his front yard, a new aluminum boat shed under his oak trees, an electric bug killer that snapped and hissed on his gallery. He did not resent his black neighbors because he considered himself superior to them and simply did not recognize their existence. Nor did he envy the rich, as he believed them the recipients of luck passed out by a society that was meant to be inequitable and often blessed the bumbling and the effete. His wary eye, instead, was directed at his peers and those among them who succeeded, he was sure, through stealth and design, and always at his expense.

He brought back a Japanese wife from Okinawa, a small, shy woman with bad teeth who worked briefly in a bakery and who lowered her eyes and covered her mouth when she grinned. One night the neighbors made a 911 call on Rufus's house, but the wife told the responding sheriff's deputies her television set had been tuned too loud, there was certainly no problem in the home.

One morning she did not report to work at the bakery. Rufus called the owner later and said she had mumps. When people saw her in town, her face was heavily made up, marbled with discolorations.

She left town on a Greyhound bus the following year. A Catholic priest who worked with Vietnamese refugees drove her to the depot in Lafayette and refused to tell anyone her destination.

For a while Rufus lived with a topless dancer from

Morgan City, then a woman who had been fired from her position as a juvenile probation officer in Lake Charles. There were others, too, who came and went, all out of that seemingly endless supply of impaired or abused women who find temporary solace in the approval of a man who will eventually degrade and reject them. As an ex-NCO, Rufus was not one to argue with long-established systems. The only constants in Rufus's life were his two hunting dogs and his squared-away, freshly painted frame house.

It was twilight when I drove up his dirt drive and parked my truck in the trees and walked behind his house. He was drinking bottled beer in his undershirt on the cement pad that served as a back porch, his knees crossed, a pork roast hissing on a rotisserie barbecue pit. Rufus's shoulders were as smooth as stone, olive with tan, a gold and red Marine Corps emblem tattooed on his right arm. At the foot of his sloping yard a half-flooded pirogue lay in the shadows, its sides soft with green mold.

As was his way, he was neither friendly nor unfriendly. My presence in his life, off the clock, had no more significance than the whir of cars out on the state highway. A brunette woman with unbrushed hair, in cutoff blue jeans, came outside, set a small table with wood salad bowls and plates, and never looked at me. Nor did he attempt to introduce her.

He slid a metal chair toward me with his foot.

"There's some cold drinks in the cooler," he said.

"I understand you drove Ruthie Jean Fontenot to the airport."

He put a cigarette in his mouth, worked his lighter

out of the watch pocket of his Levi's. It had a bronze globe and anchor soldered on its side.

"What's the problem on that, Dave?" he said.

"Are you working for the Bertrands?" I tried to smile.

"Not really."

"I got you."

"Just doing somebody a favor," he said.

"I see. You think Ruthie Jean's getting set up?"

"For what?"

"The Bertrands have their own way of doing business."

He drank from his beer, a slow, steady sip that showed neither need nor particular pleasure. He blew a cloud of cigarette smoke into the violet air. "We're going to eat in a minute," he said.

"I'm going to try to reopen the vehicular homicide case on Julia and Moleen."

"Be my guest. They weren't involved."

I looked at his rugged profile, the blond crewcut, the lump of cartilage in the jaw, the green eyes that were often filled with the lights of envy, and felt the peculiar sensation I was looking at an innocent who had no awareness of the lines he had stepped across.

"Moleen's mixed up with people who don't take prisoners, Roof," I said.

"Are you kidding? He's a needle dick. His wife slides up and down the banister all morning to keep his lunch warm."

"See you around," I said.

* * *

I woke early the next morning and drove out to the Bertrand plantation.

Why?

I really didn't know. The cement trucks, graders, and bulldozers were all idle and unattended now, sitting quietly among the swaths of destruction they had cut from the highway back to the treeline. Why had a company called Blue Sky Electric chosen this spot for its location? Access to the railroad? That was part of it, obviously. But there were a lot of train tracks in the state of Louisiana.

Maybe the answer lay in who lived here.

They were by and large disenfranchised and uneducated, with no political or monetary power. You did not have to be a longtime resident of Louisiana to understand their historical relationship to corporate industries.

Those who worked in the canneries were laid off at the end of the season, then told at the state of employment office that their unemployment claims were invalid because their trade was exclusively that of professional canners; and since the canneries were closed for the season, the workers were not available for work, and hence ineligible for the benefits that had been paid into their fund.

This was the Orwellian language used to people who had to sign their names with an *X*.

For years the rice and sugar mills fired anyone who used the word *union* and paid minimum wage only because of their participation in interstate commerce. During the civil rights era, oil men used to joke about having "a jig on every rig." But the racial invective was secondary to the real logos, which was to ensure the availability of a huge labor pool, both black and white, that would work for any wage that was offered them.

The stakes today, however, were geographical. The natural habitat's worst enemies, the chemical plants and oil refineries, had located themselves in a corridor along the Mississippi known as Toxic Alley, running from Baton Rouge down to St. Gabriel.

Almost without exception the adjacent communities were made up of blacks and poor whites.

I drove down the dirt road and stopped in front of Luke Fontenot's house. I saw his face at the window, then he opened the screen and walked out on the gallery, shirtless, barefoot, a jelly glass full of hot coffee in his hand.

"Something happen?" he said.

"No, I was just killing time. How you doing, Luke?"

"Ain't doing bad . . . You just driving around?"

"That's about it."

He inserted a thumbnail in his teeth, then folded his fingers and looked at the tops of his nails. "I need legal advice about something."

"Go ahead."

"Got to have your promise it ain't going nowhere."

"I'm a police officer, Luke."

"You a police officer when you *feel* like being one, Mr. Dave."

"I'd better get to the office."

He craned out over the railing, looked down the dirt road, measured the sun's height in the sky.

"Come on out back," he said.

I followed him around the side of the house. He paused by the back porch, slipped a pair of toeless canvas shoes over his feet, and pulled a cane sickle out of a tree stump where chickens had been butchered.

"See where the coulee go, out back of the old privy?" he said, walking ahead of me. "Yesterday they was running the grader along the edge of the coulee. The bank started caving, and the guy turned the grader out in the field and didn't do no more work here. Last night the moon was up and I seen something bright in the dirt."

The coulee ran like a ragged wound in the earth to the edge of a cane field, where it had been filled in years ago so the cultivated acreage would not be dissected by a water drainage. The sides were eaten and scrolled with crawfish holes, the bottom thick with cattails and reeds, webs of dead algae, cane husks, and through the cattails a chain of stagnant pools that trembled with insects.

Luke looked back over his shoulder at the dirt road, then slid down the side of the coulee and stepped across a pool to the opposite bank.

"See where the machine crushed down the dirt?" he said. "It look like a bottom lip hanging down, don't it?" He smiled up at me. "Mr. Dave, you gonna tell this to somebody?"

I squatted down on my haunches and didn't answer. He smiled again, blew out his breath, as though he were making an irrevocable commitment for both of us, then began working the tip of the sickle into the bank, scaling it away, watching each dirt clod that rolled down to his feet.

"What I found last night I stuck back in them holes," he said. He sliced at the bank, and a curtain of dirt cascaded across his canvas shoes. "Lookie there," he said, his fingers grabbing at three dull pieces of metal that toppled and bounced into the water.

He stooped, his knees splayed wide, shoved his wrists into the reeds and the water that was clouding with gray puffs of mud, worked his fingers deeper into the silt, then held up an oblong, coinlike piece of silver and dropped it into my palm.

"What you call that?" he said.

I rubbed my thumb across the slick surface, the embossed cross and archaic numbers and lettering on it.

"It's Spanish or Portuguese, Luke. I think these were minted in Latin America, then shipped back to Europe," I said.

"Aint Bertie been right all along. Jean Lafitte buried his treasure here."

"Somebody did. What was the advice you wanted?"

"The wall of this coulee's probably full of them coins. But we talked Aint Bertie into giving up her claim."

"This whole area is going to be covered with cement and buildings," I said. "The guys doing it don't care about the dead people buried here. Why should they care about the coins?"

"That's what I been thinking. No point bothering them."

"I couldn't argue with that. How about I buy you some breakfast up on the highway, Luke?"

"I'd like that real fine. Yes, suh, I was fixing to ax you the same thing."

Clete came into the office right after lunch. He wore a pair of seersucker slacks low on his hips and a dark blue short-sleeve silk shirt. He kept glancing back toward the glass partition into the hallway.

"Do I need a passport to get into this place?" he said. He got up, opened the door, and looked into a uniformed deputy's face. "Can I help you with something?"

He returned to his chair, looked hard at the glass again, his face flushed.

"Ease up, Clete," I said.

"I don't like people staring at me." The soles of his loafers tapped up and down on the floor.

"You want to tell me what it is?"

"Emile Pogue's trying to set you up."

"Oh?"

"You're going to step right into it, too." He paced in front of my desk and kept snapping his fingers and hitting his hands together. "I shouldn't have come in here."

"Just tell me what happened."

"He called my office. He said he wants to give himself up."

"Why didn't he call me?"

"He thinks you're tapped."

"Where is he, Clete?"

"I knew it."

Chapter 32

IT WAS LATE afternoon when we put my boat into the Atchafalaya River and headed east into the basin and the huge network of bayous, bays, sandbars, and flooded stands of trees that constitute the alluvial system of the river. The sun was hot and bloodred above the willow islands behind us and you could see gray sheets of rain curving out of the sky in the south and waves starting to cap in the bay. I opened up both engines full throttle and felt the water split across the bow, hiss along the hull like wet string, then flatten behind us in a long bronze trough dimpled with flying fish that glided on the wind like birds.

Clete sat on a cushioned locker behind me, his Marine Corps utility cap on the back of his head, pressing rounds from a box of .223 ammunition into a second magazine for my AR-15. Then he inverted the magazine and jungle-clipped it with electrician's tape to one that was already in the rifle. He saw me watching him.

"Lose the attitude, big mon. You blink on this dude and he'll take your eyes out," he said above the engine's noise.

I cut back on the throttle on the east side of the bay and let the wake take us into a narrow bayou that snaked through a flooded woods. Cottonmouth moccasins lay coiled on top of dead logs and the lowest cypress branches along the banks, and ahead I saw a white crane lift from a tiny inlet matted with hyacinths and glide for a time above the bayou, then suddenly rise through a red-gold, sunlit break in the canopy and disappear.

Clete was standing beside me now. There was no wind inside the trees, and I could smell mosquito dope running in his sweat. He wiped his eyes with the heel of his hand and swatted mosquitoes away from his hair.

"It's like being up the Mekong. It's got to be a setup," he said.

"I think he's scared."

"My ass. This guy's been killing people all his life. We can go around a corner and he can chop us into horse meat."

"That's not it. He's had too many other chances."

Clete pointed a finger at me, his eyes hard and big in his face, then went out of the cabin and worked his way forward to the bow, where he knelt on one knee with the AR-15 propped on his thigh, the sling wrapped around his forearm.

The sun fell through the canopy and illuminated a sunken houseboat and the pale, bloated carcass of a wild hog that had wedged under the porch roof. The metallic green backs of alligator gars rolled against the surface, then their long jaws and files of needlelike teeth parted as they went deep into the pocket where the hog's stomach used to be.

Up ahead was a blind corner. I began to believe

Clete had been right. Not only were the risks all ours, I had allowed myself to be convinced that an amoral, pathological man was more human, more capable of remorse, than he had ever shown himself to be previously. This bayou, shut off from light, filled with insects and gars and poisonous snakes, vaguely scented with the smells of decay and death, a place Joseph Conrad would have well understood, was Pogue's chosen environment, and so far we were operating on his terms.

I cut the engines, and in the sudden quiet I heard our wake sliding back across the sandbars into the woods, a crescendo of birds' wings flapping in the trees, a 'gator slapping its tail in water. But I didn't hear the St. Mary Parish sheriff's boat, with Helen Soileau on it, that should have been closing the back door on Emile Pogue.

I started to use the radio, then I saw Clete raise his hand in the air.

Someone was running in the woods, crashing through brush, splashing across a slough. I felt the bow bite into a sandbar and the boat become motionless. I went forward with Clete and tried to see through the tree trunks, the tangle of air vines, the leaves that tumbled out of the canopy, the pools of mauve shadow that seemed to take the shape of animals.

Then we heard the roar of an airboat out on the next bay.

"How do you figure that?" Clete said.

"Maybe he wants another season to run."

We dropped off the bow onto the sandbar and worked our way along the bank and through the shallows to the corner. The back of Clete's neck was oily with sweat, inflamed with insect bites. He put an unlit cigarette in his mouth, paused at the bend in the bayou, then stepped out in the open, his face blank, his eyes flicking from one object to the next.

He pointed.

An aluminum boat with an outboard engine was tied with a chain to a cypress knee on the bank, and beyond it a shack was set back in the willows on pilings. The screens were webbed with rust, dead insects, and dirt, and the tin roof had long ago taken on the colors of a woods in winter. The base of the pilings glistened with a sheen like petroleum waste from the pools of stagnant water they sat in. Clete pressed a wadded handkerchief to his face. The dry ground behind the shack was blown with bottle flies and reeked of unburied excrement.

I slipped my .45 from my holster, pulled back the slide on a hollow-point round, and moved through the trees toward the rear of the shack while Clete approached the front. The water had receded only recently, and the sand was wet and curled over my tennis shoes like soft cement. I heard sound inside the shack, then realized a radio was playing. It was Ravel's *Bolero*, compelling and incessant, building like a painful obsession you can't let go of.

I came out of the trees ten feet from the rear of the shack and saw Clete poised by the front entrance, his face waiting. I held up my hand, then brought it down and we both went in at the same time.

Except my foot punched through a plank on the back step that was as soft as rotted cork. I stumbled into the interior still limping, my .45 pointed straight out with both hands. Clete was silhouetted against the broken light beyond the front door, his rifle hanging from his right hand. He was looking at something on the floor.

Then I saw him, amidst the litter of soiled clothes and fishing gear and barbells. He lay on his back by a small table with a shortwave radio on it, dressed in jeans, a sleeveless green T-shirt, suspenders, his bare feet like pale white blocks of wood. A dark pool shaped like a deformed three-leaf clover swelled from the back of his neck. I knelt beside him.

He opened his mouth and coughed on an obstruction deep in his throat. His tongue was as red and bright as licorice. I started to turn him on his side.

"Don't do it, chief," he whispered. "He broke the shank off inside."

"Who did this to you, Emile?"

"Never saw him. A pro. Maybe that cocksucker Marsallus."

His eyes came together like BB's, then refocused on my face.

"We're going to put you on my boat, then get you out in the bay so a chopper can pick you up," I said.

But he was already shaking his head before I finished my words. His eyes slid off my face onto my shirt.

"What is it?" I said.

"Lean close."

I lowered my ear toward his mouth, then realized that was not what he wanted. His hand lifted up and clenched around my religious medal and chain, knotted it across his knuckles, held me hovering above the shrunken pinpoints of his eyes.

"I ain't got the right words. Too many bad gigs, chief. I apologize for the Dutchie," he whispered.

When his hand fell from my chain, his breath mushroomed out of his mouth and struck against my face like a fist. A bottle fly crawled across his eyes.

Clete clicked off the dial on the shortwave set. The dead radio tubes crackled in the silence.

Chapter 33

The next morning Helen Soileau walked with me into Clete's office on Main. The front and back doors were open, and the papers in Clete's wire baskets lifted and ruffled in the breeze. Helen looked around the office.

"Where's Avon's answer to the Beast of Buchenwald?" she said.

"What's the problem?" Clete said from behind his desk, trying to smile.

"They knew we were coming, that's the problem," she said.

"Terry? Come on," he said.

"Where is she?" Helen said.

"Getting some stuff photocopied."

"Does she have any scratches on her?" I said.

"You want me to strip-search my secretary?"

"It's not funny, Clete," I said.

"She wasn't in the office when Pogue called," he said.

"You're sure?" I said.

"She was across the street at the doughnut place."

"You didn't tell her about it?" I asked.

"No . . ." His eyes looked into space. "No, I'm sure of it. I never mentioned Pogue's name, never mentioned a place."

Helen looked at me and made a sucking sound with her teeth. "Okay," she said. "Maybe the hit was already on him. There's Marsallus to think about, too."

"Not with a knife. We're talking about one of Pogue's buddies from the Phoenix Program," Clete said. He leaned over in his chair and clicked on a floor fan, clamped his hand on top of a yellow legal pad by his telephone. The pages blew and rattled in the gust of air.

"Why would anyone try to take a guy like Pogue with a knife? Unless the killer knew we were in the vicinity?" I said.

Clete scratched at the scar that ran through his eyebrow, rested his chin on his knuckles.

"I guess you're right, you got a leak. How about that buttwipe who was in the Crotch?" he said.

"Rufus Arceneaux?" Helen said.

Clete and I drove to New Orleans at dawn, turned off I-10 onto St. Charles Avenue, and went uptown toward the Garden District, past the lovely old Pontchartrain Hotel and rows of antebellum and early Victorian homes with their narrow pillared galleries and oak-canopied yards that stayed black with shadow even in summer. We turned left across the neutral ground and the streetcar tracks and crossed Prytania, the street where Lillian Hellman grew up, then headed up Magazine, the old line of disembarkation into the Irish Channel, toward the levee and a different New Orleans, one of late-nineteenth-century paintless frame houses with ventilated shutters and hardpan dirt yards and tiny galleries propped up on bricks, clapboard corner bars that never closed or took down their Christmas lights, matchbox barbecue joints that smelled of hickory and ribs by 9 A.M., and graffiti-scrolled liquor stores whose windows were barred like jails.

I parked in front of the address Luke Fontenot had given me. A thundershower had just passed through the neighborhood and the air was gray and wet and steam rose from the roofs like smoke in winter. Clete rolled down the window and squinted at the rows of almost identical, weathered, coffee-colored houses, a ramshackle tin-roofed juke joint overgrown with banana trees on the corner, an elderly black man in a frayed suit and sneakers and baseball cap riding a bicycle with fat tires aimlessly up and down the street. I could see shadows and lights in Clete's face, like reflections that cling inside frost on a window.

"They say if you're ever black on Saturday night, you'll never want to be white again," he said.

"You usually hear white people say that after they shortchange the yardman," I said.

"Our house was one block over."

I waited for him to go on, but he didn't.

"You want to come in?" I said.

"No, it's your show. I'm going to get a cup of coffee."

"Something on your mind?"

He laughed down in his chest, rubbed a knuckle against his nose. "My old man knocked me into next week because I dropped his bucket of beer in front of that juke joint. He was quite a guy. I was never big on nostalgia, Streak."

I watched him walk toward the levee, his porkpie hat slanted on the crown of his head, his face lifted into the breeze off the river, his feelings walled up inside a private place where I never transgressed.

Ruthie Jean's address was a two-story house with a fire escape for an upstairs entrance and wash strung across the veranda and a single paint-blistered trellis that was spoked with red roses.

A police cruiser with the NOPD crescent on the door and a white cop in a sky blue shirt behind the wheel slowed by my pickup as I was locking the door behind me.

"Can I help you?" he said.

I opened my badge holder in my palm.

"On the job," I said, and smiled.

"Work on your tan if you're coming back after sunset," he said.

"Thanks," I said, and felt conspiratorial and slightly ashamed at my own response.

A moment later Ruthie Jean opened the door at the head of the fire escape. She wore a pair of new blue jeans with a silver-tipped western belt and white tennis shoes and a burnt orange blouse and gold hoop earrings. This time there was no anger or recrimination in her face; in fact, I had the sense she expected me.

"I need to talk to you about Moleen," I said.

"You surely don't give it up."

"You don't have to talk to me, Ruthie Jean."

"I know that. Come in, if you like."

The living room was airy and cool, the upholstered

couch and chairs patterned with flowers and decorated with doilies. The curtains puffed and twisted in the breeze, and you could see the top of the levee and hear boats with horns out on the river.

"Can I give you some coffee?" she said.

"That'd be nice."

I sat in a deep chair while she fixed a tray in the kitchen. A steamer trunk lay opened by the couch. In a removable top compartment, which she had set at an angle to the sides in order to pack the bottom, was a clear plastic bag with folded blue and pink baby clothes inside. A withered camellia was pressed between the fabric and the plastic.

She limped into the living room with the tray; her eyes followed mine to the trunk. She lowered the tray down on the coffee table, then reset the wood compartment inside the trunk and closed the lid.

"Why you dislike Moleen so much?" she said.

"He thinks it's natural for other people to pay for his mistakes."

"If you're talking about the abortion, it was me went over to Texas. Moleen didn't have anything to do with it."

"Moleen ran down and killed the little boy out by Cade, not his wife."

"I don't believe that."

I leaned forward with my forearms on my thighs and rubbed my palm idly on my knuckles.

"I don't know how to tell you this," I said. "But I believe Julia Bertrand may try to do you grave injury. Maybe with Moleen's consent."

"You cain't forgive him for the world he comes

from, Mr. Robicheaux. It's not his fault who he was born."

I was at a loss.

"Do you have a gun?" I asked.

"No."

Her face made me think of a newly opened dark flower about to be burned by a severe light.

"You're an admirable lady, Ruthie Jean. I hope you're going to be all right. Call me if I can ever help you in any way."

"That's why you sent that other man?"

"Excuse me?"

"The one with the red hair and the skin look like milk. He was standing outside in the rain. I axed him what he was doing in this neighborhood at night. He said he was your friend and you were worried about me. He's your friend, isn't he?"

"Yes, I think he probably is."

"Think?"

I started to explain, but I didn't. Then I simply said, "I'd better be going now."

Her turquoise eyes, gold skin, the mole by her mouth, her thick black hair that curved on her cheek were framed as though in a lens by the curtains that puffed and danced behind her head. Her eyes moved up to meet mine.

"You're a very good man," she said.

"Good-bye, Ruthie Jean," I said, and took her hand in mine. It was small and dry and I wanted to hold it a long time. I knew in a way that words could not explain that this was much more than a casual farewell.

* * *

We pulled into the circle drive of the yacht club and parked not far from the practice green. The yacht club was sparkling white in the sunlight, with flagstone terraces and tinted, glassed-in dining areas and fairways that looked like corridors of velvet between the oak trees. When we got out of the truck, Clete pulled his shirt down over the front of his slacks, smoothed it with his fingers, adjusted his belt with his thumb, looked down at his shirt again.

"How does a prick like Johnny Carp get in a joint like this?" he said.

"They recognize a closet Republican when they see one."

"How do I look?" he said.

"Lean and mean, not a bump on you."

"You sure you want to do this?"

"You got to do something for kicks," I said.

"I'm starting to worry about you, big mon."

We walked in the shade of the building toward the entrance. Sailboats were rocking in their slips out on Lake Pontchartrain. The maître d' stopped us at the door to the dining room.

"Do you gentlemen have reservations?" he said. His face and accent were European, his closed-shaved cheeks ruddy with color.

I opened my badge holder. "We're here to see Polly Gee," I said. He looked at me blankly. "That's Johnny Carp . . . *John Giacano.* His secretary said he's having lunch here."

His facial skin tightened against the bone. His eyes involuntarily glanced at a glass-domed annex to the main dining room. He cleared his throat softly.

"Is there going to be a problem, gentlemen?" he asked.

"We'll let you know if there is. Bring me a double Jack, with a Dixie on the side, and put it on Johnny's tab. He told me to tell you that," Clete said.

The domed annex was empty, except for Johnny Carp and his crew, who were eating from gumbo appetizer bowls at a long linen-covered table set with flowers and pitchers of sangria. Johnny lowered his spoon from his mouth, his face dead. A scar, like a piece of black string, was crimped into his lip where I had hit him. One of Johnny's crew, a one-thousand-dollar-a-hit mechanic named Mingo Bloomberg, started to rise from his chair. He was a handsome, copper-haired man with ice blue eyes that were totally devoid of moral light.

"The man with the badge has a pass. You don't, Purcel," he said.

"Don't get up on my account," Clete said.

"A guy's got to try. It's nothing personal."

"Put your hand on me and you're going to wear a metal hook, Mingo."

"So we see how it shakes out," Mingo said, and began to stand up.

Clete fitted his hand on Mingo's face and shoved him back down in his chair. Then he hit him twice with the flat of his hand, like a man swinging a fielder's glove filled with cement.

"You want another one?" he said. "Tell me now, Mingo. Go ahead, open your mouth again."

I cupped my palm around Clete's bicep. It felt like a grapefruit.

"I'm fed up with this shit. Somebody get security in here," Johnny said.

"You're looking good, John," I said.

"You're a lucky man, Dave." He pointed his fork at me. "You ought to burn a few candles at your church."

"That's not quite how I see it, John," I said. "You don't want to queer your people's action in Iberia Parish by killing a police officer, but then again you're not always predictable. That means I need to do something about you, like maybe squeeze Patsy Dapolito until he gives you up. You think Patsy will give you up, John?"

"What's to give? He don't work for me no more. He never really did."

"Oh?" I said.

"That's right, he's a malignant geek, a short-eyes, a freak. You gonna nail me with the testimony of a child molester? You know what my lawyer would do with a guy like that on the stand? When he gets excited he drools. Hey, you guys, picture star witness Patsy Bones drooling on the stand." Johnny stretched his face out of shape and let his tongue roll wetly in his mouth while all his crew laughed. "You two twerps get out of here."

"It's always a pleasure, John," I said.

Clete picked up a bread stick, dipped it in a sangria

pitcher, and snapped it off in his jaw, winking at me while he grinned outrageously.

Outside in the parking lot, he pulled up his shirt and removed the tape recorder from under his belt, popped out the cassette, and flipped it in his palm.

"Isn't life grand?" he said.

Chapter 34

I WAS FILLING out my time sheet the next day when Helen Soileau knocked on my office door, then sat on the corner of the desk and looked me in the face, her eyes seeming to focus on words or sentences in her head that would never become the right ones to use.

"Say it," I said.

"I just got off the phone with Fart, Barf, and Itch in New Orleans. Marsallus is dead. They've got his body."

I returned her stare and didn't answer.

"Dave?"

"Yeah."

"Did you hear me?"

"I heard you. I don't believe it."

"The body never washed up because it was wedged in the pilings of that collapsed pier."

I looked out the window. The sky was thick with lead-colored clouds, the trees filmed with dust, motionless in the trapped heat. The traffic on the street seemed to make no sound.

"How'd they ID the body?" I said.

"Dental records."

"What dental records?" I said, the irritation rising

in my voice. "Sonny grew up in a welfare project. He probably went to a dentist as often as he went to a gynecologist."

"The agent says they're a hundred percent sure it's Sonny."

"He worked for the Feds. He was an embarrassment to them. They want his file closed."

"Do you know what denial is?"

"Yeah. With me it has to do with booze, not dead people."

"You want to go to lunch?"

"No. Where's the body?"

"On its way to a mortuary in New Orleans. Leave it alone, Dave." She watched my face. "Water and fish and crabs do bad things."

I rose from my desk and looked silently out the window until she was gone. Outside, a trusty from the parish lopped a dead banana stalk in half with a machete, revealing a swarm of fire ants that fed off the rotten pulp inside.

"You sure you want to see it?" the mortician, a middle-aged black man, said. It was late and he was tired. He wore a T-shirt and rumpled slacks without a belt, and there was stubble on his chin. "Okay, if that's what you want. You say he was a friend?"

"Yes."

He raised his eyebrows and opened the door to a back room where the temperature was twenty degrees lower than the front of the funeral home. It smelled of chemicals, stainless steel, the cool odor of scrubbed concrete.

Over his shoulder I could see an elevated flat-bottomed metal trough in the center of the room.

"It's going to be in a closed coffin. His relatives will never see inside it," he said.

He stepped aside, and I saw the bloodless, shrunken form stretched out inside the trough, glowing in a cone of electric light that shone from overhead.

"There's morticians won't work on these kinds," he said. "I got a government contract, though, so I do everything they send me . . . Is that him?"

"That's not a human form anymore."

"Your friend had red hair?"

I didn't reply. He waited. I heard him put on his glasses, fiddle with a fountain pen.

"I'll show you the bullet wounds. There're four," he said. He leaned over the trough, pointing with the pen. "Two through the chest, one in the groin, one through the side. They look like dimples in oatmeal now."

"There weren't any rounds," I said.

"Believe me, Mr. Robicheaux, those are exit wounds. I worked in the mortuary at Chu Lai, Republic of South Vietnam. I took guys out of body bags been in there a long time, get my drift? . . . Look, the government doesn't make the kind of mistake you're thinking about."

"Then how'd we all end up in Vietnam?" I asked.

He walked to the door and put his hand on the wall switch. "I'm turning off the lights now. You coming?" he said.

* * *

I dreamed all night, then got up just before dawn and fixed coffee in the kitchen and drank it on the back steps. The sun was still below the treeline in the swamp and the air was moist and cool and smelled of milkweed and the cattle in my neighbor's field. I kept seeing Sonny's bloodless face and sightless eyes and red hair, like the head of John the Baptist on a metal tray. I flung my coffee into the flower bed and drove to Clete's apartment off East Main.

"You're starting the day like a thunderstorm, Streak," he said, yawning in his Jockey underwear, pulling a shirt over his wide shoulders.

"Alafair and Pogue both saw him. So did Ruthie Jean Fontenot."

"People see Elvis Presley. How about James Dean or Adolf Hitler, for God's sakes?"

"This is different."

"You want to go crazy? Keep living inside your head like that."

He slid a carton of chocolate milk and a box of jelly doughnuts out of the icebox and started eating.

"You want some?" he asked.

"I want to jump-start Patsy Dap."

"How you going to feel if he takes down Johnny Carp?"

"I won't feel anything," I said.

"Yeah, I bet."

"I won't ever believe Sonny's dead," I said.

"Don't talk to me about this stuff anymore."

"One way or another, Sonny's out there, Clete."

"I don't want to hear it, I don't want to hear it, I don't want to hear it," he said, walking into the bathroom, working one hand into his shorts.

We drove in my truck out to Patsy Dapolito's rented cottage on the edge of town, but no one answered the door. Clete shielded the sun's glare from his eyes and squinted through the blinds on the side window.

"Look at the litter in there. I bet this guy takes a shit inside his clothes," he said.

"I'll check with the landlord."

"Patsy's in a trick pad in Lafayette."

"How do you know?"

"A guy I wrote a bond on said he's got a couple of chippies at Four Corners who aren't too selective."

"That doesn't mean he's there."

"When your name is Patsy Dap, you're either thinking about getting laid or blowing out somebody's light. I'm seldom wrong about these guys. That bothers me sometimes."

I looked at him strangely.

"Be happy you got your badge, Streak. It means you get to walk on the curb instead of in the gutter," he said.

A half hour later we walked into the office of a motel at Four Corners in Lafayette. Raindrops were tinkling on the air-conditioner inset in the window. I showed my badge and a picture of Patsy Dap to the motel operator.

"Do you know this man?" I asked.

He crinkled his nose under his glasses, looked vague, shook his head.

"Lot of people come through here," he said.

"You want to get your whole place tossed?" I said.

"Room six," he replied.

"Give us the key . . . Thanks, we're putting you down for a good citizen award," Clete said.

We walked down to Dapolito's room as the rain blew underneath the overhang. I tapped with one knuckle on the door.

"It's Dave Robicheaux. Open up, Patsy," I said.

It was quiet a moment, then he spoke in a phlegmy, twisted voice: "Leave me alone 'less you got a warrant."

I turned the key in the lock, nudged the door open with my foot, my hand on my .45.

"Ooops," Clete said, peering over my shoulder.

"You guys get out of here," Patsy said from the bed.

Clete pushed the door back slowly with the flat of his hand, sniffed at the air as we both stepped inside.

"You paying for your broads to smoke China white? High-grade stuff, my man," Clete said.

She was not over sixteen, blond and beautiful in a rough way, with thick arms and shoulders, a heart-shaped face that wore no makeup, hands that could have been a farm girl's. She gathered the top sheet around her body. I pulled the bedspread off the foot of the bed, wrapped it around her, then handed her her clothes.

"Dress in the bathroom while we talk to this man," I said. "We're not going to arrest you."

Her eyes were disjointed, one pupil larger than the other, glazed with fear and Oriental smack.

"Listen, this man kills people for a living. But if

he didn't get paid, he'd do it for free. Don't ever come here again," I said.

"Why the roust this time?" Patsy said. He sat with his back against the headboard, his hard, compact body as white as the skin on a toadstool, one hand kneading the sheet that covered his loins. A bluebird was tattooed above each of his nipples.

"I think you might still want to pop me, Patsy. Earn some points with Polly Gee," I said.

"You're wrong. I'm going on a trip, all over the world, places I ain't ever got to visit."

"Really?" I said.

"Yeah, I got an itinerary, everything. A Japanese travel service put it together. They even give you a booklet tells you how to get along with everybody, what things to watch out for. Don't get on elevators with Iranians 'cause of the BO they got. Don't shake hands with Arabs 'cause they wipe their ass with their bare hand."

"Sounds great, except I don't believe you," I said. I saw the girl go past the corner of my vision, out the door. "Click on the tape, Clete."

Clete set the portable tape player on the desk and snapped the Play button. Patsy's scarred face looked confused at first as he heard Mingo Bloomberg's voice, then Clete's and Johnny Carp's and mine.

"What is this?" he said.

"I'll start it again. We don't want you to miss any of this. Particularly when they start laughing at you," Clete said.

As Patsy listened, the skin on one side of his face seemed to crinkle like the surface of paint in a bucket.

He lit a cigarette, one eye watering with the heat of the flame.

"You going to do hits for a guy like that?" Clete said.

Patsy's teeth protruded above his bottom lip like a ridge of bone. He huffed smoke out of the corner of his mouth.

"I don't want you thinking about whacking out Johnny, either. If Johnny gets capped, this tape goes to NOPD," I said.

"I can hurt Johnny in ways you ain't thought about. You're stupid, Robicheaux. That's why you're a cop," he said.

Clete and I walked outside and closed the door behind us. The rain was swirling in the wind.

"What do you think he meant?" Clete said.

"Who knows?"

"Dave, you going to be okay? You don't look too good."

"I'm fine," I said.

But I wasn't. I had no sooner closed the door to the pickup's cab when I had to open it again and vomit on the concrete. My face was cold with sweat. I felt Clete's big hand on my neck.

"What is it, Streak?" he said.

"The tattoo."

"On fuckhead in there?"

"On Sonny's shoulder. A Madonna figure. I saw it in the mortuary."

Chapter 35

LATER, I DROVE north of town to the sheriff's house on Bayou Teche and walked around his dripping live oaks to the gallery, where he sat in a straw chair with his pipe and a glass of lemonade. His house was painted yellow and gray, and petals from his hydrangeas were scattered like pink confetti on the grass; in back, I could see the rain dimpling on the bayou.

He listened while I talked, never interrupting, snuffing down in his nose sometimes, clicking his pipe on his teeth.

"Do like Purcel and Helen tell you, Dave. Let Marsallus go," he said.

"I feel to blame."

"That's vain as hell, if you ask me."

"Sir?"

"You're a gambler, Dave. Marsallus faded the backline and bet against himself a long time ago."

I looked at the rain rings out on the bayou, at a black man in a pirogue under a cypress overhang who was tossing a handline and baited treble hook into the current.

"And as far as this supernatural stuff is concerned, I think Marsallus is alive only in your head," he said.

"People have seen him."

"Maybe they see what you want them to see."

Wrong, skipper, I thought. But this time I kept my own counsel.

"Somebody knew we were coming for Pogue," I said. "Maybe we've got a leak in the department."

"Who?"

"How about Rufus Arceneaux?"

He thought for a moment, adjusted his shirt collar with his thumb.

"Rufus would probably do almost anything, Dave, as long as he thought he was in control of it. He'd be out of his depth on this one."

"How'd they know we were coming?"

"Maybe it was just coincidence. We don't solve every crime. This might be one of them."

"They're wiping their feet on us, Sheriff."

He ran a pipe cleaner through the stem of his pipe and watched it emerge brown and wet from the metal airhole.

"You're lucky you don't smoke," he said.

After work I went home and put on my gym shorts and running shoes and worked out with my weight set in the backyard. It had stopped raining and the sky was rippled with purple and crimson clouds and loud with the droning of tree frogs. Then I went inside and showered and put on a fresh pair of khakis and began poking through the clothes hangers in the closet. Boots sat on the bed and watched me.

"Where's my old charcoal shirt?" I asked.

"I put it in your trunk. It's almost cheesecloth."

"That's why I wear it. It's comfortable."

The trunk was in the back of the closet. I unlocked it and saw the shirt folded next to my AR-15 and the holstered nine-millimeter Beretta I had taught Alafair how to shoot. I removed the shirt, locked the trunk, and dropped the key in a dresser drawer.

"You still thinking about Sonny?" she said.

"No, not really."

"Dave?"

"It's not my job to explain what's unexplainable. St. Paul said there might be angels living among us, so we should be careful how we treat one another. Maybe he knew something."

"You haven't said this to anybody else, have you?"

"Who cares?"

I started to button my shirt, but she got off the bed and began buttoning it for me.

"You're too much, Streak," she said, nudging my leg with her knee.

In the morning I called a half dozen licensing agencies in Baton Rouge for any background I could get on Blue Sky Electric Company. No one seemed to know much about them, other than the fact they had acquired every permit they needed to begin construction on their current site by Cade.

What was their history?

No one seemed to know that, either.

Where had they been in business previously?

Eastern Washington and briefly in Missoula, Montana.

I called a friend in the chemistry department at the University of Southwestern Louisiana in Lafayette, then met him for lunch in the student center, which looked out upon a cypress-filled lake on the side of old Burke Hall. He was an elderly, wizened man who didn't suffer fools and was notorious for his classroom histrionics, namely, kicking his shoes across the lecture room the first day of class and gracefully flipping the text over his shoulder into a wastebasket.

"What do these guys make?" he said.

"Nobody seems to know."

"What do they un-make?"

"I beg your pardon?"

"It's not a profound concept, Dave. If they don't make things, they dispose of things. You said they had an incinerator. Who besides Satan needs an incinerator in a climate like this?"

"They do something with electrical transformers," I said.

His eyes looked like slits, his skin webbed like dry clay.

"If they're incinerating the oil in the transformers, they're probably emitting PCB's into the environment. PCB's not only go into the air, they go into the food chain. Anticipate a change in local cancer statistics," he said.

Back at my office I called the EPA in Washington, D.C., then newspapers and wire services in Seattle and Helena, Montana. Blue Sky Electric had changed its corporate name at least seven times and had been kicked out of or refused admission to thirteen states. Each time it departed an area, it left behind a Superfund cleanup that ran into millions of dollars. The great irony was that the cleanup was contracted by the same corporation that owned the nonunion railroad that transported the transformers to Blue Sky Electric.

The last place they had tried to set up business was in Missoula, where they had been driven out of town by a virtual lynch mob.

Now they had found a new home with the Bertrand family, I thought.

"What are you going to do?" Helen said.

"Spit in the punch bowl."

I called the *Daily Iberian*, the Baton Rouge *Morning Advocate*, the New Orleans *Times-Picayune*, the Sierra Club, an ACLU lawyer who delighted in filing class action suits on behalf of minorities against polluters, and a RICO prosecutor with the U.S. attorney general's office.

After work, Rufus Arceneaux stopped me on the way to my truck in the parking lot. His armpits were dark with sweat rings, his breath as rank as an ashtray

"I need to talk with you," he said.

"Do it on the clock."

"This is private. I got no deep involvement with the Bertrands. I did a little security for them, that's all."

"What are you telling me, Roof?"

"Any kind of shit coming down on their head, problems with the greaseballs, it's got nothing to do with me. I'm out. Understand what I'm saying?"

"No."

I could smell the fear in his sweat. He walked away from me, his GI haircut as slick as a peeled onion against the late sun.

* * *

That evening I helped Batist bail and chain-lock our rental boats and close up the bait shop. The air was dry and hot, the sky empty of clouds and filled with a dull white light like a reflection off tin. My hands, my chest, seemed to burn with an energy I couldn't free myself from.

"What's got your burner on, Streak?" Bootsie said in the living room.

"Rufus Arceneaux's trying to disassociate himself from the Bertrands. He knows something's about to hit the fan."

"I don't un—" she began.

"Clete and I shook up Patsy Dapolito. He said he could hurt Johnny Carp in ways I hadn't thought about."

"That psychopath is after Julia and Moleen?"

"I don't know," I said. I went into the bedroom, picked up my .45 in its holster, and drove into New Iberia.

It was dusk when I turned into Moleen's drive and parked by his glassed-in back porch. Every light was on in the house, but I saw Moleen out on his sloping lawn, raking pine needles into a pile under a tree. Behind him a shrimp boat with green and red running lights on was headed down Bayou Teche toward the Gulf.

"Is there some reason I should have been expecting you?" he said.

"Patsy Dap."

"Who?"

"I kicked a two-by-four up his butt yesterday. I

think he might try to square a beef with Johnny by going through you."

"You have problems with your conscience, sir?"

"Not over you."

"A matter of principle, that sort of thing?"

"I've said what I had to say."

"You loathed us long before any of this began."

"Your friends murdered Sonny Boy Marsallus. Either you or Julia ran down and killed a child. One of these days the bill's going to come due, Moleen."

I walked back toward my truck. Through the lighted windows I could see Julia, in a yellow dress, a drink in her hand, talking brightly on the phone.

I heard Moleen behind me, felt his hand bite into my arm with surprising strength.

"Do you think I wanted any of this to happen? Do you know what it's like to wake up every morning with your whole—" He waved his arm vaguely at the air, as a drunk man might. Then he blanched, as though he were watching himself from outside his own skin.

"I don't think you're well, Moleen. Get some help. Go into the witness protection program."

"What do you suggest about Ruthie Jean?"

"If that's her choice, she can go with you."

'You have no idea how naive you are, sir," he said.

He wore a stained white shirt and a pair of baggy seersucker slacks with no belt. For just a moment, in the deepening shadows, with the splayed cane rake propped in his hand, a drop of sweat hanging on his chin, he no longer looked like the man whom I had resented most of my life.

"Is there anything I can do?" I said.

"No, but thank you, anyway, Dave. Good night."

I held out my business card. He hesitated, then took it, smiling wanly, and inserted it in his watch pocket.

"Good night, Moleen," I said.

I woke early Saturday morning and went to Red's Gym in Lafayette and worked out hard on the speed and heavy bag, did three miles on the outdoor track, then drove back home and helped Alafair and Batist fix lunch for the fishermen who returned to the dock during the midday heat. But I couldn't rid myself of a nameless, undefined red-black energy that made my palms ring, the pulse beat in my wrists. The only feeling I'd had like it was on benders of years ago when my whiskey supply was cut off, or in Vietnam, when we were moved into a free-fire zone only to learn that the enemy had gone.

I called Moleen's house.

"I'm afraid you've missed him," Julia said.

"Would you have him call me when he comes back?"

"I've just hired an auctioneer to get rid of his things. Oh, I'm sorry, would you like to come out before the sale and pick up a bargain or two?"

"There's a New Orleans greaseball in town named Patsy Dapolito."

"I'm supposed to be on the first tee by one o'clock. Otherwise, I'd love to chat. You're always so interesting, Dave."

"We can put a cruiser by your house. There's still time for alternatives, Julia."

"You're such a dear. Bye-bye now."

Later, Alafair went to a picture show in town and Bootsie and I fixed deviled eggs and ham and onion sandwiches and ate them on the kitchen table in front of the floor fan.

"You want to go to Mass this afternoon instead of in the morning?" she said.

"Sure."

She swallowed a small bite from her sandwich and fixed her eyes on my face. Her hair moved in the breeze from the fan. She started to speak.

"I've made my peace about Sonny," I said. "He was brave, he was stand-up, he never compromised his principles. That's not a bad recommendation to take into the next world."

"You're special, Streak."

"So are you, kiddo."

After we did the dishes she walked down to the vegetable garden at the end of the coulee, with the portable phone in her hand in case I was down at the dock when Alafair called from the show.

A blue Plymouth turned into the drive, and a moment later I saw Terry Serrett walk across the grass toward the gallery. She was dressed in loose-fitting pink-striped shorts, a white blouse, and red sandals; her drawstring beach bag swung against her thigh. Before she mounted the steps, she paused, looked back at the road and down at the dock.

I came to the screen door before she knocked. Her

sunglasses were black in the shade; her mouth, which was bright red with lipstick, opened in surprise.

"Oh, there you are!" she said.

"Can I help you?"

"Maybe, if I could come in a minute."

I looked at my watch and tried to smile. "What's up?" I said. But I didn't open the screen.

She looked awkward, uncomfortable, her shoulders stiffening, an embarrassed grin breaking on the corner of her mouth.

"I'm sorry to ask you this, but I *have* to use your rest room."

I opened the door and she walked past me into the living room, her eyes seeming to adjust or focus behind her glasses, as though she were examining the furniture in the room or perhaps in the hallway or in the kitchen.

"It's down the hall," I said.

A moment later I heard the toilet flush and the water in the lavatory running.

She walked back into the living room.

"That's better," she said. She examined the room, listening. "It's so quiet. Are you Saturday house-sitting?"

"Oh, I'll be going down to work at the dock in a little while."

She was absolutely immobile, as though she were caught between two antithetical thoughts, her thickly made-up face as white and as impossible to penetrate as a Kabuki mask.

The phone rang on the table by the couch.

"Excuse me a minute," I said, and sat down and picked up the receiver from the hook. Through the front screen I saw Batist walking from the dock, up the slope toward the house.

"Dave?" the voice said through the receiver.

"Hey, Clete, what's happening?" I said.

"You remember Helen gave me a Xerox of Sonny's diary? All this time I had it under my car seat. This morning I brought it in and told Terry to stick it in the safe. A little while later I check, guess what, it's gone and so is she. I'm sitting at the desk by the safe, feeling like a stupid fuck, and I look down at the notepad there, you know, the one I took directions to Pogue's place on, and I realize the top sheet's clean. I'm sure I haven't used that pad since Pogue called. Somebody tore off the page that had my pencil impressions on it . . .

"You there?"

Chapter 36

She pointed the Ruger .22 caliber automatic at my stomach.

"So you're Charlie," I said.

She didn't answer. Her body was framed against the light through the window, as though crystal splinters were breaking over her shoulders. She looked out the window at Batist walking through the shade trees toward the gallery.

"Tell him you're busy, you'll be down at the dock later," she said. "Use those exact words."

"None of this serves your cause."

She picked up a pillow from a stuffed chair.

"You need to get rid of the black man," she said.

I rose to my feet. She backed against the front wall, the pillow folded across the top of the Ruger. Her mouth was parted slightly, as though she used air only in teaspoons. I stood in the door and called through the screen: "I'll be down at the dock later, Batist."

"The air pump gone out on the shiner tank," he said.

I hesitated, opened and closed my hands at my sides, felt the trees, the yard, the fractured blue of the sky almost pulling me through the screen. The woman named Terry raised the Ruger level with the side of my head, whispered dryly: "He won't make three steps after I do you."

"Give me a few minutes," I called.

"One of us got to go in town."

"I know that, podna."

"Long as you know," he said, and walked back down the slope.

I could hear the wood in the floor creak under my feet, the wind scudding leaves across the gallery.

"Back away from the door," the woman said.

"We've still got the original manuscript," I said.

"Nobody else cares about it. Back away from the door and sit in the stuffed chair."

"Fuck you, Terry, or whatever your name is."

Her face was as opaque as plaster. She closed the ends of the pillow around the Ruger, brought the barrel's tip upward until it was aimed at my throat.

I felt my eyes water and go out of focus.

Outside, Tripod raced on his chain up and down the clothesline. Her face jerked at the sound, then she shifted her weight, glanced quickly at the side window, an incisor tooth biting down on her lip, inadvertently moved the barrel's aim two inches to the side of my throat.

Bootsie fired from the hallway, the Beretta pointed in front of her with both hands.

The first round hit the woman high up in the right arm. Her blouse jumped and colored as though a small rose had been painted in the cloth by an invisible brush. But she swallowed the sound that tried to rise from her throat, and turned toward the hallway with the Ruger still in her hand.

Bootsie fired again, and the second round snapped a brittle hole through the left lens of the black-tinted sunglasses worn by the woman named Terry. Her fingers splayed stiffly at odd angles from one another as though all of her nerve connections had been severed; then her face seemed to melt like wax held to a flame as she slipped down between the wall and the stuffed chair, a vertical red line streaking the wallpaper.

My hands were shaking when I set the safety on the Beretta and removed it from Bootsie's grasp, pulled the magazine and ejected the round from the chamber.

I squeezed her against me, rubbed my hands over her hair and back, kissed her eyes and the sweat on her neck.

She started toward the woman on the floor.

"No," I said, and turned her toward the kitchen, the light pouring through the western windows, the trees outside swelling with wind.

"We have to go back," she said.

"No."

"Maybe she's still . . . Maybe she needs . . ."

"No."

I made her sit down on the redwood picnic bench while I walked to the garden by the coulee and found the portable phone where she had dropped it in the grass, the transmission button still on. But before I could punch in 911 I heard sirens in the distance and saw Batist come out the back door with a dogleg twenty-gauge in his hand.

"It's okay," I said. "Send the deputies inside."

His eyes went from me to Bootsie.

"We're fine here, Batist," I said.

He nodded, cracked open the barrel of the shotgun, and walked down the drive, the open breech crooked over his forearm, peeling the cellophane off a cigar with his thumbnail.

I put my palm on Bootsie's neck, felt the wetness of her hair, her skin that was as hot as a lamp shade.

"It's going to pass," I said.

"What?" She looked at me blankly.

"You didn't have a choice. If you hadn't picked up Clete's call, I'd be dead."

"Clete? Clete didn't . . . The phone rang out in the garden and he said, 'Dave's in trouble. I can't help him. It's too far to come now. You have to do it.'"

"Who?"

"I can't handle this. You said you saw his tattoo on the remains in the morgue. You swore you did. But I know that voice, Dave. My God . . ." But she didn't finish. She pressed the heels of her hands into her eyes and began to weep.

—

Chapter 37

I BELIEVE MOLEEN Bertrand was like many of my generation with whom I grew up along Bayou Teche. We found ourselves caught inside a historical envelope that we never understood, borne along on wind currents that marked our ending, not our beginning, first as provincial remnants of a dying Acadian culture, later as part of that excoriated neo-colonial army who would go off to a war whose origins were as arcane to us as the economics of French poppy growers.

When we finally made a plan for ourselves, it was to tear a hole in the middle of our lives.

I don't know why Moleen chose to do it in an apartment off Rampart, near the edge of the Quarter, not far from the one-time quadroon brothels of Storyville and the Iberville Project where Sonny Boy grew up. Perhaps it was because the ambiance of palm fronds, rusting grillwork, and garish pastels that tried to cover the cracked plaster and crumbling brick was ultimately the signature of Moleen's world—jaded, alluring in its decay, seemingly reborn daily amidst tropical flowers and Gulf rainstorms, inextricably linked to a corrupt past that we secretly admired.

At five in the morning I got the call from an alcoholic ex-Homicide partner at First District Headquarters.

"The coroner won't be able to bag it up till after eight, in case you want to come down and check it out," he said.

"How'd you know to call me?" I said.

"Your business card was on his nightstand. That and his driver's license were about all he had on him. The place got creeped before we arrived." He yawned into the phone. "What was he, a pimp?"

The flight in the department's single-engine plane was only a half hour, but the day was already warm, the streets dense with humidity, when Helen Soileau and I walked through the brick-paved courtyard of the building, into the small apartment whose walls were painted an arterial red and hung with black velvet curtains that covered no windows.

Moleen and Ruthie Jean lay fully clothed on top of the double bed, their heads wrapped in clear plastic bags. A crime scene photographer was taking their picture from several angles; each time his flash went off their faces seemed to leap to life inside the folds of the plastic.

"He was a lawyer, huh? Who was the broad?" my ex-partner said. He wore a hat and was drinking coffee from a Styrofoam cup.

"Just a farm girl," I said.

"Some farm girl. She did both of them."

"She did what?" I said.

"His bag was tied from behind, hers in front. I hope she was a good piece of ass," he said.

"Shut up," Helen said. "Did you hear me? Just shut the fuck up."

Later, Helen and I turned down an offer of a ride to the airport and instead walked up to Canal to catch a cab. The street was loud with traffic and car horns, the air stifling, the muted sun as unrelenting and eye-watering as a hangover. The crowds of people on the sidewalks moved through the heat, their faces expressionless, the gaze in their eyes introspective and dead, preset on destinations that held neither joy nor pain, neither loss nor victory.

"What are you doing, Streak?" Helen said.

I took her by the hand and crossed to the neutral ground, drew her with me into the belly of the great iron streetcar from the year 1910 that creaked on curved tracks past the Pearl, with its scrolled black colonnade on the corner of Canal and St. Charles, where Sonny Boy used to put together deals under a wood-bladed fan, on up the avenue, clattering past sidewalks cracked by oak roots as thick as swollen fire hoses, into a long tunnel of trees and heliographic light that was like tumbling through the bottom of a green well, to a place where, perhaps, the confines of reason and predictability had little application.

Epilogue

LATE FALL IS a strange time of year in southern Louisiana. After first frost robins fill the trees along the bayou and camellias that seem fashioned from crepe paper bloom with the colors of spring, even though winter is at hand. The sky is absolutely blue and cloudless, without an imperfection in it, but at evening the sunlight hardens and grows cold, as it might in a metaphysical poem, the backroads are choked with cane wagons on their way to the mill, and the stubble fires on the fields drench the air with an acrid, sweet smell like syrup scorched on a woodstove.

Bootsie and I took Alafair to the LSU–Ole Miss game that year and later stopped for crawfish at Possum's on the St. Martinville Road. It had been a wonderful day, the kind that memory will never need to improve upon, and when we got home we lighted Alafair's jack-o'-lanterns on the gallery and fixed hand-crank ice cream and frozen blackberries in the kitchen.

Maybe it was the nature of the season, or the fact that quail and dove freckled the red sun in my neighbor's field, but I knew there was something I had to do that evening or I would have no rest.

And like some pagan of old, weighing down spirits in the ground with tablets of stone, I cut a bucket full of chrysanthemums and drove out to the Bertrand plantation, down the dirt road past the tenant houses, to the grove of gum trees that had once been a cemetery for slaves. When I got out of the truck the air was damp and cold and smelled like dust and rain; curlicues of sparks fanned out of the ash in the fields and I could hear leaves swirling dryly across the concrete pad abandoned by the construction company.

I put on my raincoat and hat and walked across the field to the treeline and the collapsed corn crib where Ruthie Jean and Moleen had begun their affair, where they had been spied on by the overseer whom Luke Fontenot would later kill, where they had reenacted that old Southern black-white confession of need and dependence that, in its peculiar way, was a recognition of the simple biological fact of our brotherhood.

And for that reason only, I told myself, I stuck the flowers by their stems in what was left of the crib's doorway, then began walking back toward my truck just as the first raindrops clicked against the brim of my hat.

But I knew better. *All* our stories began here—mine, Moleen's, the Fontenot family's, even Sonny's. Born to the griff, pool halls, and small-time prize rings, he somehow stepped across an unseen line and became someone whom even he didn't recognize. The scars on his body became lesions on our consciences, his jailhouse rebop a paean for Woody Guthrie and Joe Hill.

If I learned anything from my association with Moleen and Ruthie Jean and Sonny Boy, it's the fact that we seldom know each other and can only guess at the lives that wait to be lived in every human being.

And if you should ever doubt the proximity of the past, I thought to myself, you only had to look over your shoulder at the rain slanting on the fields, like now, the smoke rising in wet plumes out of the stubble, the mist blowing off the lake, and you can see and hear with the clarity of a dream the columns marching four abreast out of the trees, barefoot, emaciated as scarecrows, their perforated, sun-faded colors popping above them in the wind, their officers cantering their horses in the field, everyone dressing it up now, the clatter of muskets shifting in unison to the right shoulder, yes, just a careless wink of the eye, just that quick, and you're among them, wending your way with liege lord and serf and angel, in step with the great armies of the dead.

IF YOU LOVED *BURNING ANGEL*, BE SURE TO CATCH JAMES LEE BURKE'S NEWEST DAVE ROBICHEAUX NOVEL, *CADILLAC JUKEBOX*, COMING IN AUGUST 1996 FROM HYPERION.

Aaron Crown should not have come back into our lives. After all, he had never really been one of us, anyway, had he? His family, shiftless timber people, had come from north Louisiana, and when they arrived in Iberia Parish, they brought their ways with them, occasionally stealing livestock along river bottoms, poaching deer, perhaps, some said, practicing incest.

I first saw Aaron Crown thirty-five years ago when, for a brief time, he tried to sell strawberries and rattlesnake watermelons out on the highway, out of the same truck he hauled cow manure in.

He seemed to walk sideways, like a crab, and wore bib overalls even in summertime and paid a dollar to have his head lathered and shaved in the barber shop every Saturday morning. His thick, hair-covered body gave off an odor like sour milk, and the barber would open the front and back doors and turn on the fans when Aaron was in the chair.

If there was a violent portent in his behavior, no one ever saw it. The Negroes who worked for him looked upon him indifferently, as a white man who was neither good nor bad, whose moods and elliptical peckerwood speech and peculiar green eyes were governed by thoughts and explanations known only to himself. To entertain the Negroes who hung around the shoeshine stand in front of the old Frederick Hotel on Saturday mornings, he'd scratch matches alight on his clenched teeth, let a pool of paraffin burn to a waxy scorch in the center of his palm, flip a knife into the toe of his work boot.

But no one who looked into Aaron Crown's eyes ever quite forgot them. They flared with a wary light for no reason, looked back at you with a reptilian, lidless hunger that made you feel a sense of sexual ill ease, regardless of your gender.

Some said he'd once been a member of the Ku Klux Klan, expelled from it for fighting inside a Baptist church, swinging a wood bench into the faces of his adversaries.

But that was the stuff of poor-white piney woods folklore, as remote from our French-

Catholic community as tales of lynchings and church bombings in Mississippi.

How could we know that underneath a live oak tree hung with moss and spiderwebs of blue moonlight, Aaron Crown would sight down the barrel of a sporterized Mauser rifle, his body splayed out comfortably like an infantry marksman's, the leather sling wrapped tightly around his left forearm, his loins tingling against the earth, and drill a solitary round through a plate glass window into the head of the most famous NAACP leader in Louisiana?

It took twenty-eight years to nail him, to assemble a jury that belonged sufficiently to a younger generation that had no need to defend men like Aaron Crown.

Everyone had always been sure of his guilt. He had never denied it, had he? Besides, he had never been one of us.

It was early fall, an election year, and each morning after the sun rose out of the swamp and burned the fog away from the flooded cypress trees across the bayou from my bait shop and boat-rental business, the sky would harden to such a deep, heart-drenching blue that you felt you could reach up and fill your hand with it like bolls of stained cotton. The air was dry and cool, too, and the dust along the dirt road by the bayou seemed to rise into gold columns of smoke and light through the canopy of oaks overhead. So when I glanced up from sanding the planks on my dock on a Saturday morning and saw Buford LaRose and his wife, Karyn, jogging through the long tunnel of trees toward me, they seemed like part of a photograph in a health magazine, part of an idealized moment caught by a creative photographer in a depiction of what is called the New South, rather than an oddity far removed from the refurbished plantation home in which they lived twenty-five miles away.

I convinced myself they had not come to see me, that forcing them to stop their run out of reasons of politeness would be ungenerous on my part, and I set down my sanding machine and walked toward the bait shop.

"Hello!" I heard Buford call.

Your past comes back in different ways. In this case, it was in the form of Karyn LaRose, her platinum hair sweat-soaked and piled on her head, her running shorts and purple-and-gold Mike the Tiger T-shirt glued to her body like wet Kleenex.

"How y'all doin'?" I replied, my smile as stiff as ceramic.

"Aaron Crown called you yet?" Buford

asked, resting one hand on the dock railing, pulling one ankle up toward his muscular thigh with the other.

"How'd you know?" I said.

"He's looking for soft-hearted guys to listen to his story." Buford grinned, then winked with all the confidence of the eighty-yard passing quarterback he'd been at L.S.U. twenty years earlier. He was still lean-stomached and narrow-waisted, his chest flat like a prizefighter's, his smooth, wide shoulders olive with tan, his curly brown hair bleached on the tips by the sun. He pulled his other ankle up behind him, squinting at me through the sweat in his eyebrows.

"Aaron's decided he's an innocent man," he said. "He's got a movie company listening to him. Starting to see the big picture?"

"He gets a dumb cop to plead his cause?" I said.

"I said 'soft-hearted,' " he said, his face beaming now.

"Why don't you come see us more often, Dave?" Karyn asked.

"That sounds good," I said, nodding, my eyes wandering out over the water.

She raised her chin, wiped the sweat off the back of her neck, looked at the sun with her eyelids closed and pursed her lips and breathed through them as though the air were cold. Then she opened her eyes again and smiled good-naturedly, leaning with both arms on the rail and stretching her legs one at a time.

"Y'all want to come in for something to drink?" I asked.

"Don't let this guy jerk you around, Dave," Buford said.

"Why should I?"

"Why should he call you in the first place?"

"Who told you this?" I asked.

"His lawyer."

"Sounds like shaky legal ethics to me," I said.

"Give me a break, Dave," he replied. "If Aaron Crown ever gets out of Angola, the first person he's going to kill is his lawyer. That's after he shoots the judge. How do we know all this? Aaron called up the judge, collect, mind you, and told him so."

They said good-bye and resumed their jog, running side by side past the sprinklers spinning among the tree trunks in my front yard. I watched them grow smaller in the distance, all the while feeling that somehow something inappropriate, if not unseemly, had just occurred.

I got in my pickup truck and caught up with them a quarter mile down the road. They never broke stride.

"This bothers me, Buford," I said out the window. "You wrote a book about Aaron Crown. It might make you our next governor. Now you want to control access to the guy?"

"Bothers you, huh?" he said, his air-cushioned running shoes thudding rhythmically in the dirt.

"It's not an unreasonable attitude," I said.

Karyn leaned her face past him and grinned at me. Her mouth was bright red, her brown eyes happy and charged with energy from her run.

"You'll be bothered a lot worse if you help these right-wing cretins take over Louisiana in November. See you around, buddy," he said, then gave me the thumbs-up sign just before he and his wife poured it on and cut across a shady grove of pecan trees.

She called me that evening, not at the house but at the bait shop. Through the screen I could see the lighted gallery and windows in my house, across the dirt road, up the slope through the darkening trees.

"Are you upset with Buford?" she said.

"No."

"He just doesn't want to see you used, that's all."

"I appreciate his concern."

"Should I have not been there?"

"I'm happy y'all came by."

"Neither of us was married at the time, Dave. Why does seeing me make you uncomfortable?"

"This isn't turning into a good conversation," I said.

"I'm not big on guilt. It's too bad you are," she replied, and quietly hung up.

The price of a velvet black sky bursting with stars and too much champagne, a grassy levee blown with buttercups and a warm breeze off the water, I thought. Celibacy was not an easy virtue to take into the nocturnal hours.

But guilt over an impulsive erotic moment wasn't the problem. Karyn LaRose was a woman you kept out of your thoughts if you were a married man.

Aaron Crown was dressed in wash-faded denims that were too tight for him when he was escorted in leg and waist chains from the lockdown unit into the interview room.

He had to take mincing steps, and because both wrists were cuffed to the chain just below his rib cage he had the bent appearance of an apelike creature trussed with baling wire.

"I don't want to talk to Aaron like this. How about it, Cap?" I said to the gunbull, who had been shepherding Angola convicts under a double-barrel twelve gauge for fifty-five years.

The gunbull's eyes were narrow and valuative, like a man constantly measuring the potential of his adversaries, the corners webbed with wrinkles, his skin wizened and dark as a mulatto's, as if it had been smoked in a fire. He removed his briar pipe from his belt, stuck it in his mouth, clicking it dryly against his molars. He never spoke while he unlocked the net of chains from Aaron Crown's body and let them collapse around his ankles like a useless garment. Instead, he simply pointed one rigid callus-sheathed index finger into Aaron's face, then unlocked the side door to a razor-wire enclosed dirt yard with a solitary weeping willow that had gone yellow with the season.

I sat on a weight lifter's bench while Aaron Crown squatted on his haunches against the fence and rolled a cigarette out of a small leather pouch that contained pipe tobacco. His fingernails were the thickness and mottled color of tortoiseshell. Gray hair grew out of his ears and nose; his shoulders and upper chest were braided with knots of veins and muscles. When he popped a lucifer match on his thumbnail and cupped it in the wind, he inhaled the sulfur and glue and smoke all in one breath.

"I ain't did it," he said.

"You pleaded nolo contendere, partner."

"The shithog got appointed my case done that. He said it was worked out." He drew in on his hand-rolled cigarette, tapped the ashes off into the wind.

When I didn't reply, he said, "They give me forty years. I was sixty-eight yestiday."

"You should have pleaded out with the feds. You'd have gotten an easier bounce under a civil rights conviction," I said.

"You go federal, you got to cell with colored men." His eyes lifted into mine. "They'll cut a man in his sleep. I seen it happen."

In the distance I could see the levee along the Mississippi River and trees that were puffing with wind against a vermilion sky.

"Why you'd choose me to call?" I asked.

"You was the one gone after my little girl when she got lost in Henderson Swamp."

"I see . . . I don't know what I can do, Aaron. That was your rifle they found at the murder scene, wasn't it? It had only one set of prints on it, too—yours."

"It was stole, and it didn't have no *set* of prints on it. There was one thumbprint on the stock. Why would a white man kill a nigger in the middle of the night and leave his own gun for other people to find? Why would he wipe off the trigger and not the stock?"

"You thought you'd never be convicted in the state of Louisiana."

He sucked on a tooth, ground out the ash of his cigarette on the tip of his work boot, field-stripped the paper and let it all blow away in the wind.

"I ain't did it," he said.

"I can't help you."

He raised himself to his feet, his knees popping, and walked toward the lockdown unit, the silver hair on his arms glowing like a monkey's against the sunset.